I0526028

RED LINE

Tosh McIntosh

Aviator Writer Press

Austin, Texas

PUBLISHER'S NOTE

This is a work of fiction. Names, characters, places, events, and incidents are either products of the author's imagination or used fictitiously. Any resemblance to actual persons, living or dead, is purely coincidental.

Copyright © 2014 Tosh McIntosh
Cover design and composite image by Tosh McIntosh
Cover thunderstorm image:
Michael Bath @ lightningphotography.com
Airplane chapter and scene-break graphic:
Tosh McIntosh via public domain
All rights reserved.

Aviator Writer Press
ISBN-13: 978-0-9840489-4-6
ISBN-10: 0984048944

Printed and published in the United States of America

ACKNOWLEDGMENTS

Ann Katherine McIntosh, light of my life, you have my everlasting gratitude for your unfailing support through years of struggle to realize this dream. And to my fellow writers, Cynthia J. Stone, Lara Reznik, and Brad Whittington, who read and critiqued countless pages of false starts and detours in a torturous journey to tame this unruly story, thank you for believing it could be done in spite of my persistent doubts. Without your wise and expert counsel, I would still be cutting and pasting my way into another dead end.

DEDICATION

To my father, may he rest in peace, who wrote short stories and kept the carbon copies in loose-leaf binders on the bookshelves in my childhood home in Dallas, Texas. I never saw the originals. They disappeared into envelopes addressed to many of the popular magazines of the day. To the best of my knowledge, none of his stories made it into print to be read by the public.

And that matters not, because I have never forgotten the experience of turning those flimsy pages and reading the words my father wrote. As for so many other things, I owe him a lifelong debt for unlocking my imagination and instilling in me a passionate love of storytelling.

CHAPTER ONE

"Tell me you're not going to fly into those monsters." Lawson McAllister, M.D., adjusted the range scale on the Victory's multi-function display and glanced at his passenger in the copilot's seat. "Which monsters would that be?"

Billy Dutton pointed at dark clouds spanning the western horizon. "If you'd get your head out of the cockpit, you might see that big black wall of trouble ahead. The one with all the lightning in it."

"Stop worrying. With skill and cunning I will save us from certain death." Lawson laughed as Billy glared at him.

"Damn it, Law. Flying isn't a joke with me. Let's turn around, find a divert airfield and wait it out. Who cares if we're late? It's just a conference."

Not hardly. Lawson's commitment to speak at the opening dinner and his report on the progress of the cancer treatment center meant far more than just publicity. Large sums of money were at stake, most of it his wife's, and he hadn't amassed a sizable fortune of his own by being timid. He'd done it the old-fashioned way. Marry rich and be very good at creative skimming.

He tapped the MFD screen on the instrument panel. "Relax. This marvelous device will keep us out of danger."

"How's it gonna do that if you fly right at it? That's like standing on the eighteenth green holding your new putter over your head with Zeus looking down at you."

Lawson shrugged. "The Greek god of thunder and lightning is a lightweight past his prime. Just sit back and watch the master at work."

The MFD provided a God's-eye, moving-map view of the terrain, airways, navigation waypoints, and his GPS course line to the Dry Springs Municipal Airport, as well as a satellite color weather radar overlay. A cluster of three red blobs, surrounded by thin bands of yellow and orange in a sea of green, indicated a classic summer afternoon pressure-cooker atmosphere turning nasty.

The message button on the GPS began flashing. He pressed it to acknowledge and glanced at the message window: APPROACHING VERTICAL PROFILE. The GPS had calculated that now was the time to leave his cruise altitude. He'd received clearance from the air traffic controller to descend at pilot's discretion, so he reported leaving 12,500 feet, canceled altitude hold and began the descent.

Radio traffic between the controller and five other airplanes ahead indicated that all were deviating to the south of the storms to approach their destination airports in the Phoenix area from behind the storms. He could follow them like a good little lamb, but that would take him even farther off course to Dry Springs. Not only that, he detested being in line at the store, a movie theater, or anywhere else. Leaders lead.

A gap between the two storm cells just to the right of his course line offered a shortcut. It wouldn't for long. When the controller denied Lawson's request to deviate in that direction, he mumbled, "Screw you, fella," and canceled his instrument clearance. He couldn't legally fly in the clouds now, but that had never stopped him before. A twenty-degree right turn set him up to thread the needle, as one of his instructors used to say, although he always prefaced the phrase with *don't*.

Billy's voice, a bit shaky now, filled Lawson's headset. "Why the hell did you turn toward the darkest one of those sumbitches?"

"That just means it's thick." He pointed at the green gap on the radar screen. "*That* means no worse than light rain. And the airplane needs a wash job." He grinned at Billy, who had begun to shiver and appeared to have shrunk into the seat cushion. "Lighten up, man . . . but tighten your seat belt first."

Billy pulled on his harness straps and glowered at him.

Continuous light turbulence had increased to moderate and would likely get worse as they approached the storm. The Victory's flight manual recommended a slower speed in rough air, but Lawson didn't want to lose the opportunity to make it through the gap before it closed up.

He selected a lower range scale on the MFD. The increased weather detail startled him. The gap was narrowing a lot faster than he thought. All three red blobs now had magenta centers, the color representing the mighty hammer of Thor ready to pound the Victory into the dirt. Lawson had chosen the airplane primarily because of its reputation as a speedster. Time to use it. He accelerated to red line, the Victory's DO NOT EXCEED speed.

With the yellow-green boundary of the nearest storm cell barely touching his projected flight path on the moving map, he began a gentle left turn to skirt the edge. The turbulence intensified, but he had confidence in the airplane's structural strength. Victory built them like tanks, and the airframe had been tested to well beyond its maximum limits during the certification process.

A sudden hard bounce drove Lawson's forehead into the cabin air nozzle mounted in the headliner. He hauled on the shoulder harness and lap belt straps as hard as he could. The autopilot began pulsing the control yoke, trying to correct for the turbulence. He pressed the autopilot disconnect button.

Heavy rain sheeted off the windshield and pounded the aluminum fuselage. A loud hissing noise filled the cabin and his headset erupted with static from all the electrical energy jammed into the nearby thunderhead. He couldn't communicate with air traffic control even if he wanted to.

He glanced at his passenger. Billy's bald head and face glistened with sweat. His hands were clasped tightly in his lap. He stared straight ahead, jaw clenched, like a sculpture. Lawson punched him lightly on the arm. "Ease up, Billy. We'll be on the ground in about five minutes. The beer's on me."

"Beer, your ass. I want champagne. Dom Pérignon."

A BEEP-BEEP-BEEP sounded, barely loud enough to hear over the deafening background noise.

Billy stared at Lawson, eyes wide behind his glasses, and yelled, "What the hell does that mean?"

Lawson yelled back, "Nothing to worry about," and pressed the button he'd had installed on the backside of the yoke to silence the airspeed warning horn. It made the Victory legally non-airworthy, but he didn't give a shit. And besides, aeronautical engineers were always covering their asses with ultra-conservative limitations.

A deep shudder rippled through the airframe.

Billy began moaning.

Lawson shouted into the mike, "Hang on, buddy. It'll all be okay in a minute."

The control yoke pulsed in Lawson's hands, went limp. The airplane pitched nose down. Negative G forces slammed him against the headliner.

A hard jolt snapped the fuselage into a right roll, pinned Lawson against the side panel. Billy came out of his seat and smashed into the console, arms flailing, hands grabbing air.

Another jolt. The roll eased.

Lawson looked out the side window at black nothingness where the left wing used to be.

With Billy's screams filling the cabin, Lawson stared out the windscreen as his shattered airplane broke free of the storm in a vertical dive and the desert came up to meet him.

CHAPTER TWO

Low clouds and poor visibility had shut down the flight school for the day, and Nick left work early. It had been just over a year since he and his wife Laurie had moved from Washington, D.C., and he wanted to celebrate their first anniversary in Cedar Valley, Colorado, along with the grand opening of Phillips Properties, Inc. Laurie had been working long hours for months setting up the business. She deserved recognition now for all her hard work, and Nick had planned the perfect menu for a special dinner.

The drive from the airport to the Valley Market took almost 20 minutes, double the usual time, the streets crowded with cars and blocked by jaywalking out-of-towners with no apparent comprehension of the word *crosswalk*. Like a plague of locusts, they had descended on the town and seemed to be devouring the privacy and anonymity Nick cherished.

The invasion had begun about a month ago soon after he rejected a reporter's request for an interview and collaboration on an article to be published in *American Vigilante* magazine, a "Where is he now?" tabloid treatment of Nick's involvement last year in uncovering a government conspiracy to murder a controversial political figure. Unfortunately, the reporter followed through with his promise to write the article with or without Nick's input, which meant transforming him into a superhero on the quest for justice at any cost, including taking the law into his own hands.

Then came the reporter's eBook titled *Airborne Justice,* which had sold over 200,000 copies to a reading public fascinated with the big mystery.

Where was the black ops assassin who had murdered Miles Larchmont, and then almost got away with it?

Did he survive the crash of his airplane after being rammed by another airplane with a tenacious aviation accident investigator at the controls?

Was he still out there, sipping tropical drinks with little umbrellas in them and swimming naked in the surf with foxy blondes?

And, most important, is Nick Phillips really a modern American vigilante?

On top of all that, ever since the rumors of a movie deal and location scouting and maybe even a casting call had stirred up the town, his normally low-key existence had become a circus.

He pulled one of his Glock .40s from under the seat and slipped it into a nylon belt-slide holster he always wore under a loose shirt or jacket, depending on the temperature, and tapped the inside of his left ankle to confirm that he had his backup, a .380 ACP Walther PPKS. These were precautionary habits born of a near-death experience at the hands of a black ops assassin and Nick's lingering suspicion that somewhere out there in the darkness, payback might be waiting for his challenging the highest levels of government. And especially for winning.

Thankful that the locusts hadn't stopped off at the market for a snack, Nick picked up all the food items on his list and stopped in the wine section. He was by no means an expert, but the market owner had introduced him to one of his favorite varietals, the Sauvignon Blancs from the Marlborough region of New Zealand. On the bottom shelf sat a bottle of Cloudy Bay.

Nick knelt, picked it up, and peered deeper into the shelf to see if there were any more. No such luck, but the owner sometimes kept some back when his stock ran low as a favor to Nick. He stood, put the bottle in his basket, turned toward the front of the store and stopped in his tracks.

The Valley Market was an old building, constructed long before the age of supermarkets with bright lights and glitz. Gray afternoon light streaming through the front windows backlit a guy standing at the head of the aisle and put him in silhouette. His size, posture, and unmoving stance raised a caution flag. Nick transferred the basket to his left hand and brushed the front of his outer shirt with his right to make sure it was unbuttoned.

The man's voice rumbled out like the sound of a locomotive, deep and heavy. "You Nick Phillips?"

"Who's asking?"

"Another American vigilante."

That sent Nick's eyes searching for signs of a weapon. The guy wore a hip-length jacket with the zipper open almost to his waist, loose fitting enough to conceal a shoulder rig or hip holster. About 15 feet separated them, and Nick engaged his personal protection limit of 10 feet until he could confirm the guy's intentions. "That article and eBook are nothing but bullshit."

The guy chuckled. "Whatever you say, podna. I promise not to tell anyone you're a fake if'n I can have your autograph. Should be worth some bucks to one o' those idiots out there who think you're somethin'."

"This conversation is over." Nick backed away, one of the

key actions taught in self-defense training for de-escalating potential confrontations. When the guy began following, Nick said, "Hold up," retreated a little faster and bumped into a stand with cardboard wine-bottle carriers and sent it crashing to the floor.

The noise distracted Nick's attention for a few seconds, and when he glanced up and saw the guy's hand disappear inside his jacket with a shadowed quick, furtive movement, he dropped the basket, flipped his shirttail out of the way with the heel of his hand, yanked out the Glock and put the front sight center mass on the guy's chest.

The guy froze, his hand still inside his jacket. Behind him, one of the market employees entered the aisle, stopped, turned and ran. Nick figured about five minutes until the cops showed up.

"Don't come any closer and show me your hands."

From inside his jacket, the guy slowly removed a magazine folded in half lengthwise. "You hadn't oughta done that. Just want your autograph."

"I don't much give a shit what you want, and I told you not to come closer."

"Oh, sure. You're gonna shoot an unarmed man?"

Nick shook his head. "Armed."

"With a magazine?"

"Check out the inside of my left calf."

The guy glanced down, squinted, looked back at Nick. "So what?"

"See that bulge?" When the guy didn't answer, Nick filled the silence with a lie designed to keep the situation static until the cavalry arrived. "It's a throwaway. No serial number. Grip wrapped in Duck tape. It'll be in your dead hand."

The guy really looked down now, spent some time, then

shook his head. "Don't believe you."

"Then come on ahead and find out."

The guy looked like he was ready to do that as a commotion at the front of the store caused him to look over his shoulder.

"That would be the cops," said Nick. "I sure hope you're not carrying illegally in Colorado."

After a moment, a deputy sheriff appeared in the aisle behind the guy, weapon drawn, and from behind Nick, the voice of a friend said, "You know what to do, right?"

"Yessir." Nick released the magazine into his off hand, ejected the round in the chamber and caught it, locked the slide back and laid them on the floor. Then he placed his hands on top of his head, fingers interlaced, and waited.

Deputy Logan gripped Nick's hands with one massive paw and patted him down with the other. It felt like he was being swatted with a sledgehammer. With the reminder that it was only for his own safety, he handcuffed Nick, secured his Glock and the PPKS, and escorted him to his cruiser. "Climb in."

Nick sat in the back seat, its unique blend of odors barely masked by pine-scented cleaner that reminded him of the harrowing trip to the rest stop with Logan a little over a year ago and finding Deputy Thornton with the back of his head spread all over the rear seat and window of his cruiser.

It was not a comforting memory, so Nick cleared his mind and thought about nothing.

TURNED OUT THE GUY was one of those secessionist nutcases advocating violent overthrow of a corrupt and oppressive government. Nick sympathized with his beliefs, but had to smile when he learned that Deputy Logan had relieved him of a .50 caliber Desert Eagle semi-automatic handgun in a shoulder holster. A smaller man would have had to bring it into the market in a wheelbarrow. And no matter their size, either man would need a Colorado concealed carry license to prevent being arrested.

After getting Nick's side of the story, Logan motioned him out of the cruiser, removed the handcuffs and looked Nick hard in the eyes. "A word of advice?"

"Sure."

"License to carry a concealed handgun does not allow you to threaten someone just because they're from out of town."

"Yessir, but—"

"Even if you *suspect* they might be a pistol-packing bad guy."

"I know that, but—"

"Don't wanna hear it. I know all about the article and the book. As a neighbor, I'm sympathetic. I don't like your notoriety any more than you do. But the next time I get a call about you putting someone at gunpoint, I won't stop at a lecture. Understood?"

"Yessir. I'm sorry."

Logan handed Nick his pistols and climbed into his cruiser. Nick leaned into the open door. "But he was carrying illegally in Colorado. How about a medal?"

"Do you really want to go there?"

Nick shook his head, thanked Logan and watched the cruiser back away from the market. He waved, got a siren chirp in reply, returned to the market and retrieved his basket, which thankfully contained an unbroken bottle of really good fermented grape juice.

Walking to his Jeep, he felt the eyes and heard the whispers of locals and strangers alike following along. The incident would be all over town before sunset.

He climbed in and stared out the windshield at nothing, wondering why such a simple objective, to mind his own business and remain below the radar, was so elusive. Was this the first in a series of visits by vigilante-justice nut jobs stirred out of the muck by the publicity? And would Nick be unable to keep them at a distance that didn't feel threatening without being thrown in jail? Jesus.

He drove home, marched into the house and put away the perishables. With an ice-cold River Rock Pale Ale, he retreated into the family room, his personal refuge from all the bullshit out there, and collapsed into his favorite chair. Covered in luxurious dark brown leather that squeaked with the slightest movement, it welcomed him home with a soft *pssss*.

Gazing at the cold remains of last evening's fire, he took that first frothy sip. The aroma and flavor of locally brewed malted barley and hops triggered memories he'd rather forget but couldn't.

His name had been in the news for months following his discovery that sabotage had downed Miles Larchmont's GoldenJet. The articles centered on a recurring theme: here's the man who risked everything to uncover the truth in spite of the danger, and look at the price he paid.

As always, the public's short attention span allowed the story to fade. Nick had directed all his energy toward reconnecting with his wife and two children. With money from his personal retirement fund added to income from Laurie's budding real estate career, they managed to pay the bills. Planning ahead for the time when Stephanie and Brad would both be in college, they decided nothing bound them to Washington, D.C., and ample reasons existed to push them away.

In the end, although returning to the site of so many dreadful events seemed incongruous with starting a new life, they chose Cedar Valley, Colorado for its gorgeous scenery, small-town atmosphere, no flight school at the airport, only one real estate company, and the inevitable growth spurt on the near horizon.

For about a year now, he and Laurie had built a new life under the radar. Until now, that is. Nick easily ignored the glances, the questioning eyes, the barely concealed curiosity of the locals. But the quiet anonymity of Cedar Valley, where folks understood what the desire for privacy meant, had suddenly disappeared all because of one reporter/author's tale of fiction disguised as *truth according to speculation*. Quite a concept. Make up something and call it a fact.

He slipped the Glock from its holster and set it on the lamp table. The weapon had become a part of him, along with a dedication to caution in his daily life. Never again would anyone waltz into the world of Nick Phillips and fool him so completely. And although he didn't really believe that any of the original conspirators were hiding out there in the shadows plotting revenge, the fact that he thought about it at all justified vigilance.

Which apparently didn't mean pointing Glocks at autograph-seeking vigilantes, even if they were carrying .50 caliber Desert Eagles.

CHAPTER THREE

Nick put the afternoon's incident behind him by concentrating on one of his relaxation hobbies.

When he was with the NTSB, boiling water was a challenge. Cook a meal? Forget about it. But with Laurie working long hours at her firm, Nick had donned a virtual apron and become a more than passable everyday chef.

He leaned over the stew pot and inhaled the aroma of onions, garlic, and green pepper sizzling in olive oil. Marvelous. And the Cloudy Bay Sauvignon Blanc in his glass was definitely worth a case or two. All was right with the world of his own making.

When the onions had lightly browned, he added plum tomatoes in purée, tomato juice, Worcestershire sauce, salt, pepper, oregano, basil, and two bay leaves. He increased the heat and measured a half-cup of the wine. Offering a silent toast to the memory of his mother, he added it to the pot.

He had once asked her for the secret of gourmet cuisine. Her answer carried a simple message: *Always put a little of what you're drinking into what you're cooking.*

Nick drained his glass and helped himself to another. Then he added cubed red snapper. When the stew began to boil, he covered the pot, lowered the heat to simmer, and started the salad.

Five minutes later, he put a half-loaf of crusty Italian bread in a low oven to reheat and set the table. He admired his work and glanced at his watch. Perfect. Laurie was due home at seven for dinner, and this would be Nick's surprise.

Laurie would be proud of him. Not so much for the stew, it was her recipe after all, but for what else Nick had planned: homemade Caesar dressing, Bananas Foster for dessert, a champagne toast to her business success, and a commitment from Nick to have her dinner ready on time every work night. A Glock-carrying house hubby. She should like at least part of that.

One last stir, turn off the heat, and just enough time for a quick shower.

THE OVEN CLOCK STARED back at Nick with a glowing green 8:45. Two bowls of cold snapper stew, a wilted salad, and hockey-puck-hard Italian garlic bread sat on the table. He picked up the wine bottle to pour another glass, but it contained only air.

He snatched the phone handset off the table and speed-dialed Laurie's office. For the third time, the same irritating message filled the earpiece. Another call to Laurie's cell went directly to voicemail. He cocked his arm to throw the phone into the fireplace, then took a deep breath and tossed it on the table.

She knew better than to be out of touch, how easily he got worried for her safety. He'd tried for years, and especially in the aftermath of the Larchmont investigation, to instill in her an automatic security awareness. But the laid-back, no-one-ever-locks-their-doors atmosphere of Cedar Valley had turned his efforts into a Don Quixote deal. He'd given up nagging her about it, but the least she could do—

Tires crunched on the gravel driveway. Bright light squeezed through thin cracks between the blinds covering the front windows, then disappeared.

Finally. He relaxed into the chair. He didn't want to greet her with confrontation, but this was a matter of simple courtesy. You don't do this to the people you love. All it takes is a—wait a minute.

Laurie would drive into the garage.

The doorbell rang.

Oh, shit. Please don't let this be the cops.

He scrambled up, ran to the foyer and peered through the security peephole. His trepidation about Laurie vanished at the sight of a stranger standing under the soft glow of the porch light. An idiot who couldn't read the NO SOLICITORS sign.

Nick turned away from the door and stopped. Was that a bulge under the guy's armpit?

He opened the drawer in the lamp table by the front window, pulled out one of his Glocks, checked the chamber and magazine. Through the peephole he studied the guy.

He wore a plaid sport coat over a striped shirt with a polka-dot tie. Nick couldn't imagine a salesman, or low-life reporter, or even a self-respecting criminal would be caught dead in that outfit. On the other hand, he'd learned through bitter experience that a dark suit and tie, white shirt, and fake ID could camouflage a stone-cold killer as a federal agent.

The doorbell rang again, with the insistent repetition of someone pissed that you aren't responding. What an asshole. Nick looked through the peephole again. The guy's jacket fit too poorly to tell whether he was carrying a weapon.

Nick held the Glock behind his back, unlocked the door and snatched it open. "Whatever you're selling I don't want."

The man held up a photo. His eyes flicked from it to Nick.

He slipped it into a jacket pocket. "Mr. Phillips, my name is Cliff Yates. May I come in?"

"Based on your name alone? No. What do you want?"

"To hire you."

Nick's anger and attitude eased a bit. "Come by my office at the airport in the morning. I don't do much teaching personally, but I know a nice young man who would be more than happy to provide flight instruction."

"This has nothing to do with taking flight lessons."

"Then you have the wrong person. I run a flight school. If you don't need to rent an airplane or hire an instructor, go away."

Nick slammed and locked the door, returned the Glock to the lamp table, and went back to the family room. He added another log to the fire and sat down. After a few minutes of staring at the flames, wondering if he should be out checking the places where Laurie might be, the front window lit up again with approaching headlights. The garage door hummed open and clunked to a stop. He glanced at the grandfather clock. The brass pendulum reflected soft light from the fire and tick-tocked away the seconds.

9:15. About time.

The tension in his shoulders eased. She was safe, but now the irritation gained traction. He resisted the urge to confront her and propped his feet on the leather ottoman. Familiar sounds broke the silence: the Suburban door slammed shut, the garage door buzzed down, the kitchen door opened and closed, high heels clicked on wood flooring, paused, then clicked again. The new business owner returns.

"Nick?"

"In here."

Laurie appeared at the kitchen doorway. Meticulously

dressed in her usual work attire, she carried a filing cabinet disguised as an overloaded leather attaché case. "Why didn't you eat your dinner?"

"Lost my appetite."

"That's a first." She walked into the family room, laid her attaché case and keys on the sofa, and slipped out of her heels. "Sorry I'm late."

Nick nodded. "A call would have been nice."

Laurie paused, her jacket halfway off. "I mentioned last week I would probably have a meeting with Frank this evening about the new zoning."

"And I told you this morning I was planning a special dinner. You said you'd be home about seven."

Laurie tossed her jacket on the sofa and sat down in her chair beside Nick's. "It appears we both forgot what the other said about this evening. Is that why you didn't eat?"

Nick shrugged. "You want me to heat up the stew?"

"No thanks. I ate with Frank. Are you going to answer my question?"

Nick's jaw tightened. Laurie had been spending an increasing amount of time with her office manager. Long days and late evening arrivals were becoming more common. He clasped his hands in his lap. It seemed to keep his voice under control. He didn't know why.

"I didn't eat because I lost my appetite. I lost my appetite because I was so goddamn worried about you. I was worried because ever since you started this business, you've been staying out later and later."

Laurie nodded and locked eyes with him. "Oh, I get it. You're pissed about me pursuing a career, something I want to do, rather than being at home."

"I have no problem with your career, Laurie, and I'm glad

that real estate has provided you with this opportunity. But from where I sit, you've gone off the deep end, and—"

"Whoa, there, Nick. Your family treaded water for about twenty-five years while you immersed yourself in the NTSB. Welcome to the world of living with a spouse dedicated to an activity outside the home."

"So what is this? Payback?"

Laurie's face turned stone cold. "Sure. I chase a career not because of what it might do *for* me, but what it will do *to* you." She stood and snatched her jacket and attaché case off the sofa. "You haven't changed a bit. You think *I'm* getting worse? Take a look in the mirror. You can't get over the collapse of your career even with the satisfaction of knowing you proved a man was murdered."

"My career didn't really collapse."

Laurie stared at him. "What does that mean?"

"They offered me the Director's slot. I turned it down."

The room fell silent, except for an occasional pop from the dying fire.

Laurie nodded. "So that's it. You finally achieved your goal and decided to put your family first. Now you regret the decision. You feel trapped in this valley. Deep down, you blame us for your not accepting the offer."

"That's not true."

"Maybe not. But ever since we moved, you've been . . . I don't know . . . agitated . . . restless. Unhappy here with me."

Nick stared at the glowing embers, unwilling to accept Laurie's words but knowing that a morsel of truth lay hidden there.

When he finally glanced up, she was gone. He returned his gaze to the dying fire and tried not to read anything into the undone button on her blouse.

CHAPTER FOUR

Nick drove to work the next morning in the ten-year-old Toyota Tacoma he used to indulge his hobby as a handyman. Last night's quarrel with Laurie nibbled at his thoughts as he stopped by the post office. Passing the airport café, the aroma of cinnamon and yeast drifted through the open driver's side window, weakening his commitment to eat healthy. He parked and stepped inside. The little bell attached to the upper doorframe announced his arrival.

From the kitchen, a raspy greeting. "Come on in, stranger, and have a seat. But don't sit in them booths. Hurts my back to clean 'em."

He eased into a stool at the counter.

Loretta Barrett, seventy years old before she quit counting, pushed though the swinging door backwards with a pot of steaming coffee and a tray of fresh doughnuts. She turned, looked at Nick and stopped in her tracks. Her eyebrows furrowed, like they always did just before she playfully lectured a young whippersnapper.

Nick didn't give her a chance. "Why are you calling me a stranger?"

Loretta shook her head and continued behind the serving counter. Nick couldn't take his eyes off the starched hat perched on her nest of gray hair. It looked like origami. A bird, maybe.

Ready to fly away.

She put the coffee pot on a warmer and began layering the doughnuts on a serving dish. "Loyal customers come in here regular, stay and chat, support a local business."

"That's not fair. I'm busy trying to keep my own local business out of bankruptcy."

Loretta snatched the coffee pot off the warmer and grabbed a coffee mug. "Don't gimme no excuses. It don't take but a few minutes to walk over to this here café from the flight school." She poured Nick a cup of her legendary coffee. Rumor had it the cups were so heavy because her "mud" would dissolve anything with less bulk.

He chose a chocolate-covered doughnut and opened a copy of the *Cedar Valley Gazette*. Harvey "Hotel" Sweet's latest column dealt with the controversy still raging over Nick installing the flight school. The airport authority and local government had welcomed the investment. But nearby homeowners complained about the noise, the pollution, and the danger of crashes. Hotel had written a solid, impartial piece, not an easy task considering his personal bias. He'd recently begun flight lessons, and the flying bug had bit him hard.

Nick finished the article just as Loretta came out of the kitchen with a fresh pot. "More mud, gent?"

He accepted and carefully took his first sip. Loretta served her coffee hot and with no apologies.

She poured herself a cup and leaned against the counter. "That guy ever find you?"

A strange feeling, a kind of nakedness, settled on him. The Glock was still in the truck where he'd left it when he visited the post office. He excused himself, retrieved the weapon, and returned to his seat. "What guy?"

"Showed up here 'bout dawn yesterday. Didn't even have

the first pot brewed."

"What did he want?"

"Didn't say. Asked where you lived, if you worked at the airport, that sort a thing."

"What did you tell him?"

Loretta began wiping her hands on a dishtowel. "I told him you lived on a big spread out west a ways, didn't work at nothin' far as I knew, and you carried a shotgun in the back window of your pickup. I also told him you wouldn't take kindly to strangers askin' questions. I didn't tell him 'bout you packin' heat."

This gal was full of surprises. "What are you talking about?"

She began wiping the counter, which didn't need wiping. "A girl my age has had to learn to be aware of bulges on men, sonny."

Nick slapped a hand over his mouth to stifle a laugh. After a moment, he said, "What did you really tell him?"

"Just told you." Loretta waved over her shoulder and disappeared into the kitchen.

Nick sipped the last of his coffee and eyed the sugary treats under the glass lid of the serving dish. He countered the desire by pinching a roll of flab sneaking over the top of his belt.

Loretta always insisted she didn't want tips, they're for the hired help and she owned the place. Nick ignored her as usual and laid a five-dollar bill on the counter. He pushed open the door into the kitchen. Loretta was busy with something in the pantry.

"Hey Loretta?"

"Hmmm?"

"Did you see what kind of vehicle the guy was driving?"

"Ugliest car on the planet. An LTD looked like it was held together with duct tape and cable ties. Out-of-state plates."

Nick thanked her, drove to the flight school, opened the front door and stepped into bedlam. Students and instructors filled the room, everybody talking at once. Ashton Halder stood behind the counter facing the scheduling board. He wrote an aircraft N-number on the first line.

A student groaned, turned toward the door and stopped. "Oh. Good morning, Mr. Phillips."

Nick scowled, having fun. "Would you prefer a different airplane?"

"Yessir. That one doesn't have any good landings left in it."

The student's instructor patted him on the back. "Don't worry. We'll stop at the good-landing pump on the way out and fill 'er up."

Nick laughed and opened the door for them. "Fly safe." Then he stood in the corner and watched Ashton at work.

The kid was determined to fly airliners. Nick had taken him under his wing because he recognized the passion for flight that consumed those destined to be aviators. All major air carriers required substantial flight experience and ratings before they'd accept an application. Instructing was a common method of acquiring flight hours. Let a student pay for them and make a few bucks in the bargain.

Ashton stayed at the flight school from dawn to dusk, ready to teach anyone who walked in the door. He'd spent over an hour one evening trying to convince a stranger to get a private license. Turned out the guy was the new janitor, who spoke very little English. Ashton's well-known skill with a lasso had embellished the incident to create an airport mantra: If you see that instructor with a rope, watch out.

Aircraft assignments made, including for a flight with Sweet/Halder as the crew, Ashton turned around. "Hey there, Mr. Phillips. I'll leave the register unlocked if you'll be around for an hour or so."

"No problem. What's going on?"

Ashton looked at Nick as if he had spoken in tongues. "We canceled all of yesterday's flights. It's a nice day. There's a front due tomorrow with a forecast of low clouds and rain. We've got students wanting to do some flying before the weather turns."

Hotel's voice spoke up from behind Nick. "Don't bother explaining it to him, Ashton. He's not a real pilot any more."

Nick turned around. "And I suppose with less than ten hours of total flight time, you are."

"No, but it won't be long now."

Ashton nodded. "Absolutely, Mr. Sweet. You'll be flying for the majors in no time."

"Hear that, Nick? I'm going to be an airline pilot."

Nick shook his head. "You'd never want to fly for an airline with standards low enough to accept you."

"Hear that, Ashton? He's disparaging my flying skills and he's never flown with me."

Ashton snatched his flight bag off the counter. "I'm not getting involved in this. See you at the airplane, Mr. Sweet." He charged out the door.

Nick pointed at the door. "You better hurry. He's so eager he might take off without you."

"That's why I like flying with him. See you later."

Nick went to the snack bar for a cup of coffee. Through the picture window he watched the flight line come alive. Soon the drone of aircraft engines and throbbing props announced the beginning of a good day for the flight school, maybe put the month in the black for a change.

In his office, with all the airplanes in his fleet airborne and the building as quiet as a museum, Nick reviewed the financials and scheduled maintenance projections until someone opened and closed the front door. Before Nick could get up, Cliff Yates appeared at the entrance to his office.

Nick closed the folder on his desk. "Ever consider knocking?"

"It didn't work last night. Thought I'd try something different."

"Are you always this much of a pest?"

"Only when I have to be. Mind if I sit down?"

Since it might be the only way to get rid of this cockroach, Nick motioned toward a chair facing his desk.

Yates sat down and crossed his legs. His shoes looked like they were made from a polish-rejecting material with an affinity for dust.

Nick couldn't resist pimping the guy. "Where'd you get that sport coat?"

Yates held his arms out and examined them. "On sale. Sleeves a little long, but I got a good deal. Bought two."

This has *got* to be an act. "I'll bet. What can I do for you, Mr. Yates?"

"I want to hire you, and I'll make it worth your while."

"I guess you didn't hear me last night, so I'll repeat it. I run a flight—"

"I know all about you, Mr. Phillips. What you do now, what you did last month, last year, you name it."

"Really? Then perhaps you'd better tell me more about *you* before we discuss anything about a job."

Yates leaned forward and placed a business card on the desk. The card appeared used, as if he had presented and then retrieved it more than a few times. A phone number had been scratched through, replaced by another written in the hand of a child. Classy.

Nick picked it up. "Private investigator. With an Arizona

business address and area code. You licensed in Colorado?"

"This isn't about investigating anything in Colorado."

"You apparently investigated me."

"I didn't have to come to Colorado to do it. Ever hear of the information highway?"

Nick leaned back in his chair. "What's this about?"

"Finally," said Yates, "the right question." Then he stood, closed the door to Nick's office, and sat down. "I'm working a case to find proof that an airplane was tampered with so as to cause a crash. I've made some progress, but I need your expertise to finish up."

"I've already told you I don't do that any more."

"You aren't doing it *right now*. My guess is, you might be persuaded to do it again. Unless, of course, running a flight school in a hick town fulfills you. Gets the old heart pumping." After a pause, "That's bullshit, and we both know it."

"The bullshit is thinking that searching the Internet can tell you anything about me. Just out of curiosity, do you have any experience investigating air crashes?"

"Nope."

"Then why did someone hire you for this job?"

Yates smiled, a toothy grin that Nick found disturbing. As if his teeth demanded to be looked at. "Because I'm very good at what I do. Am I supposed to turn it down because it involves aviation?"

"I suppose not. But in case you ever decide to, just say, 'No.' It's really simple."

"I'll keep that in mind. Now—"

"You also have to recognize a rejection when you see one." Nick stood. "I'll escort you to the door."

Yates remained seated. "Sit down, Mr. Phillips, and let's talk about this. You haven't heard what I want and what it's worth to my employer for us to get it."

Nick snatched the phone off his desk. "You're right, and I don't intend to." He pretended to punch in 9-1-1 and waited for a moment, then said, "I'd like to report a criminal trespass, please."

Yates gestured with both hands, palms down. "Chill out a second. I just came here to—"

Nick glared at Yates. "Are you leaving? Right now? Or would you like an armed escort? Big guys, sporting Smoky Bear hats and mirrored sunglasses. Who like using their tactical batons."

Yates' face turned a fiery red. He jumped up, grabbed his business card off the desk and stormed out.

Nick hung up the phone and sat down. He stared at the financials folder, filled with numbers and graphs and lists and . . . *Jesus*. Talk about boring. Sometimes he missed investigating so much he could scream. And although a tiny bit curious about why Yates' employer needed Nick's skills, he'd started this business, local wannabe aviators had walked in the door with their pocketbooks, and Nick owed it to them to keep trying.

After about an hour, sounds of returning aviators filtered in from the reception area. He picked up his coffee cup and strolled into the break room. Multiple conversations provided images of practice maneuvers, stalls, and landing practice. The nuts and bolts of knowledge transfer. An amazing process, really.

Someone walks in the door with a dream to slip the surly bonds, and a few weeks later walks out wearing a huge grin and half a shirt, the back cut out and nailed to the Initial Solo board to commemorate the first time a student goes up without the security blanket of an instructor in the right seat. Nick really enjoyed being a part of that, even if it no longer charged his batteries.

Hotel and Ashton stood in front of the drink machine. Nick walked up behind them. "How'd it go?"

Hotel selected a Coke. "My instructor says I'm a natural."

Ashton twisted the top off a Mountain Dew and drank half the bottle in four swallows. He gasped, belched, and said, "Mr. Sweet's got the gift, all right. Show him something once, he's right on the money."

Hotel smiled at Nick and sipped his Coke. "I told you so. Who was the guy in the horse blanket?"

"A dapper dresser, for sure."

Ashton perked up. "I've got an opening this afternoon, Mr. Phillips. Is he going for a private license?"

"I don't think he's aviator material. Best forget about that one."

Ashton's face clouded. He seemed unable to understand why anyone wouldn't jump at the chance to fly with him.

Hotel clapped Ashton on the shoulder. "Let's debrief. Then you can rush outside and see if the guy is still hanging around. I'll help you tie him in the cockpit."

Ashton rolled his eyes. "I'll *never* be able to shed that reputation."

After the break room cleared out, Nick poured another cup of coffee, returned to his office and sat down. The decision to leave the NTSB had been so easy, but with a year of clarity, he knew in his heart that he needed to be more fully engaged. Hands-on instructing could fill some of the void, but he couldn't run a successful business from the right seat of a trainer. Welcome to the desk and the purgatory of ownership.

"Don't you have anything better to do than stare at a coffee cup?"

Nick looked up from his desk at Hotel. "What a coincidence. I was just thinking about that."

"Good. How about teaching me to fly a taildragger?"

"Lord almighty, we have unleashed a monster. You don't even have your private yet."

"Ashton tells me that people get their initial flight training in taildraggers all the time."

"Back in the old days, sure. They were a lot more common. But now only *real* pilots fly them."

Hotel grinned. "When do we start?"

Nick stood and headed toward the door. "Come with me."

"I'm due at the *Gazette*."

Over his shoulder, Nick tossed a challenge. "I knew you were a pussy." He kept walking as the sound of Hotel's footsteps hurried to catch up.

From a hallway storage closet, Nick got a kid's tricycle he bought at Goodwill. Pink and white, it had a basket on the handlebars and tassels on the grips. He stepped into the parking lot, walked to an area clear of cars, set the trike on the asphalt and looked at Hotel, who stared back and shook his head.

"I am *not* getting on that."

"A real man would, but it takes time to make the transition from being a pussy. Now pay attention." Nick placed his hand on the seat and shoved the trike. It swerved left and right as the handlebars wiggled back and forth, and came to rest against the curb about 10 yards away.

Then he retrieved the trike, returned to the starting point, and this time shoved it backwards with his hand on the handlebars. It began swerving again, but this time the oscillations increased until the trike tipped over, flipped, and skidded to a stop.

Nick looked at Hotel. "See that?"

"What are you—?"

"Did you *see* that?"

"Yes!"

"Good. Make sure you remember it." Then he explained the term *ground loop* and its cause, allowing the tail of a taildragger to swing far enough to either side so that the center of gravity of the aircraft moved outside the footprint of the main tires on the ground.

"In academic training for your private pilot's license, you learned that the velocity of the aircraft always moves through the center of gravity. In this situation, that velocity will continue shoving the tail around the pivot point of a main tire, which usually tips the aircraft so much that the wingtip, and in extreme cases the prop, contact the ground. Hello, engine overhaul. Still interested in flying taildraggers?"

Hotel nodded. "That ground-loop thing sounds like fun."

Nick picked up the trike. "You won't be that flippant if you ever let it happen."

Back in his office, Nick plopped down in his chair and made three short-term promises to himself: finish analyzing the financials, review the maintenance schedule, and try to repair the damage to his marriage from last night's argument.

CHAPTER FIVE

Caitlin Monroe snatched her phone off the passenger seat of the Mercedes and glanced at the screen: *Yates Enterprises.*

Always putting on airs, that guy. Like he was a wheeler-dealer with business interests around the world and annual revenues that would make Michael Dell drool with envy.

Truth was, she'd hired an ex-Albuquerque narc whose only current enterprise, as it were, involved the sleazy world of private investigation and his specialty: getting the evidence of adultery to be used by divorce lawyers to emasculate husbands and toss unfaithful wives out on the street where they belonged. Which is why Caitlin knew about him, actually.

He'd followed her and Lawson around like a shadow on a cloudy day. And in spite of her well-developed commitment to vigilance, an unwanted gift from an abusive childhood, she never knew he was there until he offered to sell her the photos that Lawson's wife had hired him to get. That competence, combined with his bargain-barn rate and the fact that he didn't appear the least bit reluctant to get his hands dirty, got him the job and gave Caitlin a headache.

She answered the call with, "Speak."

"ARF! ARF!"

"Not bad for a castrated ex-cop, Cliff. Anything else you'd like to tell me?"

"Funny girl. I'm cracking up here."

"Did you call for the joke of the day, or do you have news for me?"

"News, and it ain't no joke. He refused. Twice."

"I didn't send you to fail. Keep trying."

"Won't work. He called the cops, and he'll do it again."

"What good are you if you can't do what I ask?"

"You didn't have any complaints about the results of my work in Arizona."

"I do now."

"Then maybe I should handle what I do best, and you do the same. No way he could decline an offer from you."

Caitlin knew better than to ask, but curiosity about what Cliff would say next made her do it. "Why's that?"

Yates made a kissing sound. "Be like butter in your hands."

The jerk was right. Caitlin had the body to capture a man's attention and the brains to use it wisely. The combination gave her a distinct advantage as a drug rep. Walking into a room and a little harmless flirting had been useful tools for building a lucrative account list with male physicians eager to hand her their business. They *wanted* to please her. With female doctors, she left the flirting at the door and let her brain do all the talking.

Dealing with Yates required an entirely different approach, which was her reason for the tough talk now. "That's a good idea. Probably the first one you've ever had. Take a few days off. See the sights. But stay out of his way and do not cause *any* trouble out there or I'll harvest your balls for souvenirs."

"You can have them any way you want."

Caitlin could picture Yates' lascivious grin, the gap in his front teeth looking like one black piano key amid a host of yellowed ivory ones. "You bet I can."

She disconnected the call, climbed out of the Mercedes and walked to the edge of the overlook. Faint sounds of airplane engines drifted up from the valley. Tiny specks that looked like gnats buzzed around the Cedar Valley airport.

She picked up a rock and threw it as far as she could, watching it disappear into the trees far below and suddenly wondering why she did that.

A memory from childhood? Except that she had so few fond ones.

Or maybe it was a genetic thing, deep in her DNA. Young kids will do that, won't they? Like stomping their feet in a puddle of rainwater?

Fatigue settled over her. She sank onto a bench beside the railing.

Reading the *American Vigilante* article and the reporter's book had convinced her that if anyone could find the evidence of sabotage and prove that Lawson was murdered, Nick Phillips was the guy. His tenacity, even when a hired assassin began cleaning up the loose ends from a conspiracy and came after him, had more than proved his mettle. All she had to do was convince him to help with her plan, formed in the immediate aftermath of the crash.

But according to the article, he'd resigned from the NTSB to put his role as husband and father above that of being an aviation accident investigator. Throwing Yates out of his office without even considering the job offer indicated a continued commitment to keeping the home fires lit.

But if any truth lay beneath the book title *Airborne Justice*, the ember of a different fire smoldered there and Caitlin needed to fan it.

IT HAD BEEN A good day for the flight school, especially welcome since most of yesterday's schedule had been canceled for weather. Nick arrived home late, greeted by a dark house as he entered the driveway. The garage door rose to reveal two empty spaces. He parked the Jeep and went into the kitchen, found the stovetop light on dim, breakfast dishes in the sink, a half-full pot of cold coffee on the counter. He prepared it for the morning, pressed the AUTO button, then remembered the weather forecast and pushed it again. An empty building wouldn't need supervising. Lowering clouds, gusty winds, and the hint of rain foretold another day of lost revenue.

While a serving of snapper stew heated up, he opened a bottle of Kim Crawford unoaked Chardonnay, another of his favorites from New Zealand, made a salad and tried to resuscitate two pieces of rock-hard garlic bread in the steamer. As he ate a solo Friday night dinner, his mind kept dredging up the memory of the argument with Laurie, sifting through the words on both sides and trying to make sense of how he really felt.

From the moment Laurie had begun preparations for starting a business in Cedar Valley, she tackled the undertaking with the same driven will to succeed that had characterized Nick's career goals for almost twenty years. He honestly believed in and supported her right to do that. But at the same time, he struggled with the feeling of being left out, sitting in the stands, unable to compete with Laurie's commitment to working outside the home.

Sour grapes? Maybe, although he didn't completely buy into that conclusion. Envy? Probably, because he yearned for the rush, that eagerness to dive into an endeavor with abandon and swim for the wall. Laurie had it now. He didn't. Running a flight school felt like a holding pattern, or being in a sailboat minus sails and a rudder.

He sighed, carried his dishes into the kitchen and stared at the empty bottle of wine he had just placed on the counter. He couldn't remember pouring more than two glasses, but he obviously did.

The oven clock's 8:42 mocked his mood with an irritating reminder that Laurie's day had still not ended. She was probably having dinner with Frank again, mapping out another piece of strategy for growing Phillips Properties into a kick-ass real estate firm.

Nick rinsed the dishes and carried two fingers of cognac in a snifter into the family room, sank into his favorite chair and stared at the cold fireplace. He loved a good fire, but decided against it. He'd just get it going and fall asleep.

He held the snifter with both hands for a few minutes to warm the cognac and then swirled it. With his nose buried in the glass, he took a deep breath and sipped, let the liquor remain in his mouth to evaporate. How someone could make grape juice taste so good baffled him.

Nick sipped the cognac and picked up today's *Cedar Valley Gazette* to read Hotel's column. His latest series addressed the ongoing clash between the no-growthers and the Cedar Valley Real Estate Board. Laurie's bid for president was about to bring the battle to the Phillips family doorstep. As if they needed any more tension in the house. Nick had declined to be interviewed about his opinion. Smart growth or dumb growth, it didn't matter. He preferred that Cedar Valley remain just the way it was.

A faint squealing of tires drifted in the room. Probably a car going too fast on one of the many curves on the street that passed in front of his house. He walked into the living room and peered through the blinds. Laurie's Suburban, following the sweeping arc of twin high beams, careened into view around the nearest curve and turned into the driveway without slowing very much and disappeared into the garage. He hurried into the kitchen and reached for the doorknob.

The door swung open. He backed up a step. Laurie stood in the doorway. Her tousled hair and disheveled appearance startled Nick so much he couldn't speak.

She blew a strand of hair away from her eyes. "You won't believe what happened!"

Her words had a liquid quality, obviously lubricated with alcohol. Laurie enjoyed wine and an occasional beer or mixed drink, but Nick couldn't remember the last time he had seen her the least bit tipsy. "I'd believe you've been drinking. And driving."

"Just a small celebration." She stepped into the kitchen and pushed the door closed with a high heel.

"With Frank, I presume?"

She dismissed the question with a wave of her hand, got a snifter out of the cabinet and poured it half full with cognac. "Bring the bottle, please."

He followed her into the family room, where she tossed her attaché case on the couch, slipped a heel out of a shoe, flipped it across the room with a swift kick, followed it with the second one, collapsed into her chair facing the fireplace and propped her feet on the ottoman.

Nick stared at the back of her head, expecting it to rotate 180 degrees. He put the cognac on the lamp table beside her chair and sat down on the hearth facing her. "Why didn't you call me? Or take a cab?"

"You apparently killed that bottle of Chardonnay in the

kitchen all by yourself and started in on the cognac, so spare me the lecture."

Nick's temper almost took control, but he stuffed it back in the box and didn't point out that he wasn't the one who'd been driving. "You want to tell me what's going on?"

"Just been waiting for you to ask, darling. This has been a red-banner day for Phillips Properties. Frank has agreed to become a partner and invest in the firm. That provides the working capital we need to acquire the parcels and take advantage of a market that is bound for the *moon*." After a moment, she sipped her cognac and stared at him. "You don't seem very happy for me."

"Of course I am. It just seems kind of sudden."

"So what? Opportunity doesn't have to creep into your life."

This conversation had all the makings of an argument-bomb ready to explode, but Nick didn't feel like tiptoeing around the issues. "I hope Frank is the real deal, Laurie, and the partnership works. But I'll be surprised if it does."

Laurie's voice took on an edge. "And why is that?"

"You're so committed to balancing growth and concern for the environment, and—"

"What makes you think I'd accept an incompatible partner?"

"You wouldn't. But you're not a typical real estate developer. The pursuit of maximum return on the investment emphasizes growth corridors and big-box concept commercial properties over residential areas."

Laurie nodded and drank most of her cognac in one swallow. "So now you're a real estate investment expert."

"That's not what I said."

Laurie's complexion flushed red. "Do me a favor, Nick.

Keep your opinions out of my business. I'm a big girl, and I can take care of myself."

"Okay, let's talk about how you do that. Buy low, sell high, right?"

"So that's the extent of your financial knowledge?"

"No, but it's all I need. You talk about this as a unique opportunity to purchase properties while demand is low and realize the appreciation when buyers are lined up at your doorstep."

Laurie nodded. "Sounds like the perfect concept to me."

"Sure, but not for the long-time residents of the valley whose families have owned property for a century or more."

"So what? They probably paid close to nothing for it. They'll walk away with a bundle."

"But they could make a lot more."

Laurie shook her head. "Would you please stick with running a flight school and let me deal with the investment decisions in *my* business?"

"Okay, but not without pointing out that you could choose to be a successful real estate tycoon and a good neighbor at the same time."

Laurie laughed. "This is wonderful. Let's say I agree that I'm not a good neighbor. How would you suggest I become one?"

"You're turning a profit now as a broker and doing better all the time. Keep it up while you find property owners who might be interested in selling and get their commitment for you to handle the sales. They get a more profitable bottom line and you make a very nice living while protecting the valley. It's a win-win."

Laurie stood, walked to the stairs and turned as she reached the lower landing. "You might consider selling the flight school and start investigating again. That's apparently the only way you can fulfill your need to be in control."

Nick fought the urge to reply in kind as Laurie climbed the stairs. He drained the last of his cognac, savored the sweet burn, stared at the fireplace and the cold, gray ashes that matched his mood.

Chapter Six

The pproaching dawn backlit the eastern ridgeline as Nick climbed out of his Jeep on Saturday morning. Clouds capped the mountains to the north. The sky had the unsettled look of an impending weather change, but the forecasted cold front had not arrived.

He had to operate the flight school with little regard for weekends or holidays. Few student pilots had the luxury of paying for flight instruction without working full-time jobs. Weather in southern Colorado could shut the doors suddenly and for long periods. Whenever clear skies and student availability coincided, he made certain the place was ready to roll.

He opened the reception area, started the coffee, and checked the flight schedule. It reflected an average day, but when he listened to messages, three pilots wanted to add their names to the list. More would probably call in when they realized the meteorologists had tricked them once again. The maintenance summary indicated only one trainer out of service. It might be a good day for the bottom line.

Someone entered the reception area through the front door. Probably Ashton. Nick got a cup of coffee from the snack bar and went to his office. Then he noticed the silence. Ashton never did anything quietly. Maybe a new customer?

Nick returned to the reception area.

A woman stood a few feet from the ops counter. Shoulder-length black hair framed a movie-star face above a red turtleneck. Designer jeans molded to curves in all the right places. A small handbag hung from her left shoulder, her hand curled around the front of the bag. No wedding ring.

Nick approached the ops counter. "May I help you, ma'am?"

She smiled. "Do you always call younger women 'ma'am'?"

"Learned it from my dad."

"How times have changed. Might you be Nick Phillips?"

"Yes, ma—I mean—yes."

She laughed. Perfect white teeth glistened in the overhead lighting. "Old habits die hard."

"That they do. What can I do for you?"

"How about a moment of your time?"

"Okay, Ms. . . . ?"

"Caitlin Monroe. Please call me Caitlin."

"Very well. What's this about?"

"In spite of your commitment to being polite, Nick, you haven't offered me coffee."

"My apologies. I even have a fresh pot." He led her into the break room and poured a cup.

She sipped the coffee. "Can we sit down?"

"Sure." Nick pulled out a chair for her.

She declined with a wave of her hand. "Somewhere more private, perhaps?"

"Certainly. Follow me."

Nick closed the door to his office on the first sounds of activity drifting in from the reception area. The building would fill up quickly, and he hadn't yet reviewed the schedule, a regular morning ritual. He offered Caitlin a chair and sat down behind his desk. "I need to begin my work day soon, but how may I assist you?"

She sipped her coffee and with a finger teased her hair behind an ear. "First, promise you won't call the cops."

"Why would I do that?"

"Maybe for the same reason you did yesterday."

The sudden contrast between the image of Cliff Yates and his stripes, checks, and polka dots compared to the woman on the other side of the desk sitting in the same chair paralyzed Nick's tongue for a moment. He would never have guessed a connection. He cleared his throat. "That's a deal, but I'm going to tell you the same thing I told your accomplice, or whatever he is. I'm not interested."

"Sure you are."

"Excuse me?"

"You just don't know it yet. You know why?"

"Can't wait to hear it."

"Because you haven't listened to the facts. At least give me that much."

Nick glanced at his watch. "You have twenty-five minutes."

A HALF-HOUR AND ANOTHER cup of coffee later, Caitlin sipped from a bottle of water and said, "Well? How about it?"

"Your facts are mixed with intriguing speculation, but the answer is still no. Unlike my response to your partner, I'm going to explain why."

"He's *not* my partner."

"Fair enough, but I don't care one way or the other." Nick twisted the top off a bottle of water and sipped it. "I have a Google alert on a number of keywords and phrases, one of which is *pilot error*. Stripped of speculation, the facts of this

Victory crash paint a classic picture of an *accident* that wasn't any such thing. Two people lost their lives, and there's absolutely no question that their deaths were totally avoidable. It's a slam-dunk conclusion. Want to know why?"

Caitlin sipped more water and settled into the chair. "Go ahead."

"What do you know about the V-Tail Beechcraft Bonanza?"

"Nothing. Do I need to?"

"Yes." Nick related a Cliff's Notes version of the airplane's history and emphasized the original design flaw that caused hundreds of fatal crashes due to inflight failure of the tail section. He touched only briefly on the efforts of Beechcraft to deny that a problem existed and their various methods of harassment to silence the critics. And he made it clear that when forced by the Federal Aviation Administration to deal with the issue, Beechcraft's design changes were effective and tail failures had become quite rare.

Caitlin frowned. "That story might be fascinating to some, but why are we talking about a type of airplane that Lawson wasn't flying?"

"Because I'm not done yet. In spite of all the skeletons in the V-Tail's closet, and I mean that both figuratively and literally, most pilots will tell you that it's one of the most beautiful airplanes ever built. Beechcraft stopped making V-Tails in 1982, which is why Victor Sebastian invested so much money in development of the Victory. He wanted to provide a brand-new version of this classic airplane."

"An airplane that has none of the design flaws of the original V-Tail."

Nick smiled and nodded. "His copycat effort didn't go back quite that far."

"Which brings *me* back to the question of why all this

history is relevant to Lawson's crash."

"Because no design change to a V-Tail can address the fact that it has ruddervators." Before Caitlin could ask the question he fully expected, Nick continued, "Conventional airplanes have a rudder and elevators in a "T" or inverted "T" configuration to control the aircraft around two of three axes, pitch and yaw.

"V-Tails utilize a unique flight control that combines those two functions, hence the name. And even with the earlier design flaws eliminated, there exists the potential for a combination of inflight conditions to create aerodynamic forces that can rip a V-Tail airplane apart more readily than its conventional-tail cousin."

"Do what?"

"We call it inflight breakup. The tail separates from the fuselage."

Caitlin's face turned white as she put her hand over her mouth and gasped.

Nick couldn't believe that he'd been so insensitive not to think for one second of how distressing the image he'd described would be. He snatched a box of tissues off the credenza beside his desk and placed it within Caitlin's reach.

After a moment, she pulled out a couple of tissues, dabbed the moisture from her eyes and cheeks, and appeared to will herself free of the emotion as if flipping a switch.

"I'm sorry for your loss, Caitlin, but the facts documented in the preliminary NTSB report clearly indicate pilot error caused this crash."

"Then I need you to prove that to *me*."

"I just did."

"That was a history lesson. I want evidence. The kind you found a year ago that you can hold in your hand."

Nick shook his head. "There won't be any."

"Then show me that *you* couldn't find anything rather than confirming that someone else didn't. A slam dunk, as you call it, shouldn't take any time at all."

Nick picked up the water bottle sitting on his desk beside two framed photos: one of a GoldenJet just like the one Miles Larchmont was flying when he was murdered, and the other of his father standing beside the airplane in which he died.

As always, Nick's eyes focused on the watch on his father's left wrist. Without conscious thought, he opened his desk drawer and looked at the very same Glycine Airman, with a shattered crystal and the hands frozen forever at the instant Nick crashed into a mountain a little over a year ago.

"Have I lost you, Nick?"

Caitlin's voice brought him back to the moment. "Uh . . . no. Sorry." He closed the desk drawer.

"You're thinking about it, aren't you?"

"I'll let you know tomorrow."

"What's wrong with right now?"

Nick stood. "I've got a flight school to run." He escorted Caitlin out of the building and stepped up to the ops counter as Ashton swapped two tail numbers on the scheduling board. "Why the change?"

Ashton pointed to one of the student-instructor pairs. "This is an instrument ride. They need an attitude indicator that doesn't tumble every few minutes."

"Okay. Let's put that airplane down ASAP and fix it."

"Will do." Ashton nodded toward the front door. "Who was *that?*"

Nick couldn't resist the opportunity. "A new student."

"Holy sh—excuse me, Mr. Phillips—really? I'm available for the next year or two."

"I'll bet you are, but you need to cool your jets. She's not really here for lessons."

"Let me talk to her. I'll sign her up before noon."

"Be my guest, but be careful. When she sees the rope, you're going to be in *big* trouble."

"No ropes, Mr. Phillips. Just my irresistible charm."

"And although you have gobs of that, may I offer a word of advice?"

"Yes, sir."

"Read up on black widow spiders."

"What for?"

"To learn that after they mate, the female often eats the male."

Ashton nodded. "It'd be worth it."

Caitlin drove from the airport to her motel in a daze, her mind trying to deal with the possibility of failure.

With a pony bottle of Chardonnay from the mini-bar, she sank into the armchair to ponder her next move. Or decide if she even had one. Other than waiting for someone else to do something, which was not an option.

Nick had seriously challenged her belief that Lawson was the victim of murder. It sounded like he'd committed unintentional suicide by stupidity. What other conclusion was there considering the history of the V-Tail and the design change and how that still didn't eliminate the potential for certain conditions to be so dangerous?

She didn't know much about piloting an airplane, but Lawson always seemed so competent and in charge that she'd never questioned her safety. How could she possibly wrap her mind around accepting that his own pilot error killed him, and he could have taken her with him to the grave just to save a few minutes of flight time?

Caitlin thought about that for awhile and realized that she didn't have to mind-wrap anything. The quality of Lawson's piloting skills and judgment had no bearing on their relationship, and she wasn't going to let Nick's opinion or anyone else's diminish the memory of her faith in Lawson or his commitment to her and their future together.

Abandoning her quest would be the equivalent of accepting weakness as a soul mate, resigned to a life far too reminiscent of her childhood and the vulnerability she endured for years. The foster homes. Fighting off the groping hands of men expected to nurture and protect. A vicious punch to the face during a horrific attack. The acrid legacy of betrayal. And not a woman anywhere strong enough to step between her and sexual deceit.

No other choice remained than to do whatever was necessary to remain free of the helplessness and fear that had defined what should have been the springtime of Caitlin's life. To be true to herself and the vow made so long ago. To be resolute in the face of adversity no matter the cost. And to never again be resigned to a fate of another's choosing.

ON SATURDAY NIGHT, NICK ate leftovers. By himself. Again. He cleaned up the dishes and noted that if Laurie made a permanent habit of arriving home so late, his promise to have dinner ready in support of her career wouldn't mean much. He couldn't remember the last time they sat at the same table for a meal like normal folks, and he had no clue when that might happen again.

He completed his usual perimeter security check of the house, which meant every window and door because to Laurie, locks were nuisances. After watching a little TV and reading the *Gazette,* he went into their home office about 10:00 p.m. to check email.

One of Laurie's leather business folders was resting on the keyboard. He picked it up, set it aside, noticed the corner of what appeared to be an airline boarding pass poking out of the top. Feeling a little like a snoop, he opened the folder.

Laurie Phillips was flying to Las Vegas next Thursday afternoon.

Nick's skin felt like fire ants were crawling over every square inch. They weren't biting, but he got the distinct impression that they were sharpening their pincers.

After a moment he shed the feeling by telling himself that it had to be a Phillips Properties trip. She hadn't told him about it for the same reason that the rest of her business activities came as complete surprises: preoccupation. Yeah, that was it. Had to be.

He closed the folder and went upstairs to take a shower. Although he preferred to set the alarm at times when he felt less capable of defending himself, and being in the shower more than qualified, he couldn't do that with Laurie not at home. Both the INSTANT and AWAY settings increased the potential for triggering an inadvertent alarm. And the one he had installed was *loud.* Heart-attack loud.

He was in the bathroom drying off when a thumping noise penetrated the whirr of the exhaust fan. He turned it off, opened the bathroom door and listened.

Someone downstairs?

Recommended tactics for home defense never advised confronting an intruder while wearing nothing more than flip-flops and a towel.

Nick locked the bedroom door, removed a Glock from the

bedside table, checked it, threw on a shirt and jeans, shoved his feet into running shoes and went to the head of the stairs.

He thought about dialing 911, rejected the idea. It could be nothing more than a raccoon in the garbage. Besides, protecting his life and property was his responsibility. Forget about cowering upstairs in his own house.

Another home-defense tactic was to make it very clear to a possible intruder that you were prepared to blow someone's shit away.

He started to call out, then remembered that he'd left one of his Glocks on the lamp table beside his chair in the family room. For an intruder to steal and use on someone else, or lie in wait for him to show himself and get blown away.

He descended the stairs, peeked around the corner and thought he heard a rustling of some kind. Or whispers? All the lights were off except over the stovetop. On dim. But the glare from the kitchen was brighter than that.

A peek into the kitchen revealed an open door into the garage. And a faint whiff of cigarette smoke. Friends and acquaintances knew the Phillips household was smoke-free, and that if Nick had his way, the zone would extend to the property line. Or in truth, to the edge of the known world.

Who the hell was out there asking to be forcibly ejected from his castle grounds?

With his Glock at the ready, Nick advanced through the kitchen, looked into the garage.

No Suburban.

Nick backed away, followed his nose to the front door, slightly ajar.

A shadowed figure stood at the bottom of the porch steps, the glow of a cigarette in his left hand.

Nick reached for the door handle, heard the door to the

study open behind him, swiveled around with the Glock coming up.

Laurie screamed, dropped a file folder, papers scattering everywhere on the floor, and stood motionless with her hands over her mouth.

Silence. Then from behind him, "What happened?"

Nick jerked around.

Frank Talbot stood framed by the front door, his eyes flicking down to the Glock and back up.

"Jesus, Nick. It's just us."

AFTER FRANK HURRIED OUT to his car, Nick followed Laurie into the family room, where she walked to the opposite side of the coffee table and turned to face him.

He immediately detected the change in the room. No longer comforting, their mutually favorite refuge felt as if a thunderstorm had parked itself above the ceiling fan, electrifying the atmosphere, raising the hair on the back of his neck and arms and stinking of ozone. Global warming had reached the Phillips household.

Looking at Laurie's expression, however, Nick wondered if global war might be a better description. He'd seen hard stares from her flint-steel eyes before, but not like this.

She crossed her arms, held herself in an embrace that whitened her knuckles. "I can't believe you pulled one of your goddamn guns on us."

That opening salvo made it clear that this was not going end well, but at this point Nick didn't give a shit. "Knowing full well that I keep guns in the house, and that unlike you I pay attention to the security of our home, you should have known better than to sneak in here like a common criminal."

"Of course. It's our fault for trying not to wake you."

"Interesting that you should use the term *our*. Talbot phrased it as *us*. As in, *a couple*."

"Fuck you, Nick. If you think there's something going on between Frank and me, your security paranoia has spread like a cancer and poisoned the rest of you."

"One reason might be that the Suburban is missing. Most nights it comes home with you."

"Ever hear of a dead battery?"

"Okay, so Talbot gave you a ride home. How does that end up with him smoking a cigarette on our front porch?"

"Just so we're clear, I'm not going to endure an interrogation. But to answer this *one question*, he was waiting for me to print some documents I had forgotten to put on my laptop and take to the office."

"So you won't answer when I ask if you're going to Vegas alone?"

That startled her into a momentary pause. "I told you about the convention coming up and that Frank and I decided to attend. It's especially important now that we're going into partnership. We can't engage in that kind of networking without being there."

"You didn't tell me anything about that."

"I'm not going to argue the point."

"Nor will I. What I will do, however, is build a box in this room, right here, right now, and invite you to climb inside it with me to find out which one of us is the first to leave." The challenge reflected a common saying within their marriage about any disagreement when one or both partners has had enough.

Laurie shook her head. "I'll save us both the aggravation and leave right now."

"Of course you will. Anything to avoid a topic that we've lived with for over a year now and you absolutely refuse to address."

"And what would that be?"

"The gorilla in the room and you know goddamn well what I'm talking about."

In the silence, with each of them glaring at the other, Nick knew the time had finally come to deal with what Laurie considered to be a cancer and he thought of as essential to long-term health. And the only way to do that was to do it. "Want to sit down?"

"Not on your life."

"Okay, let's talk about life. About how your failure to do something so simple as set the alarm allowed a stone-cold killer to terrorize *our* daughter for over a half hour. Ever think about what it would have been like to find her—?"

"Of course I do! Every single day."

"Really. Well I gotta tell you, Laurie, I find that extremely hard to believe. You open up the back door, windows, then walk out of the house without setting the alarm and call that *thinking*?"

Laurie's face hardened even more, which Nick didn't think possible. Her eyes glistened, and a single tear flowed down each cheek. "Maybe not. But here's what I call *not* thinking." She walked around the coffee table and stopped a few feet away from Nick.

"You have yet to acknowledge that your failure to come home when your daughter asked for her daddy has forever altered not only your relationship with her, but with your son. His hero failed the family once again by putting career ahead of us. He never lashed out, but I promise you his love now has a footnote. The same one as Stephanie's. They didn't want a fucking *alarm* system!"

As Laurie brushed by him, tears streaming down her face, he reached out to stop her.

She slapped his hand aside and ran out of the room.

Nick stared at her back as she reached the stairs and took them two at a time out of sight. He couldn't ever remember seeing her so eager to put distance between them. To leave his presence. Like an escape.

He was trembling slightly and his knees felt weak, so he sat in the armchair. And tried to make sense of the conflicting emotions fighting for predominance as the memories began to play.

After the Larchmont investigation and his retirement from the NTSB, Nick dedicated himself to reconnecting with his kids, even though he understood that they both had long since passed the point at which dependence on family had lessened and been replaced by a more peer-oriented approach to life.

Looking back now, he realized that the diminished connection to them he'd felt at the time, and attributed to the natural transition from child to adult, was a coward's way of hiding from his reflection in the mirror.

He had failed his daughter, and his son noted the neglect. Both had lost faith in their dad and drifted away without even trying to reconcile their disappointment with previous acceptance of his faults and their willing forgiveness.

How could he have been so blind to the impact of danger added to the equation? He'd secured the protection of his family at home by trained professionals and considered that sufficient, then accepted becoming the target of an assassin's bullet without a moment's thought about how that might affect his family. Especially Brad.

The irony of it saddened him to the core. Devote his

professional life to the cause of flight safety, motivated by the emotionally charged personal goal of preventing any other sons from losing their fathers to pilot error, and as a consequence forfeit an essential connection to his own.

He stood and hurried up the stairs to acknowledge his failures and apologize and make it all better between them and not let this happen. He knocked on their bedroom door. "Laurie?"

No answer.

He knocked and called out again, tried to open the door. Locked.

"Open the door, Laurie, I—"

"If you try to come in here, I swear to god you'll regret leaving one of your pistols in the nightstand."

"Oh, come on. You don't mean that."

"Go the *fuck* away."

CHAPTER SEVEN

Nick spent a restless night in the guest bedroom, tormented by a brain that wouldn't quit running at full speed. A little after 6:00 he gave up, showered and shaved in the guest bathroom, dressed in yesterday's clothes and set up the coffee for Laurie.

Their marriage had survived some heated disagreements over the years, but she seldom used profanity. Based on that alone, last night's argument had reached a new level of confrontation, and Nick figured they both needed more space and time before making any attempt at reconciliation.

The Jeep's tires hissed on wet pavement as he pulled off the highway and passed through the airport main gate. Rain blocked his view of the rotating beacon, and low clouds chopped off the top of tree-covered mountains to the north. No wheels would turn today. He parked at the café and entered to the aroma of doughnuts. Any willpower he brought with him sprinted back outside to the Jeep. He didn't try to stop it.

Loretta's voice carried into the dining area from the kitchen through closed swinging doors. "Have a seat. Be with you in a second."

He sat at the counter directly in front of the coffee pot, thought about what flavor he wanted, couldn't make up his mind. A waistline-threatening predicament.

Loretta charged out of the kitchen with the doughnuts on a serving platter and poured him a cup of her famous mud. "You decided yet?"

Nick sipped the hot coffee. "What makes you think I want something else?"

Loretta smiled, a gold bridge gleaming in the harsh overhead florescent lighting. "I can always spot a doughnut low-level light."

Nick nodded. "Then let's turn it out with one of each. Where'd you learn pilot talk, Loretta?"

She put a plate with three doughnuts on the counter. "From pilots. Airports tend to attract them."

"You're right. Foolish question." He bit into the chocolate doughnut, still warm from the fryer. His taste buds responded with a million little *thank you*'s as he sipped the coffee and figured that if Laurie ever threw him out of the house, he'd take up residence right here and become a booth bum.

He finished his doughnuts, got a coffee to go and laid a ten-dollar bill on the counter.

Loretta stared at it. "That's too much money."

"Put it on my account."

"Nobody has a damn account."

"Then keep the change."

"Why don't nobody listen when I tell 'em no tips?"

"Because we love you, Loretta."

He left the café, climbed into the Jeep, stuck the key in the ignition and paused when the thought occurred to him that he held another key, the one that could unlock the door to a better future for Caitlin.

She would never be able to put Lawson McAllister's death behind her without accepting the reality of what had almost certainly happened. It had taken Nick more than 25 years to accept the NTSB's conclusion that the death of his father was due to pilot error. The tragedy had defined his career goals and elevated them above and beyond commitment to Laurie and their children. He had lost so much and could never get it back.

So why not accept the job and thereby do Caitlin a favor? Help her move on without the past dragging her down, poisoning relationships, filling her with anger and resentment.

He could use a break from running the flight school, which in many ways seemed to run better when he wasn't second-guessing Ashton's decisions.

Nick stared out the rain-streaked windshield at the gray mist, so depressing that it was shoving his mood under the floor mat, and decided that he and Laurie could also use a longer break to let their emotions subside before standing together in the box and working it out.

And then there was that other thing. The buzz he felt whenever memories resurfaced of each discovery during the Larchmont investigation. And how, one by one, the clues ultimately leading to the truth charged his depleted batteries with new energy.

He reached for his phone and realized he didn't have Caitlin's number. Or Yates'. He went back into the café and found Loretta on her way to the kitchen.

"Got time for another question?"

She lurched to a halt with the screech of tennis shoes on polished linoleum. "Shoot."

"Remember that fellow wearing—?"

"Yup."

"How can you answer a question without hearing it?"

"Only one guy woulda caught my eye by his duds. I ain't no fashion maven, but this fella bad needs some wardrobe intervention."

Good old Loretta, the local straight shooter. "Any idea where he's staying?"

"My guess would be the Sleepy Time. He ate all three meals here yesterday, and he don't look like the type who'd drive far to find a feed bag."

THE SLEEPY TIME MOTOR Court dated from the '50s, a building frozen in another era. A neon sign with a flickering NO in front of the VACANCY could have meant that room availability was changing rapidly, but Nick doubted it.

The office, according to another sign trying to die, sat at the end of the long portion of twelve units arranged in an "L" shape. Dark, shuttered windows indicated no one was in attendance. From the look of things, Nick suspected the owners might have abandoned the place years ago.

One car sat parked halfway down the building. Nick eased the Jeep forward and stopped near the rear bumper. The Ford LTD's age and condition matched the surroundings perfectly. Arizona plates indicated that Cliff Yates might still be in town.

Nick turned off the engine and got out. Not a sound broke the silence. Pale, gray light and misty rain blended the building, parking lot, and surrounding forest into a homogenous scene, like an old black-and-white movie. His boots crunching on wet gravel seemed especially loud as he approached to the door of the unit in front of the LTD.

Room 137. He'd never understood numbering systems for motels. The 37th unit on the first floor seemed incongruous with a single-story building that had only 12 rooms.

His knock opened the door about two inches. Nick stared at the thin vertical stripe of dark interior. A piece of duct tape held the bolt flush with the edge of the door. A shiver of apprehension climbed his spine as he unzipped his jacket and nudged the door open.

"Anyone here?"

No answer.

He called out again with no response, then leaned into the doorway. Closed drapes blocked the intrusion of ambient light. With his right hand gripping the butt of the Glock, he patted the wall just inside the doorjamb to his left, found a light switch, flipped it on. A single bedside lamp struggled to brighten the dark interior. He stepped inside.

Yates was no housekeeper. Clothes, towels, and snack wrappers lay scattered about. Snickers bars and Lay's potato chips apparently sustained him between café visits.

Should he wait? Or leave and forget all about—?

"Don't move."

Nick stilled his body and sensed a person move up close behind him. "I'm looking for Cliff Yates."

"That hand under your jacket?"

"Uh . . . I need to—"

"It so much as twitches? Last thing you'll see is a chunk of your spinal cord coming out your navel."

Something hard pressed into Nick's back. A hand eased his jacket away, gripped his wrist.

"Loosen your fingers and let your arm go limp. I'll do all the moving."

The hand guided Nick's arm to the top of his head.

"Slowly now, bring your other hand up and interlace your fingers."

Nick complied. One hand clamped both of his. Another took the Glock, then a few seconds later patted him down. The hand let go of his.

"Turn around."

Nick faced an elderly man holding his Glock and what looked like a .357 magnum revolver with the hammer cocked. The guy had the look of someone who took no guff from anyone, never mind his advanced age. "I didn't break in," said Nick. "The door was open."

"Bullshit. It may have been unlatched, but that's because the lock's broken. You from the government?"

"No, sir. I'm looking for a guest." His use of the term surprised Nick with a mind picture of the little chocolates left on pillows in classy hotels. An absurd image under the circumstances, but the revolver pointed at his guts might explain it. He swallowed, his mouth as dry as burned toast. "His name's Cliff Yates."

The man shook his head. "Only got one. Signed in as John Doe."

"Okay. Perhaps I'll just leave—"

Yates stepped into the room. "What the hell's going on?"

The old man gestured with the revolver. "Found this guy in your room, Mr. Doe. I think he's from the government."

Yates smiled. "We'll just see about that. Thanks for looking after my things." He glanced at the handguns. "You came prepared, old timer."

"Call me that again and I'll shoot your nuts off, sonny."

Yates laughed. "I believe you might do just that."

"You can count on it." The man held out the Glock. "He was packing this."

"Ooooh. It's a big one, too. How about I take it just in case this gentleman is tougher than he looks?"

The man handed Yates the Glock. "You don't want me to call for backup?"

Yates gently guided him out of the room. "That's not necessary. Thanks again." He closed the door and turned to

Nick. "I wondered if I might be hearing from you. Have a seat."

Nick's knees suddenly abandoned their job. He collapsed into a rickety wooden chair beside a small table that wobbled when he leaned on it.

Yates offered him the Glock. "You might reconsider carrying this if you let an old man get the drop on you."

Nick could still feel the barrel of the revolver jammed into his back. He accepted his pistol and holstered it. "Thanks for the advice, but I had him right where I wanted until you showed up."

"Uh huh." Yates sat on the edge of the bed and placed his elbows on his knees, hands clasped together. He stared at Nick with alert eyes.

Underestimating this weasel might be dangerous, and Nick decided that he ought to compare Yates' story to Caitlin's. "I was thinking about your visit the other day."

"I bet you were. For now, why don't I do the talking?"

"Go ahead."

"My employer wants to hire you to investigate a plane crash. We believe sabotage was involved, and two people were murdered. Your reputation led us here, particularly when we read that article in *American Vigilante* and that book. Along with your expertise, it's your tenacity we want. Somebody who'll stick with it, not get discouraged or chased off."

"By whom?"

"I'll get to that after you sign on."

"Are you saying you know who did it but not how?"

Yates nodded. "You'll be working with me, and—"

"Tell me about your employer."

"That's none of your business."

He nodded. "For now, maybe. What have you done so far?"

"Mostly beat my head against a stone wall. I had no idea how the NTSB works, and those investigator types are a tight-lipped bunch. The on-scene investigation is almost done. Or it might be by now, come to think of it. Preliminary conclusion of pilot error. Kind of like another investigation you're familiar with."

"Without being a part of the official inquiry, I can't gain access to all they have until it becomes part of the public record."

"That's a load of crap. With your connections, there has to be a way."

"What makes you so sure?"

"Because that's the way the world works. I used to be a cop. I have friends here and there, owe me favors, expect them in return. You can do the same thing."

Nick had no doubt he could *try*, but the NTSB wasn't law enforcement and operated on a completely different mindset. "What's your employer's phone number?"

"That also is none of your business."

"Then tell her to get in touch with me."

Yates frowned. "I never said my employer was a girl."

Nick stood, got in Yates' face, and grinned. "Don't forget I'm one of those tight-lipped investigator types. Bye."

ABOUT FIVE O'CLOCK SUNDAY afternoon, Nick finished the work interrupted by Caitlin's visit to the flight school on Saturday and locked up the deserted flight school building. His empty stomach and sagging energy reminded him that he hadn't eaten anything since over-dosing on Loretta's doughnuts, and a dinner plan formed without thinking about it much.

A peace offering, maybe? To keep the home fires lit for a

few weeks until he and Laurie had cooled off a little? Or just because they both liked the meal and had to eat something?

Whatever Nick's reason, Laurie seldom worked late on Sundays even during the recent months of intense effort, and that boded well for his chances.

Standing in the Valley Market checkout line, he politely endured the surreptitious glances and whispered conversations about him being *that guy* they were going to make the movie about, the one who pulled a gun on a dangerous stranger *right over there in the aisle with the wine.* One customer even said something about *Dirty Harry lives in Cedar Valley.*

As Nick swiped his credit card, he asked the clerk if he knew whether those Hollywood types had really conducted a casting call.

The young man shook his head. "I heard it was just location scouting."

From the line behind Nick, a transplant from another state said, "I's over to The Cellar that night 'fore they got outa here, and looked to me like they had one o' them call things goin' on in the party room."

Then another, apparently from the same area of the country: "Don't think so, Alvin. That was them just havin' a good time."

"Well," said Alvin, "might o' been. But they was doin' some readin'. Ya know, like the same line more'n once."

A third voice, probably a Colorado native, cleared it up. "That was just old man Thatcher in his cups again."

When the laughter died down, Nick declined the offer of help out with his groceries, lifted his two sacks and decided to stir the pot a little. He turned to face the customers in the checkout line.

"Don't tell anyone this, but I got turned down." Then into the resulting silence, "I couldn't believe it. They want Hotel in the lead role. Go figure." He hadn't taken more than three steps toward the exit before the murmurs began.

Fifteen minutes later, Nick pulled into an empty garage and wondered if Sunday evening dinners were a lost cause as well. Then a pervasive feeling of emptiness settled into the Jeep's interior when he noticed folded packing boxes leaning against the house along with a roll of butcher paper.

He climbed out of the Jeep with the groceries and stared at the door into the kitchen. His feet didn't want to move. When he finally forced them into action, time appeared to have slowed way down. It took him forever to enter the kitchen.

Open boxes lay on the floor and countertop, a stack of newspapers nearby, along with a few glasses, some silverware, cooking utensils, pots and pans, dishes, and the spare toaster.

Nick set the makings for dinner on the countertop. "Laurie!"

A silent house answered, just as he knew it would.

Walking to the living room felt like a trip across a space-time continuum, passing a before-after boundary through a door that slammed shut behind him.

On the other side of a lamp table beside his favorite chair was an empty space where Laurie's chair used to be. The place where she always sat to read, watch TV, chat with her husband about life, love, children, dreams, anything of consequence in their universe.

In its place, only a layer of dust on the oriental area rug, lit by a shaft of late-afternoon diffused light slanting through the picture window. Nick stared at the dust, a symbolic reminder of the emptiness that had begun to settle into his heart.

His knees weakened and he sat down. But someone had swapped out his chair. This one was a stranger, an interloper in his own home, no longer the familiar, comforting place to rest his body and mind from the turmoil out there.

Silence, interrupted only by the ticking of the grandfather clock in the foyer by the front door, assumed the function of a barrier against the future for Nick. If he didn't say anything to break it, maybe this wouldn't be happening.

He leaned back in the chair, stared at the forest outside the window and waited, but it didn't work.

CHAPTER EIGHT

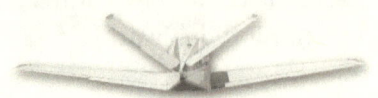

Trapped in a maze with deadly creatures who know every twist and turn, Nick struggles to find the exit while keeping his head on a swivel.

Closer and closer they come to surprising him with their stinking breath and foul odor before he can point the Glock and fire to stop them from ripping into him with razor-sharp teeth. His arms grow weary as the pistol becomes heavier and heavier, his reflexes dulled by the constant attacks.

When one of them finally gets close enough to bite off the end of the barrel, Nick throws the destroyed Glock at the beast and closes his eyes to await the end.

A PHONE RANG AND Nick bolted upright, drenched with sweat and shaking, in a room that had grown into a lonely cavern overnight. He found the phone on the floor. Caitlin Monroe asked where he was so she could meet him there.

"Not on your life."

"What does that mean?"

"It isn't neutral territory."

"You aren't making sense."

"Not to you, maybe."

"And I suppose my motel room is hostile as well?"

"Oh, yes."

"How about my car? Or your car? Or the overlook above the airport where we could park both cars and sit on a neutral bench."

"Thirty minutes."

CAITLIN PULLED THE MERCEDES into the overlook and parked beside the bench. The view didn't include anything more than low clouds, and a brisk wind from higher terrain to the east carried a fine mist that settled onto her windshield and coated everything in the visible world with a sliver-gray sheen. She could barely see the highway in her rearview. If Nick wanted to keep their meeting privately neutral, this should suffice.

After a few minutes of fidgety waiting, she needed to get out and stretch her legs. She opened the Velcro closure on her shoulder bag and pulled out the Walther, checked it, and slipped the pistol in the pocket of her jacket. She had no reason to think she'd need it for protection against Nick, but events in her past demanded unwavering caution. She'd grown up surrounded by predators, and once free of their fangs, she had vowed *never again*.

Standing by the railing, she pulled up her collar, released the hood and draped it over her head against the chilly, wet wind. After a few minutes the sound of an approaching car drifted toward her from the direction of Cedar Valley. She turned in time to see the vague outline of a vehicle pass the overlook. She couldn't tell what kind. According to her watch, Nick was over 20 minutes late. Another 10 and she was out of there.

About the time she was ready to leave, rustling in the forest below the overlook caught her attention. She gripped the Walther inside her jacket pocket and peered over the railing.

The slow advance of moving branches up the hill marked the path of someone, who turned out to be Nick when he finally appeared from behind a tree. He wore head-to-toe camouflage and she couldn't make out much more than his face. She smiled. "Sneaky. Question is, why?"

"Trying to regain what little anonymity I once had."

"Is it working?"

"We'll find out."

"Okay. In the meantime, I'm not going to talk to a tree while standing in the rain."

"Get in the Mercedes and I'll join you there."

A minute or so later, a tap on the passenger-side front window startled Caitlin. She unlocked the doors.

Nick slid into the seat, dripping water all over the leather, and flipped back his hood. "Sorry about the mess."

"No problem. I'll have my valet take care of it."

"Good. Let's talk about what I'm going to do for you."

"Before we get to that, what changed your mind?"

Nick fixed Caitlin with a warning glare. "We won't ever get to that if you keep asking me questions." After a moment, he continued, "First, I need to find the wreckage, and that introduces three scenarios.

"One: I doubt it's still under the control of the NTSB. But if it is, that won't be easy unless I can call in some favors.

"Two: It's better if the NTSB has released the wreckage to the family, unless they've already sold it for salvage. Then I'll have to hunt it down before they start reclaiming any usable parts and send the rest to recycling. The good news is that your money in my hand can buy me unrestricted access for as long as I need it, *unless* they get suspicious and cut me off."

Caitlin frowned. "Why would they do that?"

"Because they make their living as scavengers, and I don't

mean that as a derogatory comment. Any aircraft wreckage usually yields high-dollar parts that can be sold, but most of it is nothing more than scrap metal. If I go in there acting like I'm trying to find something *really* valuable, it won't take long for them to take a look for themselves."

"And the third scenario is?"

"The family has control of the wreckage but they haven't made arrangements for salvage. Then we have the possibility of two sub-headings to deal with."

Caitlin shook her head. "I'm getting a little confused. How about the short version?"

"There's no such thing in aviation. Sub-heading number one: The crash was a slam-dunk case of pilot error like the NTSB says. I can probably talk my way into examining the wreckage and prove that to you once and for all. Then you can get on with your life and leave this tragedy behind.

"Or two: We're dealing with a conspiracy to murder. The family, which according to you is represented by the murderer, will either want that wreckage to go to salvage and be crushed into a lump of junk as soon as possible; or, get to it first and remove any evidence of sabotage to make discovery by anyone an impossibility."

"I was with you right up until the end."

"What?"

"I wasn't expecting that last sub-heading to have two parts."

"Okay, here—"

"I was joking. And I have a question for you."

"What?"

"If you had sabotaged an airplane and murdered someone, which sub-heading of part two of the third scenario would you choose?"

Nick almost smiled. "Three-two-B."

"Finally," said Caitlin. "We're on the same page." When Nick reached for the door handle, she touched his arm, noticed the slight flinch, wondered about it. "What did you mean by getting on with my life?"

Nick looked down at his lap and brushed a few drops of water off his camo rain pants. After a moment he said, "I know all about holding onto something destructive for too long and the price you have to pay. My father died in his airplane when I was a kid. The NTSB called it pilot error. I refused to accept their conclusion for almost twenty years. And by denying the truth, I allowed career to supplant family and push away the ones I love." Then he looked at Caitlin with an expression that seemed to plead with her. "I hate to think that you would make the same mistake."

Before Caitlin could respond, he climbed out of the Mercedes, hopped over the railing and disappeared down the slope into the gray forest. She sat very still, afraid to move and break the comforting spell that had joined her in the sedan.

What were the odds that an ex-aviation accident investigator she just hired to prove that Lawson was murdered would know through personal experience the emptiness she'd felt every day since the crash? And also be only the second man she'd ever known who seemed more interested in what he could do *for* her than *to* her?

Caitlin didn't believe in luck, fate, or destiny, but this moment seemed to contain a little bit of all three.

CHAPTER NINE

The day after meeting with Caitlin, Nick left his half-empty house for the airport at 6:00 a.m. based on a forecast indicating that weather conditions would improve. The current cloud ceiling and visibility met legal requirements for departure, but he had a personal rule never to takeoff unless the weather met or exceeded landing minimums, which were typically higher.

More than a few pilots he'd known over the years didn't share his caution, the product of having crashed his first experimental amateur-built airplane after departing this airport in bad weather about a year ago during the Larchmont investigation. A combination of eagerness to get home and a stupid mistake had very nearly killed him when his airplane iced up and Cedar Valley was the only airport within reach.

Soon thereafter, he'd crashed another airplane he borrowed—well, *stole* would be more accurate—when chasing down a hired assassin. The way Nick figured it, any aviator's luck he may have accrued in 20-plus years of safe piloting without incident had been all used up within a couple of weeks.

Blanketed in low clouds this morning, the airport was deserted except for Loretta, who waved at him through the front window of the café. It didn't matter to her that the weather would probably keep all her regular customers away. She'd have fresh doughnuts and coffee ready just in case for *her boys*.

He parked the Jeep in front of his hangar, disabled the alarm and flipped the switch to open the bi-fold door. The airplane that slowly came into view had a direct connection to the aftermath of the Larchmont investigation

Much to Nick's surprise and relief, the builder of the airplane he destroyed did not pound him into the dirt with his fists. Instead, he extended a hand and congratulated Nick on "taking it to those jerks who killed Larchmont." It seemed only fitting to pay the builder for a replacement, which Nick did with some of the assassin's blood money, along with an additional amount for the builder to construct a second one for Nick, a single-engine, tandem two-seater, the pilot in front and a passenger behind. With a turbocharged 350-horsepower engine and retractable landing gear, it could peel Nick's eyelids back.

Preflight inspection completed, Nick loaded his bags in the compartment behind the aft seat and checked the weather one last time. Clouds obscuring the high terrain in three quadrants around the airport dictated a takeoff to the south. He received his departure clearance from Air Traffic Control on the phone so he could enter the weather prior to establishing radio contact with ATC, typically possible only when above 7000 feet MSL at the Cedar Valley airport.

Lined up on the centerline of Runway 17, Nick scanned the instrument panel, confirmed all engine instruments in the green, and that his navigation display was set to maintain runway heading for the climb to his assigned altitude of 10,000 feet MSL.

Stick full back in his lap, release brakes, throttle full forward with right rudder to keep the nose straight down the runway, relax back pressure on the stick as the wings begin to produce lift and the airplane gets light on her wheels, one little skip and liftoff.

Nose up to 15 degrees on the attitude indicator, retract the landing gear, confirm up and locked, enter the clouds at 500 feet above the ground and on the gauges with his world reduced to a primary flight display of attitude, heading, vertical speed, altitude, and airspeed. Passing 1000 feet above the ground, reduce the throttle and propeller to the climb setting.

He called Denver Center and received clearance to 12,000 feet and on course.

Once clear of the clouds shrouding the valley, Nick climbed into a brilliant blue sky and leveled off for cruise. With good weather ahead, he canceled his instrument clearance, bid goodbye to the air traffic controller, engaged the autopilot and settled into the peace and quiet of his own special universe.

Yesterday, Nick had called the airport manager at the Dry Springs Municipal Airport near Phoenix, Arizona, introduced himself as a private investigator, and confirmed that the NTSB Go Team had chosen the airport as headquarters for the investigation. And more importantly, the wreckage was still there, and the manager had not heard anything about when it would be removed.

The ease with which that pretense rolled off his tongue had surprised Nick at the time, and it still did. Maybe because that's what he was. A private *air crash* investigator. Sounded good, anyway, and the manager had no reason to be suspicious. A pile of mangled metal had been sitting in one of his hangars for a couple of weeks surrounded by a security perimeter that disappeared when the team went home. Who cares if a stranger wants to look at it now?

Nick's agreement with Caitlin was simple. For an advance of $5000 to cover expenses and $500 a day paid in arrears, he would search the wreckage for any indication of tampering. And although he expected his physical examination to confirm the online preliminary report's conclusion of pilot error, a tiny bit of the old Nick had crept to the surface. If he found anything suspicious, nothing stood in his way except the obstacles he failed to overcome.

After an uneventful flight and landing, Nick opened the canopy for taxiing to the parking ramp and appreciated the fact that he'd cold-soaked himself and the airplane at altitude for the better part of three hours. He arranged with the line guy to have the airplane stored in a hangar so it wouldn't melt.

When he asked about where the NTSB had set up shop, the guy pointed to the largest hangar on the field. The airport manager had gone to lunch, so Nick decided to grab a bite, find a room, and return about 2:00 p.m. to assume his new role.

With a rented Jeep's air conditioner on maximum and directions to the closest accommodations, he left the airport and 15 minutes later approached the reception desk at the Bargain Suites Motel.

"I need a room, please."

"How long you staying?"

Nick thought the desk clerk had said the words, but he'd never seen anyone speak without moving his lips. "Put me down for three days."

"Have to ask, but it don't really matter. We're not full or nothin'." The clerk tilted his head toward keys hung in rows in an open cabinet on the wall. "Help yourself."

Nick hadn't seen anything but a motel keycard in years. That didn't bode well, but this wasn't a vacation, and convenience trumped quality. "What room number?"

"Your choice."

Nick grabbed a key and walked into the bright sunshine. Heat radiated off the asphalt in shimmering waves. Approaching fall hadn't done much to lower daytime temperatures in Phoenix, but the locals probably considered 96 degrees cool compared to what they had endured during the summer. He fully expected to hear a resident say, "Oh, but it's a dry heat" before the end of the day.

He opened the door to his room with memories of a frequent traveler's uncertainty: What's this one going to be like? He stepped inside and sniffed. Ah yes. Another home away from home magically transformed into non-smoking by removing the ashtrays. Wonderful.

Back at the office, he couldn't see the clerk's head. Closer inspection found him face down on the counter, arms hanging limp by his sides. Nick grabbed a handful of keys and went looking.

After trying more than a dozen rooms, he found the lemony aroma of cleaning solution and relatively fresh air. He unloaded his bags from the Jeep, stopped by the office, and dropped the unwanted keys on the counter.

He'd been in the room only a few minutes when a knock rattled the door. Nick opened it and found Yates standing in the blast furnace heat wearing his signature eye-torture outfit minus the polka dot tie. Caitlin hadn't said anything about sending along a babysitter, but Nick decided to go along with it. "Aren't you warm?"

Yates marched into the room and sat in a desk chair. "I'm used to dry heat. Ready to start?"

"How did you know where I was?"

Yates looked at Nick with an *Are you shitting me?* expression, shook his head and propped his feet on the desk. The sole of his right shoe had a hole in it, the left one not far behind. "I find people every day who are *trying* to hide."

Nick sat in an armchair and decided not to mention that he had met with Caitlin. Let Yates think that Nick needed him. It would also serve to compare their stories. "Go."

He listened to Yates prattle on for five minutes without providing anything Nick hadn't learned from Caitlin, and he figured that she hadn't told Yates about their meeting. Nick had no clue what that meant, if anything, but he filed it away. He also noted that Yates said nothing about suspicions of murder. He also seemed to know more than the average person about aviation details.

After another few minutes, Nick interrupted with, "Why not accept the NTSB's conclusion?"

"A year ago you proved that Larchmont was set up to die as a result of what everyone expected would kill him sooner or later. Same thing is true here."

"So McAllister's piloting skills were suspect?"

Yates shook his head. "He was a doctor. And he owned a Victory. That sets the stage right off."

"That might be the basis for suspecting pilot error, but not sabotage."

"Except," said Yates, "that he *loved* to go fast and routinely operated the airplane past red line."

Hello. "How do you know that?"

"It's what investigators do."

"Are you a pilot?"

"I got my private license a few years back when I was a cop. Thought maybe I'd apply to the aviation division."

That explained Yates' familiarity with the deadly V-Tail/doctor combination and use of the aviator's term for maximum allowable airspeed. Nick looked up from his notes. "Didn't work out?"

Yates shrugged. "Among other things."

"Okay, so how does knowledge about how he operated the airplane tie in with the crash?"

"Well, duh. That's why *you're* here."

No shit, fool. "Thanks for the info. I'll be in touch."

Yates stared at him. "The hell you talking about? We're a *team.*"

"Like hell we are. This is my world, and I don't need a tag-along sidekick."

Yates stood, the blood vessels on his forehead looking like a roadmap of welts. "Watch your step, Phillips. I've eaten milquetoasts like you for a snack."

He stormed out of the room, leaving Nick with the nagging impression that to take Yates lightly might not be wise. The guy seemed to exude contradiction. Why would any serious professional with competence at anything but being a clown dress like that? No telling.

To Yates' credit, however, Nick's preconceived notion that the crash was due to pilot error had just developed a tiny crack in the form of a *not so fast* feeling, ironically based on the revelation from someone other than Caitlin that McAllister was an *always-fast* aviator. If Yates could come up with that, who else knew and would be able to connect the dots and create a smokescreen for hiding sabotage?

The person would have to understand that the V-Tail configuration produced less aerodynamic drag, improved performance, allowed more rapid acceleration, particularly nose-low in descents, and pilots could get into serious trouble by exceeding red line.

And that excessive speed by itself wasn't the problem, because manufacturers had to prove during flight testing that an airplane could fly 30 percent faster than red line without exhibiting any dangerous aerodynamic characteristics, and test plans never called for flying into thunderstorms.

But most important, the killer had to figure out how to tamper with a Victory to increase its vulnerability to inflight structural failure.

If someone knew all those things and had access to McAllister's airplane? They'd be a standout person of interest for Nick's microscope.

He stood and began pacing around the room, which felt like it had suddenly received a shot of high-voltage static electricity that raised the hair on his arms and filled his whole body with a familiar tingle of excitement. Like when discovering the first piece of evidence that opened the door to solving a crash puzzle.

And here he was, sitting in a cheap motel room doing a bit of simple math: excessive speed plus turbulence plus tampering equals *flutter*.

Okay, then. The time had come to do a little role-playing.

IN SPITE OF THE name, Nick doubted that surface water had ever existed within hundreds of miles of the Dry Springs Municipal Airport. Just looking at it made him thirsty. Dust devils twirled in the distance, the horizon distorted by heat waves climbing from the desert.

He turned off the highway past a faded metal sign mounted between two posts, with a saguaro cactus and a cartoon cowboy, one arm outstretched, pointing the way. A large hangar with a small terminal building attached to one end sat on the edge of an aircraft parking ramp and taxiway. Two runways in an "X" pattern baked in the afternoon sun. They appeared to be overdone.

He drove up to the terminal building and peeled himself

out of the Jeep. The unrelenting heat sucked any remaining moisture from his mouth and throat. A small trainer engaged in landing practice touched down with a double chirp of rubber meeting concrete, followed by a full-power takeoff and a painfully slow climb for altitude and another attempt.

A tattered sticker in the front window of the terminal building announced the presence of air conditioning inside. Nick shoved open the door. Soggy expulsions of a swamp cooler enveloped him. Dry heat outside and moist semi-cool in here. Wonderful.

A man dressed in soiled coveralls stepped out of an interior office. "Help you?"

"I'm looking for the NTSB team."

"They're gone."

Nick hoped the guy bought his feigned astonishment. "What?"

"As in outta here."

"Damn! The team chief—can't remember his name—promised me they'd be here through Thursday."

"Looks like he lied."

Nick smiled. "I hate it when that happens. But I don't really need him if that Victory wreckage and the logbooks are still here. He asked me for an opinion about something. Where's the wreckage?"

"Down this hallway to the end. They used the last two rooms on the right and the whole south end of the hangar."

"Thanks." Nick turned toward the hallway.

"But I can't let you in there, mister."

So much for it being easy. He faced the guy. "It'll be okay. Really. I'm authorized access."

"That may be, but the head guy on that team never said anything about it. And the way I figure it, you'd be able to remember his name if you were here on his authority."

Busted. "If I get him to call you and he says it's okay?"

"You're in."

"Good. What's his name?"

The guy smiled at that. "Persistent, aren't you? Even when tap dancing."

"Always."

"Then you can always consider me *re*sistant when confronted with tap dancing."

So much for role-playing. Nick thanked the guy, returned to the Jeep, began making a mind list of possible next moves and stopped at number one. *Of course.*

Playing dangerously with speed limits on the way to the motel, he called James Dickson, the current director of the NTSB's Aviation Division. James had been Nick's second-in-command on the Larchmont investigation and a former protégé of the previous Director, murdered by the same assassin who almost took Nick's life as well.

ARIZONA'S DECISION NOT TO observe Daylight Savings Time meant only a two-hour difference between Nick's watch and James Dickson's in D.C. That forced Nick to stare at the Skype contact page on his laptop waiting for James to arrive home from his office at the NTSB, grab a beer, and get the hell online for a video chat.

When it finally happened, James appeared against a background of floor-to-ceiling shelves with lots of books, knick-knacks, and pictures. Probably a home office. He took a sip of beer from a mug and initiated the conversation with, "Nice digs, Phillips. Have your fortunes diminished over the past year?"

Nick's eyes were glued to Dickson's mug. It had frost all over it, and he could almost taste the beer, those first few sips with the foam against his lips. His bottle of beer from the mini-bar didn't come close. "No. I'm just staying in this dingy motel room to relive all the good times with the NTSB."

"How's that working out for you?"

"It's a trip down memory lane." They both laughed at that in spite of the fact that their mutual past didn't contain very much in the way of memories worth keeping, then spent a few minutes catching up on each other's news.

James had been offered a promotion to Director of the Aviation Division, which was a good fit for his bureaucratic talents, but he turned it down. When Nick asked why, James said, "Wasn't ready for it. Hadn't earned my spurs. And I can honestly say that for years I didn't appreciate the true importance of what we do. Working under Lars was so seductive, and I got lured into the easy way. Career advancement fueled by connections. After he died, it was like a release that allowed me to understand why you were always so intense. What's up with you?"

Nick finally managed to recover from hearing James' report of having morphed into a real investigator and related a short version of the period immediately following the Larchmont investigation and the move to Colorado.

"A flight school?" said James. "Like it?"

"There's satisfaction in seeing young pilots improve, but I miss investigating."

"Working your ass off in a dump for a few weeks? Are you nuts?"

Nick chuckled. "Undoubtedly. But to the purpose of my call, did you happen to see a magazine article a while back about my involvement in the Larchmont investigation?"

"Heard some talk about it around the office, but *American Vigilante* isn't on my subscription list."

"What about the book?"

"I might be interested, but it's only an eBook. I'm a paper kinda guy."

"Well, somebody who's read both wants me to look into this crash."

"Look into as in . . .?"

"Sabotage leading to murder."

Dickson shook his head. "Jesus, Nick. That's a pretty strong statement. I can understand why they'd come to you, but you were on the investigation team in Colorado and had direct access to the evidence. You told this person that, right?"

"Sure."

"So what do you think you can do for them?"

"There's a private investigator representing the family. He's an ex-cop, made the point that he's got back-channel sources. That got me to thinking. You know . . . curious about what it would be like to be involved again. Even if on the fringes. I decided to look into it."

"And you came to me for info. Unofficially."

"Of course."

Dickson picked up a pen, tapped his against his lips for a moment, tossed it on the desk. "We've had our differences, Nick. Far as I'm concerned, that's over with. But I could get in a shit load of trouble by—"

"No one would ever know."

"There's no way to guarantee that."

Nick considered his words carefully. "Sure there is. Unless you think the NTSB is monitoring the private communications of their employees, we're the only two people who know about this conversation. And everything we discuss will ultimately be in the public record anyway."

James leaned back in his chair, clasped his hand behind his head, and stared at the ceiling.

Nick started to say something, thought, *Shut up and let him decide on his own.*

After a moment, James centered himself on the screen and stared into it. "I guess it's time to find out what you want and how much I can tell you."

"Fair enough. How about an overview?"

James related much of what Yates had said. When he paused for a drink of beer, Nick asked about the weather conditions.

"Typical summertime convective activity. Thunderstorms, turbulence, high winds, hail, you know the drill. The pilot had filed a flight plan under instrument flight rules, but the audiotapes indicate he didn't want to continue accepting vectors to follow slower traffic to circumnavigate the storms. He canceled his IFR clearance, and we think the crash occurred less than five minutes later."

"Who reported it?"

"No one. The flight plan was closed, so Air Traffic Control didn't look for him. People expecting the occupants contacted the fixed-base operator where the pilot had arranged for parking and fuel. The airplane was more than three hours overdue before they finally got a search going. The next day, a Civil Air Patrol pilot spotted the wreckage in remote areas."

"Areas, as in plural?"

"Yeah. The airplane broke up in flight, pieces scattered all over hell and gone."

Nick asked about the pilot's qualifications. Dickson's answer verified Yates' description of McAllister's reputation as a speed freak. Nick looked up from his notes. "How much of the wreckage did you find?"

"Enough to determine that all the major systems were working normally."

"The tail section landed first?"

"Yeah. We plotted the location of each piece, of course, and the last known direction of flight is consistent with an in-flight breakup."

"So you think the pilot flew too close to a thunderstorm at high speed, encountered turbulence, and the tail ripped off?"

Dickson paused a moment. "After giving you the standard comment that we're still studying the evidence and it's too soon to tell, everything points to it. No other explanation is even remotely plausible."

"Did you personally inspect pieces of the tail section?"

Dickson nodded and sipped his beer. "I'm not a structural engineer any more than you are, but the experts decided that the inciting event had to be a combination of high speed and severe turbulence."

"What about flutter?"

"Could have been, but it doesn't matter. If the pilot hadn't flown the airplane the way he did, we wouldn't be having this conversation."

Nick couldn't agree more. He also knew that determining whether an in-flight breakup had been caused by high speed and turbulence alone or in combination with flutter required attention to specific telltale evidence. Unlike Nick, NTSB investigators had no reason to do that.

Another possible cause they would have addressed involved structural weakness. If McAllister had exceeded g-limits and overstressed the airframe, logbook entries and/or physical evidence might provide documentation. "Any evidence of pre-accident stress fractures?"

"None that we found."

"Okay. How about a special favor?"

"I can tell I'm not going to like this, but what now?"

"I need to look at the logbooks and wreckage. The airport manager out here says he has no objection if you authorize it."

Dickson frowned. *"That* would put me in a spot."

"How so? Either you say 'yes' or you don't."

"I'm well aware of my choices. I'd like to help, but your past official status has no bearing on legality. Anyone finds out, I'm toast."

"We could do this without anyone knowing."

Dickson shrugged. "Except for the airport manager. But that's not the point. You have enough to tell your employer that this crash was totally preventable."

Don't push this. "I understand, James, thanks. Can I contact you again if I need anything more? Information, that is?"

"We'll see. But you might want to wait to receive my bill. Not sure you can afford me. Bye."

Nick closed his laptop, got another beer from the mini-bar and sat down just as someone knocked on his door. He checked the security peephole, sighed, opened up. Yates stood there in dusty shoes, pumpkin-and-green-striped slacks topped by his trademark plaid sport coat, his mouth full and chewing. A half-eaten doughnut leaked red jelly onto his hand.

"Your doughnut is bleeding."

"I like them fresh from the hunt." He waved Nick aside and took a step toward the door.

Nick blocked his way. "What do you want?"

Yates shoved the rest of the doughnut in his mouth, swallowed it one gulp and licked the filling off his fingers. "First, where have you been?"

The urge to have it out with this asshole right there in the doorway almost took over, but Nick shoved it down, turned, and walked into the room. "Close the door." He waited until Yates did that, then leaned toward him, nose to nose. "I'm not working for you. To what degree I work *with* you is up to me. You've got nothing to say about it."

"Okay, tough guy. *Our* employer wants results. If I have to bird-dog you to get them, that's what I'll do."

Nick nodded. "Looks like an impasse." He went into the bathroom, soaked a washcloth with tepid water and began wiping his face and neck.

Yates' reflection appeared in the mirror. "What the fuck is your problem? All you have to do is keep me in the loop so I can report some progress."

Which confirmed again that Caitlin wasn't telling Yates everything she was doing any more than Nick was telling either of them. His best tactic appeared to be more role-playing, which gave him a buzz he couldn't quite define. He faced Yates.

"You can relay that I'm setting up an information source."

"Who are you talking to?"

Nick turned around, pushed past Yates and sat down at the small dining table. "That's my business."

Yates followed, stood over him. "When will we get something worthwhile?"

"Maybe never. So far, everything confirms your description of what happened. I asked to see the wreckage, and he'll get back to me."

"Goddamnit, Phillips. Does everything you do take this long?"

Nick glared at Yates. "I can't push him."

"That's bullshit. What good's a source if you can't get what you want?"

"He's got to offer it, and I have to protect him in the process."

"How long we talking about?"

"He'll think about it for a day or so, then come around."

Yates leaned over, lowered his voice. "Just so you know, I'm not fooled. Up to me, I'd pound your ass in the dirt so far only your eyeballs would show. Leave you there until you agree to quit stalling and find some *evidence*."

Nick eased his hands under the table, palms up against the underside, ready to shove it toward Yates. Back him up and get room to maneuver. "But it isn't up to you, is it? Somebody else is calling the shots. You're just a messenger. An errand boy."

Yates hitched up his belt. "Believe what you want. But there'll come a time when you answer to *me.*" He formed a child's rendition of a pistol with his hand, pointed at Nick and dropped his thumb with a soft, "Pow," turned on a heel and walked toward the door.

"Don't try any of that PI shit," Nick said. "Follow me, you and your employer are on your own."

Yates yanked open the door, said "Yeah, yeah" over his shoulder, slammed it closed behind him.

Nick got up, freshened the washcloth, lay on the bed, and covered his face with it. Two showers already today, the sweat kept pouring out. He could be lounging on his deck in a day or so, surrounded by the dry cool of a Colorado autumn, sipping River Rock Pale Ale from a frosty mug.

All he had to do was tell Caitlin she's damn lucky that Lawson McAllister didn't take her on that trip. His arrogance, spawned from the expert syndrome so common with over-achievers, would have ended her life as well. Face the reality, mourn the loss and put it behind her.

And he'd do that soon. But first, dig a little deeper to make certain the NTSB investigation hadn't missed something that was nudging Nick's curiosity out of a deep slumber.

It began with a simple question, *How would you have done this?*

Dickson wasn't going to offer more than he already had to help Nick find the answer, but at least the mutual antipathy they had shared over many years no longer fouled the relationship. Having finally shed Lars Nordstrom's bureaucratic twaddle and learned to be a real investigator, he might be willing to do more if Nick could bring him something.

Okay. Decision made. Time to go a'hunting.

THE WESTERN HORIZON GLOWED with the last rays of a departing sun as dusk cloaked the desert. Nick pulled off the airport road and drove about fifty yards into the scrub. The dashboard clock showed 8:02; the thermometer on the rearview read 91. He climbed out and stood by the Jeep. A stiff breeze blew his drenched shirt against his chest with a welcome hint of coolness.

Earlier that day, he had asked the desk clerk if it ever cooled off in Dry Creek. Oh, yes. The winters here are very nice. Maybe so, but I'd never survive a summer here to enjoy it. Yeah, 110 degrees is hot, but it'll be 40 degrees cooler at five a.m. Wonderful. I'll just get up earlier.

Nick leaned against the fender to wait for the night to deepen. Although relatively sure nothing in the hangar would prove sabotage, he needed to confirm that before trying to convince Caitlin. With the NTSB investigation completed and control of the wreckage and responsibility for security shifted to McAllister's estate, the window of opportunity for a personal inspection could close at any moment, especially if there were any truth to Caitlin's accusations. Mrs. McAllister would likely have already made arrangements to promptly wipe the earth clean of her philandering husband's precious Victory.

An hour passed with no sign of human activity. The airport appeared deserted, but he couldn't shake the feeling he might be wrong. He stared at the hangar in the distance. A single window in the office area glowed yellow. A forgotten switch or someone working late? No cars in the parking lot didn't mean much. Airport business owners and employees often parked their rides in hangars.

But the real concern came from a line of four rectangles of brilliant light spilling from windows in the old-style Quonset-hut hangar. It took enormous overhead fixtures to illuminate that large an area. Expensive to leave on. Small operations like this had to watch every penny. There had to be someone—

A section of hangar lights went out, then three more in quick succession until darkness claimed the interior.

That answered that. On second thought, maybe it didn't. The lights could be on a timer, or someone might be spending the night.

Nick stood in the silent darkness and decided to give it another couple of hours . . . then changed his mind.

If he found someone there, just act his way out of it. Spur of the moment, play it by ear, go with the flow. An essential skill for investigators. At least the private kind.

Or better yet, have a story ready. Something like . . . the Jeep broke down. The battery on my phone died. How about a ride?

He drove back to the airport road and parked on the shoulder. Glock on his right hip, extra magazine and flashlight in a holder on his left and both concealed under a light jacket, he got out, locked the Jeep, and walked to the office at the front of the hangar.

The door was locked. He pounded on it. "Hello? Anyone there?"

After a moment he walked toward the back of the hangar and peered in each window as he passed. At the rear of the hangar he found a personnel entrance built into the huge sliding doors for moving airplanes in and out. All hangars had them. They were frequently overlooked when closing up for the evening.

But not this time. Nick peered into the small window in the door. Through the larger windows in the hangar walls, soft light from a quarter moon coated pieces of a Victory spread out on the floor. His stomach tightened, still affected after all these years by the aftermath of violent forces in brutal contact with metal.

The feeling didn't last long, replaced by the excitement born of curiosity. A single clue could be hidden in that wreckage, invisible to the untrained eye and undiscovered by expert NTSB investigators because they had no reason to suspect that hands of any human other than the pilot had played a role in ripping the Victory apart.

On the other side of the hangar he found another locked door, but with an ancient lockset that didn't hold the door tight against the jamb. The lock held when he pulled on it, but just barely.

Nick slipped the blade of his Spyderco knife into the space between the edge of the door and the jamb and worked it between the latch and the strike plate, which had also seen tighter days. Careful not to use too much force and snap the blade, he wiggled and pried it up and down, side to side, and suddenly the door popped open.

He stuck his head inside, listened, heard nothing to indicate he'd triggered an alarm. The door opened farther with a rusty squeal that sounded way too loud in the silence. Nick stepped inside, closed the door and stood motionless in a short hallway with restrooms and what appeared to be a utility closet. No security cameras. At least that he could see.

After a few minutes, he checked that the door handle would turn from the inside in case he had to leave in a rush, walked to the end of the hallway where it connected with another one and peered around the corner in both directions.

To the right, an office area. On his left a door labeled AUTHORIZED PERSONNEL ONLY, access to the hangar.

But it was locked. Wishing for a few cat burglar tools and the skill to use them, he found the office the NTSB had been using. The door was open. Taped boxes stacked in a corner had to be the aircraft records, which would have been thoroughly examined by the team, copied for the final report, and boxed for return to McAllister's estate along with the wreckage. He'd have to cut the tape, and that gave him pause until he shook hands with the reality that breaking and entering could get him in a lot more legal trouble than opening a box sealed by the NTSB. Which he didn't think was a felony. Or was it? No matter.

Inside he found standard airframe, engine, and propeller logbooks. No saboteur would document his tampering, but examining them was necessary to search for specific types of discrepancies and corrective action that might relate to vulnerabilities of the airplane to turbulence. Nick had looked at so many aircraft records over the years that he was able to skim through the pages in about a half-hour, especially since he expected to be interrupted at any minute by a security guard or gung-ho deputy sheriff with insomnia. It added a little urgency to his task.

Masking tape from a roll in the desk drawer resealed the boxes. It didn't match the original tape, but he doubted anyone would notice or care even if they did.

Back in the hallway, Nick used his flashlight to look closer at the lock on the door into the hangar. It was the same kind as the one he forced open before and just as old, but in a little better condition. He rummaged around in the desks of three offices and found a cheap tool kit in a plastic pouch. The lock didn't give up as easily, but the screwdriver in the kit stood up to more force than his Spyderco could take, and he managed to pry open the latch.

The physical evidence of V-Tail inflight breakups was so well documented that Nick was able to quickly examine the aft fuselage and tail section and find all the classic indicators. Now came the sleuthing, by asking himself how someone might alter the flight controls or weaken the airframe to increase the probability of structural failure. As he stood back from the wreckage and pondered that question, light flashed from the hallway through the open door, probably the headlights of a car in the parking lot at the front of the hangar. Nick hurried out of the hangar into the hallway, heard a door slam—no, two or three—what was this? A midnight convention?

Voices, someone at the front door, the snap of a deadbolt, lights flooding the front office.

He turned toward the hallway to the door he entered, but approaching footsteps behind him signaled *No time.* He ducked into the closest office and crouched behind a desk.

Two or three men passed in the hallway. The one speaking sounded like the guy on the phone who wouldn't allow Nick access to the wreckage. He wasn't happy, something about why can't you show up during normal business hours? What's the goddamn rush?

Then another curse, louder this time, the guy angry that the door into the hangar had been left unlocked and he was going to put someone's balls in a vise and make an example out of them.

Nick waited about ten minutes until all the activity appeared to be concentrated in the hangar, low-crawled out of the office down the long hallway around the corner into the short one and up to the door he'd entered. He opened it a little and glanced outside, where a semi had backed into the hangar with only the tractor visible, the name of the company printed on the door.

He stepped out, eased the door closed, and sprinted into the desert. After about 30 yards, he jumped into a depression and lay down behind a low bush to catch his breath. No one appeared to have seen him, so he pondered his next move, which had to be finding out where that wreckage was going.

He could call the company and ask. They might tell him, but probably wouldn't unless he could act his way into convincing them he had the right to know.

A tracking device would be handy, sit back and follow the truck from a distance. But unlike all the movie action heroes, he didn't always have one tucked away in a handy pocket.

After a moment, he turned to face away from the hangar, got out his phone and pulled his jacket up and over his head into a tent. With the backlight dimmed almost to nothing, he Googled *Southwest Shipping & Salvage* and found an address in Tucson, Arizona.

If Nick were a betting man, he'd wager good money that their salvage operation was located there. The process required specialized equipment, tools, storage facilities, and trained employees, and could only be profitable with a centralized location.

He brought up the mapping function and confirmed that they'd probably travel southeast on Hwy 60 into Phoenix and then connect with either I-10 South toward Tucson for salvage, or I-17 North to Flagstaff and I-40 East to Albuquerque to deliver the wreckage to McAllister's widow.

Committed to the role of manual tracking device, Nick dimmed the backlight on his phone to nothing, un-tented himself from his jacket, and settled down to wait.

Either destination presented problems to a private crash investigator with no authority to compel anyone to do anything. But all things considered, he probably had a better chance with the salvage company, especially since the likelihood that they had recently murdered anyone was so remote.

DAYBREAK HAD NOT YET begun to backlight the ragged outline of mountains defining the eastern horizon when Nick pulled into the Bargain Suites Motel parking lot. He turned off the engine and yawned. Fatigue had been dragging his eyelids closed, dulling his senses, demanding rest as he sat in the desert watching the activity in the hangar, waiting, finally tailing the truck until it turned northeast, then returning to his motel without running off the road with his chin resting on his chest.

The door to his room opened into a refrigerated heaven. He'd hidden the knobs so the housekeepers couldn't turn off the air conditioner. As he opened a bottle of water, someone knocked. He checked the peephole, saw no one. "Who is it?"

"Yours truly," said Yates. "Open up."

The SOB had to be following Nick around to show up here like this. He jerked the door open.

Yates was leaning against the doorjamb, one foot crossed over the other. A toothpick between two front teeth oscillated rapidly in time with rapid jaw movements. Nick considered inviting him inside, decided no.

Yates spit the toothpick onto the sidewalk. "Got some news for me?"

Nick leaned against the opposite doorjamb and mirrored Yates' stance, coughed up some saliva and spit at the toothpick. He missed. "Damn. Never was much good at that."

"You'll be spitting teeth, you keep up with the talk, dickhead. I asked you a question."

The urge to grab Yates by the throat rose up in Nick so fast he almost couldn't control it. He clenched both hands into fists, fingernails digging into palms. Caitlin didn't have enough money to make up for Nick having to work with assholes. "Tell your client I'm out of here early tomorrow morning. This crash is a slam-dunk accident with nothing except a pilot's poor judgment and a thunderstorm to blame."

"I told you—"

"And I'm telling you that whatever you think you have is bogus. There's no evidence of tampering or sabotage. Period."

"You confirmed that yourself, did you?"

"Yes."

"Which means you examined the wreckage, right?"

"What I did or didn't do is no concern of yours."

Yates lurched away from the doorjamb and stuck his face about an inch from Nick's. Onion-laced breath accompanied his words. "Some investigator you turned out to be. All press release and nothing to back it up. I was watching when you hightailed it out of that hangar and failed to put your eyeballs on that wreckage and do what we're paying you to do."

It had been a long time since anyone had confronted Nick so forcefully. The memory of a dark night in Colorado surged up, with images of a killer's snarling face, the smell of blood and fear, and a panic born of impending death. He reached out for Yates' jacket lapels.

Yates brought his arms up in an uppercut motion and knocked Nick's aside. He grabbed Nick's throat, yanked him away from the doorjamb, and shoved him into the room.

Nick tripped, fell backward, and landed on the bed. He tore at Yates' wiry hands choking off all the air but couldn't dislodge his grip. He went for Yates' eyes and punched at his face until his arms went limp and the world turned fuzzy and faded to black.

CAITLIN SNATCHED HER RINGING cell phone off the bedside table, glanced at the caller ID. "This better be good, Cliff, especially this early in the morning."

"The son-of-a bitch says there's nothing to find and he's done. But he's lying."

"About finding nothing or quitting?"

"No way he put eyes on that wreckage long enough to know what is or isn't there."

Caitlin knew that might not mean Nick was quitting, but she had no reason to share that. "Where is he now?"

"His room."

"Okay, I'll handle it. In the meantime, stay away from him." Caitlin waited a moment. "Did you hear me, Yates?"

"Yeah . . . but we had a . . . well . . . a fight. Sort of."

Through clenched teeth, Caitlin hissed, "What the hell were you thinking?"

"Thinking didn't enter into it. I'm getting sick and tired of playing pussyfoot with this bastard. He's not being straight with—"

"I'm coming out."

"Don't bother."

"What did you say?"

"He's not going anywhere for awhile."

"What do you mean by that?"

"His departure time is delayed. That gives me time to change his mind."

"Don't, and I'm not going to tell you again." Caitlin disconnected the call and hit the speed dial for Phillips' cell number. Voicemail. Damn it. She'd been home less than a day and felt out of control already.

And if that truck was there to load up the wreckage . . .

Chapter Ten

Nick woke up, swallowed. His raw throat reminded him of Yates' hands. He eased off the bed, found a bottle of water in the bathroom, sat down and took a long drink.

What the hell was he doing here, dealing with a maniac? He ought to file charges. But on second thought, Yates was only defending himself. Leave it be.

After two cups of coffee and a little time to think, Nick knew he wasn't going to walk out on Caitlin until he'd done what he promised. Or at least give it his best shot and put eyes on the wreckage again. Which meant getting his ass to Albuquerque. When he had his larger duffel filled, he hauled it outside to the rented Jeep and found the right rear wheel resting on a pancake-flat tire.

Sonofabitch. Another new life experience: changing a tire in an oven. But unwilling to wait for the rental company to respond, he hauled out the spare and the tool kit. He was loosening the lug nuts when someone behind him said, "Gotta flat?" The word "flat" had two syllables, like "fly-yut."

A barefoot man in greasy coveralls, torn Arizona State University Sun Devils T-shirt, and wearing a tattered "Lambert's Seed and Feed" baseball cap stood beside a grocery cart piled high with junk. Nick was positive the man hadn't chewed food with teeth in a very long time.

Nick nodded, couldn't resist the sarcasm. "Everything was fine until the other three suddenly inflated on me."

The man stared at Nick and pointed to the right front tire. "Looks to me like only two done that." *Tha-yut.*

Only then did Nick notice the second flat tire. He turned to apologize for being a smart ass, but the man was shuffling away and appeared to be having a conversation with himself. Nick tossed the spare and tools in the Jeep, locked it, and trudged back to the motel room. After a call to the rental car company's emergency number, he made a third cup of coffee and sank into the armchair for a game of mental tug-of-war. It felt like playing a solo game of chess in which he had to make a move, stand up, change seats, make a move, and repeat the process until he checkmated himself into staring at the board with no place to go.

GRUMPY AND FEELING AS if the wrinkles in her clothing had made it through to her skin, Caitlin walked out of the jetway into the terminal at the Phoenix Sky Harbor International Airport. Airline travel sucked. Lawson's Victory wasn't the lap of transportation luxury, but they just went to the airplane, loaded up, and took off.

None of that TSA crap, either. She was convinced they hired nothing but perverts to conduct the female pat downs. Talk about profiling. And Caitlin's Walther way out of reach in checked luggage.

Lawson had taught her a little about what he called "stick and rudder," so their flights passed quickly. She had begun to enjoy her time at the controls. Then it all crashed around her. Literally.

Waiting in line for a rental, she remembered how the cars would be sitting on the ramp where they parked the airplane. Lots of guys scurrying around, carrying bags, smiling at her and ignoring Lawson. She used to tease him about it. He'd laugh, say something about that being the price he had to pay for being with such a good-looking *chick,* and the memory of those days, lost forever now, almost brought her to tears.

But not today, when she needed to focus on her goal and make it happen. While giving the air conditioner a chance to transform the Cadillac's interior into something other than a sweat lodge, she entered her destination in the GPS, expecting the bitch-in-the-box to exclaim, "You want directions to *where?*" To her surprise, someone had put Dry Springs in the database. She headed north on I-17 in relatively light traffic, the only advantage of getting up so early.

About two hours outside the city, a turn off to the end of the universe appeared out of the shimmering haze. A two-lane blacktop secondary road led into the distant west. She pulled onto the shoulder and got out to stretch her legs.

Heat immediately pounded her senses into submission. Her legs could wait. She retreated to the refuge of her mobile refrigerator and accelerated into the furnace, the road ahead wavering, a black ribbon with silvery mirages of standing water, leading to what she hoped would be the next step in building a trap for Elizabeth Blaine McAllister, black widow spider times two.

"**THEM TIRES WAS SLASHED.**"

Nick turned to the tow-truck driver kneeling beside the Jeep. "Say again?"

"That cut didn't come from no road hazard. Your warranty

won't cover the—"

"This is a *rental.* I don't care about the warranty. Are both tires cut?"

"A knife done it."

A slow fury began to work its way up Nick's spine. "How long before my ride to the airport shows up?"

"I ain't the one handles that sorta thing."

"But the rental company hired you to take care of this, right?"

"We gotta contract. It pays—"

"Tell you what, partner." Nick handed the man ten bucks. "Call whoever it is at the rental place that sent you out here and tell them I need that ride an hour ago. There's another of those in it for you if they're here when I get back."

He stalked off toward the motel office. The clerk in his normal pose greeted him, face down on the counter, snoring. Nick jostled him awake, added a couple of extra shoves just for spite. When he had the man's groggy attention, he asked, "What is Cliff Yates' room number?"

"I'm not supposed to give out that information."

Nick shoved his hands in his pockets and saved himself from an assault charge. He felt some bills in his right hand, yanked them out and tossed the ten bucks he promised the driver on the counter. "What's . . . his . . . room . . . number?"

The clerk blinked a few times, then tapped at a keyboard and stared at a computer screen that looked kind of melted, like it'd been left out in the heat. "Two twelve. But I gotta call first."

"Go back to sleep. If you call him, I swear to God you'll have to wait until your next crap to spend that."

He scrambled up an outside staircase and found the room. Hand poised to knock, he hesitated, then stood to one side of the security peephole. With the key to the Jeep, he rapped on the door and in a high, screeching voice, yelled, "Housekeeping!"

A muffled, "In a minute." A toilet flushed.

The security bolt snapped open. The door began to move. A wall mirror visible in the widening space between the door and the jamb reflected the image of Yates looking down to check his fly.

Nick charged shoulder-first. The door caught Yates on top of his head and knocked him backwards, legs and arms flailing. Nick followed the door and slammed Yates to the carpet with his whole body. Rage and frustration poured out in a flurry of blows.

Yates covered his face with both hands, arms pressed tight against his chest and stomach.

Nick turned and punched him as hard as he could in the crotch.

Yates screamed and drew his legs up.

Nick hopped up to ease the door almost shut, just in case he had to make a quick exit, knelt beside Yates and snatched out a folding-blade knife that was clipped in his left front pants pocket. He flicked it open with his thumb and sat down on the bed. "Is this what you used?"

Yates opened his eyes, glared at Nick, and between ragged gasps shouted, "You fucking asshole! I'll kill you for this. You'll wish—"

The door swung open. Sunlight streamed in, backlighting the person in the doorway. Nick raised his hand with the knife to block the glare, noticed a smooth, quick movement of shadowed hands.

A woman's voice said, "Drop the knife."

Nick couldn't see a gun, but her stance told him all he needed. "Hold on a min—"

"Drop it!"

Nick obeyed and held both hands out to his sides.

The woman stepped into the room, closed the door with a backward kick, and the face of Caitlin Monroe framed a small pistol aimed at Nick's heart. "Slowly now, move over there." She nodded her head toward the corner at the head of the bed and farthest from the door.

Nick did that and watched as Caitlin bent over Yates and said something to him. He began screaming obscenities. She ordered him to shut up and quit acting like a baby. Yates glared at Nick with hate-filled eyes as he stood and hobbled toward the bathroom with both hands cradling his crotch. Caitlin slipped the pistol in the outer pocket of her shoulder bag, grabbed the ice bucket from the counter above the mini-bar and tossed it to Nick. "Fill that."

When Nick got back to the room, Caitlin took the bucket, set it down in front of the bathroom door, knocked twice, and turned to Nick. "Want to tell me about this?"

"Let's just say Yates and I are even. What are you doing here?"

"Preventing you two from killing each other, apparently. I find my employee lying on the floor in *his* room, balls damn near crushed, and you're holding this nasty little item." She waggled the open blade, dim lamplight glinting off shiny steel. "What happened?"

Nick took a deep breath, let it out. "That sonofabitch slashed the tires on my Jeep."

"What the hell for?"

"You'll have to ask him, but probably to keep me from leaving Dry Springs before you showed up."

"We need to talk about that."

"So talk."

"Privately. And if I were you, I wouldn't want to be here when Yates comes out of that bathroom."

Cliff Yates sat on the closed toilet lid with the ice pack between his legs. He'd frozen his nuts off on stakeout a few times, but never in a motel room.

Through the closed bathroom door drifted the voices of Monroe and Phillips, not clear enough to understand the words, then the sound of his room door closing. When he could no longer endure the cold, Cliff tossed the ice bag into the sink, eased himself up, and waddled out of the bathroom.

His knife lay on the table. He picked it up, slipped it into the right front pocket of his jeans, and promised himself that sooner or later, Phillips would taste the bite of an edge that Cliff kept scalpel-sharp.

He got a beer from the mini-bar, sat in the armchair beside the desk and propped his feet on the desk chair. It eased the discomfort in his crotch, which he intended to forget all about in short order by taking multiple doses of the bottled medicine in his hand.

Getting kicked off the force was the dumbest thing he'd ever done. He had the perfect setup, carrying a badge and a gun, roaming back alleys filled with sleazeballs and scumbags just asking to get ripped off. Accommodating them was so easy, retaliation out of the question, and that immunity had tempted Cliff to push the limits one rip-off too far. His last bit of luck had been all used up when he avoided prosecution and was allowed to fade from sight, disgraced and relegated to the role of *Private Snoop of the Unfaithful Spouse Patrol.*

At least he was good at it, enough so to pay the bills, and his reputation for results had landed him a job with Lawson

McAllister's wife. She wanted evidence of her husband's infidelity to prove the validity of the saying, *When you have them by the balls, their hearts and minds will follow.*

Ever alert for opportunity, Cliff tried to double-up the bucks by selling a single set of compromising photographs to both McAllister's wife and her husband's lover. That didn't work, but one of the benefits of being a private dick was the number of times the *subjects* of his clandestine camera work were so impressed with his sneaky ways that they hired him to do the same to someone else.

Like now. It had put him on this job and led him here, sitting in a motel room nursing sore nuts and with the distinct impression that Monroe and her pet aviation sleuth were pushing him into the role of flunky.

Cliff still had a significant advantage, however, in that with every mundane job came the potential for bringing him one step closer to a life-altering payday and a change of residence to a new address on easy street.

CAITLIN FOLLOWED NICK INTO his room and sat in the chair he offered at the small dining table. He got two bottles of water from the mini-bar, offered one to Caitlin and sank into the chair opposite her. "For the record, I don't like people pointing guns at me."

"Then don't go around threatening people with knives."

"I wasn't threatening anyone."

"Maybe not." Caitlin slipped the bag off her shoulder, set it on the table, and patted it. "But my Walther made sure of that, didn't it?" Then she leaned toward Nick. "Yates thinks you're quitting. Which means you've confirmed in one day that sabotage had nothing to do with Lawson's crash?"

Nick shook his head. "I was following the wreckage to Albuquerque and would have left by now if it weren't for Yates."

"What can I say? He's unpredictable. But I need him for awhile yet."

"Use him however you want, Caitlin, but I'm through with both of you unless we agree that he never speaks for you when dealing with me and vice versa."

"Fine. Where does that leave *us?*"

Nick gave her an account of his Skype session with Dickson, filled with technical detail she tried to understand. Then he summed it up with a bottom line she grasped all too well. "That's not absolute confirmation, because with all the circumstantial evidence pointing to pilot error and nothing to contradict it, the NTSB had no reason to be suspicious."

"But you do."

"More like curious, based on speculation and conjecture."

"Which you can validate or dismiss based on physical examination of the wreckage."

"Maybe. Not being able to find the evidence won't prove it doesn't exist."

"When can you do that?"

"I already have. Last night. At least partially."

"What does that mean?"

"The salvage company showed up and almost caught me in the act of breaking and entering."

Finally. "Ah, yes. A little of the pit bull I've read about. Where are they taking it?"

"Don't know for sure. But if you're right about what happened and why, it's probably headed to the Adobe Wings Airport where it was maintained."

Caitlin settled back in her chair. "You said *if.* I need the guy I read about. Not some NTSB flunky checking off boxes in an accident report. What's it going to take to get you on board?"

Nick paused a moment to drink some water. "I need you to convince me I'm not wasting my time. Because what I have now is really simple. A reckless pilot died when he flew his Victory at high speed into a thunderstorm. His lover refuses to accept the obvious. For reasons that appear too loosely based on fact, she thinks the guy's wife wanted him dead, and I'm supposed to find evidence to prove she killed him."

The tears came, stinging Caitlin's eyes as her lower lip quivered. She hated herself for being so weak and spineless, got up, walked into the bathroom and closed the door. It took a handful of tissues to stem the flow and dry her eyes.

After a moment, she breathed deep, checked her appearance in the mirror, and cursed under her breath. Waterproof mascara? They lied. She cleaned her eyes and dropped the stained tissues in the wastebasket. At the door she paused, then picked up the tissues out of the wastebasket, tossed them into the commode and flushed it. Good riddance to evidence of emotional fragility.

Back at the table, she sat down and locked her back as straight as a board. Something about doing that helped her deal with the flood of memories, good and bad, which were about to drown her.

"I don't *think* she wanted him dead. I know it."

"What was her motive?"

"Spite, vengeance, retribution, whatever, but don't look for any logic in it. Lawson was the heart and soul of the cancer center. It was the pinnacle of his career, not just another rung up the social ladder. She *needed* his full attention on it, but he was going to divorce her and marry me. She threatened to cut him out of the whole project. Like she brought anything more than money to the table. He told her to go to hell, and she promised to bury us both in a smoking hole. That's a direct quote."

"Yeah, but people say things like that in the heat of the moment and don't really mean it. What makes you think this is any different?"

"Her reputation as a black widow."

"What?"

"Her first husband died young, under suspicious circumstances. She was a person of interest from day one, but I guess they never had enough to charge her." Caitlin watched Nick's face and was pretty sure that this revelation had gotten his attention.

He took a deep breath and exhaled, a kind of exasperated sound. "So . . . the basis for your hypothesis about conspiracy to murder is the rumor mill?"

"Think of it as the cornerstone."

"It takes a hell of a lot more to support a conclusion that Lawson's wife murdered him, Caitlin."

Caitlin nodded. "Then ask your questions, and be prepared for me to tell you it's none of your goddamn business."

"Fair enough. And if I think for a second that you're playing me? I'll put you, Lawson, and the Victory in my rearview mirror."

"And Yates."

Nick chuckled. "Naw. I may take him home as a pet."

"Don't forget to use a cage. What do you want to know?"

"First, why would a brilliant cancer surgeon marry a woman who supposedly had already put one husband in his grave?"

"Because he had a career and didn't pay any attention to the tabloids and Facebook and Twitter and all that nonsense."

"Okay, but how does the guy not become aware of the scuttlebutt? Hard to believe he could remain oblivious to the publicity circus after their wedding."

Caitlin thought for a moment about how best to answer.

"I don't know when he found out. But I can tell you that Lawson was confident to the point of arrogance. He wasn't lacking in ambition, either. The center would validate his entire career. She wanted to climb to the top of the social pyramid on the back of her dead husband's philanthropy.

"It was a marriage consummated in a checkbook. Her seed money, combined with his expertise, would create a world-class facility with his name on it."

"So you think his arrogance and ambition outweighed any concerns about black widow rumors."

"Yes."

"Rumors *you* believe are credible enough to support a conclusion that she killed husband number two?"

"Nope. I called it the cornerstone. And that's all I could point to until she made her next move." Caitlin paused to let Nick's legendary curiosity kick in. It didn't take long. He did a little *let's have it* move with the fingers of one hand.

"With no warning," she said, "Lawson's wife announced a new name for the project: the Elizabeth Blaine McAllister Cancer Treatment Center. He frequently argued with her about that, until one evening when she went postal. Scared the hell out of him. That's when he realized he should have paid more attention to the rumors. That he was in fact married to a very sick and dangerous woman capable of almost anything. Including murder."

"Why the hell didn't he leave?"

"He was planning to."

"What's to plan? Open the door and slam it on the way out."

Caitlin shrugged. "Two factors. No, three. The first was that arrogance. He never believed she could hurt him physically. But she damn sure could financially. And she could cut him off from the culmination of his life's work. He needed time to set up an exit strategy he could live with."

Caitlin's eyes stung as her mind added . . . *and he ended up dying with.*

Nick seemed to sense her discomfort as he got up, turned his back and took his time getting two more bottles of water out of the mini-bar.

She went into the bathroom for a couple of tissues, dried her eyes, and returned to the table. Nick handed her a bottle. She drank about half of it at one time, very un-lady like, but this was thirsty work.

He waited for a moment longer, staring at his lap, as if pondering what to say next, then looked at Caitlin. "We know Lawson's wife had the means to murder him by sabotaging his airplane, although that is a far more complicated scenario than using a gun, or a knife, or putting rat poison in his food. But let's assume she enlisted the help of his mechanic by offering him a life-changing payday.

"She also had the opportunity, because Lawson not only flew his own Victory, but he regularly played chicken with the consequences of flying past red line. She wouldn't have any way of knowing that, but the mechanic certainly would, and that goes back to means.

"Motive, however, is a more difficult to pin down. Except for the difference in value, to yank Lawson's dream of the cancer center away from him is like a wealthy wife taking the houses, the cars, and all of her husband's play toys. It's a scenario as old as failed marriages. But you're asking me to accept that Lawson's wife wasn't content with any revenge short of murder."

"Absolutely. And you know, Nick, this may come down

to whether or not you believe me about how crazy that bitch really is. But if you could have seen Lawson when he told me about that . . . *conversation* isn't even close to the right word. It was an ultimatum.

"And I can tell you that he believed his life was in danger. And after that night I did too. Psychopath, sociopath, antisocial personality disorder, it doesn't matter what you call it when it's sitting in your living room."

Except for the snapping of plastic bottles as Caitlin and Nick sipped water, silence filled the room. She stared at nothing, almost afraid to breathe. Nick was looking toward the window and appeared to be lost in thought, which would hopefully result in a decision to climb on the vengeance express Caitlin had planned for the Balloon Bitch. Just about the time she was ready to ask what the hell was his problem, he drank the rest of his water and crushed the bottle in his hands.

"Okay. I'll be happy to take your money and do *everything* I can to uncover whatever there is left to find. But I have to be clear that I still *expect* to confirm the NTSB's conclusion of pilot error."

Caitlin's hands began to tremble slightly. "So you still aren't convinced otherwise?"

"*Right now*, I still believe that's what happened. And if you want me to investigate with the tenacity you expect, I can't have any doubts. Do you understand that? *None.*"

It took all of Caitlin's self-control not to scream at the top of her lungs and shed at least some of the frustration and anger that had been building since Lawson's death. She looked down at her hands, balled into fists, the knuckles white with tension. Tears tried to flow. She willed them to retreat. A calming breath or two helped ease her off the edge.

When she finally managed to look at Nick, and thought

her voice wouldn't crack, she nodded. "Doubts about what?"

"*Your* motive. Because on the surface, this could easily be nothing more than the case of a gold digger who lost her sugar daddy and wants to shakedown the wealthy widow for a retirement fund. Why isn't that you?"

Caitlin's body went rigid in the chair. Her fingernails felt like razors cutting into her palms. The urge to lash out and make Nick take back his words almost won out until she got control and forced herself to think about how to change his mind.

As she began breathing deeply, Nick started to say something, and before she could stop it, her right hand shot out, forefinger about an inch from his nose. "Shut. The fuck. Up." Then she stood and marched to the window, looked down at a planter bed next to the building, and concentrated on the beautiful clusters of white flowers on spikes sticking up from a lower mound of pointed green leaves that looked dangerous. She'd seen plants like it before, knew the name at one time, and tried to remember it. Anything to keep from turning around, walking over to Nick Phillips, and clawing his eyes out.

Time didn't mean much. But after a while, she'd calmed down enough to tell herself that Nick couldn't help being infected with stereotypical male attitudes toward younger women having affairs with older, wealthy men. She returned to the table and sat down. "First off, forget the gold digger and sugar daddy clichés. This is real life, my life, not some made-for-TV movie.

"I could have gone that route if I wanted. I'm a pharmaceutical rep. I make a nice living, and had been doing so for a couple of years before I met Lawson. It's a profession dominated by men, and most of my clients suggested some after-hours activities to close the deal. I know some reps that do that kind of thing, but I don't play those games. And I still top the sales charts.

"And Lawson *never* asked me to, either. In fact, he kept it strictly business until my third visit, and even then it wasn't about him. He asked how I had broken my nose. A very personal question. You know what he said? 'I know a surgeon who can repair that single flaw in an otherwise perfect face.' He even offered to pay for the operation, but I refused."

"He had to do a lot more than that to begin an affair."

"Agreed. But the next time, he crossed the line with a dozen roses. And twice more after that. Each time I told him I had no interest in dating a married man."

"So what changed?"

Caitlin lost the battle for emotional control as the memories surged out of the dark recesses where she'd stuffed them. She buried her face in her hands and sobbed, vaguely aware of Nick getting up. After a moment, she felt the gentle touch of his hand on her shoulder. She looked up, accepted the tissues, dried her eyes, and looked at Nick.

"He was the first man who didn't treat me like an object. Given my history, where I come from, to be able to trust him . . . not to be expecting betrayal . . . meant everything. I told him things I've never told anyone . . . terrible things . . . about my childhood."

Caitlin lowered her head and cried into the tissues for a moment, then sat up straight, collected her emotions and shoved them back where they belonged. Once again she looked at Nick. "And you haven't asked me, but it's written all over your face. Yes. We truly loved each other."

Nick met her eyes for a few seconds and then began looking around the room, down at his lap, back to her face, finally nodded and stood up. "I haven't eaten any breakfast. You hungry?" When Caitlin nodded, he handed her the takeout menu from a café next door to the motel. "Hard to believe, but the food in the healthy section is pretty good. Pick something you like, order for two and a pot of coffee. I've got to clean up."

Caitlin smiled, in part to see if it might reflect inward and cheer her up a little.

CHAPTER ELEVEN

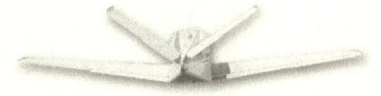

When they finished eating, Nick put the DO NOT DISTURB sign on the knob and sat down at the desk. "How are you doing?"

"You've had a free pass for all the personal questions you're going to get. How do we get your eyes on the wreckage and reduce some of that conjecture you keep talking about?"

"There's no 'we' to it. And before I do anything more, you need to understand that I've talked with the current head of the Aviation Division about the preliminary report. They looked at every possible cause and found no evidence of sabotage."

"That wasn't good enough for you in Colorado."

"I was an NTSB employee on site with access to everything from the very beginning. Big difference."

"But if you were able to inspect the Victory wreckage completely you might have another opinion?"

"*If* there's something to find, and *if* I can find it, absolutely."

"That's all I'm asking you to do."

"Fair enough. But don't forget that the tampering on Larchmont's GoldenJet was ingeniously hidden. I was lucky to have found it."

Caitlin shook her head. "You discovered the secret because you refused to give up. I'm certain the investigators missed something, and I'm asking you to use that legendary Phillips tenacity and find it. Answer my question."

"Which one?"

"The one you keep ignoring."

"Oh. That one. Depending on where the salvage company is taking the wreckage, the window of opportunity to learn anything more about what caused the crash may have just slammed shut. But even if it didn't, two considerations need to be addressed before we take the next step. The first is that *my* examination of the aircraft records and wreckage, although interrupted, brings me to the same conclusion the NTSB came up with."

Caitlin's crossed leg began to bounce. "How can you possibly know that with only a few hours to investigate? The NTSB spent over a week. And the whole point is not to let what they *didn't* find lead you to believe there's nothing *to* find."

"If we were starting from scratch, I'd agree with you. But we know enough to concentrate on the most likely causes. The tail section provides all the information we need to—"

"Why don't you have to look at the *whole* airplane?"

Nick settled back in his chair. Caitlin's emotional reaction to the first mention of inflight breakup in their initial meeting at the flight school made him cautious now. But he needed for her to understand this, and he couldn't accomplish that by softening the reality of the horror Lawson and his passenger must have endured when the Victory came apart around them.

Caitlin touched his forearm. "If you're worried about me, forget it. Tell me what I need to know and I'll deal with it."

Fair enough. "Okay. When all the wreckage is confined to a small area, it tells us the airplane was in one piece when it impacted the ground. The Victory crash site covered a few square miles. That's conclusive proof of an in-flight breakup. Individual pieces separated and fell at different rates based on their size and shape. We can determine the direction of flight by mapping the debris field. The first pieces came from the tail section and give us the best clue about the precipitating event."

Caitlin sniffed, drank some water, and stared past Nick's shoulder for a moment before taking a deep breath and exhaling in a rush. "So all or part of the tail broke off. How the hell does that happen?"

Nick explained that catastrophic atmospheric turbulence powerful enough to break an airplane apart was very rare and could only be caused by large, fast-moving frontal systems with massive storms. The NTSB found no reports of widespread unusually rough air from other pilots in the area at the time.

Caitlin shook her head. "But that could be misleading. Lawson once told me that for all the power contained within thunderstorms, the most severe conditions tend to be very localized."

"That's true, but—"

"So maybe he flew into the worst area and never had the chance to report it."

"That's a possibility."

Monroe pursed her lips and frowned. "What else might have caused it?"

"Structural weakness. Airplanes can be overstressed. Cracks develop in crucial components and remain undiscovered. Then under the right conditions, something gives way, but there's no evidence of that with the Victory."

"Why are we talking about things that didn't happen?"

"Because you questioned me about not being thorough enough. I'm trying to explain why the existing evidence suggests there's no need to look at any other possibility."

She leaned her head back and closed her eyes. Her crossed leg bounced rapidly, like a frustration meter spiking off the scale. After a moment, she appeared to regain control. "Well, then. Does that finally bring us to what *did* happen?"

"Yes, but first I need to explain something more. Remember our discussion about ruddervators?" Caitlin nodded, and Nick continued with, "The V-Tail design produces less drag, which in part means the airplane accelerates faster. The bad news is that ruddervators are very sensitive to balance. Any disparity becomes especially critical when approaching maximum allowable airspeed."

Her face clouded up. "What happens if you exceed it?"

"Nothing, hopefully. Regulations require manufacturers to flight test their airplanes up to red line plus thirty percent without demonstrating any adverse effects. Did Lawson ever discuss speed with you? How fast he liked to fly, anything like that?"

Caitlin stared at the table. "A broker tried to talk him into a different airplane, but Lawson insisted on the Victory because it was a . . . a *speed demon*, I think he called it. He was always asking controllers for clearance to go faster. He *hated* following slower airplanes."

Nick nodded and reached for his water bottle. Caitlin had given him the perfect opportunity to address the topic of speed without giving the impression that he had jumped to a hasty conclusion that would disparage her lover's flying abilities.

After a moment of silence, she said, "What if he did? You just said they build in a safety margin."

Thank you. "And usually it's more than sufficient. But there's another factor we have to consider. Flutter." Nick let the word hang between them in the pale yellow light from the overhead lamp.

Caitlin stared at him. "An airplane can flutter?"

"Not the whole airplane. But a flight control surface, like

an elevator or rudder, certainly can."

"What causes it?"

"High speed. Not by itself, but it's always the common denominator. It creates a very unforgiving aerodynamic environment." Nick paused again.

"What other factors are involved?"

"Turbulence." Nick held his hands horizontally side by side, fingers pointed at Caitlin. "Let's say this," he waggled his right hand, "is the movable control surface attached to the fixed portion in front. The control gets displaced up sharply. Aerodynamic loads shove it down, but it overshoots the neutral position and travels farther down than it did up. See what I mean?"

Caitlin's eyes were transfixed on Nick's hands. "Yes."

"When a flight control flutters, each displacement from neutral is farther than the preceding one." Nick demonstrated an exaggerated, slow motion flutter event. "At some point—this all happens in a split second—movement of the flight control exceeds design strength and something breaks. From that point, it's a chain reaction."

"Is that what happened to Lawson?"

"Very probably. And there's something else."

Caitlin recoiled from the table, as if to retreat from the upcoming news.

Nick realized that what he was about to say would be especially hard for Caitlin. He softened his voice to ease her into accepting that Lawson had most likely caused the crash. "It's not a design flaw, per se, but the V-Tail configuration of the Victory is especially susceptible to flutter. When pilots combine high speed and turbulence, they are playing a dangerous game."

"Are you telling me Lawson bought an airplane he shouldn't have?"

Nick wasn't about to mention the V-Tail Bonanza's nickname of "Doctor Killer," but he couldn't ignore the issue. "Not at all. But sometimes, when people successful in fields other than aviation become pilots, they exhibit the expert syndrome. These folks consider flying an airplane as nothing compared to what they've accomplished elsewhere. Piece of cake, right? Can't be that difficult. Too often they learn the hard way how wrong they are."

Caitlin tried to swallow and couldn't seem to complete it.

Nick jumped up, got another bottle of water and handed it to her.

She drank eagerly.

Nick backed away from the table and waited.

Her eyes filled with tears. "So this was his fault?"

Nick sat back down. "I don't know that. It's like a jigsaw puzzle. His attitude toward flying might be one piece of the answer. Which leads me to the next topic."

Caitlin stared at him as if she couldn't stand to hear much more. Then she took a deep breath and sighed. "Another bombshell?"

Nick spoke softly as he explained that ruddervators have weights attached to an extension called a "horn" to balance them aerodynamically. "The balancing procedure is critical, and it doesn't take much of an imbalance, combined with high speed and turbulence, to dramatically increase the chance of encountering a flutter event."

"Are you telling me that the ruddervators on Lawson's plane were out of balance?"

"There's no way to tell after the fact because they're too badly damaged. And in some cases the weights are thrown clear during the event and never recovered."

"Did that happen here?"

"One of the weights was missing."

Caitlin stood, paced around the room for a few moments, snatched the water bottle off the table and drank most of it, and finally sat down. "What if someone wanted to alter the balance? Like mess around with one of those weights? Or remove it?"

"But we have to consider what is most likely. Speed, even higher than red line, turbulence and an altered or missing balance weight would change probabilities for the worse, but they aren't enough to *guarantee* catastrophic flutter."

Caitlin's body appeared to deflate, like all the life had been yanked out of it. She lowered her head, eyes closed, hands balled into fists. After a moment, she drank more water and stared at Nick with moist eyes. "You said a weight was missing. What if it wasn't there to begin with?"

Nick didn't want Caitlin to be put in the mode of defending Lawson, but he couldn't avoid the next issue. "Did you ever notice how much time Lawson spent preflighting the airplane?"

"Not really. Why do you ask?"

"Victory pilots know the ruddervators have to be carefully balanced. And while they rely on a mechanic to do that, they can test the balance on preflight by manual feel. Any significant deviation outside of normal limits would be noticed."

Caitlin jumped up like she'd been catapulted out of the chair, crossed her arms and began pacing. "Lawson failed to notice a missing weight?"

"I'm not saying that. But you want me to determine cause, and that's one logical explanation. Did you usually arrive at the airport with him, or show up after he was there?"

"I never met him where he kept the airplane. He usually flew into an airport near my home. What does that have to do with anything?"

"I'm looking for something to explain how a missing weight might have escaped notice. If he was casual about performing preflight inspections, that would be another piece of the puzzle."

Caitlin sat down and leaned close to the table. "I feel it in my bones, Nick. Lawson was murdered, and I escaped only because I had to cancel out of the trip. I don't know why that other guy got on the airplane and I don't care. He's collateral damage. What I need is total commitment from you to help me find out how Lawson's bitch wife pulled it off so well that the NTSB and you both come up with nothing. I thought we'd gotten past your reluctance, and now it feels like you're back to second-guessing everything."

At that moment, all of Nick's doubts faded into the background: about Caitlin and her intentions; about the possibility that Lawson might have been the victim of foul play at the hands of his wife; about the underlying source of his current dissatisfaction with life; and about whether his yearning for involvement in an endeavor he considered especially worthy deserved to be recognized and acted upon. The time had come to be truthful with himself about what he really wanted to be doing, and by extension, with Caitlin Monroe.

He lifted his water bottle and held it toward her in a "let's drink a toast" gesture. "I'll do whatever I can. But you need to realize that the chance of finding something is very remote. Don't get your hopes up."

Her face softened. "You still don't understand, do you? You *are* my hope." Then she tapped her crushed water bottle against his, said, "It's a deal," and simulated taking a drink. Her eyes never left his.

After an uncomfortable moment in which Nick wanted to look away and couldn't, he faked a cough. "Okay. Then I need to confirm that airplane is headed where I think it is."

"Where might that be?"

Nick reminded her of their discussion in the Mercedes, explained that the wreckage was now under the control of a shipping and salvage company, and it depended on what they were hired to do. "My guess is that the last option we talked about is the one in play. McAllister's widow paid the insurance company salvage value out of the insurance proceeds. In other words, she bought the wreckage from them. It's on the way to the Victory's home airfield and point of origin, which is the most logical place for her to take control of it. And more important, where someone had maximum access and opportunity for tampering."

Caitlin closed her eyes and paused for a moment. Nick figured that she was digesting all the information he'd just dumped on her. Then she asked, "I'm still bothered by the question of why you can't involve the NTSB after you find what we need. Wouldn't they trust you to present untainted evidence?"

"It's not an issue of trust. The investigation is closed."

"Can't it be reopened?"

"I've never heard of that happening. Even if it's possible, the NTSB wouldn't make the decision because they can't pursue investigations into criminal acts."

"So the cops would have to be involved."

"FBI. And they wouldn't touch this because chain of custody doesn't exist."

Caitlin tapped the table with her palm. "So it's just you and me. What can I do to help?"

"Nothing. And if I were you, I wouldn't go anywhere near that wreckage."

Caitlin frowned. "That sounds like a warning."

Nick shrugged. "What would you do if you had murdered Lawson McAllister by sabotaging his Victory, and his lover showed up towing a private crash investigator with the reputation for being a pit bull, and he's currently being publicized in a magazine and an eBook, and in the future maybe even on the big screen?"

Caitlin picked up her shoulder bag and held it up between them. "Let her come. I'll—"

The sound of a big V-8 invaded the room. Nick leaned sideways and looked out the window just as Cliff Yates' LTD charged into view and screeched to a stop. The PI climbed out and slammed the door shut. Mouth set in a grim line, he marched toward Nick's room.

He turned to Caitlin. "Guess who."

Yates pounded on the door. "Do not disturb, my ass! Open up, goddamnit!"

Nick and Caitlin both stood. Nick opened the door and backed up a little. As Yates stepped inside, Caitlin moved between them, held her hands out in front of her body, palms down, with a couple of quick up-and-down motions. "Now, now, boys, let's stay calm and keep things civil."

"Tell you what," said Yates. "Why don't I return a favor to this asshole first, then we can discuss civility?"

Caitlin shook her head. "We don't have time for this. Way I figure it, you're both to blame. Nick's throat still looks like a hangman failed to do his job, and Cliff? Well . . . you seem to be walking okay."

Nick peered around Caitlin at Yates. "Truce?"

After a tense moment, Yates offered a quick nod. "For now."

"Good," said Caitlin. She winked at Nick. "Stay in touch. Let's go, Cliff."

Nick closed the door behind them, got a beer out of the

mini bar and plopped down at the table.

The Victory had been based at a small airfield near Albuquerque rather than the much larger international airport. Lawson McAllister could have kept it there for any number of reasons. Although the cost of hangar space, fuel, and maintenance probably wasn't a factor in his decision, Caitlin had mentioned his impatience when dealing with air traffic controllers. He may have preferred the ease of departing and arriving at an airport without a control tower.

But of far more significance to Nick's investigation, the absence of additional security measures at large airports would have made tampering with the airplane less complicated, as well as disposing of any telltale evidence remaining in the wreckage.

Drive time from Dry Springs to Albuquerque was about seven hours at highway speeds in a car, longer for a semi hauling the remains of a Victory. He needed to be there when it arrived and talk his way into examining the wreckage. Or get it done after hours, and be careful while doing it.

Okay. Check out of the motel, turn in the rental Jeep at the Dry Springs Airport, fly his airplane to an Albuquerque airfield that *didn't* likely have a resident mechanic-saboteur, and rent another Jeep. He lifted the bottle to take his first long swallow of beer, stopped, stared at it. *What are you doing?*

Federal Aviation Regulations required a minimum of eight hours "bottle to throttle" and no smoking within 50 feet of the airplane, which pilots revised to: No smoking within eight hours of flying and no drinking within 50 feet of the airplane.

Nick poured the beer into the bathroom sink, grabbed his belongings and left the room to pursue a goal that he hoped would reconnect him with his long-lost professional identity, but which in his heart he felt would probably lead only to a dead end.

Caitlin had taken a room at the Bargain Suites only for the convenience of meeting with Nick and regretted it now as she sensed Yates moving up close behind her, spouting more of his sickening pseudo-coolness.

"Hey, there, gorgeous. How's about you and me playing hide the salami?"

Caitlin whirled around. "Shut your filthy mouth, Yates, and remember you're here for only one reason. Keep your distance."

"Fine. Pay me what I'm owed, and you and Nickie lover boy can do this by yourselves."

"You'll get paid nothing more until the job is finished." She marched to her room and opened the door before Yates caught up. Inside, she slipped her hand in the shoulder bag and hurried to the far side of bed. The hammer tab came loose with a flick of her thumb. She gripped the Walther and faced the door.

Yates slinked into the room. His eyes flashed to the bag and back to her face. "You going to shoot me now?"

Caitlin stared at him. "Decide right now whether you can keep this professional. If not, back your miserable ass out of here for good, minus the last payment." Talk of money lost usually got Yates' attention.

After a moment, during which Caitlin was sure she could hear rusty mental gears engaging, Yates sniffed and smacked his lips. "What do you want me to do?"

Something to keep you away from me. "Tail Phillips and make sure he doesn't see you."

Yates chuckled, a kind of *yuck, yuck* sound like a cartoon character. "You never saw me, and he won't either. Speaking of which, where will you be?"

She opened her eyes wide. "I'm a will-of-the-wisp. I go when and where I please. Now leave."

His jaw clenched, he backed to the door, opened it without turning around, and retreated from the room.

Caitlin fastened the security chain and sank into an armchair. She had needed Yates and might again. Problem was, it felt a little like carrying a loaded gun, cocked but not locked, ready to shoot off one of her own toes. In the meantime, she had no choice but to deal with a fact she knew all too well.

Once a leech smells blood, he never stops.

CLIFF STORMED INTO HIS room with his jaw clenched so tight that it hurt. Not as much as his balls, but close.

Monroe and her lap dog were making a big mistake if they thought he was going to let them keep him on the sidelines. Cliff had dealt with being excluded, alone and invisible to others, ever since he was a kid, and he'd had enough of it to last a lifetime.

After guzzling two beers, he popped the top on a third and quit pacing so he could calm down, sit down, and double down on his bet that opportunities for regaining the upper hand were never far away. Especially when everyone around him bought into the doofus act and dismissed him as a joke.

All he had to do was bide his time and stay alert. Sooner or later the joke would be on them.

CHAPTER TWELVE

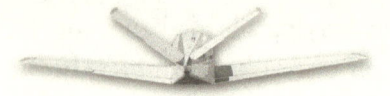

Nick propped himself up in the way-too-soft bed and squinted against the sunlight intruding through a gap in the shabby drapes. A broken innerspring poked him in the spine. Although the office clerk had been awake when Nick checked in, the Albuquerque Los Orcones Motor Inn could be a clone of the Bargain Suites in Dry Springs, Arizona.

Feeling almost human after a shower and the first cup of coffee buzzing through him, he sat at the flimsy excuse for a writing desk. Entries in the airframe, engine, and propeller logs for the Victory indicated a single shop had performed all routine and unscheduled maintenance since the major overhaul and refurbishment accomplished five years ago. A mechanic named T. L. Parker had signed off the individual work orders, with Leonard Stillwater adding his signature as the inspector.

Nick powered up his laptop and Googled *albuquerque + aircraft + servicing + maintenance* and found a listing for Stillwater Aviation at the Adobe Wings Airport. His road map showed the airport symbol about 20 miles southwest of Albuquerque International Sunport. He poured a second cup and considered how best to approach the problem.

Although committed to the task, he couldn't shed the lingering thought that this effort was destined to produce nothing definitive. Caitlin's insistence that the Victory had been sabotaged and all her reasons for believing it couldn't produce evidence out of nowhere. That said, Nick knew all about gut feelings and the persistent obsession that compels action in spite of the risk.

Even if she was correct, the chance of finding hard evidence of sabotage had to be like winning the lottery. And then tracing a smoking gun back to the shooter? Powerball jackpot remote.

He knew that, and yet it simply didn't matter. Sitting in this motel room, with nothing but the indicators of pilot error visible, he felt the rush of getting close. The craving to peel back the layers covering the truth that *might* be under there. And the eagerness to do something significant again.

In addition to personal reasons, Nick wanted to help Caitlin leave behind the tragedy of Lawson's death and look to the future without him rather than being trapped in the past. And then there was the other thing. The desire to please a mysterious beauty wrapped in milk-and-honey skin. Admitting his attraction did not sit well, but he couldn't deny it. She exuded a kind of aura that filled a room.

Nick raised his left hand and stared at his wedding ring. The symbol of his commitment to the woman he'd loved since that first date. The mother of his kids. Partner for life. Or so he thought.

But even now, with her moved out and their marriage likely done for, as long as he wore this ring, he couldn't cheat on Laurie any more than he could have for the last 25 years.

Nick closed the drapes and opened the closet. For his new role, he put on a pair of pressed jeans, white shirt with a button-down collar, blue-and-gray patterned tie, and a pair of smooth ostrich ropers with matching belt. A lightweight navy blazer completed the ensemble.

The reflection of Nick Phillips, a *private* aviation crash investigator dressed in western business casual, stared back from the mirrored closet door. He gathered his notes, shoved them into his old leather attaché case, and paused.

Barely visible as an outline in the soft leather of an interior pocket, a slight bulge had caught his attention. With a thumb and forefinger, he pulled out his credentials, forgotten in the hectic aftermath of the Larchmont investigation and his retirement from the NTSB.

He probably should have turned them in, but no one ever asked.

What if he'd used them when he approached the guy at Dry Springs?

If he used them now and got caught, what would he be charged with? Impersonating who he *used* to be? Or was he simply reclaiming the role of who he *was, is now, and always will be?*

And what about the deception? Would it stain him somehow and make it easier the next time? Creep into other areas of his life like a virus? Or was it justified by his good intentions?

After a moment, Nick slipped the creds into the outer breast pocket of his blazer, snatched his keys and wallet off the dresser, and marched outside to the Jeep.

THE AROMA OF SOFT tacos rose from the paper bag and filled the Jeep with mouthwatering temptation before Nick had driven a block from Don's Juan and Only Taco Stand. By the time he turned into the entrance of the Adobe Wings Airport, he was ready to eat all six, bag included. But that would not be wise. When you walked in on a man at noon, bringing lunch was a great way to get his attention.

The sign for Stillwater Aviation pointed Nick to a large hangar at the south end of the field. He parked in a space marked for visitors and climbed out of the Jeep into a comfortable 75 degrees. What a difference 4000 feet of elevation could make.

Stillwater's care and attention to detail immediately impressed him. The hangar sported a recent coat of paint. The area around it had been swept free of gravel, not an easy chore in the desert, and two airplanes parked on the ramp were tied down and chocked. Safety covers and windshield shades minimized the damage from a merciless sun.

Cleanliness didn't necessarily signify good maintenance, but it didn't hurt. He peered into the open hangar door. Spotless floors, tools put away except for those in use, supplies stored in bins and on shelves against the perimeter walls, and clearly marked safety equipment indicated the owner had his shit together.

Nick entered the office and noted more of the same: the aroma of fresh paint, clean floors, no years of dirt packed into the corners, current magazines fanned out on a coffee table, a sofa and armchairs new or freshly recovered. Unusual signs of prosperity for an operator at a small airport. Did Stillwater Aviation receive a recent infusion of cash, perhaps?

A second, smaller office was deserted. A door to Nick's right labeled NO ADMITTANCE WITHOUT ESCORT—NO SMOKING obviously opened into the hangar. He walked toward it. A voice from nowhere halted him.

"What's that smell?"

Nick glanced around the empty room. "Latex paint."

"Oh, good. A comedian. I meant the *other* one."

"Tacos. Anybody hungry?"

A muffled bump, followed by a whispered, "Goddamn it."

Nick peered into the smaller office. A man in gray work clothes knelt behind a gleaming wooden desk, rubbing his head. Nick said, "I heard that all the way out here."

The man looked up. "I'll bet you did. Help you with something?" The words STILLWATER AVIATION were embroidered in red above the man's left breast pocket and the name LEO above the right.

Nick held up his credentials in one hand and the bag in the other. "My name's Nick Phillips, Mr. Stillwater, and I've got too much food here."

Leo stood and laid a rag and a bottle of furniture wax on the desk. "Since when do you guys deliver food?"

"It's a common practice, actually, whenever we show up at noon on official business."

"And I suppose that should overcome my natural reluctance to break bread with a total stranger?"

"Not by itself, but these are from Don's Juan and Only and I've got more than I can eat."

Leo nodded. "You won't for long. I'll supply the beverages."

Nick followed Leo down a narrow hallway to a room labeled CANTEEN. Vending machines lined one wall. Three round tables with chairs filled most of the floor space. A long counter on the opposite wall had a sink, coffee maker, microwave oven, and built-in refrigerator.

Leo pointed to the table by the window with a view of the flight line. "Have a seat. Your choices are iced tea, cold water, or a soft drink."

"A Coke, please. Water back."

Leo acknowledged the joke with a grin and a nod, got the drinks and sat down. He must have been as hungry as Nick. Little talk interfered, and it didn't take long. Leo crumpled up the paper wrappings, stuffed them in the sack, and lofted it in a high arc to a perfect three-pointer in the trashcan. He drained the last of his Coke and leaned back in his chair.

"What can I do for you, Mr. Phillips?"

Nick felt like crossing his fingers behind his back until he reminded himself that he wasn't telling black lies. "We recently began a quality control program in which a senior Investigator-In-Charge who no longer leads Go Teams in the field will conduct a follow-up evaluation on how investigations were conducted. I probably don't need to tell you I'm here about the fatal crash of Lawson McAllister's Victory. I'll need to examine the aircraft records and the wreckage and interview your mechanics about the maintenance history for those small details that never make it into the logbooks."

Leo nodded. "Just for the record, no matter what you think you might find, you won't. That Victory was in as fine a mechanical condition as any airplane I've ever seen. Mr. McAllister spared no expense, and this shop did all the work. I'll stand behind my mechanics one hundred percent."

"No one is suggesting otherwise, and let's be clear that my only purpose is to evaluate NTSB procedures and employees."

"Fair enough. The wreckage and records are in transit. Got a call this morning that the truck broke down with engine trouble about halfway between Holbrook and Gallup, and they don't know exactly when it will be delivered. In the meantime, what can I tell you?"

How about that? Nick had guessed right about the salvage company truck's destination, and now he had some extra time to prepare for when the wreckage showed up. "I'm familiar with the maintenance history since the airplane was first based here. But I'm looking for that elusive, nagging problem that never made it into the records. Anything come to mind?"

Leo stared at the ceiling for a moment. "Not right off. Like most shops, we never log the small stuff. But nothing major goes out the door without all the paperwork done. Every invoice I sent Mr. McAllister had the work order and a copy of the maintenance discrepancy sheet. And he didn't just file it away. He'd call, ask questions, wanted all the details. Initially I thought he didn't trust me. It didn't take long to realize he was just meticulous."

"Was he signed up for factory tracking of unscheduled maintenance and inspections?"

"No, and I'm not sure why. My guess is he figured that his personal attention would be at least as thorough and probably more."

Nick noted that as worthy of further attention. Owners who took an active interest in how their airplanes were maintained normally took advantage of using the manufacturer's computerized record keeping. Leo's assumption of why McAllister didn't *need* it might be accurate, but Nick couldn't ignore the possibility that he might not have *wanted* it. That question was best left private, so Nick shifted to another topic.

"Was he the kind of pilot who wouldn't report that he'd exceeded g-limits?"

Leo smiled. "Absolutely not. You may have heard that he loved speed, and I can confirm that. We all cautioned him about how fast the Victory can accelerate. 'Yeahyeahyeah,' he'd say, real fast like that, as if he knew everything you were going to say before you even thought about saying it.

"After his third solo flight in his Victory, he crawled out of the airplane white as a sheet and admitted he'd let the speed get away from him during a descent. Pulled out of the dive with about five g's. We inspected it and found no evidence of damage."

Nick sipped his water. "Okay. The airplane was repainted

before it arrived here, right?"

Leo nodded. "A shop in Texas did all the exterior and interior refurbishment and avionics upgrades."

Repainting any flight control, particularly ruddervators on the Victory, required rebalancing prior to flight. From the logbooks, Nick knew the answer to his next question, but he needed Leo to confirm it. "And since that time you've had no reason to repaint the ruddervators?"

"Uh . . . yes, as a matter of fact. The left one."

That revelation hit Nick in the solar plexus. He'd seen nothing in the logs about that. He could have missed it, but—

"Mr. Phillips?"

"Uh, sorry. My mind sometimes has a mind of its own. Do you remember the reason?"

"Hangar rash. Somebody not paying attention."

The term commonly referred to nicks, scrapes, and small dents that seemed to germinate on airplanes kept in community hangars. "Who performed the rebalancing procedure?"

"Tommy Lee Parker, and he's a fine mechanic."

Nick didn't want his questions to come across as interrogation, so he paused to drink some water. The ruddervators pivoted around a point much closer to the leading edge than the trailing edge. Like an adult on one end of a playground seesaw and a child on the other, the heavier trailing edge would fall sharply if released from a level condition. Lead weights bolted into the horn, an extension on the leading edge, offset most of the imbalance. Lead washers added to the weights fine-tuned the ruddervator to be slightly tail heavy, which meant the trailing edge of the flight control would tend to fall if held level and then released.

And the most important fact: even a single coat of paint could alter the balance, and standard Victory maintenance practice called for rebalancing even if nothing else was done to a ruddervator.

He spent another five minutes asking questions about a number of maintenance issues he cared nothing about, just in case Leo noticed Nick's interest in topics that might drift outside the NTSB's official purview. "All of this confirms what I've suspected, and I thank you for your time." He pushed away from the table. "I noticed in the logs that Parker did all the work on McAllister's airplane. I need to talk with him."

Leo picked up the empty water bottles and stood. "You're welcome to do that. If you can find him."

CHAPTER THIRTEEN

Ever since the Victory crashed, Tommy Lee Parker had been hiding out at Buster's house, built by his grandfather and apparently designed for a creature that lived in the dark because light hurt its eyes. Tommy Lee had worn a pathway all around the threadbare area rug in the living room, the largest in a house that couldn't be much more than a 1,000 square feet total. His own home wasn't any larger, but he expected that when living in a trailer park. A real house should offer more room, for chrissakes.

At one of the front windows that looked out onto a covered porch, he eased the curtain back and peeked into the front yard. He didn't see anything he hadn't seen before: dead grass, dirt, with twin grooves worn from the highway to the house and out of sight past it to the detached garage where he'd hidden his truck. But staying out of sight was about to drive him nuts, and he just wanted to see something other than the walls.

In the kitchen he got a beer and sat down at the small table where he'd had a lot of time to think about how life used to be pretty damn simple. Maintain a low profile, stay out of trouble with the law, and milk his job as Lawson McAllister's mechanic for all it was worth. The guy had given him an opportunity to earn a pilot's license, and Tommy Lee was grateful. But it had been a constant struggle to keep from throwing it all away.

McAllister wrote the book on being a tough guy to work for. He wanted the Victory in perfect condition all the time, which was physically impossible. And the way he complained about a bug on the windshield, it's as if he expected Tommy Lee to arrange for all the insects along his boss's proposed route of flight to stay on the ground.

But being a good employee, Tommy Lee had gritted his teeth and put up with the aggravation as a price to pay for having the job. Then, in a stroke of personal genius, he found a way to make dealing with the frustration easier by socking away some cash.

Tommy Lee had never been part of the local biker scene, but close enough through his friendship with Buster not to be considered a threat. Which meant he could drink with Buster in a popular biker roadhouse, but don't even think about sitting with any of the other dudes. And late one night, everybody in the place tanked up and loud, he overheard a conversation from the next booth about problems transporting product.

It took a couple of weeks and a year's worth of nerve to ask Buster about it. After a bunch of hemming and hawing about not knowing much, Buster confirmed that yeah, these guys dealt a little meth to make ends meet. Tommy Lee wasn't buying that bullshit, and it didn't take long to talk Buster into making the connection. The result? Access to the Victory became the key to a lucrative startup he called Mule Air, and it filed no tax returns.

McAllister's flight schedule usually firmed up a week or more in advance, and the procedure became comfortable, low-key routine: fabricate a reason to work late; transfer the drugs in privacy to hidden compartments in the Victory; fly the next day to a pre-arranged airport with overnight hangar space; show up that evening having forgotten something in the

Victory, or needing to check out a malfunctioning instrument, whatever; remove the drugs, being sure to chat with whoever was manning the operations desk, real casual like; use his rent car to make the delivery and return to Adobe Wings the next day.

And then Tommy Lee had turned monumentally stupid.

He suspected that McAllister was using the airplane for something other than business, or in combination with it. About a year ago, the typical aromas in the interior gained a companion, the hint of something exotic, mysterious, and that had nothing to do with aviation. This scent was all woman, and none of Tommy Lee's business, of course, until McAllister's wife made it so.

He should have never agreed to meet with her privately. But he did, and a simple question about whether her husband had ever taken female passengers on trips ended up with Tommy Lee being rode hard and put away sweaty by a woman who obviously wasn't getting any at home and enjoyed the hell out of getting it on with her husband's airplane mechanic.

And not long after, his stupidity became a lot closer to insanity.

After an evening of steamy, uninhibited sex, she asked, *Have you ever wanted more from life than being Lawson McAllister's mechanic?* Of course. *What would you like to do?* Own my own shop. *How much would that cost?*

Tommy Lee didn't have a clue then any more than he did now, but his spur-of-the-moment answer of a million bucks led to her proposal: *Help me get rid of him and it's a deal.*

Her idea was that Tommy Lee would get some of his contacts in the biker community to take care of the dirty work, pay them whatever it took to get the job done, and keep the rest.

The problem was, he didn't have any contacts like that or know the first thing about where to get them. But more important, the thought of not sharing a million tax-free dollars with anyone was way too tempting.

Sitting down with a bottle of Jack Black one night, Tommy Lee came up with an idea that startled him with its simplicity and potential for getting away with it. He convinced Beth to accept the lack of predictability about when it would happen in return for hiding the murder so well that Lawson's death would be ruled an accident.

But then it all had turned complicated and unpredictable in less than 24 hours.

After putting the finishing touches on his modification to the Victory, he was strolling to his truck in the midnight darkness when he noticed a faint glow inside the cab.

The dome light? He'd closed the driver's door. Or had he? Couldn't remember. Then he noticed that the light was shining up from below.

He reached behind his back for the Beretta—*shit*. He'd left it under the front seat. Dumb-ass move. What now?

After a moment, *Jesus, Parker. You afraid of the dark now?*

He strode to the truck and yanked open the door and froze.

Looked like his portable GPS navigator had up and left the glove compartment for a more comfortable resting place on the console. All by its lonesome. Plugged itself in, even.

Why now, for chrissakes?

Tommy Lee climbed in, closed the door, picked up the GPS, stared at the destination: Scottsdale Airport, north of Phoenix, AZ.

He laid his forehead on the steering wheel as his brain frantically tried to deal with this unforeseen development.

Under the false floor of the storage box welded onto the bed of the pickup, he would find the standard four-bag shipment, all wrapped up neat and tidy, delivered to him like always. He never knew in advance when it would happen or saw who made the deliveries.

Tommy Lee *could* leave the stuff right where it was and drive to Scottsdale. Problem was, he hadn't sold a local drug dealer named Leland on the idea of Mule *Ground* four years ago, and messing with success didn't seem very smart considering Leland's rep for being fair only until somebody failed to deliver as promised. And *especially* since the New Mexico State Police and Arizona Highway Patrol were experts at finding probable cause to stop vehicles and ask for consent to search. Deny it and end up in cuffs.

But the thought of making one last Mule Air trip in *that* Victory made Tommy Lee's skin crawl, even knowing that the chances of the modification resulting in his own death were slim to none. He'd never flown faster than red line, certainly wouldn't now, and that should protect him.

Problem was, he couldn't get his mind off *slim* and *should.*

Then it dawned on him that he couldn't use the airplane tomorrow even if he wanted. McAllister was going to . . . *what did the schedule say?* He closed his eyes and pictured it:

Date: Tomorrow
Departure time: 0800
Destination: KDSP *Where the hell is KDSP?*
Return date: *Who gives a shit?*
Arrival time: *Ditto*

Tommy Lee pulled out his phone, entered the airport identifier into his aviation app, and his brain ended up on the only option that made any sense, even as little sense as it made.

The Dry Springs Municipal Airport sat to the northwest of the Phoenix metropolitan area. Not within spitting distance of

Scottsdale, but close.

McAllister would fly the Victory fast like always, but speed alone wouldn't do it. What was the probability that all the other factors would come together *tomorrow?*

After a few moments of furious what-if-ing, he decided that the tiny risk of the Victory crashing with the drugs on board was more than offset by the potential reward waiting after he completed this last delivery, shut down Mule Air, quit his job with McAllister, and put some distance and time between him and the big event.

He grabbed the pistol from under the seat, stuck it in his waistband, and hopped out of the truck. With four packages of drugs from the storage box, he rushed back into the hangar and concealed them in the Victory. Back in the truck, he changed the destination in the GPS and accelerated into the darkness toward one final delivery rendezvous.

He'd been so relaxed on the drive to Dry Springs, singing along with his favorite tunes mainlining into his brain through earbuds and not a care in the world. He didn't even have to speed. A 1:00 a.m. departure from Albuquerque would put him in the Phoenix area about seven hours later at 7:00 a.m. local, because Arizona didn't observe Daylight Savings Time. McAllister's scheduled departure plus a two-hour flight to allow for weather and/or traffic delays meant he would land about 9:00 a.m. local. No sweat.

Tommy Lee stopped at a Circle K in Peoria for coffee and a breakfast burrito, napped in his truck for about three hours, and arrived at the Dry Springs Municipal Airport at 10:00 a.m. He didn't see the Victory on the parking ramp, but McAllister always arranged for hangar space.

In the small terminal building, Tommy Lee found the airport manager sitting behind the operations counter. "I'm looking for a Victory that arrived this morning from Albuquerque."

"Haven't had one o' those in, let's see . . . musta been . . . July, no . . . it—"

"Excuse, me, sir. Did a Mr. Lawson McAllister arrange for overnight parking for a Victory with the tail number of November Three Two Five Lima Mike?

"Yup."

"And he hasn't arrived?"

"That's what I been tryin' to tell ya."

Tommy Lee sighed, struggling not to ask this idiot where he'd left his brain, and walked into the pilot's lounge. He checked the flight tracker on his phone, found the Victory's flight path history, and had to sit down to keep from falling down.

The line on the screen just stopped. In the middle of goddamn nowhere. The next few minutes had been a blur as the questions peppered him over and over like jabs from a champion welterweight.

Is it a problem with the flight tracking application or did McAllister crash?

If he crashed, did the sabotage cause it?

What the fuck do you care?

Will accident investigators find the drugs?

Is the world big enough for you to hide from Leland, the law, and Mrs. Elizabeth McAllister?

Tommy Lee's mental and emotional confusion continued until he confirmed the crash and a clear goal had shoved every other consideration aside. And here he was, two weeks later, walking out of Buster's kitchen into the living room and pacing again, wondering for the millionth time when it would be safe to come out of hiding. To join the ranks of regular folks going about their business and not expecting the FBI to show up, in their dark suits, white shirts, and conservative ties, grilling Tommy Lee about a particular Victory that had crashed. He had no idea how he would answer their questions without sweating through his clothing, never mind the temperature.

Of course he knew the airplane. He'd maintained it, kept it spotless and discrepancy-free for the owner. Why did they want to know? *Well, sir, the NTSB found evidence of—*

Tommy Lee's phone rang, probably someone from Stillwater again, wanting to know where the hell he was. But when he checked the caller ID, it was a strange, yet familiar area code. Where the hell had he seen . . .? Oh yeah. Of course.

In the aftermath of the crash, Tommy Lee had told Beth to let the insurance company know she wanted to pay salvage value out of the insurance proceeds. When he gave her the number of the salvage company, she had burst out laughing and barely managed to say, "I hated the airplane when it was in one piece. What the hell do I want with the wreckage?"

"I'll explain later. Give them my cell number as the point of contact. It's important."

And now, he answered the phone and listened to the manager of the Dry Springs Airport relay the best news Tommy Lee could have received. The NTSB had released the Victory wreckage, and the manager wanted to let him know that the salvage company had picked it up.

Tommy Lee thanked the guy and almost tossed his phone into the next room from celebrating with a couple of fist pumps. The NTSB hadn't found the tampering. He had tippy-toed through the minefield of his deal with Beth like one of those dancers in tights and a puffy skirt that she liked to watch on some stuck-up artsy-fartsy channel.

And maybe even more important, they hadn't found the special cargo. Which meant he would be able to get it back and keep all of his body parts where they belonged. He'd wait until the wreckage showed up at Adobe Wings, where the shipping company would offload it into McAllister's hangar. Then some midnight real soon, Tommy Lee would go in there, recover the product, and make sure nothing that remained could point a finger at him.

Free and clear, he could then collect the big payday Beth had promised and boogie out of town for one of the millions of places in the world where nobody knew who he was, where he was from, where he might be going, nothing.

Or maybe he'd stick around for a while. Let things cool off, no lingering suspicions, and see what the future might hold with Beth. He didn't mind the sneaking around, kind of preferred it, actually. Especially if it meant the opportunity to get his hands on some more of Beth's greenbacks.

The ringing of Tommy Lee's phone interrupted his fantasy, a call from the same number.

"Yes?"

"You hung up before I could tell you."

"Tell me what?"

Tommy Lee's carefully imagined daydreaming about the future began to disintegrate into dust as the guy told him about a visitor who showed up and wanted to examine the wreckage.

"You didn't let him, did you?"

"Hell, no."

Whew. "Thanks."

"That's not all. As the shipping company was leaving, I realized I hadn't given them the boxes with the records."

"But they've got them all now, right?"

"The boxes, but I'm not sure about the records."

"Why the hell not?"

"Those boxes were sealed with special tape. But they had

been opened and re-taped sometime after that investigation team hauled ass out of here."

"You're shitting me."

"No, but this might. Two door locks in the office and hangar look like they've been jimmied. If so, whoever it was had access to the wreckage."

The living room seemed to shrink even more as Tommy Lee thanked the guy and ended the call.

To sabotage the Victory and get away with it, he'd known from the beginning the camouflage would have to conceal more than the tampering itself. No way he could complete it in one solitary night in the hangar. He wouldn't be able to explain why he was removing the ruddervator. And most important, failure to complete the paperwork would have Leo all over his ass asking, *What the hell you doin'?*

With no other choice, Tommy Lee had filled out the maintenance log for Leo to sign off as the inspector just like always, and then he had to erase the paper trail.

Each logbook page was numbered and bound in triplicate so he could tear out the two perforated carbons, one yellow and one pink. Victory owners could sign up for factory tracking of maintenance and send in the pink copy for the information to be entered into computer records, and retain the yellow copy for other uses or toss it.

McAllister didn't want the factory or anyone else snooping into how he maintained his Victory, but he was so meticulous about how Tommy Lee did everything that he wanted all the records retained, duplicate or not. So to prevent leaving a signpost that read TAMPERING in the primary source logbook, he'd scrubbed the records by removing a couple of white, original pages, which took some careful work with a razor blade.

To discover that these pages were missing, an investigator would have to pay close attention to the page numbers, relatively small and insignificant among all the other information pre-printed on the pages, which were filled out in pen to document the discrepancy and corrective action required to fix it. Absent that, no one would ever notice the cut edges of the pages buried deep in the binding, and they didn't. They'd done exactly what Tommy Lee planned by latching onto the most obvious answer to the riddle of why the Victory had crashed.

And now, someone was snooping around. Who the hell was it and what were they looking for? Tommy Lee wasn't worried so much about the bound logbook. But the incriminating copies in the looseleaf binders were a carbon paper trail pointing a finger directly at Tommy Lee in spite of his precautions.

He sank into the sofa, an ancient relic of the past that had seen much better days. It tried to swallow him, which wasn't a bad idea, come to think of it. Maybe he could hide in there. Stick his head between two of the cushions like Tommy Lee Ostrich.

He dialed Buster's number and hoped his buddy wasn't charging down some highway out there with his cell phone ringing its heart out, crushed between his butt and the seat of his Harley with that patented roar filling his ears.

Chapter Fourteen

Nick sat in a chair in the canteen at Stillwater Aviation and twisted the top off a bottle of cold water. He drank some, slipped his cell phone out of its holster and speed-dialed Caitlin.

Her silky voice answered on the third ring. "What have you found?"

"More like what I haven't. The mechanic who did all the maintenance on the Victory hasn't showed up for work since the day after the accident."

Silence for a moment, then, "What does that tell you?"

"It *suggests* a scenario I'm familiar with. Tampering with an airplane requires access and specific knowledge about the particular make, model, and in the best case, the serial number. If you wanted to kill someone and disguise it as an accident, recruiting the mechanic is the logical first step. It's also the most obvious."

"Any indication that foul play is involved in his disappearance?"

"We don't know he's disappeared, Caitlin. He just hasn't been at work."

"Like maybe he took the money and ran."

"Makes sense to me. Can't imagine that an airplane mechanic would become a killer for hire and then keep on fixing airplanes. The payoff has to be a life-changer."

"Have you tried to find him?"

"That's a little out of my area. I'm just an ex-accident investigator, and—"

Caitlin scoffed. "Spare me the excuses. Not being *in your area* didn't stop you from sticking your nose deep into the Larchmont conspiracy."

"That was then. Besides, I got my nose tweaked really hard."

"Okay. I'll send Yates out there. He's an asshole, but he knows his business."

"Not a good idea. He and I—"

"You both need to get over that. He'll contact you when he arrives."

The line went dead. Nick stared out the window at the flight line. An instructor with a bored expression trailed a student performing a preflight inspection on a small trainer.

Nick could be doing that in Colorado. Part of him wondered why the hell he wasn't, but the alpha-dog part demanded that he finish what he'd started. He sighed, drank the rest of the water, and left the canteen. Standing just inside the hangar door, he studied the maintenance area. No one paid him any attention.

Airplanes filled the space from wall to wall, fitted together like a jigsaw puzzle. He counted at least six mechanics engaged in various tasks and watched each one individually. In every workplace all over the world, some percentage of employees appeared beaver-busy while doing as little work as possible. But in this business, sloughing off could kill people. After about thirty minutes, he'd seen nothing that raised a red flag.

A wall clock read 3:45. He didn't want to interfere with work in progress. Closer to quitting time would be better. But not too close. Give a mechanic a reason for coasting near the end of a hard day and learn a lot. Being nice to people can lower suspicion and loosen up tongues.

Nick turned to leave and noticed a man sitting beside a workbench. He was eating a granola bar and appeared to be on break.

As Nick approached, the man nodded in greeting. "Are you Nick Phillips, the NTSB guy?"

"Is it that obvious?"

The man grinned and extended his hand. "Ronnie Cox. Leo told us you'd be in here."

"I'd appreciate a moment of your time."

Ronnie glanced at the clock on the wall. "The boss knows we get the work done and isn't too picky about breaks. What can I do for you?"

"I'm looking into how the NTSB investigated the crash of Mr. McAllister's Victory. I need to speak with T. L. Parker. Leo said he hasn't shown up for a while. Any idea why?"

Ronnie shrugged. "Tommy Lee is—or was, whatever—a fine mechanic. But he didn't really *like* fixing things. Most good mechanics do. He always seemed to be waiting for something better to come along. My guess is he found it."

A sack full of cash, maybe? "Did you know him outside of work?" When Ronnie shook his head, Nick said, "You think any of the other mechanics might have?"

"Tommy Lee was friendly enough, got along okay with everybody. But he never stayed around after. You know, have a beer or two. Quitting time, he's out of here."

"Any thoughts on why he wasn't more sociable?"

Ronnie hesitated, brushed some crumbs from the granola bar into the palm of his hand and wrapped them in a napkin. "It may have less to do with him than the rest of us." After a pause, Ronnie lowered his voice as he said, "Tommy Lee had a really sweet deal that any mechanic here would want. It's not easy to move past being jealous of a guy who gets to fly his boss's airplane around."

Whoa. Nick filed that tidbit away for the future. "Did he have his own work area?"

"Sort of. Each mechanic has his own tools and a cabinet. Without planning it out, we've staked out our territories where we do most of the work assigned to us." Ronnie pointed to a long workbench flanked on one side by a standing metal storage cabinet and on the other by a huge tool chest on rollers. "Tommy Lee's is right over there."

Nick thanked him and walked to the workbench. The top surface had the look of hasty abandonment. Pegboard fastened to the hangar wall behind it held a vast array of tools, with about ten empty spaces. He mentally paired the tools on the workbench with the unused pegs. Looked about right. Did the mechanic not clean up his work area because that was his normal habit? Or was he in a hurry?

Materials lying about suggested Tommy Lee had been in the process of fabricating a doubler plate to reinforce a sheet-metal component. Nick turned on an overhead light and took a closer look at the work product. He rubbed his fingers along a line of rivets to check for proper countersinking and seating depth. The guy did nice work.

The toolbox had an integral locking system, but an open padlock hung from a slot in the top compartment. A bit strange. A mechanic makes his living with tools and usually guards them carefully. Inspecting each drawer confirmed Tommy Lee liked organization and neatness. He had also spent a small fortune.

The cabinet was also unlocked. Shelves stacked with supplies in labeled boxes filled the interior. The bottom shelf served the standard purpose of catchall storage. He'd never known any handyman or professional mechanic who didn't save loose nuts, bolts, and washers.

He knelt, pulled out the box on the far left, heavy with a mixed assortment of hardware, and rummaged through the contents, looking for anything that might be part of a Victory's balance weights. Nothing. Seven identical boxes contained only miscellaneous hardware. But the last one, although just as full, felt lighter. He bent over to peer inside.

The box was shorter. He pulled it all the way out, set it on the floor and reached deep into the locker. His hand closed on the front edge of another small box.

His heart beat a quick double time. He took a deep breath and glanced over each shoulder. No one seemed the least bit interested.

In the box rested three airfoil-shaped pieces of lead, balance weights from a Victory ruddervator. The flat rear surfaces had empty threaded holes where bolts could be inserted and tightened to hold lead washers for the fine balancing of the flight controls. Extra bolts and washers lay alongside the weight.

Nick picked up one of each, slipped the washer over the bolt, and threaded the bolt partway into the hole in the weight. Then he reversed the process, returned the materials to the box, pushed it to the back of the cabinet, and replaced the front box. He stood and closed the locker door. Pretending to examine something on the workbench, he considered this find.

Could one of these be a balance weight removed from the Victory? Was there any way to prove it? Why didn't he think before he touched the weight with bare hands? What if Parker's fingerprints are on it? Compromised evidence? What now?

Nick's phone rang and jerked his thoughts back to the moment.

Cliff Yates growled, "Where the hell are you?"

NICK ARRIVED AT THE Los Orcones Inn about 6:00 p.m. and idled the Jeep through the parking lot. Caitlin had said she *would* send Yates out here, but Nick was pretty sure he was being shadowed. Not because he knew how to recognize it, but because Yates was as predictable as the sun and displayed all the characteristics of a bad penny.

No elderly Ford LTD with Arizona plates, a car as distinctively Yates as his sport coat. The PI hadn't shown up yet . . . but on second thought . . . he might be using a rental. Nick parked in front of his room.

A six-pack of Michelob and a paper bag lay in the front passenger's seat. The tantalizing aroma of another daily special from Don's Juan and Only filled the Jeep. He stared at the bag. Had he again bought more tacos than he could eat? A peace offering, maybe? Get Yates' mind off revenge and on his stomach?

Nick removed his tie, just in case he walked into a war zone. He'd prefer to shed the sport coat as well, but he couldn't legally carry the Glock in the open. He grabbed the bag, the beer, his briefcase, and climbed out of the Jeep. Head on a swivel, he walked to his room and paused with the key in the door.

PIs knew all kinds of sneaky tricks. Especially *this* one.

He transferred the beer and tacos to his left hand with the briefcase, unbuttoned his coat for easy access to the Glock, unlocked the door and eased it open.

Semi-darkness and silence. He flipped on the first of three light switches by the door. The entrance spotlight contracted his pupils and turned the rest of the room into a black cave. *Shit.*

The last switch turned on a floor lamp beside the far wall that cast enough light for Nick to confirm that Yates wasn't lurking within the living area. He checked the bathroom, and feeling a bit foolish, yanked open the closet door and said, "Boo!" The ironing board didn't flinch.

He bolted the door and sat down for another taste of spicy heaven. He'd just finished eating three of the six tacos when someone knocked. Dirt from countless years blocked any chance of seeing out the peephole. He slipped the dead bolt and turned the knob. Holding the Glock beside his leg, he jerked the door open.

The housekeeper jumped as if hit with a cattle prod. Her eyes flicked down and back up. She retreated a step and covered her mouth with both hands.

Nick spent the next few minutes calming her down. He didn't hear her announce housekeeping, thought she was someone else, he was one of the good guys who could legally carry the weapon and yes, he really did want her to turn down the sheets. Could he please have an extra set of towels? And does the Inn offer guests those little chocolates?

He cleaned out the peephole as best he could and turned toward the kitchen for a second bottle of Michelob. Another knock stopped him. The distorted face of Cliff Yates filled the peephole, which confirmed he'd already been in Albuquerque and Caitlin didn't have to *send* him from anywhere. Wondering if she had known that when they talked earlier today, Nick released the hammer tab on his holster, eased the Glock up about an inch, and opened the door.

Yates held his hands out to his sides, palms up. "Relax. I'm unarmed at the moment."

Nick rubbed his sore throat. "It's not your gun I'm worried about."

Yates lifted his hands. "I can't leave these outside, Phillips." He smiled, his lips a thin, tight line. "But I promise not to use them."

They glared at each other for a moment.

As if from a director's chair, Nick suddenly pictured what this testosterone-filled confrontation would look like in a movie. A bad one. He stepped aside.

Yates strolled in and stopped at the foot of the bed. "Nice room. I particularly like the bedspread."

Nick hadn't yet paid much attention, but it was a gaudy, brightly colored pattern. He closed the door. "Goes well with your sport coat."

Yates nodded. "I may steal the one in my room and have someone make me a couple out of it." He tilted his head back and sniffed twice, exaggerated and quite loud in the stillness. "Is that food?"

"Help yourself."

Yates smiled, big and toothy, and sat down. He helped himself to a beer and attacked the tacos like he hadn't eaten in a week. Nick sipped his beer and watched the man gulp his food with the manners of a Viking.

Yates finished with a belch. "Damn good. Thanks."

"You're welcome. Why are you here?"

Yates drained the last of his beer and opened another. "Our employer figures the two of us should join forces. Get faster results thataway. *Podner.*"

Yuk, yuk. A cowboy clown.

"And what exactly is *your* role, Cliff?"

"You'll find out soon enough. Exactly."

"Like when?"

Someone knocked on the door.

Yates smiled. "Like right now, maybe?"

CAITLIN STEPPED INTO A motel room that seemed to be electrified with male posturing.

Yates' sport coat reminded her a circus clown. All he needed was an orange wig, some makeup, and a pair of floppy-toed shoes. Nick was . . . well . . . Nick. Solid, reliable, if rumpled a bit in a cowboy-casual sort of way after a hard day on the job. Investigating, hopefully.

She stepped between them. "Whatever this is, you both need to keep a lid on it." She sat in an armchair and pointed to the two chairs by the small dining table. When they were seated, she continued.

"We have to assume McAllister's widow and an accomplice, probably the mechanic, arranged for the wreckage to be delivered here for something more than sentimental reasons. Nick is the only one who has publicly shown any interest in it, and we need to keep it that way for as long as we can."

"So," Nick said, "I'm like . . . bait?"

"A diversion. To give Cliff and me the freedom to move around. And even if they find out about us, your expertise is the real threat."

"That's comforting."

"Not to worry," said Yates, "Two people who conspire to murder and neither of them gets any blood on their hands? They don't suddenly become do-it-yourselfers. And even if she got the mechanic to send some kind of message, they'd plan a limited-response deal. Escalate only if she has to."

"Good," said Nick. "Just a sledgehammer to the knees?"

Caitlin smiled. "You carry a Glock. So what if some goon shows up to a gunfight with a sledgehammer? In the meantime, we've got two problems to solve. Both require special skills.

One, find out what caused the crash. And two, tie the sabotage to BB. That's the only—"

"BB?" said Nick.

"Balloon Bitch," said Caitlin. "My personal nickname for the not-so-grieving widow. She lives in Santa Fe where the money is, but the cancer center is here in Albuquerque where they have this annual hot-air balloon fiesta. She sponsors entries, hosts parties, really gets into it."

"Sounds exciting," said Nick. "Like watching those exposed elevators going up and down in hotels."

"Be a cynic. But I dare you to watch one mass ascension and then tell me it's not a spectacular sight with all those bright colors against a clear blue sky." Caitlin tilted her chair away from the table. "You said the key to proving sabotage is to focus on the most logical source of tampering. The mechanic is either lounging in the sun on a tropical island counting his blood money, or he's rotting in a shallow grave with maggots feasting on his eyes. Either way, we need to find him."

"There's a third and more likely possibility," said Yates. "He might be holed up locally. We need to toss his residence. Find something to point us in one direction or the other."

"Dead or alive," said Nick, "his trail is going to be hard to follow. That takes special knowledge and access, both of which we don't have."

Yates laughed. "Who says? PIs can trace people as well as anyone."

"Really? You found him yet?"

"No, and I might not. Bribing someone to kill your husband and then leaving the killer alive, no matter how much you paid him, is dumb-as-a-stump stupid. Guys like that will go through a bankroll faster than you can fan the bills. Then they get greedy. Start asking for more. It never ends. That sonofabitch is probably dead."

Caitlin began clapping. "Bravo, Cliff. I'm glad we have your conclusion on the matter. Now we can—"

"What you can do," he said, "is stop with the sarcasm. I know what I'm talking about. Let's concentrate on finding him and the sabotage evidence. People always leave trails."

Caitlin's jaw muscles tightened, an involuntary precursor to losing control of a temper with a mind of its own. She took a deep breath, nodded at Yates and focused on Nick. "What else did you find at the maintenance shop?"

"It's what I didn't find that tells us the most."

"What the hell does that mean?" asked Yates.

"That shoddy workmanship isn't the most likely probable cause. Which supports a suspicion of tampering."

"Why?"

"Because people fail much more often than critical components. An expert mechanic reduces the probability of human error, the most common reason for system malfunctions. And I found a tantalizing bit of lead."

Nick pronounced it "leed." which confused Caitlin. "You found a lead?"

"It's a piece of lead."

She glared at him. "A leading piece of lead. Do I have that right?"

He nodded. "You remember me telling you about balancing the ruddervators?"

Yates said, "Doing what?"

Nick gave him the short version of what he'd previously explained to Caitlin and told them both about his find in Parker's locker at Stillwater Aviation. "Those balance weights couldn't have been shoved any deeper in the locker. Coincidence or intentional?"

"What do you think?" asked Caitlin.

"I don't put much faith in coincidence. What if the mechanic removed an original balance weight from the ruddervator and altered it? The weights are large chunks of lead. Fine-tuning the balance requires adding or subtracting lead washers attached to the outside of the weights. He could remove all the washers off one side. Maybe add extra ones to the other side and create more asymmetry. Or he could be really sneaky and hollow out the weight to imbalance it."

When Nick paused, Yates held his hands out, palms up. "Why not just remove it?"

"That would work."

Caitlin shook her head. "Hold on a second. We talked about this. Even with Lawson's casual approach to preflights, wouldn't that be hard to miss?"

Nick shook his head. "Not from just looking at it. The weights are installed behind access panels."

"If these weights are so important," said Caitlin, "why hide them so the pilot can't make sure they're installed?"

"Because other indicators provide confirmation of proper balance." Nick reminded Caitlin of the manual check on preflight and explained that the pilot is supposed to move the ruddervators full cycle from one stop to the other. Once by hand when outside the airplane, and a second time in the cockpit with the yoke. A properly balanced ruddervator should be slightly tail-heavy. "To a conscientious pilot who does a thorough preflight, a missing weight would create a very different feel."

Caitlin winced at the word "conscientious." As far as she'd known, Lawson was a good pilot. She wouldn't have flown with him otherwise. After a moment she said, "BB probably had no clue about what kind of pilot Lawson was. She hated the airplane. Accused him of spending more time involved with it than he did his obligation to her and the cancer center. I can personally vouch for that. But the mechanic wouldn't leave signposts pointing to the tampering."

Yates crossed his arms. "Whatever it was, we know the pilot failed to catch it. Government investigators did no better. That tells me the mechanic came up with a way to make that airplane come apart under conditions he anticipated McAllister would operate in."

Caitlin looked at Nick. "So the balance weights are the most obvious culprit?" When Nick nodded, she said, "Which means that investigators would have looked closely at that part of the wreckage? And—"

"Not necessarily," said Nick. "Remember that they had no reason to think of a balance weight problem as *causing* the Victory to breakup. They'd examine the ruddervators, of course, and a missing balance weight would only be anecdotal evidence that tells them *what* happened, not why."

"Okay," said Caitlin. "Is there any way to determine if the weight was missing before the accident or ripped out during the event?"

Nick leaned back in his chair. "That's a great question, and it goes directly to something the investigators would pay particular attention to. The answer is yes, but not to an absolute certainty."

He explained that the balance weight was much denser than the aluminum or composite fiber structure surrounding it. A violent event, like an airfoil shape encountering the severe gusts of a thunderstorm, might accelerate the ruddervator in one direction, building inertia, then almost instantaneously reverse direction.

Yates' eyes had opened up a bit more than his normal sleepy

lids allowed when he wasn't doing the talking. "That could rip the weight out?"

Nick nodded. "Especially if the weight wasn't bolted securely to the surrounding material. That would allow it to build up additional inertia."

"We've strayed from my question," said Caitlin. "How do you tell what happened with *this* Victory?"

"We start by examining the ruddervator horn. Let's say the skin is splayed outward and the ripped edges are curled away from the ruddervator. An exit wound, if you will. This would indicate something came out with enough inertia to overcome the containing strength of the skin on the horn."

"But," said Yates, "if the horn is crumpled inward, like with impact damage, and it appears that the skin collapsed into an empty space, that would indicate the weight was missing at the time of the event."

Nick stared at Yates. "I'm impressed, Cliff. You actually listen on occasion."

Yates sat up from his trademark slouch and placed both hands palms down on the table. "Keep that up, dickhead, and—"

"Shut up," said Caitlin, and to Nick, "What did the damage to this ruddervator horn look like?"

"I never got the chance to find out in Dry Springs because the salvage guys showed up."

"Could the balance weight in the mechanic's locker have come from the Victory?"

Yates laughed and slapped his knees with both hands. "Wouldn't that be friggin' great? Find that weight hidden in the guy's locker? Hells bells! What have we here? Wasn't this boat anchor supposed to be balancing those V-Tail thingys on that Victory? What do you suppose this means?"

"I doubt it will be that simple," said Nick, "but you never know."

"We've been at this a while," said Caitlin. "How about some food, then I want to see what we can do about tying a rope around the Balloon Bitch's nipped-and-tucked neck."

SANDWICH WRAPPERS, EMPTY SNACK-CHIP bags, soft-drink cans, and a scattering of crumbs from a takeout meal covered the small table in Phillips' room.

Caitlin tossed a couple of used napkins in a wastebasket, picked an empty Coke can and wondered if there might be a recycling bin close by—*What the hell you doing?*

She put the can back on the table along with the napkins, plus two empty potato chip bags from the wastebasket. Why she succumbed to an infuriating personal tendency to clean up after men, usually without thinking, remained a mystery. Maybe from her childhood . . . trying to be the perfect orphan so the current foster family wouldn't send her back into circulation.

Whatever, these two guys could clean up their own trash, and hers too, come to think of it. She waited for Yates to decide that nothing worth grazing for remained on the table. The guy was like a vacuum cleaner when it came to food. She half expected him to get on all fours and sniff the carpet looking for crumbs.

Caitlin tapped the table with the palm of her hand. "Looks like you got it all, Cliff. Let's assume we find evidence that one balance weight was missing prior to the event, and the resulting imbalance ripped off the Victory's tail section. And further, the weight in the mechanic's locker turns out to be the one. How do we tie the sabotage to BB?"

Yates pulled a mangled toothpick from his mouth and appeared to swell up with importance. "When you're looking for connections between people, first thing to check is the possibility of physical contact. It's like with your infidelity cases. I get a series of shots with some housewife coming out of an apartment building on the arm of a man looking nothing like the husband who hired me? Doesn't take much to conclude they didn't meet for a spot of tea."

"But," said Nick, "even if we find the mechanic alive, he's not going to be running around with BB."

Yates drained his Pepsi and shook the can, as if that would dislodge the last of the soda hiding inside. Apparently satisfied, he slapped the can down on the table. "Unless they're stupid, and I doubt she is. But somebody may have seen them together. I get my hands on pictures, canvas around, talk to the guys at Stillwater, maybe BB was out there. We know she never flew with her husband. What's she doing at the maintenance facility? Parker's friends and family might know something."

Nick shrugged. "Sounds like a long shot."

"A PI's life is made up of long shots. Sooner or later one comes up short, and bingo, you got what you came for."

"Okay," said Nick. "What else do we have?"

"Money," said Caitlin. "There has to be a trail."

Yates pointed toward the ceiling. "Following the money is usually a key. Something as simple as timing withdrawals from one account to deposits in another."

Nick frowned, a look of disbelief distorting his features. Caitlin decided to remain a bystander to the conversation, content to let the two alpha males hash it out while she looked for opportunities to get Nick even more personally involved. Not only to prove the sabotage, a task that he had already accepted, but also to go after the black widow. Based on

Nick's reputation, if Caitlin could focus his attention on the righteousness of her goal to seek justice for Lawson's death, it would be like removing the chain on a guard dog. And Nick would charge. She could see it in his eyes. Love of the hunt smoldered inside him.

She sipped her mineral water as Nick said to Cliff, "You can hack into bank records?"

"I have sources, remember? You'd be surprised how easy it is to get information nowadays. But the mechanic may not have been a good banking customer. Guys like that, bachelors, working the trades, live hand-to-mouth. They spend whatever they get before they get it. So what would he do with a sudden cash payment, probably more money than he's ever seen in his life? I bet we'd see an expensive car, a fishing boat, fancy clothes, a brand-new fifty-inch plasma in his living room. But if he's even half smart, he stuffed it under the mattress like BB probably told him to. Wait a while, let things cool off before making a lifestyle change."

"Okay," said Caitlin. "Hopefully we can find a direct payoff connection. You have a plan for that, Cliff?"

"You can count on me."

"Good. What's the deal with the wreckage, Nick?"

"One of the mechanics at Stillwater is going to give me a call when it arrives."

"Good. I want to know immediately what you find."

As they left Nick's room, Cliff said, "Wanna play house with your daddy?"

Caitlin turned away from him and walked in the opposite direction from her room. "Save it for one of your regular sluts."

"But I'd really like to do the dirty deed with an *irregular* slut. Are you available?"

Caitlin rounded the corner out of Cliff's sight, used her

key card to enter the building and hurried up the stairs. Once inside her room she tried to calm down but couldn't.

Keeping the guys focused on their individual roles felt a little like preventing two predators from eating each other. She hated working with Cliff because it left her with a slimy feeling. But she needed him, especially when he shed the clown persona that lived in the outfit and got down to serious business. Reminded her of a chameleon. In reverse. The ability to become more visible rather than less so, indicative of private agendas under that coat, maybe?

But none of that mattered to Caitlin if Yates could find physical evidence of a payoff connection and locate Parker while Nick searched out the proof of sabotage. Their combined efforts would arm her with power over the future of Elizabeth Blaine McAllister, AKA The Black Widow, AKA The Balloon Bitch.

CHAPTER FIFTEEN

Cliff parked the LTD in the desert about 100 yards from the trailer park and checked his watch: 3:47 a.m. Thirteen minutes to go, only because he had a rule never to break into anyone's residence prior to 4:00. Supposedly, the average person slept the most soundly between then and the big wake-up call in the sky. Sounded like good info, anyway.

Earlier that day, he used Google map and satellite views to reconnoiter the layout of the park and terrain around it. A single dirt road separated two rows of trailers, 21 per side. A street view couldn't confirm which trailer Tommy Lee Parker called home because many of them had no addresses. But a visit to the phone validator website with the number listed for Parker proved that his trailer had a landline. Cliff had called it to make sure it was a working number. It also had no answering machine or service.

At 3:50, he checked that the dome light was off, grabbed the pry bar, got out of the LTD and approached the trailer park from the side opposite Parker's row. In the darkness between two trailers, he crept forward and peered across the street.

About ten yards down on the opposite side of the road, a single outside bare bulb cast a yellow circle onto a lopsided wooden porch and stairs and barely illuminated a row of white pickets, most of them leaning. Behind them, the trailer he thought was Parker's looked as if a tornado had at one time taken it for a turbulent flight and performed an atrocious landing.

Cliff retraced his steps, worked his way around to the other side of the park and crept up to the rear of Parker's trailer. A wire from a phone box on the back of the trailer climbed a pole and extended to an overhead feeder line that ran the length of the street. He knelt beside a set of wooden steps leading up to the back door and dialed Parker's listed number.

A phone rang inside the trailer. After 15 rings, Cliff climbed the steps and slipped the pry bar between the jamb and the door at the level of the lock. A quick shove toward the door and push on his end of the pry bar toward the jamb popped the door open. He dropped the pry bar, drew his .45, stepped inside and closed the door. Diffused light from the outside bulb through the filthy front windows coated the interior in a ghostly gray film.

Visual scan: living room, couch, two armchairs, entertainment center with big screen TV on the opposite wall, small kitchen and dining table to his left. A pile of mail below a slot in the door. The ringing phone rested in a cradle on a lamp table beside the couch, with what looked like the business end of a computer power cord hanging almost to the floor. Cliff ended the call with his phone and in the silence listened for any sound inconsistent with an empty trailer. Nothing.

Odors: dust, stale air, no indication of recent cooking or even takeout food.

He did a quick walkthrough to check every room. The owner cared little about housekeeping. Clothes, beer cans, the remains of fast-food containers, newspapers, magazines, and the miscellaneous debris of a life gone to slob covered every square foot of space.

He holstered the .45 and pulled out his penlight. Over the years of being a cop, he'd developed a search routine that considered every common hiding place and a lot of really sneaky ones, many of which he'd seen kids use to hide drugs from their parents.

Tonight's search had nothing specifically to do with drugs, but the principle was the same, and he was looking for anything to help answer two questions.

Was Tommy Lee Parker missing, as in a victim of foul play, hiding out in the local area, or gone for good?

Had he hidden anything in the trailer that might connect him directly to McAllister's widow in terms of money or incriminating communications?

Moving from room to room, Cliff remained alert for crawl spaces, loose flooring, drop-ceiling panels. He checked under the bed and mattress, behind bookcases, inside desk drawers and chests of drawers, and in battery compartments of electronic devices like remote controls and portable players. He looked for modified furniture, such as hollow areas in the legs of a chair, behind electrical outlet plates, in air conditioning and heating ducts; and a favorite most folks thought would fool anyone but seldom did, a closet, especially in the pocket of a jacket or stuffed in the toe of a shoe.

He stepped into the second bedroom, obviously used only to store more junk. In the beam of his flashlight, cardboard boxes sat in two floor-to-ceiling stacks. Just the sort of thing someone might do to give the impression he never had overnight guests. It's a small trailer, he's got lots of stuff and needs all the space just to hold it all. But a bedroom with no closet?

Cliff walked over to the boxes and tapped them, one at a time, and got hollow, empty sounds in reply. So if Parker didn't need the boxes to store things, why aren't they broken down to save space? Cliff shined the flashlight beam behind the stack. *Maybe this explains it.*

He tossed the boxes on the bed, which already had a bunch of linens and towels and clothes on it, and opened the door to an almost empty closet. Parker didn't have enough room to hold everything, and yet he left this closet unused?

A long overcoat, called a duster, hung from a rod at one end of the closet and reached all the way to the floor. He lifted the hangar with the duster off the rod and tossed it on the bed.

The closet was lined with the same cheap, fake paneling that covered all the walls, but the narrow end that had been hidden behind the duster had a strip of plastic running horizontally across it. All the other 4x8 panels only had vertical strips at the junctions between sheets.

Cliff knelt and used the pliers in his multi-tool to pull the strip away from the wall, revealing a seam between the upper seven or so feet of paneling and the bottom foot. Then he slipped his fingers into the seam and gripped the bottom piece. A couple of tugs and twists, and the false panel came up from behind the baseboard. Bending it outward in the center, he removed it from the plastic strips on each side.

Tucked into a hollow space within the interior wall, a laptop computer propped vertically on top of bundles of cash.

Cliff removed the computer and pulled out one of the bundles, used bills of various denominations held together with a rubber band. He removed ten more bundles and whispered, *Thank you, Mr. Parker.*

He found a garbage sack in the kitchen, tossed in the cash, returned to the living room and put the computer power cord in the sack, then picked up all the mail on the floor and put it on the dining table. With his penlight, he examined each of the envelopes.

Postmarks indicated that the mail began accumulating within a day or so of the crash and was still being ignored. Mr. T. L. Parker hadn't paid his electricity bill, renewed a subscription to *Sports Illustrated*, responded to a bill collection agency, or cashed a paycheck from Stillwater Aviation.

Cliff examined the walls, found no telltale holes and less-faded areas to indicate recent removal of photographs. Flat surfaces that might have had freestanding frames where people generally keep family photos were all covered with a uniform layer of dust. None of Parker's possessions appeared to be cleared out as might be expected when someone was hauling ass out of town for good, not to mention that he hadn't returned for his computer and cash.

Standing in the living room, Cliff considered whether he should cover his tracks and decided no. He stacked the mail neatly on the table to leave a message because he needed to see what Parker did when he came back.

Because there was no *if* about it.

CHAPTER SIXTEEN

Nick's phone rang and woke him up. Ronnie Cox, the mechanic at Stillwater Aviation, slapped him alert with the news that the Victory wreckage was being offloaded at that very moment. Nick performed a supersonic rendition of his morning ritual and hurried out to the rented Jeep. Ten minutes later, his third cup of coffee had him wired for sound when he stopped at the Sugar Time Doughnut Shop.

Aromas of chocolate, cinnamon, and yeast tantalized his taste buds while he waited for a very large woman to order six boxes of mixed treats, which emptied the trays lining the display counter. She decided to pay by check, and of course couldn't find her checkbook, didn't have a pen, how much was that again? Do you have a stamp or should I write it in?

As Nick finally got his turn and stepped up to the counter, stacked trays of freshly baked doughnuts on a wheeled cart clanged through a set of double doors, trailed by a short, dumpy man in a white uniform. He looked like the Michelin Man. Without the puppy. Every time he slipped a tray out of the rack and plopped it onto the counter, a puff of flour dust rose from his shoulders, highlighted in the bright glow of overhead florescent bulbs.

The Doughboy turned, stepped to the counter. "What's your pleasure, sir?"

"Two of everything you've got and a large cup of coffee."

As Nick was leaving with the boxes of fat pills, he thanked the Doughboy and said, "You may not realize this, but doughnuts are one of the four major food groups."

He smiled. "At the Sugar Time, they're the *only* one."

Driving to the Adobe Wings Airport, Nick ate an apple fritter with absolutely no regrets. After he parked at Stillwater Aviation, he chased the first course with a chocolate-covered éclair loaded up with Bavarian-vanilla-creme and finished his coffee. He climbed out of the Jeep feeling like he'd just mainlined a half-pound of sugar, jitter-walked into the office, and put the boxes on the operations counter.

After a moment a familiar voice said from somewhere in the back, "What's that smell?"

Nick yelled, "Tacos!"

Leo Stillwater appeared in the hallway. "Bullshit. You've been to the Sugar Time."

Nick smiled. "Good smeller, Leo."

"Bring those on back here so I can grab my favorite before the guys catch a whiff." Leo led the way to the canteen, poured himself a cup of coffee into a huge mug with no handle, which just happened to have the Victory logo on the side, and plopped down at a table. "Any apple fritters?"

Nick found the box with the remaining fritter and handed it to him, got a bottle of water out of the dispensing machine, and sat down.

Leo all but inhaled the fritter, pulled a handkerchief from his coveralls and wiped his mouth and hands. "Whassup?"

"Examine the Victory wreckage, and I was wondering if you know why it isn't being taken directly to salvage."

Leo sipped his coffee. "Mrs. McAllister must be paying salvage value."

"Why would she do that?"

"Maybe she's sentimental, although I really doubt it."

Nick paused, drank some water and considered how to approach this. Based on Caitlin's description of how she and McAllister arranged meeting for trips, Nick doubted Leo knew anything of the affair.

He reached for the doughnut box and opened the lid. A cinnamon roll beckoned. With his other hand, he pinched the persistent roll of flab trying to hide his belt. He dropped the lid, tapped it closed and said, "Have you ever met Mrs. McAllister?"

"Sure."

"What kind of woman is she?"

"Other than physical appearance, I have no clue. She wasn't in the habit of talking to mechanics. At least to this one. Very classy, and reserved to the point of a stone statue around the hired help. But I've seen her on TV, and you'd almost think she changes skins when the cameras are rolling."

"Did she come around the airport often?"

Leo's face hardened, eyebrows narrowing over steel-gray eyes. "You're looking into the NTSBs investigation, right? But your interest seems to have shifted to a dead man's widow. Makes me wonder why." He got up, refilled his cup, and stood at the window, staring at the flight line and sipping coffee, his other hand in the side pocket of his coveralls. The clinking sound of coins drifted into the silence. His words bounced off the glass, clear and distinct.

"Mr. McAllister helped set me up in business. That sort of history generates a good bit of loyalty, and I'll do nothing to betray *his* confidence and trust in me." Then he turned and walked to the table, opened the doughnut box, and lifted out a cinnamon roll. Holding it close to Nick's face, he said, "I saw you looking at this. I'm going back in my office to eat it and save you from yourself. And off the record, I hope you find what you might be looking for along that line of inquiry."

Nick watched Leo disappear into the hallway. What the hell just happened?

In Nick's experience, most pilots were smart enough to treat the mechanics who worked on their airplanes with courtesy and respect for the vital role they played in keeping flights boring. But far too often, passengers copped an attitude of superiority and privilege. Mrs. McAllister didn't talk to the hired help. No love lost, maybe? Or was it something else?

Nick wrapped two doughnuts in a paper towel and walked into the hangar. A typical day of activity bustled from wall to wall. He spotted Ronnie Cox talking with another mechanic. When the conversation ended, Nick made his way through an obstacle course of parked airplanes to Cox's work area.

Cox was riveting a piano-hinge plate into the oil filler access door opening on an engine cowling. Nick waited until he looked up. "How's it going, Ronnie?"

The mechanic nodded and laid the rivet tool on his workbench. "Same old, same old. Those wouldn't be from the Sugar Time, would they?"

Nick smiled and shook his head. "Made them myself."

Cox wiped his hands on a shop towel and accepted the doughnuts. "Sure you did. Follow me." He led Nick to a small table tucked against the rear wall of the hangar. "Have a seat." He poured a cup of coffee from a Thermos and ate one of the doughnuts in about three bites. "We used to trade off bringing doughnuts every morning, but it got too expensive. Calorie-wise. What can I do for you?"

"Leo mentioned that Mrs. McAllister is—and I'm paraphrasing—kind of aloof around the hired help. I'm curious to know if you ever met her, or saw her around the other mechanics. Parker, in particular."

Cox sipped his coffee. "Never had the pleasure of being introduced, but yeah. I've seen her with Tommy Lee."

A tingle of discovery climbed Nick's spine. "Did she get involved with maintenance decisions on the Victory?"

"Can't say. Tommy Lee did all the work on it. He and Mr. McAllister seemed to be on good terms—not outside of work, of course, they weren't drinking buddies—but I'd see them around the airplane a couple times a month, at least. McAllister played a pretty active role in taking care of it."

"Maybe she paid the bills? Brought him checks?"

"Doubt it. McAllister probably paid the company, and Tommy Lee got his checks directly from Leo like the rest of us."

"I just seems curious that she would . . . you know—"

"Deal directly with a mechanic?"

If Cox was insulted, he didn't show it. Nick said, "In so many words, yeah. Any talk around the shop?"

Cox tilted his head and shrugged. "You could say that."

"Maybe they met outside of work?"

Cox took his time to remove the inner cap on the Thermos, pour another cup of coffee, and replace the cap. He sipped an ebony liquid that looked like sweet crude. "I didn't say I saw them together around *here*."

Big tingle. Nick kept his expression neutral and waited to let the mechanic offer more.

Cox brushed sugary doughnut residue off his dark blue work trousers. "Before this goes any further, I need to make it clear that I'm not much for gossip. Don't give a shit about what people do on their own time. But you quote me on any of this, we'll have a problem."

Nick had no reason to doubt Cox's words, or that the man

would back them up. "Fair enough."

Cox leaned back in his chair. "You can't walk around with earplugs and blinders. I've heard rumors, seen things. It's pretty much common knowledge that the McAllisters weren't a *Good Housekeeping* couple. Each had outside interests, and the marriage didn't mean much. Let's just call it a union with extensive extra-marital activities."

That wasn't news to Nick based on what Caitlin had told him, but she hadn't said anything about who McAllister's wife might be hooked up with. If they could find a between-the-sheets connection between her and the mechanic? Dynamite. "You have any idea where Parker might be?"

"Not a clue. He has a buddy who's thick with a crowd of biker types. They might know. But be careful."

"Just a bunch of bad boys, or into serious stuff?"

"Serious enough to repeat the warning."

Nick figured the lead would be perfect for Yates. Let him follow up, maybe be rid of the jerk for good when the bikers tied him to a couple of hogs and drove off in opposite directions. "Okay, Ronnie, thanks. Don't tell anyone, but there's two more boxes of doughnuts in the canteen."

Cox smiled. "Maybe I'll just reserve me a couple for my next break."

They shook hands. Nick mentioned he would be taking another look around Parker's work area and asked about the Victory wreckage.

"Every dude on that salvage crew must have a hot date waiting for tonight, because they were damn near out of here before they arrived." Cox reminded Nick that they would be closing the shop early this afternoon for inventory, gave him the code for entry into McAllister's hangar and went back to work on the cowling.

Nick checked his watch and figured he might have enough time to finish looking at everything, but he couldn't waste any. Especially given that a watch he couldn't see was ticking away the minutes until access to the wreckage would be gone forever.

He opened Parker's parts cabinet and searched for a box of latex gloves. Mechanics used them to protect their hands from all manner of substances, and Parker was no exception. Nick slipped on a pair and knelt on the floor. With the smaller parts box from the right rear corner of the cabinet lying in front of him, he removed one of the Victory ruddervator balance weights and examined it.

A series of numbers stamped into the lead confirmed what he'd suspected. The weights were important enough to warrant tracking with part and serial numbers. He copied the numbers on each of the weights in a small notebook and replaced the weight. In the unlikely event the police became involved, at least he didn't add any fingerprints this time.

With the cabinet contents restored to their original state and the doors closed, Nick left the shop, walked outside to the personnel access door into McAllister's hangar and paused. Instructors and students filled the flight line with activity. Cooler temperatures and lighter winds always made mornings a favored time for learning. His presence appeared to generate no curiosity. Ignoring a niggling apprehension, he punched in the code, hauled open the heavy door, and stepped inside.

Semi-darkness filled the hangar, broken only by shafts of bright sun pouring through windows on three sides. The wall to his left held a row of switches. He flipped one up. A section of the ceiling erupted in brightness that flooded about a third of the hangar floor.

The Victory wreckage lay scattered about, randomly placed by hands hired to move it with no regard to relative positioning of the pieces. Nick waited a moment to allow his usual emotional reaction to subside and be replaced by an investigator's detached objectivity. He'd never managed to do that completely when he was with the NTSB, but every little bit helped. Then he turned on the remaining two banks of lights and approached the remains of a once-beautiful airplane.

The forward portion of the fuselage with one wing attached lay by itself. The wing that had broken off rested nearby. Although Nick's primary focus would be on the tail section, he felt an obligation to look at everything. Inspecting cockpits and cabins where lives were lost always took the greatest toll on him, so by habit formed over many years, he began there to minimize the time spent dreading it.

The interior of the mangled fuselage was too dark to see much detail. Nick appreciated that when it came to the lingering physical evidence of death due to blunt trauma, but he used his flashlight to look for anything that might catch his attention. Within a few minutes, the beam had found an unusual push-button switch mounted on the back of the left arm of the pilot's control yoke. Nick stared at it, wondered what the hell it was for, and let his mind transport him into the cockpit to consider the possibilities.

He's manually flying the Victory, left hand on the yoke, right hand free to manipulate the engine controls, enter navigation commands, tune radio frequencies, or perform any of the other tasks necessary in flight. His left thumb adjusts the trim system for relieving air-load pressures on the controls. His forefinger keys the microphone to transmit over the radio. The position of the extra switch below the microphone button puts it within easy reach of his middle finger on that hand. To do what?

Any switch located on the control yoke, whether by original

manufacturer's design or retrofitted by an owner, was put there for the pilot's convenience in performing a recurring function. Nick had never flown a Victory, so he didn't know exactly what switches were on the yoke when the airplane left the factory. But the beam of his flashlight soon found telltale evidence that this was a rogue.

A single wire, probably multi-conductor with two or three wires within an insulated outer covering, snaked from the switch down the yoke and out of sight under the boot at the junction of the yoke with the floor. Where the hell did it go?

Nick had no way of answering that question before the wreckage disappeared for good. Which meant the only two options for ascertaining the purpose of the switch were to find an entry in the logbooks that documented the retrofit, or to determine if the NTSB found the switch and traced the wires to their source.

It took over an hour to go through the logbooks, beginning when McAllister had all the upgrades done by the shop in Texas and ending with the last entry. Nick pulled out his phone and texted James Dickson: *Did team discover function of non-standard switch on Victory yoke?* James would either answer or he wouldn't, but Nick would never know unless he tried.

Back to his investigation, he skirted the edge of the debris field and stepped up to the tail section. The portion of fuselage still attached to it displayed the twisting and tearing of metal common to Victory in-flight breakups. The remains of the tail section told its own story.

The left ruddervator had been ripped completely off the stationary portion of the tail that supported it. Nick couldn't see the ruddervator among the wreckage, which wasn't surprising. It would have been the first piece to depart the Victory during the breakup sequence, and first to separate meant first to impact the ground. Not in time necessarily, but in position along the flight path of the debris following the breakup.

Investigators would have realized they were missing a major piece of wreckage that clearly indicated what probably had happened. If an expanded search didn't turn it up relatively quickly, they would have to decide how much more time to spend looking for it.

Nick was speculating even further afield now, but he knew from extensive personal experience that the totality of evidence drove many decisions during the course of an investigation. As soon as the team had even the most basic information about this crash, they would make a crucial assumption that this Victory had been flown into a violent thunderstorm at high speed.

Every member of the team would also know it doesn't take a flutter event to cause an inflight breakup. Any airplane, V-Tail or not, flying at a speed high enough to generate greater g-loads than the airframe can handle, is like an empty beer can on the dance floor of a honky tonk. It's only a matter of time until it gets crushed by some shit-kicker in a pair of Tony Llamas.

Speculation aside, the ruddervator wasn't with the wreckage, which meant it was still out there in the desert. Did it contain any secrets worth trying to uncover? An investigator who suspects a sabotage-generated flutter event might find the answer to that question. The time had come for Nick to be that guy, and the place to begin lay on the hangar floor at his feet.

He knelt and examined the two fixed portions of the Victory's tail section. Like the vertical and horizontal stabilizers of a conventional-tail airplane, they served as attachment points for the Victory's single flight control that served as both rudder and elevator. And like many other airplanes, mechanical stops on these stabilizers prevented the ruddervators from being damaged by traveling too far in either direction.

By definition, catastrophic flutter resulted in rapid, excessive movement of a flight control that exceeded structural limits. And there, on all four of the stops, Nick found the telltale evidence of fluttering ruddervators as they battered themselves to death.

Then he examined the horn of the right ruddervator. The access panel was missing, with torn edges indicative of overstressed containing skin. He trained the flashlight beam into the shattered horn. Reflected light from the interior confirmed that the right balance weight was gone. Examining the crumpled outer skin, he tried to form a picture of an event sequence.

Did the weight shed during the breakup, not uncommon in cases of aerodynamic flutter? Or was it missing to begin with, which would have created a seriously out-of-balance condition in that ruddervator?

The skin on the horn appeared to be crumpled inward from impact forces as well as being split outward by the weight as it violently departed the structure. This evidence supported the conclusion that the weight was installed, tore through the skin during the flutter event, and some portions of the exit wound were subsequently crushed inward toward the cavity on ground impact.

But if the left balance weight had been removed, the two ruddervators would have reacted very differently. Anti-symmetric aerodynamic forces on either side of the fuselage could easily create the torsional twisting evidenced here.

Laboratory analysis might be able to answer these questions. But if McAllister's wife had arranged for the sabotage, she'd never allow anyone to examine the wreckage now that she had physical control of it. The fact that Nick had gained access probably meant she didn't know it had arrived. This visual inspection might be the only opportunity he'd get, and a speculative conclusion was better than none.

Nick stood and looked around the hangar. The cardboard box from Dry Springs with the aircraft records rested on a workbench along the back wall. Beside it, a black plastic document storage container with the Victory logo embossed in white.

He opened the cardboard box to examine the maintenance logs for a third time. Going back a full year, nothing indicated that any work had been performed on the ruddervators. But Leo said that the left ruddervator had been damaged and repaired. No way would the paperwork for that level of maintenance have been ignored, especially by a shop that had all the outward appearances of being run by a man who knew his business. Nick returned the logbook to the box and closed it.

The black box contained two looseleaf binders, one with pink pages, the other with yellow. These were the perforated carbon copies that the mechanic would have torn out of the primary logbook. Finding both copies in the logs confirmed what Leo had said about McAllister not having signed up for factory maintenance tracking. That wasn't unusual and didn't mean much, but it was important to Nick because either binder should reflect *exactly* the same sequence of maintenance actions as the original white pages.

He opened one of the binders. Thumbing from the most recent entry and backward in time, he once again looked for any indication of maintenance on the ruddervators. It took only a few minutes to find an entry that reactivated the adrenaline tingle.

Scribbled notes on two maintenance transaction reports documented the incident of damage to the left ruddervator horn that Leo had mentioned. Parker had removed the ruddervator and replaced the dented skin, which required removal and reinstallation of the balance weight.

Nick laid his notebook on the workbench and compared the part and serial numbers from the balance weight in Parker's parts locker to those in the logbook. The numbers matched those on the weight supposedly installed in the Victory's left ruddervator at the time of the crash. Which told Nick what?

Parker made a mistake with the paperwork? Or did he remove the weight entirely to create a dangerously unbalanced flight control?

Nick made note of the dates on the carbon copies, replaced the logbook in the box and closed it, then reopened the cardboard box, removed the bound logbook with the original white pages, and found two adjacent pages with dates on either side of the dates the ruddervator maintenance had been performed. And unlike during his previous examinations, the two-page gap in the page numbers appeared to be virtually highlighted in bright yellow.

His hands trembled as he removed his flashlight from the holder on his belt, pressed hard into the open binding of the logbook with the fingers of one hand, and directed the flashlight beam into the gutter.

And there he found evidence that someone had very carefully removed two pages.

In all the years of officially investigating airplane crashes, Nick could count on the fingers of one hand the number of times he had without warning stumbled across something that seemed to leap out at him and grab his throat.

But now for the second time in a little over a year, an unofficial investigation had turned 90 degrees in a split second and opened a new door, beyond which lay an unknown result.

Nick removed two carbon pages from one of the binders, put them in his jacket pocket, and returned the logbooks to where he found them. Leaning against the workbench, he pondered how events in a conspiracy might have played out and where this discovery left him.

Mrs. McAllister decides to murder her husband and his lover. She may have been involved with Parker before, but in any event she recruits him into her scheme. He has to be the one who came up with the idea of sabotaging the Victory as the way to get it done, or at least the specifics of how to do it.

He could have done all the tampering behind the scenes, but for some reason he didn't. He dings the ruddervator, something as simple as hitting it with a hammer. Goes to Leo, says, Hey, boss, my fault, I'll fix it right away.

When the repair is finished, with new paint and no balance weight installed or some kind of modification to it hidden within the ruddervator horn, he signs off the work and re-balance procedure as the mechanic who performed the required tasks. Leo trusts Parker and signs off the repair as the maintenance inspector without personally verifying every single detail, particularly when the result is hidden behind an access panel. Happens all the time. Then Parker modifies the logbooks to avoid alerting investigators to the maintenance and focusing attention on the ruddervators.

What he fails to do is remove the carbon pages from the looseleaf binders. Probably an oversight, due in part to the fact that Parker knows all the maintenance performed on the Victory for years has been in-house and under his direct control. Leo has never paid any attention to the carbons because they are superfluous to the primary white pages in the bound logbook. Or Parker may have intended to get rid of them and never got around to it.

McAllister's casual approach to preflights is well known. He's always in a hurry to get airborne, and he fails to notice the change in ruddervator control pressures on the ground. Airborne, he wouldn't feel any difference because air loads would hide any imbalance caused by the sabotage.

Parker can't predict any better than the Larchmont conspirators could when the necessary combination of factors would merge. But he knows that McAllister's proclivity to fly the Victory past redline predisposes him to encountering aerodynamic flutter.

It's summer. Turbulent air, thunderstorms, and all the attendant hazards abound throughout the southwestern US. The altered ruddervator is like a time bomb, eager to shake itself to death. Sooner or later, McAllister is going to die.

It happens sooner, and probably surprised the Parker/Mrs. McAllister coalition as much as it did McAllister himself. Well, maybe not that much, but they had another surprise to deal with. Lawson's wife knows Caitlin flew with her husband on most flights and would likely end up in the same smoking hole. But Lawson had taken a business associate instead. Oops.

So Caitlin wants Nick's help to prove it, but all they have is circumstantial indications of the tampering, hindered by serious chain-of-evidence issues.

Nick stared into the hangar, weighing the possibilities. No matter how hard he tried, the scale of justice kept coming up light on the side of the law. Again. So why not tell Caitlin one more time that it's hopeless and boogie back to the boonies? The question hung there, begging for a reply, and the only answer that made *any* sense didn't make much.

He craved exploring the possibility that more definitive clues might lie hidden just beyond the next turn of events. That Yates might find evidence of payoff links between McAllister's widow and Parker. And in an orgy of wishful thinking, that they might build a case strong enough to pursue a civil case based on the preponderance of evidence and make two conspirators pay the price. Even considering the odds against it, the thought stirred Nick's blood.

His phone rang. Caitlin wanted to meet for a late lunch. Nick glanced at his watch. About two hours until Stillwater Aviation closed for the day. He needed more time than that to finish up and make sure he hadn't missed anything. But it would have to be tonight, hopefully before Parker reappeared with whatever cover-up he might have planned.

He asked Caitlin to text him the address of the restaurant, thanked Ronnie and Leo, and climbed in the Jeep, eager to discuss the possibility of a very unlikely connection between a wealthy widow and the mechanic who performed all the maintenance on her dead husband's Victory.

Then Caitlin could unhook the leash and sic Cliff Yates on the trail of a link that smelled a lot like conspiracy.

CHAPTER SEVENTEEN

I n spite of the luxury sedan's charcoal interior and a day in the sun, Caitlin hadn't driven more than a few miles from the motel before goose bumps appeared on her bare arms and her nipples pressed through the drape of her silk blouse. She smiled at the thought: if the Mercedes-Benz engineers were really good, they'd have installed a tiny camera to detect her physiological reactions to cold air and designed the air conditioner to turn down the fan about now.

She'd looked online for a list of restaurants in Albuquerque that offered fine dining and discovered a wide variation in definition of the word *fine*. But after scouring the links for one that met *her* expectations, she stumbled onto a relatively new restaurant that appeared to be trying the hardest.

The Oasis sat in the high desert countryside at the crest of a small rise barely visible from the highway. Quickly known for its excellent cuisine and extensive wine list, the restaurant's splash of green landscaping beckoned patrons inside to enjoy a cool one. Caitlin followed the winding road to the top of the hill and parked well away from the entrance.

She flipped down the visor and peered into the vanity mirror. Perfection stared back. She sent herself an air kiss in appreciation. Black pearls adorned her ears, with a matching necklace supporting a diamond-studded monogram, a gift from Lawson. It was an especially nice touch considering the background glimpse of cleavage.

Caitlin draped her handbag strap over her left shoulder. With her right hand, she released the Velcro closure and removed the Walther. A round in the chamber, a full magazine, and the safety off confirmed the pistol ready for instant use. Just in case. As always.

She slipped out of the Mercedes and walked toward the entrance. A multi-tiered fountain splashed to her left, nestled among planting beds packed with color and separated by walkways formed with pavers, each surrounding a diamond-shaped center of green. She paused for a closer look, and realized that short-bladed grass filled each one. The owners must employ an army of miniature landscapers to snip each tiny section of lawn by hand. Totally impractical, and it spoke to an attitude of, *Who cares?* Perfection goes way beyond the necessary, and that's why she loved it so.

As she continued toward the entrance, her phone chimed. A text from Nick: *Have I missed linch?*

Caitlin laughed and replied: *Not yit.*

A twenty-something doorman almost forgot his job. Caitlin had to slow up to let him fumble with the door. She smiled, whispered a thank you and entered the cool, dim light of the restaurant. Directly behind the hostess's station, a massive curved counter encircled three bartenders catering to a full crowd. A weekday at 2:00 p.m. Did any of these people work?

An attractive young woman stepped toward Caitlin. "May I show you to a table?"

"Along the far wall, overlooking the garden."

The hostess picked up a large menu covered in mahogany leather and a thinner companion folder that promised to list the wine selection. "Follow me, please."

Caitlin stayed put. The hostess advanced about 10 feet into the bar area before realizing her guest hadn't moved. She turned, polite irritation masking her face. "Ma'am? May I show you to your table?"

With her hand extended, palm up, and moving her first finger in a come-here motion, Caitlin drew the young woman to her. She leaned forward, her mouth a few inches from the hostess's ear. "Do you honestly think I'm going to lunch by myself?"

The young woman's face reddened. "How many will there be?"

Caitlin held up two fingers.

The hostess picked up a second menu and led the way to a secluded corner table overlooking the garden. Caitlin refused the proffered chair and pointed to one with an unobstructed view of the restaurant, bar, and front entrance. She had also noticed the location of the restrooms, kitchen, and emergency exits, an automatic survey whenever she entered an unfamiliar environment.

The hostess handed her a menu and placed the other one and the wine list on the table. "Raphael will be your server. Enjoy your meal." Within a few seconds a middle-aged man dressed in black, his dark hair slicked down and glistening in the soft overhead lighting, materialized as if out of thin air.

Caitlin ordered a glass of Chardonnay and thought about how good servers hover close by without announcing their presence or trying to establish a personal relationship with customers. Raphael soon reappeared with the wine. A thin film of condensation embraced the sides of a crystal glass. Caitlin sipped, nodded at Raphael, rewarded him with a heartbreaker of a smile, and sent him back into the ether.

Nick showed up about 15 minutes later and spoke to the

hostess, probably describing Caitlin.

Watching them walk toward her table, Caitlin considered how she might describe Nick: a good-looking man, mid-forties, about six feet tall, brown hair, blue eyes, slightly pudgy, and confused as to whether he's going to a rodeo or a restaurant. She couldn't imagine how anyone could find a shred of redeeming virtue in urban-cowboy casual. The fact that it appeared to be the national dress of the Western United States didn't affect her opinion in the least.

As Nick sat down, Raphael appeared beside the table. Nick pointed to Caitlin's glass, ordered the same, and looked at the garden. "I'd hate to pay their water bill."

"You won't have to. I'm buying."

He laughed. "In that case, may we look to see how much they're going to get?"

Caitlin ordered a rare Ahi tuna steak served with mango chutney and sautéed baby vegetables. Nick chose a chicken Caesar salad. As Raphael walked away, Caitlin shifted in her chair to give Nick a profile view.

His eyes flicked down, back up, and registered his appreciation.

Good. He's not really an automaton. She sipped her wine. "Anything to report?"

"A visit to Adobe Wings." Nick described his examination of the logbooks and the discovery that the missing balance weight had been installed in the Victory at one time, but the required paperwork had been altered. "Doing the work, filling out the logbooks, then removing the pages makes no sense. Unless you've just sabotaged the airplane."

Caitlin almost dropped her wine glass. She carefully set it down and took a deep breath as the realization settled in that this was evidence she could hold in her hand. "Why complete the paperwork and then have to do something to hide it?"

"It does seem counter-intuitive. But without going into all the details about documenting aviation maintenance, suffice it to say that the way he did it helped avoid suspicion before and after the crash."

"I'm still having a hard time understanding why the NTSB didn't find anything."

Nick started to answer and paused while Raphael served their meals.

Caitlin glanced at her plate, a striking presentation from a chef who paid attention to even the smallest details. Unfortunately, her appetite had vanished. For food. She sipped the last of the Chardonnay and motioned to Raphael for another.

With two fresh glasses on the table, between bites of his meal, Nick said, "The records tampering was very well done. As for the wreckage, even if there were something to notice, safety investigators don't approach any accident looking for a primary cause of sabotage. Their mindset is completely different from that of law enforcement. And as I've told you, if they find anything to indicate foul play, the FBI takes over."

"And no matter what we find now, the Feds are out of it?"

Nick nodded and sipped his wine. "No way they would step in once the NTSB has concluded the investigation."

"But the final report takes months. If it's not finalized—"

"Doesn't matter. The gathering of evidence is complete and they don't have physical control of the wreckage." He dipped a piece of crusty bread in a mixture of olive oil, balsamic vinegar, and spices and popped it in his mouth. Wiping his hands on a linen napkin, he said, "Another crucial factor is that airplane accident investigation involves a team of individuals, each with specialized scientific knowledge. No single investigator can stay current in all areas, and few, if any, NTSB employees have the expertise to confirm the presence of aerodynamic flutter and in-flight breakup. That's not a criticism of their talent or dedication, just a statement of fact. It's like a tracker giving a bloodhound a scent. You have to be tuned in to the telltale signs."

"But now *you* have the scent?"

"Absolutely. It's like this paperwork discrepancy is the gun, but it isn't smoking. I need to take another look at the wreckage to see if I can positively determine whether the balance weight was in place or missing at the time of the crash. And there's another factor I'm probably a fool for bringing up, but you hired me to find evidence to put McAllister's widow in prison for murder. Now you know that's not going to happen."

"I thought you had something new to tell me."

"How about this? I'm certain that Beth McAllister doesn't know anything about the chain-of-custody issue, and I very much doubt that Tommy Lee Parker does either. But if they *think* that new physical evidence can be used to prosecute them for conspiracy to murder, you have a powerful weapon in your hands."

"You mean in yours."

Nick shook his head. "We're talking about using the perceived threat of prosecution to make something happen, and I'm not going to be involved with anything like that."

"Like what?"

"Whatever you've planned for the endgame. Blackmail, maybe?"

Caitlin had to grip the edge of the table and clamp her jaw tight to maintain control. After a moment, she took a deep breath, exhaled, and said, "So you think this is about money?"

"No. It's about revenge, or retribution, or justice. But

whatever you call it, it's not going to be legal. I've taken some risks to get you this far, and I'll probably do so again, but I'm not going end up in handcuffs for you or anyone else."

Caitlin would call her final goal any and all of those things without knowing how she was going to achieve even one of them. And if the man sitting across from her was the same vigilante she'd met in the book *Airborne Justice,* his use of the words *legal* and *handcuffs* seemed disingenuous at best.

But rather than challenge him, she chose to send the message with a little word emphasis. "Nobody's *asking* you to break the law, Nick. Anything else?"

"The mechanic and Mrs. McAllister may have had something going on the side."

"Why tell me? You didn't put any faith in rumor and speculation about Lawson marrying a black widow, and now you think gossip points a finger at something we can use?"

"That depends on what you mean by *use.* Who's sleeping with whom isn't the point, except maybe for scandal-mongers who think a wealthy widow's sexual involvement with her husband's airplane mechanic is of interest.

"But even without confirmation, it's hard to ignore the possibility when it might be more evidence of conspiracy. You've heard the advice to keep your friends close, but your enemies closer? How about someone who conspired with you to commit murder? It doesn't get much closer than the bedroom. Following up on that, however, may not be easy."

Caitlin smiled. "Except for Yates."

"My thoughts exactly. And did you know that the mechanic who maintained the airplane *you* flew in with McAllister was involved, even if on the fringes, with rough characters who deal in illegal substances?"

"Why should that concern us?"

"Because if he thinks the threat of going to prison is real, he might not be timid about preventing someone from digging up what he'd rather keep buried."

"He's got to show up to do that."

"What if he's laying low nearby with his buddies? It'd be like kicking a fire-ant hill."

Caitlin shook her head. "Don't worry about it. Yates is the one—well, speak of the devil." He was standing at the greeter's desk.

Nick looked over his shoulder. "Did you invite him?"

She scoffed. "What am I? A glutton for punishment?"

"How the hell did he find us?"

"He's a very good private investigator, Nick. Be nice."

Yates strolled past the bar checking out the action, his head bobbing like one of those dogs in rear windows of cars. He sauntered up, hauled a chair over from an adjacent table, collapsed into it and stared at Caitlin, then Nick. "How cozy. Having a nice, quiet, romantic *repast*, are we?"

Raphael stopped short of the table. Yates' sport coat probably scared him. "A glass of wine, sir?"

"Wine's for women and pussies. Bring me a beer."

Raphael's distaste visibly deepened now that he had a display of boorish manners to go with the coat. "We have over two-hundred-fifty kinds of—"

Yates waved a dismissive hand. "Some of the cold kind."

"Would you prefer a draft or bottled beer?"

Yates scoffed. "Only daft people drink draft." Then he laughed, a braying guffaw that reminded Caitlin of a donkey.

Tight-lipped, Raphael nodded and glided away.

Yates leaned over the table. "What's good in this joint?"

"Anything you order will suit you just fine," said Caitlin. "What brings you here?"

Yates smiled, a splintered toothpick doing the flutter kick between clenched teeth. "News, little lady. Just news."

Raphael arrived with the beer. Yates ordered a cheeseburger, extra onion, a double order of fries, and another beer. He tilted the bottle back and drank about half in a series of loud gulps.

Caitlin watched the show with amusement. Raphael had brought the beer without a glass and with the cap removed. Waiters who knew their business never did that, partially to show the customer that the bottle had not been tampered with. He'd probably spit in it. Or worse. "How's the beer?"

Yates peered at the bottle. "Never had this kind. A little salty for my taste, but it'll do in a pinch. You want my news, or not?"

Caitlin nodded.

"I got friends all over this town. Grew up here for the most part, then spent a bunch of years as a cop. You get to know all types of folks on both sides of the law, and it pays to keep in touch. I went to the library—"

Nick sat forward in his chair, his face contorted in mock surprise. "You know a real librarian?"

Yates' face turned crimson. "Screw you, Phillips. I don't have to take—"

"You're right," said Caitlin. "Nick," she cooed, knowing he would pick up on the sarcasm, "mind your manners and don't interrupt. Cliff has a job to do just like you."

"Damn straight," growled Yates.

After Raphael had served Yates' food and retreated from the table, Caitlin said, "So, what's your news, Cliff?"

He attacked his food with the ferocity of a starving animal, chased a huge bite of cheeseburger with beer and slobbered, "Information security today is a joke. There's hell of a lot more hackers out there rooting around under the firewalls than there are people manning the gates. But when you got a guy on the inside, you know, who does this shit for the government, man, it's like stealing pablum from a baby . . . not that anyone would want to do that, mind you." Then he broke out laughing. "You ever eat pablum?"

Caitlin couldn't help herself. "No. I usually don't partake of over-simplified or tasteless writing."

Yates stared at her and shook his head. "I'm talking about baby food and you're off in outer space. Jesus. Anyway, my contact did a little digging around and found a well-worn money trail." Yates shoved his plate to the center of the table, hunched forward in his chair and glanced around. "We got e . . . vi . . . dence, the kind that ties withdrawals from the McAllisters' account by date and amount to deposits into Parker's. How about that shit?"

"McAllister's account?" said Nick. "He could have paid Parker for—"

"You didn't hear me right. The payments were from their *joint* account."

Caitlin said, "Any way to know who authorized the payments?"

"Yeah, and ain't this the kicker? Both of them were paying the bastard."

The revelation hit Caitlin just as she sipped her wine. She choked, snatched a napkin off the table to cover her mouth and rushed to the restroom. Standing at the sink, she stared into the mirror.

The face that stared back could not hide the internal struggle between conflicting emotions vying for control: excitement over the money trail; shock that finding it may have finally wiped away any speculation and replaced it with proof that Lawson's wife really was a murderer; and monumental sadness at having lost forever the man she loved.

An elderly woman on her way out paused at the door. "Are you okay, honey?"

After a moment, Caitlin made eye contact with the woman in the mirror and shook her head. "Thank you for asking, but only time will tell."

WORRIED THAT CAITLIN MIGHT have choked on something and need help in the restroom, Nick looked around for a waitress. When an elderly woman rounded the corner below the restroom sign, Nick jumped up from the table and intercepted her.

"Why, yes," she said, "The lady appeared to be fine. A little shell-shocked, maybe."

"A little what?"

"Confused. Is she your wife?"

"Uh . . . no. Business acquaintance. Thank you." Nick returned to the table and sat down. Yates started yakking right where he'd left off, like he'd hit the pause button when Nick left the table. A few minutes later, Caitlin appeared from behind a potted palm at the entrance to the hallway with the restrooms. Nick stood and held her chair.

She touched his arm and leaned close. A whispered "Thank you" caressed his ear.

"Aren't we the gentleman?" said Yates.

"Common courtesy," said Nick as he sat down. "You might try it sometime."

Yates laughed. "If you knew what I know, you might be less courteous and more careful. This lady is not—"

Caitlin pointed at Yates. "Shut up." She sipped her wine and dabbed her lips with a napkin. "What else did you find?"

Yates smiled, pleased with himself, which seemed to be a

perpetual condition. "Parker thought he could hide his laptop, but he has no idea who's dogging him now. Even left me a power cord. I took it to a guy, he plugged it in, opened the lid, the damn thing was sleeping, and not too soundly. And guess what?" Yates opened his eyes wide, both hands palm-up in front of his chest.

Nick glanced at Caitlin, and the looks they shared communicated a mutual distaste for Yates and his clown act. Nick couldn't tell if the guy picked up on it, but he doubted it. "Would you just get on with it?"

Yates shrugged. "You guys are no fun. Anyway, he found emails to and from the same addresses going back about a month. They didn't make much sense, which means they're probably in some kind of simple word code, but it's not what they said that got my attention."

"And what would that be?" asked Nick.

"Parker answered the latest one yesterday."

"From *that* computer?"

"Probably not. He's got local cable service. I saw the bill in a pile of snail mail. He uses a computer-based email program. Emails wait on the server until he accesses them, then exist only on his computer. When I brought his laptop out of sleep, a bunch of messages chimed in, all in bold print. The latest one wasn't in the new batch and it wasn't in bold."

"Could he have accessed it on his laptop remotely?" asked Caitlin.

"Sure, assuming emails are that important to an airplane mechanic. Under the circumstances, they probably are."

"And the Balloon Bitch sent those emails?"

"That's what my source says."

"How did he confirm it?"

"If I knew, I'd be doing what he does for a living."

Caitlin hated relying on other people, especially for second-hand information. This scheme could self-destruct with one mistake. But for the moment, she had no other choice. "So, we still can't confirm where Parker might be."

"Correct, based on the emails. But I can tell you for certain that the dude hasn't been in there since the crash, and he hasn't flown the coop for good."

"How do you know that?" said Caitlin.

"Trust me. There's stuff in that trailer he wouldn't leave behind."

"Like what?"

"What don't you understand about the words 'trust me'?"

In the silence, Nick stared at Yates, who had dropped the comedy act, then at Caitlin. She chewed her lower lip for a few seconds and sipped her wine. Nick had assumed all three of them believed Parker was out of the picture, and now the possibility of coming face-to-face with a conspirator to murder and his drug-dealing friends didn't appear to sit well with lunch.

Caitlin said, "So why not go on about his business rather than draw attention by his absence? And then stick around. That makes no sense."

Yates nodded. "Unless something scared him. And he's got unfinished business."

"Like what?" said Caitlin.

"I'm working on that," said Yates. He snapped his fingers and motioned to Raphael, who appeared to have become one with the potted palm. He nodded at Yates' waving of an empty beer bottle and meandered between the closely packed tables toward the bar. Yates set the bottle on the table. "This is pretty good beer."

Caitlin sneered at him. "I thought it was too salty."

"Must be getting used to it. Anyway, we ought to be

looking for Parker. I'd much rather find him than the other way around."

"Caution is required in either case," said Nick.

Yates looked at Caitlin, then Nick, and smiled. "But the three of us can handle him, right?"

CAITLIN DROVE FROM THE Oasis to the Los Orcones Motor Inn in the mental fog of too much Chardonnay, after-lunch drowsiness, and emotional turmoil: lingering rage from a broken childhood; pride in breaking free; the promise of love shattered by deceit; hope for reconciliation, and the grief of permanent loss.

She opened the door to her room and stepped into the stale, lukewarm interior. The housekeepers had once again switched the air conditioning completely off. Not even a fan. It wasn't their fault. Some penny-pinching manager had told them to do it, but it made her so mad she fantasized about paying him a visit. Let him know how close he was to eating the business end of a Walther. She'd never do that, but the mind game helped her deal with the frustration.

After setting the tired unit on maximum cold, the fan blowing the curtains like another Monroe's famous skirt, Caitlin got a bottle of water from the refrigerator and sat at the table.

What an emotional roller coaster it had been.

Initially, confidence in a simple plan that flowed from Caitlin's firm belief that Lawson had been murdered. She would orchestrate the efforts of Cliff Yates for any sneaky stuff and Nick Phillips to find the key evidence, based on the assumption that an NTSB investigation could be reopened and lead to criminal prosecution.

Then came the fear. That she would fail because Nick thought this was nothing more than the case of a gold digger looking for a big payday before moving on to the next sugar daddy.

Then the optimism as he became less suspicious of Caitlin's motives and began a proactive investigation reminiscent of the Nick Phillips she'd read about.

Then depression arrived on a pale horse when Caitlin finally had to face the reality that nothing Nick found could be used to threaten the Black Widow and her lackey. They'd gotten away with it.

But now, optimism had returned with Nick's discovery of real evidence that changed speculation into fact. And he handed Caitlin a valuable gift by pointing out that both the conspirators were probably worried about what they believed to be a very real threat of hearing the dreaded knock on the door, followed by the opportunity to wear a pair of linked, ratcheting bracelets.

The potential usefulness of that revelation gave Caitlin goose bumps. Nick had cautioned her on more than one occasion about the possibility of a violent reaction to their snooping. He had a point, but she had no intention of being careful. Quite the opposite, actually.

She received her concealed carry license in Florida. Currently, New Mexico was one of the 21 states that honored Florida permits. Reciprocity agreements required out-of-state permit holders to comply with all the restrictions governing concealed carry in any state within which reciprocity privileges were being exercised. That could potentially result in misdemeanor violations of the more obscure provisions, but the biggie was universally chiseled into stone in all states: Lethal force was always justified when faced with the imminent threat of serious bodily injury or death. Period.

Let them come. And although Nick had undoubtedly been referring to Parker or one of his drug-dealing crowd as the threat, Caitlin had heard too many stories from Lawson not to believe that Elizabeth Blaine McAllister was capable of far more than hiring someone else to do the dirty work.

One way or the other, Caitlin would avenge Lawson's death. All she had to do was keep her two pit bulls focused on the scent and the Walther close at hand.

CHAPTER EIGHTEEN

Nick needed to convince himself no evidence of sabotage was hiding under the next rock, waiting to be discovered if he would only turn it over. The unknown timing of Mrs. McAllister's plans for disposing of the wreckage had brought him back to the Adobe Wings Airport last night. But cars in the parking lot and bright lights in the offices and hangars evidenced an inventory effort still in full swing. He'd waited until after midnight before deciding no one would be messing with the wreckage until the following evening, which gave him about 24 more hours to work with.

Just in time for mid-morning break, he stepped into the front office of Stillwater Aviation carrying two boxes of tasty treats from the Sugar Time Doughnut Shop.

Leo looked up from the desk behind the counter, waved, and went back to whatever he was doing. "Save me a cinnamon roll and one of those éclairs."

"Gotcha covered." Nick strolled into the canteen and set the pastries on the counter. He'd already put Leo's favorites in a bag, which he placed on the desk in his office. Then he walked into the hangar and found Ronnie Cox with both hands and most of his head stuffed in the engine compartment of a two-seat trainer. Mumbled curses indicated the task was not going well.

As a matter of courtesy, Nick stopped a few feet away, and in this case it had a practical side: don't startle a mechanic concentrating on work.

After a moment, Ronnie glanced over his shoulder. "Hey, Nick. Where's my treat?"

"In the canteen."

"What can I do you for?"

"Just a few answers. You guys do all your sheet metal work here?"

"Yeah. Each mechanic has his own hand tools, but the heavy machines are in a common area. In that far corner." Ronnie pointed a greasy hand and index finger toward the rear of the hangar.

"What about other private lockers?"

"Through the door near the sheet metal machines."

"You know if Parker has one?"

"We all do."

Nick thanked him, walked to McAllister's private hangar, entered the security code Ronnie had given him and stepped inside.

The Victory wreckage appeared undisturbed since he'd last seen it. The thought had occurred to Nick that McAllister's widow might not be aware of the sabotage details, or if she was, she hadn't realized the importance of restricting access to the wreckage. Which raised the question of where in hell Parker was, and why he wasn't actively protecting them both. Whatever the answers, Nick knew that the situation could change in a heartbeat once either one of them found out that someone was snooping around. Which might have already happened, all the more reason to get this done.

He let his eyes roam over the debris pile, looking for one of those elusive indicators that years of experience had taught him might point to something not quite right.

The right ruddervator intact, but with the typical rash of dents and scratches from uncontrolled impact with the ground. The horn crumpled and bent, balance weight missing. The left ruddervator ripped off and missing. Jagged metal edges, signs of tearing, evidence of the massive forces associated with aerodynamic flutter. Clear evidence that one ruddervator had reacted very differently than the other, creating torsional tearing of the aluminum skin and twisting the aft fuselage like a soda can until it broke. Anti-symmetric forces had instantaneously ripped the tail off the airplane.

And yet every clue was consistent with the undeniable fact that turbulence and high speed could have caused identical damage without criminal human intervention. If a mechanic tampered with the ruddervators, how did he camouflage it so well?

Nick paced around the hangar for a few moments to free his thoughts of the question and stopped about 10 feet away from the wreckage. He'd learned over the years that the old saying about not seeing the forest for the trees applied to accident investigation. Without looking for anything in particular, he began at one end of the debris pile and studied it. After one pass in each direction, he was on third sweep when he noticed something about the aft fuselage that didn't look quite right. He walked over to it and knelt down.

A section of skin about twelve inches long and six inches wide had been pulled away on one corner. He peered closer and realized that it fit flush onto the surrounding skin like an access panel.

But it had been riveted on. Access panels were called that for a reason, and they weren't designed so that using them required drilling out rivets. What the hell was this?

He bent over and looked closer at a rivet. It had a hole in the center, like pop or "blind" rivets, which were seldom used in structural applications unless they were special CherryMax rivets designed for that purpose. These did not appear to be that type.

He pulled a small halogen flashlight from a nylon holster on his belt and lay down on the hangar floor. With the beam pointed directly at one of the rivets, he peered into the hole, adjusted the light to make sure . . . Well, I'll be damned.

The hole through the center of the rivet wasn't circular, but hexagonal. He'd never seen a rivet like this because it wasn't a rivet. This panel had been designed to be easily removed and replaced without looking like it. He examined the opposite side of the fuselage and found an identical panel.

Nick returned to the main hangar and grabbed a handful of Allen wrenches from Parker's tool kit and returned to McAllister's hangar.

He found the correct size, inserted it into the hole in one of the false rivets, and applied pressure until it began to rotate. In about five minutes, he had unscrewed all the false rivets and removed the panel to reveal a hidden compartment. The beam of his flashlight revealed two packages wrapped in duct tape. Just like in the movies.

Lying on the floor beside the fuselage, Nick began a rapid what-if and what-now debate.

Lawson McAllister?

No way.

Tommy Lee Parker?

Had to be.

Take them now?

Don't be an idiot.

He replaced the access panel, checked the Victory's

logbooks to confirm that no paperwork existed to document FAA approval for the modification, and returned the Allen wrenches to Parker's tool kit in the main hangar.

Leaning against Parker's work bench, Nick noted the sheet metal work area was laid out with the same attention to detail evident everywhere else. He pictured the sequence of a typical task and how he would move from one machine to the next to cut, shape, grind, and polish a piece of aluminum. Overhead lighting bathed the area and eliminated shadows. The efficient work environment reflected Leo Stillwater's years of personal experience, and Parker could have done almost anything to a metal component right here. None of the other mechanics would have paid any attention. Just another day at the office as he sabotaged an airplane.

The door at the rear of the area opened into a room packed with storage cabinets on all four walls. In the center sat two rows of lockers, one with PARKER stenciled on the front. Padlocked.

Shit. Now what? He had to be sneaky, but that was nothing new.

He examined the lock, a common medium security device found in any hardware store. As he left the hangar, Nick mentioned to Leo that he'd be back later and received a casual wave in reply. A quick search on his cell phone found the closest hardware store, about half a mile from the taco stand. He glanced at his watch. Perfect.

As he walked to the Jeep, a text from James Dickson chimed into his phone.

Cutout switch for airspeed warning horn.

Nick felt that little tingle and smiled. An unauthorized modification to the Victory that rendered it unairworthy according to FAA regulations, and whose only purpose was to facilitate operating the airplane faster than red line without having to tolerate an obnoxious warning, had just risen to the top of the list of suspicious findings.

A pilot dies under conditions that shout *pilot error,* and that divert the NTSB's investigation?

Nick climbed in the Jeep trailed by the familiar odor of *smokescreen.*

CHAPTER NINETEEN

At ten minutes to noon, Nick carried four sacks of tacos into the break room at Stillwater Aviation. A new padlock weighed down his jacket pocket. A bolt cutter hung under his armpit from a cord across the opposite shoulder. The word about free food traveled faster than the aroma, and whether Leo liked it or not, every mechanic in the place took a lunch break at the same time.

One of them dumped two sandwiches into the trash and smiled at Nick. "If I come home with these, she'll find something worse than bologna to slap between two pieces of bread." He lifted two tacos out of a bag and nodded his thanks.

Nick strolled into the hangar and hurried to the storage room. The bolt cutter did the trick on Parker's lock. He searched the shelves. In the bottom right rear corner of the locker, he found a cardboard box with a very unusual balance weight in a plastic baggie. It looked to be about half size, cut down the center longitudinally. And there was something else in the bag.

He knelt, lifted out the bag and held it up to the shaft of sunlight slanting through a single window in the hangar wall. It took a moment for his brain to register *black fingerprint powder and a piece of lifting tape.* Sitting on his haunches, Nick pondered this latest discovery.

If the missing portion of this weight had been installed in

one of the Victory's ruddervators, McAllister's casual preflight regimen could easily have missed the change in control pressures caused by the lighter weight. And he couldn't have detected the difference in weight between the two ruddervators, because they moved in tandem. To fly this airplane at high speed into turbulence was a prelude to disaster. Hello, sabotage, we meet at last.

The presence of the lifting tape revived Nick's earlier concern about touching the weights in the parts locker. Why would Parker fingerprint this half weight and hide it in here?

Well, duh. It certainly wasn't to prove *he'd* touched it.

Nick slipped the weight into his jacket pocket, replaced the box in the locker and snapped the new lock on the door handle. No one but Parker would notice, and he was probably long gone. If not, what were the chances he'd come in here? *Pretty good, actually, if this half balance weight proves sabotage.* That thought unsettled Nick a bit. He put the cut lock in his other jacket pocket and the bolt cutter back under his jacket.

Three final, crucial pieces of evidence remained: the left ruddervator and both balance weights installed in the Victory when it crashed. If one of the weights was half size, and Yates knew someone in a CSI unit, maybe the tool marks could be matched to the blade of a power tool at Stillwater Aviation. And what if the cut edges of the two halves matched? The noose would tighten, and the thought raised goosebumps on Nick's arms.

Leaving the storage room, he realized the supply of tacos must have run out. Mechanics were returning to work, and near the door from the front office into the hangar, a woman stood talking to Leo Stillwater. Nick peered at them through the gap between two airplanes parked close together. Leo had lost his typical easygoing demeanor and appeared to be paying close attention. The woman's elegant appearance, erect bearing, Leo's obvious deference, and the fact that she was doing all the talking suggested that Nick was looking at none other than Mrs. Lawson McAllister.

He glanced at the emergency exit door twenty feet away. It didn't appear to be on an alarm. He should just walk over there, step onto the parking ramp, get in the Jeep and boogie. *Do it now before—hold on.*

Leo motioned toward the front of the building with an *after you* gesture. The woman disappeared into the hallway with Leo in trail.

Nick walked to a window where he could see all of the parking lot except for visitor spots by the entrance. After a few minutes, a black sports coupe backed into view, turned, and accelerated out of sight. Nick crossed the hangar and stuck his head in Leo's office. "Got a moment?"

"Come on in."

Nick sat in a chair facing Leo's desk. "Just wanted to thank you."

"You're welcome. Find what you needed?"

Nick had already triggered Leo's suspicion once before with a question about Lawson's widow. He glanced down at his jeans, brushed away an imaginary piece of something, looked around the office and back at Leo.

Leo nodded. "Is that it?"

"I was wondering . . . well . . . I'm just curious—"

Leo held up a hand, leaned forward with his elbows on the desk. "Mrs. McAllister stopped by to tell me two things. One, the salvage company will be here tomorrow to pick up the wreckage, and two, she wanted to know if I'd seen Tommy Lee in the past couple weeks." He stood and extended his hand. "I guess you'll be on your way."

Nick knew a hint and a dismissal when he heard them. He thanked Leo again and left the office. Walking to the Jeep, the weights and bolt cutter pounded his body with every step. He put the evidence of sabotage and the burglary tool under the driver's seat and climbed in.

How about that? Yates said Mrs. McAllister and Parker had been in contact within the past day or so. Who was playing whom? At this point, did Nick care? And the answer was, *Not really*, because it didn't affect what he needed to do next.

He was, however, extremely interested in what role, if any, drugs played in the death of Lawson McAllister. It seemed improbable in the extreme that a renowned cancer surgeon married to a multi-million-dollar fortune on two legs would be screwing around with cocaine or meth or whatever that stuff was. Being wealthy, however, offered no defense against stupidity, and he had to check it out. And it had to be tonight, with one final visit to Stillwater Aviation before the salvage company showed up.

Then he'd do his best to find that missing ruddervator, hand all the evidence over to Caitlin Monroe, and wish her well.

At least that's what he told himself, in spite of a nagging curiosity about whether he could bring to justice the architects of a conspiracy to murder.

FRUSTRATION FILLED THE INTERIOR of Beth McAllister's Jaguar F-Type R. She had every available option, including a supercharged 550 HP 5.0 liter V8 capable of 0-60 mph in 4.0 seconds, but it still wouldn't leave her annoyance behind at that damn airport. She wasn't even sure a jet would be fast enough. *Goddamn Tommy Lee Parker.*

He'd been so insistent she had to pay salvage value for the

wreckage of an airplane that she would have gladly given away when it was all in one piece. He told her to have it delivered to Adobe Wings, and they'd send it off to be cut apart and recycled as soon as possible. When she challenged him to explain why they couldn't skip the first step, he settled the issue with five words: *To avoid going to prison.* And he promised to take care of everything.

So here she was, doing what he wanted, but without knowing whether he'd done his part. Or why the hell he'd dropped out of sight the day after the crash and hadn't been Tommy-Lee-on-the-spot answering most of her emails.

How soon the crash happened surprised Beth as well, but she didn't change her routine one little bit. Lawson's sudden death barely sent a ripple through the organization, probably reflective of his inattention over the recent months and a staff prepared to pick up the slack. But the Center needed Beth's attention to maintain momentum, and she couldn't do that while hunting for Tommy Lee.

Where *was* that boy? Should she cancel the pickup of the wreckage?

The question nagged at her as she accelerated down the airport road until she happened to glance in her rearview and noticed one of the hangars. She slowed to a stop and tried to remember where she'd seen a structure that looked like half of a huge corrugated metal cylinder lying horizontally on the ground. Then it came to her.

Quonset hut. And a local variation that has nothing to do with aviation.

Albuquerque's proximity to Kirtland Air Force Base and Sandia National Laboratories had made it a potential first-strike target for Soviet ballistic missiles during the Cold War. A few years back the *Journal* or the *Tribune,* she couldn't remember which, published a look-back feature with photographs about a family that had built a fallout shelter. After the Berlin Wall came down, they became even more obsessed with survival and started a business selling bunkers that could be partially buried for protection from the apocalypse.

Tommy Lee's best friend Buster grew up in a house that had one. They had played war and other mayhem there as kids, and it sounded like the perfect place to disappear for a while. Familiar, comfortable, and private. Beth had no idea why Tommy Lee felt the need to hide, but she was going to find out.

An iPad search found the article. With the address entered in the Jaguar's nav system, which she felt was always trying to take her to Buckingham Palace, she cracked the whip on all those horses and charged down the highway in search of her absentee partner in the nefarious business of ridding herself of one Lawson McAllister, brilliant cancer surgeon, mediocre businessman, and philanderer extraordinaire.

THE HOUSE SEEMED TO be shrinking over the past couple of days, driving Tommy Lee stir crazy while he waited for Buster to return his calls and cover his back while he took care of four nagging problems.

First, get rid of any and all evidence linking him to the crash of the Victory, which would effectively eliminate the second complication of someone snooping around the logbooks and wreckage. Beth couldn't understand why he was being so secretive now that it had been released, but Tommy Lee wasn't about to mention his third concern, that one of Buster's neighbors ran around with a local meth dealer. Or why that should be of concern to him.

And if she found out? Tommy Lee would need to solve his

fourth dilemma and recover the insurance policy he arranged for protection against the wrath of a woman who frightened him more than the NTSB, FBI, and Leland combined. He'd never seen Beth display the ruthlessness that lay at the core of conspiring with him to murder her husband, but he *felt* it, close to the surface and ready to strike.

As had become his habit, he peeked out each of the windows to look for signs someone might be watching the house. At one of the front windows he saw a silver car rocket by on the highway. Looked like Beth's Jag, but no way she . . . *uh oh*. The Jag drove back to the driveway in reverse, screeched to a stop and paused. The damn thing had tinted windows, and even if it didn't, he was too far away to see the driver.

How many silver Jags were there in Albuquerque? The question became irrelevant when it turned into the driveway and sped toward the house with a cloud of dust in its wake.

Tommy Lee snatched his pistol out of his belt just in case and ran into the kitchen and out the back door onto the porch. The Jag had turned off the driveway and stopped in the back yard. The driver's door opened, out stepped Beth McAllister, and she looked pissed.

"Put that pistol away, you sonofabitch, before I shoot you with it!" She charged up on the back porch and got right in his face. "What the hell do you think you're doing?"

"You shouldn't be here. The neighbors—"

"The closest ones are over a mile away."

Very gently, Tommy Lee guided Beth into the kitchen, thinking, *You've got to sell this.*

"These people have nothing better to do than look out their windows and see *everything*. It's hard enough to avoid attracting attention with my pickup. That Jag—"

"What do you have to fear from neighbors knowing you're

in this house?

Use the other thing. "It's not that *they're* interested so much as whoever's sniffing at the Victory."

"But you said the investigation was over."

"This isn't official."

Only the ticking of a clock above the kitchen table broke the silence as they stood by the sink, Beth's expression unreadable. "If you've done your job, we have nothing to worry about."

"I have, but we still might. And this could be serious."

"We'll deal with that later. What's serious *now* is that the salvage company is picking up the wreckage tomorrow."

"But I haven't been able to—"

"How well I know. You've been hiding out in this dump while I'm doing exactly what you told me to, spending money to purchase the wreckage of an airplane so you could send it off to be crushed into scrap."

"But that was so I could get to it *before* it went to salvage."

"Exactly my point," said Beth. "And it has to be tonight unless you want me to cancel the pick up."

"I'll take care of it."

"You better." She slapped him, so fast he couldn't even think about ducking. "That's for disappearing." Then she kissed him so hard he thought his teeth would break. "That's to make it all better. And now," as she grabbed his crotch, "let's get out the best tool in your tool box. I need a tune-up."

CHAPTER TWENTY

From the Jeep, parked on a slight rise in the desert about a mile from the front gate of the Adobe Wings Airport, Nick watched activity wind down. Every car he saw was leaving. And for the last hour, no lights had moved in the gray-black of night under a crescent moon. A few outdoor lamps glowed in the distance and a couple of windows cast patches of yellow onto the desert floor.

Although security measures in the aftermath of 9/11 had undergone a period of intense scrutiny and renovation, safeguards at smaller airports remained much less restrictive, designed primarily to keep law-abiding folks out of areas where they shouldn't be. It bothered Nick a little bit that he needed to do this, but not enough to keep him from trying. He wore the darkest clothing he had and felt like a kid playing ninja. Especially with the Men's Teenage Mutant Ninja Turtle backpack he'd bought at Target to carry the drugs.

More than once since discovering the ingenious compartments built into the fuselage of the Victory, he'd changed his mind about what to do with them. Tonight's sneak attack on the hangar reflected his most recent decision, using the justification that without knowing if they had anything to do with the murder, the best way to prepare for learning they did was to make certain they didn't disappear.

He picked up the jack handle from the tire-change kit, climbed out of the Jeep and tried not to think about snakes. It was a big desert. What was the likelihood he would encounter one of the slithering devils? If he stumbled onto one, of course, probability no longer mattered.

At a slow trot, he advanced toward the airport, keeping his eyes trained close in front to avoid cactus, rocks, ankle-snapping holes, and whatever else lay in wait for someone foolish enough to try this. He was in pretty good shape and exercised at a comparable altitude, so the trip to the perimeter fence didn't take more than ten minutes. He turned at the fence and followed it to the front gate, closed at night and controlled by a sensor that responded to vehicles. The fence had no concertina or razor wire, and he'd planned to scale it if he had to. But just in case, he stepped onto the road, moved around in the right lane and waved his arms.

Click, then the squealing of hinges crying out for grease. He hustled through the opening and waited. After a minute, the gate closed and Nick trotted down the middle of the road on the center stripe. It occurred to him that in cooler weather snakes often used the heat stored in paved roads during the day to help warm up for night foraging, but this still seemed like a better option than the desert.

Stillwater Aviation owned the third large hangar along the main airport road. Light poles ringed the individual parking areas, but the lights weren't on. Same for those on the perimeter of the aircraft parking ramp. They might be on sensors, so he avoided them as he worked his way around to the rear of Stillwater's hangar where McAllister's private hangar had been added.

At the rear corner where he had unlatched the window, he forced the flat end of the jack handle into the junction of the frame and the window, pried it up enough to get his fingers inside, yanked the window open, and dropped the jack handle on the ground.

Crawling through head first, he lost his grip on the windowsill and fell onto the concrete floor. His flashlight slipped out of his jacket pocket and clattered against the wall. So much for ninja stealth. The left side of his face stung. He touched it, held his fingers up in the pale moonlight slanting through the window. No blood, but he'd probably have a bruise. He rolled into a kneeling position and listened. Nothing. *Be careful, fool.*

At the wreckage of the fuselage, he placed the flashlight on the floor and turned it on and off quickly. Too much. He rummaged through a trashcan nearby and pulled out a soft-drink cup, cut a small hole in the bottom, and slid it over the flashlight to concentrate the beam. Better.

From his jacket pocket, he removed a set of Allen wrenches he'd purchased that afternoon. Using the narrow beam of the flashlight to illuminate each access panel in turn, he unscrewed the fasteners, removed a total of four packages of drugs, and replaced the panels. As he stuffed the last package into the book bag, the snap-click of a deadbolt being thrown broke the silence in the hangar.

Nick snatched the flashlight off the floor, turned it off, jumped up and looked around.

The storage room? No. The front office? Too far. What's closest? A Cessna 206. Some have large cargo doors. He scrambled to it. *Yes!* He crouched down and prayed for it not to be locked—they normally don't for airplanes in hangars—slipped his hand inside the door handle and pulled . . . thankyouthankyouthankyou!

The rear seats had been removed. Nick crawled inside and pulled the door closed as he lay down on the floor and wished himself small and invisible.

Silence in the hangar, then rustling, someone moving about, voices, coming closer.

TOMMY LEE HELD UP his hand to stop Buster. "Shhh."

"What?"

"I said shut the fuck up."

"No, you *didn't*."

"Well, I am now." He stepped farther inside, lit only by moonlight slanting through the windows. A cluster of airplanes sat in dark silhouette against the gray background. The only sound, Buster's boots shuffling on the floor. The guy was like a giant Energizer Bunny on meth, and he hadn't gotten any of Tommy Lee's messages because he'd let the battery on his phone run down. He wouldn't make a good mascot even if he could play a bass drum.

Tommy Lee glared at him, whispered, "Stand still, goddamn it." He'd always been pretty good at sensing things around him. A threat nearby. Or something out of place. An anomaly. McAllister had used that word once. Tommy Lee looked it up, liked it. Maybe because that's what he felt like most of the time.

Then he noticed the open window on the far wall. He reached for the Beretta, remembered that he'd left it behind to avoid getting busted with the drugs *and* carrying a concealed weapon. Let his friend take the heat. "Buster?"

"Yeah?"

"Bring me your pistol."

Buster walked up, handed over the weapon and started to say something.

Tommy Lee held up one finger to his lips and again motioned for him to stay put. The guy usually couldn't move ten steps without knocking something over. But his loyalty to Tommy Lee made him useful, and his duties seldom required tiptoeing.

At the window, Tommy Lee found fresh scrape marks on the rusted metal frame. He knelt, put his head close to the floor, looked toward the center of the hangar. A trail of dusty footprints led away. They had to be recent. Leo kept the place so clean that Tommy Lee had often wondered if he ought to abandon his trailer and move in here.

He stood, let his eyes wander around the hangar, looking for one of those anomalies. Nothing caught his attention, although the unsettled feeling stayed with him. He motioned for Buster to join him and patted the air with his hands palm down in a "be careful" motion.

Buster hadn't gone 10 feet when he rammed his head into the wingtip of a Cessna. Sounded like a baseball bat striking a 50-gallon drum. As the brute approached, Tommy Lee said, "Now I'm going to have to fix that airplane."

"Huh?"

Tommy Lee sighed, shook his head, and handed the pistol to Buster. "We might have a visitor. Wait here and keep your eyes open for anything. Movement, flashlight, whatever."

Buster grinned and held up the pistol. "Can I shoot 'em?"

"Just don't shoot me." Tommy Lee approached the tail section, confirmed the left ruddervator had been ripped off, and it wasn't in the wreckage. Which meant the NTSB didn't find it. And the balance weight in the right ruddervator was missing. If they'd found it, the wreckage wouldn't be lying on the floor in front of him. The NTSB would be crawling all over Tommy Lee wanting to know how the fuck did a balance weight cut down the middle lengthwise end up at our crash site?

He smiled and added a couple of NFL-quality fist pumps.

The whole plan had involved a series of guesses, and it worked better than he would have ever predicted.

From his workbench he picked up a portable drill and Allen head bit and froze. Someone had been messing with his stuff. He'd forgotten to lock up when he left in such a hurry, but that hadn't worried him at the time. Mechanics respected the boundaries of co-workers when it came to workspace and tools. This was someone outside the Stillwater group. Tommy Lee glanced at the open window, the Victory wreckage, and . . . *Goddamn it.*

He ran to the storage room in the main hangar, got his key ring out of his pocket and shoved the locker key into the padlock. It didn't turn. He jiggled it, tried again, pulled it out, stared at the stenciled PARKER on the door.

Big anomaly here. He lifted the padlock. It was brand new. Tommy Lee didn't have *anything* new, which was the main reason he got involved in this whole mess.

Who the hell was it?

Leo? Tommy Lee didn't owe him anything, except maybe an apology for not giving notice. And Leo would have first confiscated Tommy Lee's tools in the hangar, worth a lot more than anything in this locker. To someone else, however, a piece of lead might be a valuable find. Who might that be? Tommy Lee didn't know, but he damn sure needed to find out.

In the meantime, he had more immediate concerns. Recovering misplaced property belonging to Leland meant Tommy Lee might get to keep all of his fingers. Unless whoever came through that window . . .

He rushed out of the storage room and back into McAllister's hangar. Ignoring Buster's repeated, "What the hell ya doin'?", he knelt beside the Victory's rear fuselage. With the small light on his key ring, he examined one of the special access panels.

A tiny piece of fishing leader placed between the panel and the fuselage had disappeared. *Holy shit, don't tell me . . .*

He jumped up and dashed to his workbench for the drill and bit.

Back at the fuselage, he frantically began removing the modified fasteners.

NICK LAY IN CLOTHING soaked with sweat. Voices, thudding footsteps on the run, and now a whirring sound made its way into the Cessna cargo compartment.

A drill? An image of a movie scene flashed before his eyes, involving a drill and kneecaps. He clenched his muscles. A few moments of deep breathing helped.

Just wait. They aren't searching the hangar. Yet. Maybe you should get out now.

He eased up from the floor of the Cessna, took a peek through a cabin window and ducked.

A man-mountain stood about thirty feet away, facing toward Nick, aiming a pistol. Did the guy see him? Nick's heart rate surged. He began breathing rapidly, felt like shrinking into himself as he waited for the gunshot. After a few moments, he had to take another look . . . and stared at a scene that could be from a comedy.

Silhouetted against the moonlight through the window, the guy stood still for a few seconds, then ducked, whirled around, and brought the pistol up in a combat stance. His lips appeared to mouth, *POW! POW!* Then he shoved the pistol back into his waistband and repeated the move in another direction.

Nick lowered his forehead to the floor of the Cessna and sighed. A fast-draw wannabe trying to shoot himself in the foot. Nick had only two options. Hide and wait, or run for it and use the airplanes as cover.

A few more quick peeks found the pistolero still preoccupied with imagined adversaries. Nick slipped his arms through the straps of the book bag and rotated his body to face the cargo door on the side of the Cessna opposite from the shooter. He eased open the door and crawled out headfirst by using the boarding step to help support his body weight.

Lying facedown on the hangar floor, he looked over his shoulder and couldn't see more than the guy's lower legs and heavy boots as they moved, paused, moved again. He was still shooting people, apparently.

Nick low-crawled toward the other side of the hangar and the door into the front office. With every movement, he expected a bullet to tear into him, spill his blood onto Leo's clean concrete.

TOMMY LEE FRANTICALLY REMOVED the last rivet, held his breath and paused. *Please let it be here.*

The panel came away to reveal an empty compartment. He closed his eyes and whispered, "Goddamn it all to hell."

From the dark hangar, "You talkin' to me, Tommy Lee?"

Tommy Lee had often thought Buster could probably hear ants crawling inside a mound. Maybe because his ears were so damned big. "You'll know it when I do."

He checked the other compartment, same deal, went back into the storage room and stared at the padlock. If his insurance policy was gone, the shit storm of his life might have turned perfect. When he got his hands on the motherfucker who—

"Tommy Lee!"

He hurried out of the storage room. Buster's dark shape ran toward the front office. Tommy Lee rushed to the emergency exit door and slammed through it shoulder first—hurt like hell—and sprinted toward the front of the hangar. As he rounded the corner, Buster stood in the empty parking lot waving his pistol.

His friend had always been a bit too trigger happy for Tommy Lee's taste. He skidded to a stop in the gravel close to the hangar and looked around the parking lot. "What happened?"

Buster looked like a robot suffering from energy overload, running around in circles. "He was in one of them planes! Has to be around here somewhere! Where's his car?"

Good thing I don't rely on Buster for his brains. "Maybe he's on foot. Who the hell we talking about?

"Some guy. Saw him sneakin' into the hallway like a fuckin' snake. Shoulda shot the prick."

"Put away that gun before you shoot me, goddamn it."

Buster wound down to a nervous fidgeting, little jerks in his head, arms and shoulders that made Tommy Lee expect to see sparks flying out of his eyes. He stared into the darkness and wondered who he was dealing with and what could he do about it.

One thing he knew for sure. The time had come to either get so close to Beth that she couldn't do anything without him knowing about it, or far enough away to not give a shit one way or the other.

In the meantime, that padlock had to come off. Tommy Lee told Buster to take his pickup, which was equipped for serious off-road work, turn on that blinding light bar and try to find the snake he saw hightailing it for the cactus. It would also get Buster out of the hangar and prevent him from looking over Tommy Lee's shoulder asking, "Whatcha doin'?" Not that he didn't trust him, but the fewer people who knew, the better.

Bolt cutters weren't common tools in a typical aircraft maintenance shop. But a few years ago, one of the mechanics had been killed in an auto accident. Leo bought his tool chest from the family and had to cut off the padlock.

Tommy Lee found the tool in the common work area, cut the new lock that some asshole had put on his private locker, opened the door and felt his pulse throbbing in his ears as he stumbled backwards against the wall.

NICK KEPT REMINDING HIMSELF it was a big desert and snakes couldn't be everywhere at once. After five minutes of hard running, the book bag heavy with drugs slapping against his back, he coasted to a fast walk, then stopped and turned around.

Gasping for breath, he scanned the desert for pursuit. It might be two guys with flashlights, or an off-road pickup with a thousand-candlepower light bar mounted on the roof and a couple of shooters standing in the bed with assault rifles. In either case, he could be in deep cow paddy. Figuratively speaking. He already had some on his boots.

That had to be Parker, but he wouldn't know who Nick was. Or would he? If he had drug connections, he probably ran a pretty good intelligence network. Could Caitlin, Yates and Nick have done all their snooping under the radar?

CHAPTER TWENTY-ONE

Tommy Lee slumped down in the seat of his Dodge Ram and stared out the windshield at the front door of Stillwater Aviation. The sun not even up yet, no sleep last night, and he could barely keep his eyes open. He felt like shit for running off like he did without saying anything because Leo was a good man and didn't deserve to be treated with disrespect. But choosing between that and what Leland might do to him hadn't been a choice at all.

Headlight beams appeared in the rearview, tracking the airport road to the front gate. Tommy Lee eased lower in the seat as Leo's F-150 passed him and coasted to a stop in the boss's usual parking spot. He climbed out, opened the front office door, and disappeared inside.

Tommy Lee yawned again, decided to wait for Leo to make the coffee. Anything to put this off a little longer. He'd almost drifted off to sleep when someone tapped on the driver's side window and sent Tommy Lee's heart into his throat. The questioning eyes of Ronnie Cox peered into the cab.

Tommy Lee opened the door and climbed out. "Hey."

"The hell you been?"

"Long story. Has Leo said anything? You know, like he's pissed?"

"Even if he was, he wouldn't and you know it."

"Yeah. Are you pissed?"

"Why would I be?"

"Extra work, for one thing, having to—"

"I'd kill for overtime, so any work you don't want? Lemme know." Ronnie turned on a heel and disappeared into the office.

Tommy Lee deserved Ronnie's attitude. As a favored mechanic around a shop, with an airplane assigned to him by the owner and that no one else even touched, much less worked on, he was bound to ruffle some coveralls.

Not only that, being able to fly the airplane whenever he wanted was a privilege any mechanic would envy. Even if they'd never flown an airplane in their lives. Special treatment set him apart from everyone else in the shop, but he hadn't become an airplane-and-powerplant mechanic or accepted the job with McAllister to win any popularity contests.

Tommy Lee took a deep breath, let it out in a rush and marched toward the office. He found Leo in his usual pre-workday pose in the records room, sitting in an old military surplus office chair with his feet resting on a matching decrepit desk.

Leo peered at him over the rim of his coffee cup, lifted it slightly and lowered it. "Yours is still on the rack."

Tommy Lee nodded, relieved beyond measure at not having to block verbal or physical blows just yet. "I'll get some. Got a moment?"

"What's up?"

"A more private moment?"

"Meet you in my office."

Tommy Lee got his coffee, went to Leo's office, such as it was, and closed the door.

Leo motioned to a chair stacked with papers. "Toss that stuff on the floor and take a load off."

When Tommy Lee was seated and trying not to meet Leo's always direct-to-the-point gaze, he sipped his coffee and finally set the cup on Leo's desk. "I wanted to apologize for leaving without giving you a heads up."

Leo shrugged. "It did seem a little unusual for a guy who's always on time. If you'd ever done anything like that before, I'd be tossing your ass out on the ramp. But you still got a job if you want, minus McAllister's Victory and the extra privileges."

Tommy Lee nodded his appreciation. "It's time for me to move on. I think we're square on my pay, unless I cost you anything by walking off like that?" When Leo shook his head, Tommy Lee said, "All right if I collect my tools?"

Leo nodded, stood up, and extended his hand.

Tommy Lee shook hands and paused. "Is my money any good for renting an airplane?"

Leo laughed. "If it's good, it's good for renting an airplane."

At the front desk, Tommy Lee put his name on the schedule for the Maule M-5, a rugged short-takeoff-and-landing taildragger designed for off-runway operations. This airplane was an early serial number manufactured in the mid-70s. But like all of Leo's rentals, it was in superb condition where it counted. Which meant that Leo didn't worry about faded paint and skin rash from takeoffs and landings on gravel roads, sand bars, flat desert and the like.

Tommy Lee stopped by the records room. "I've scheduled the Maule today for about two hours of flight time. If I need to do an overnight, is that going to cause a problem?"

"Anyone got it tomorrow?" When Tommy Lee shook his head, Leo waved a dismissive hand.

Tommy Lee turned to leave, and then in his best I-forgot-to-ask-you manner, paused at the door. "One of the guys mentioned there's been a stranger poking around, asking questions. He seemed especially interested in me. Anything you can tell me about that?"

Leo looked up from an aircraft log and peered over the top of his reading glasses. "NTSB investigator."

Tommy Lee's legs threatened to collapse under him. "But . . . uh . . . they're finished, right? What's he doing here?"

"Investigating the investigators."

"What?"

"He's a senior guy looking at how well the team did its job. Why should that worry you?"

Because I'm not an investigator. "Just curious. See you."

Walking to his truck, Tommy Lee felt like another of those anomalies had just paid him a visit.

AFTER A NIGHT OF hide-and-seek with the pistol-packing, fast-draw cowboy and a desert 5K escape, Nick figured he might never sleep well again. So he didn't even try and gave in to an irresistible craving for sugar and caffeine.

Even with the driver's side window open, the aroma of fresh-baked Sugar Time Donut Shop fat pills still filled the Jeep as he crumpled the empty bag and popped the lid on his third cup of French Roast. He had to hold it with both hands to take a sip. *Jittery? Who, me?*

He glanced at his watch. He had called Caitlin about an hour ago and gave her coordinates to a remote highway intersection in the desert. Figuring that from the motel she would approach the spot from his left and at a right angle, he parked on the gravel shoulder about a mile distant and slightly higher with a good view in both directions.

This needed to be a private meeting. No more Yates surprises. The guy had proven to be as unpredictable in behavior as he was proficient at surveillance. Nick never knew what to expect in either case, and Yates might well have hidden a tracking device on Caitlin's Mercedes. Assuming he wasn't connected to a geek in a dark room staring at computer screens with images from satellites all over the world, he would have to be following her close enough to pick up the signal, which he'd be hard-pressed to do undetected out here in the open.

Nick was brushing the residue of a cinnamon-sugar donut off his cargo pants when he heard a soft hiss punctuated by snaps, like tires on asphalt with gravel on it. Or maybe on a shoulder.

Well . . . shit.

In the rearview sat the snout of a black Mercedes. Any other car, he'd have heard the engine. The damn things must be designed for sneaking up on people.

He picked up the balance weight and the book bag with the drugs, climbed out and approached the sedan. The driver's window hummed down an inch and her voice drifted out into the silence. "Get in."

Nick motioned to the trunk. "Pop it." The lid clicked open. Nick put the drugs inside, closed it, and slipped into the front passenger seat. The interior felt like a refrigerator. "You keeping meat in this thing?"

"I could if I wanted," said Caitlin. "Something to tell me?"

Nick shifted in the seat to face her and reached behind his back to adjust the Glock without thinking about how that might appear.

Her hand disappeared into her concealment shoulder bag so fast that Nick almost couldn't believe it.

He held out both empty hands. "Easy, big girl. We're on the same team, remember?"

She nodded and removed her hand, minus the Walther.

"But you can't trust free agency."

Nick related the events at the hangar. Caitlin's face never changed expression at hearing about the evidence of sabotage with the balance weights.

When he mentioned the drugs, however, she frowned and shook her head. "Lawson would never have been involved in anything like that."

"I believe you, but this is about Parker hauling drugs in the Victory and cutting up balance weights, which makes him a drug dealer, or a mule for one, and a killer. That adds up to dangerous."

"I couldn't care less about him. He didn't suddenly decide to murder his meal ticket. A better deal came along, and I want the bitch who offered it."

"Then go get her. On your own. But there is something I can offer as a parting gift, so long as you understand that whether I'm successful or not, we're done."

"What kind of gift?"

"A search for the missing ruddervator. It's lying out there in the desert, maybe with the other half of this," Nick slowly removed the cut-down balance weight out of his pocket and set it on the console, "If it has tool marks to match, proof of sabotage is a slam dunk."

"What makes you think you can find it when the NTSB didn't?"

"Like I've said, they had no reason to expect sabotage, and they found direct evidence of Lawson's addiction to speed. An unauthorized modification to the overspeed warning system pointed them directly to a conclusion of pilot error."

"Modification to *what?*"

Nick explained the purpose of the horn and the switch. "The only explanation is that Lawson had Parker, the only mechanic who ever worked on the airplane, install it so he could routinely fly faster than red line without having to put up with the aggravation in his headset."

Caitlin's face clouded over, and the moisture in her eyes glinted in the morning sunlight streaming through the windshield. "Why would he take that risk?"

"Overconfidence. And I can tell you from personal experience that it's one of the most dangerous attributes a pilot can have."

She stared out of the driver's window for a moment, took a deep breath and sighed. "Back to this gift, when can I expect it?"

"Don't. Trying to find it isn't like looking for a flight data recorder at the bottom of the ocean, but close enough to be problematic. All I can do is try."

"And then you're out of here."

"Count on it. And let's be clear that finding those drugs complicates the hell out of whatever you do next, which has nothing to do with me."

"You're dreaming. When the evidence ties Parker to the sabotage, and Yates produces a few eight-by-ten glossies of him and the Balloon Bitch together, and Parker realizes the drugs are missing, if he hasn't already, we're both going to be potential targets."

"You've got photos?"

Not yet. But when I do, it will be so sweet!"

"What?"

"Imagine my surprise when he offered to sell me photos that BB had paid for so she could confront Lawson. Said he'd tell her he didn't find anything and get paid twice in the bargain."

"Why didn't you?"

"I wasn't about to use my hard-earned money for that."

"Why not use Lawson's? He had a vested interest in keeping his wife from learning about the affair."

Caitlin shook her head. "That would have meant trusting Yates, and even without the photos, she knew. I may have also indulged in wishful thinking. That if she confronted Lawson, it might nudge him in the direction he said he wanted to go. But this time, the same guy who took photos for her works for me."

"Until he offers them to her."

"Who cares? I'll still get them because he likes to double up on paydays, and the effect is the same when she finds out, no matter who delivers the bad news."

Nick nodded and got out of the Mercedes, paused, leaned into the open door. "Don't speed. Around this part of the country, a speck of dust is considered probable cause for a traffic stop."

As Nick drove away with Caitlin's Mercedes shrinking in the rearview, he knew without a doubt that it had been way too long since the hunt beckoned. And at this very moment, that ruddervator might be lying out there in the desert northwest of Phoenix.

TOMMY LEE HAD LOGGED about 50 hours in the Maule and loved flying it.

First conceptualized by B. D. Maule in 1956, the airplane had undergone years of improvements to create this M-5, a real bush-flying workhorse when it came to hauling heavy loads into and out of unimproved airstrips and rugged environments. Tommy Lee had no doubt B.D. would be much distressed to learn his airplane served drug dealers. But when you design something so well, you can't expect to limit its uses.

After departing Adobe Wings, he climbed to a comfortable

cruise altitude above the turbulence. He had about an hour to kill, and a little sneaky head-faking to do.

Over the course of their clandestine affair, he and Beth had taken insane care to keep it that way. By now, she would have received his coded message, and at this moment, she was somewhere in the middle of a sequence that involved driving the Jag to the Coronado Mall in Albuquerque, where the layout, size and multiple entrances allowed her to blend in to the point of disappearing. He'd taught her some tricks about how to defeat a single tail, and figured that if anyone wanted to monitor her movements tightly enough to assign a team, they were busted sooner or later no matter what either of them did.

She'd get a taxi, give the driver two or three changes of destination en route to a car rental agency, where she would rent an SUV using the fake credit card and driver's license he'd given her. She wouldn't pay with the card because it didn't access a real account, but cash plus the credit card/driver's license combo always worked with not an eyebrow raised behind the counter. Just another matron wanting to keep her fling with a young buck a secret from the Mister.

Then she'd take a circuitous route into the desert, eventually leaving hard surface for a destination on a portable GPS, consisting of about 2000 fairly straight-and-level sandy feet in a ravine. Dry streambeds crisscrossed the terrain all over the Western US, remnants of a time when water ran freely. Balloon tires on the Maule were tailor-made for sand, and the meet-up would be consummated. Not literally this time, however, which Beth loved because it was so deliciously exciting to be out there in the open directing her love toy in just what she wanted him to do and when. Too much going on for that. Maybe later.

Tommy Lee entered the pattern at a non-towered airport

near a range of low-lying ridges that extended all the way to his intended destination. He performed a few practice touch-and-go landings, just like he always did. After the last one, he kept the Maule a few feet off the runway, just like he always did, showing off, nothing new about that, and departed the airport. Once out of sight behind the terrain, he hugged the desert all the way to the ravine. All of this an excess of caution, maybe, but no one could find a radar trail if he didn't leave one.

At the north end of the ravine sat a white SUV, looked like a Range Rover for chrissakes. He'd told Beth to rent nondescript vehicles for meet-ups. When she complained about the possibility of being seen by an acquaintance while driving a car made for everywoman, he reminded her that the whole point of renting one rather than using her own was to remain anonymous. Lot of good that did.

Two passes over the ravine confirmed the absence of other vehicles. He did a third flyby and waggled the wings. As he set up for the approach, she got out of the SUV and waved a New Mexico flag as a last confirmation of everything being okay on her end.

Flaps down, mixture rich, prop to high pitch, Tommy Lee settled into the groove on final and pegged the airspeed at 70. Passing his personal "threshold-marker" tree that confirmed he wouldn't land short, he eased the throttle to idle and let the speed drop to about 65 as the tailwheel touched an instant before the mains. The control yoke back in his lap planted all three tires into the sand and brought him to a stop with most of the runway unused. A 180-degree turn to the approach end of the runway followed by another 180 to runway heading positioned him for a quick takeoff. Just in case.

Beth had followed his advice about wearing functional, average clothing and leaving the jewelry in the safe, but he had no doubt she'd changed since leaving the mall. He didn't want to know how.

She greeted him with, "I guess that arrival means you are no longer in hiding."

"For the moment, but that may change."

Her face clouded over. "What's that supposed to mean?"

"Does the air conditioner work on *that* over-priced British attention-grabber?"

"Oh, stop it. I can't help it if I like luxurious cars. And yes. It would probably freeze anti-freeze."

"After you."

With both of them settled in the front seats, Tommy Lee tried one last time to come up with a good way to say this, but there wasn't one. "I've not been entirely truthful with you."

"I haven't with you, either, so I guess we're even."

"Probably not." After a moment of staring out the windshield at the Maule, sitting in the sand as if waiting to carry him away to another life, Tommy Lee told her about his deal with the head of the biker gang and the shipment of drugs hidden on the Victory when it crashed.

Beth's expression never changed, but Tommy Lee was well aware she could mask her feelings without giving away even a hint of what was going on inside.

She smoothed the fabric of her khakis, then fixed him with the cold stare he'd seen before when she wanted his undivided attention "You're right. We're not even. I didn't jeopardize our arrangement by running a side business with the potential for setting up Lawson, the public face of *my* center, to be busted for transporting drug quantities that could put him away for a long time"

"I was in a bind—"

"Of your own making! No one forced you to put drugs on

the airplane after you modified it."

"You're right. But that doesn't solve the problem."

"Only one?"

"One's enough."

"And I guess that means the investigators found the drugs."

"Hardly. I had a foolproof method, ingeniously deceptive, if I do say so myself."

"And I say that your brain has either gone on holiday or there's a key detail missing. The salvage company is scheduled to pick up the remains of Lawson's toy this afternoon. If they do, those drugs, so creatively hidden, are lost to history forever in a smelting plant. If they don't, go recover them. Surely you can get in that hangar after hours."

"I can get in that hangar anytime I want. But it won't do any good."

"You're messing with me, Tommy Lee, and I'm beginning not to like it."

"Sorry. The drugs are missing."

"But you said—"

"The *investigators* didn't find them, but someone else did."

Beth shook her head and sighed. "I can't *believe* you let this happen."

"If I don't come up with them, or the money, I'm fish food."

"That's what they do on the coasts. Here, it's a drier option. They stake you out in the desert with no eyelids and cover you with honey. Ants love it."

"I appreciate the details, but are you going to help me or not?"

"I may. First, how can they be missing if you hid them so well? Who would have the knowledge to know where to look?"

Tommy Lee wasn't about to reveal the name of Nick Phillips, because that asshole had also stolen Tommy Lee's insurance policy against being hung out to dry. Wearing his best straight face, he said, "When I find out I'll let you know. In the meantime, those biker dudes aren't known for their patience."

"How much to get them off your back?"

"Don't know yet. These guys usually deal in crank. There were four packages, probably a kilo each. For markets out West, I'm guessing less than thirty thousand, but that can change in a heartbeat."

"That's all?"

"Money-wise, probably. Look, Leland—"

"Who?"

"Forget I said that. These guys keep a very low profile and deal in quantities that pretty much stay below the radars of the big boys. It's not about getting rich. Give them beer, some weed, harder stuff on occasion, and enough dough to fix up a Harley and they're in hog heaven, no pun intended."

"That doesn't sound like much of a problem to me."

"Because they don't know about you. But me and that Victory? We're on the front lines."

"But if you pay—"

"That may not solve it."

"Why not?"

"Because the drugs are still out there, and whoever took them knows where they came from."

Beth sighed, an exasperated sound she often used that made Tommy Lee feel like he was behind the conversation. "So what? They can't *prove* it With the Victory wreckage gone, any physical evidence to connect drugs with it, you, me, Lawson, whoever, goes with it. What are you worried about?"

"The unexpected. I'd like to know who took them, because I don't think it has anything to do with stealing drugs. Whoever was in that hangar was looking for something else."

That visibly slowed Beth up, put her in a processing mode, and Tommy Lee knew exactly when she stopped on the something else that worried *him* the most. And that he hadn't brought up, because it was his little secret.

She shook her head. "No way."

"You're sure about that?"

"You set it up, so there must be something you're not telling me."

"I have no reason to hide anything from you now, but I'd feel a lot more confident of protecting my—uh, our asses if I knew who was doing all the snooping." Tommy Lee picked up a bottle of water from the console and drank some, waiting for the significance of the word *our* to sink in. A few quick blinks might have been the indicator he was looking for. "You hired a guy to get the juicy details on Lawson's rutting with his trip bunny, right?"

Beth winced at Tommy Lee's description, as he knew she would. Rutting was fine with her under the right circumstances, which meant actually *doing* it. Talking about it, however, was to be avoided like the plague. She nodded. "I know a private investigator."

"How do I contact him?"

"You don't."

"Why not?"

"Because that's my little secret."

Tommy Lee stared out the windshield at the Maule.

You just keep thinking that, sweetheart.

CAITLIN COULD AFFORD TO stay wherever she wanted and had told Nick he didn't need to sleep on the cheap. But in Both Dry

Springs and Albuquerque, he'd let convenience drive his choice of motels, and that seemed so sensible under the circumstances that she followed suit. The Los Orcones Inn was old and tired, but clean enough that she didn't worry about sleeping on last week's sheets.

She sat at the small dining table that tilted precariously every time she touched it. Resting in the dim glow of an overhead swag lamp of a design long since obsolete lay a sheaf of papers containing copies of Parker's banking statements for the past few months and a series of emails between him and BB. Nearby rested a chunk of lead in a plastic baggie along with what appeared to be black fingerprint powder and a single piece of lifting tape. Beside the baggie, four surprise packages of drugs. Didn't matter what kind. The only significance to Caitlin was where they came from and if she could use them to her advantage. *Where* was the easy part.

Lawson's mechanic had modified the Victory with hidden storage compartments. You call, we haul your product from here to there. The cops won't have a clue. A sweet deal anyway you sliced it.

Caitlin had never met the guy and didn't want to. But she had his stuff . . . well, maybe not his exactly. If he only transported it, the loss would likely stir up a hornet's nest of trouble she'd best avoid. As she thought about how, a delicious possibility came to mind, a way to rid herself of two problems at once.

Yates had probably outlived his usefulness. And even if she cut him loose and later had need for his services, his reputation for greedy acceptance of all manner of odd jobs meant he'd be available on short notice.

Caitlin owed him money. But why give him cash when she had the drugs, of no personal val;ue to her and dangerous to have around? She had no clue about what they were worth, but Yates had been a narcotics cop. And a crooked one.

I'm sorry I don't have the rest of your fee, Cliff. But lookee here. That bad boy Parker left us a gift. It's yours, and we'll call it even. Deal?

It might work. And work even better if that diverted onto Yates whatever trouble came looking for the drugs. Couldn't happen to a more deserving guy.

The bank statements showed six weekly $9,950 deposits into Parker's account and images of the checks drawn on the account of Elizabeth Blaine McAllister. Neither of them could possibly be stupid enough not to realize the connection this created. There had to be an explanation, and the only conclusion that fit suggested the intentional laying of a paper trail to serve one of the two parties . . . which had to be the Black Widow. Keeping her partner close to the web.

The emails contained nothing obvious about planning and committing a murder, an error not even the most inept conspirator would commit, but neither did they appear to communicate anything of substance. Caitlin suspected they contained some kind of code to schedule clandestine meetings, with all the details previously arranged in person.

That didn't mean the communication footprints were useless, however. They began suddenly, within a week of the first deposit, and with no previous history of contact between a wealthy woman and her husband's airplane mechanic. Coincidence? Sure.

Now what about the final weapon?

Caitlin picked up the chunk of lead and peered at it through the baggie. Five of the six sides looked the same. Smooth surfaces, slightly rounded edges, just the way they appeared when the casting was made. But the sixth clearly showed evidence of a lengthwise cut, the only way to produce the saw marks on the face and the sharp edges.

Caitlin put the weight back on the table and paced around the room, letting her mind play out a scenario that Nick had hypothesized.

The Victory took off with the other half of this balance weight installed in one ruddervator. Nick had explained how dangerous that was under certain flight conditions, which came together as Lawson tried to beat the odds like he always did. Any pilot who has an unauthorized switch installed to cancel an airspeed warning horn undoubtedly planned to use it. And that thought put Caitlin into the armchair as her knees weakened.

She never paid any attention to details like that. If you can't trust your pilot, you've got no business flying with him. She also couldn't remember ever hearing the warning horn. Nick might know why. Maybe Lawson used the switch in advance of reaching red line to prevent it.

Parker couldn't reliably predict when the accident would occur, and that uncertainty was an essential part of the sabotage. Like a time bomb with an indefinite fuse planted in a moveable object. All they had to do was be patient, and Lawson would kill himself in that airplane sooner or later. And when he did, it would be so far removed from the sabotage in time and space that the connection would be tenuous at best.

But why would Parker keep the other half, which clearly tied him to the sabotage? All the effort to distance himself with the pilot error smokescreen would be worse than ineffective if someone found it. That's stupid, and Parker is no dummy. He had to have a good reason and—*Ohmigod*.

Caitlin held the weight close to the lamp, stretched the baggie tight against the lifting tape and examined the single fingerprint preserved in black powder. After a moment, she smiled and said to no one, "You sneaky sonofabitch."

Could an airplane mechanic have been savvy enough to protect his backside with the undeniable physical proof of sabotage that connected his lover directly to the murder?

This was perfect. Like the slam-dunk, put-the-needle-in-the-arm CSI evidence of a killer's fingerprint in the victim's blood at the crime scene.

Caitlin's plan had been a long shot from the beginning, but the world belonged to those who grabbed their piece of it and held on. As of this moment, everything she hypothesized had been confirmed, even if Nick didn't find the missing ruddervator.

Lawson died because his wife hired Parker to help murder him. She'd escaped justice once for lack of proof, and would do so again because the evidence had been hidden behind a veil of ingenious sabotage and had no legal standing.

But that didn't rule out a less-than-legal method, particularly since Caitlin was willing to leave justice in the hand of fate and seek vengeance by her own. If and when a self-defense situation presented the opportunity, of course, which would then be conveniently judged as legal.

Absent a personal application of the death penalty, Caitlin had a backup plan to destroy the one possession Lawson's widow cared about only slightly less than life. She lived in a world oblivious to the obvious, as he put it, by refusing to recognize that the attention she sensed when entering a room derived not from admiration and respect for her many charitable activities, but from scorn. The black-widow hearsay had made her the local laughingstock.

And on the rickety table in front of Caitlin sat what might be the keys to transforming the Balloon Bitch into a social pariah, to be actively shunned by those she so desperately wanted to impress.

And the best part? It would effectively be a life sentence.

Three sharp raps on the door startled Caitlin. She checked the security peephole.

Ah, yes. Time to rid myself of some gum on my shoe.

She hid the balance weight, left the drugs on the table, and opened the door.

Chapter Twenty-Two

Cliff had been worried about taking the LTD off-road into the dry riverbed, but so far the hard sand was crisscrossed with the shallow tire tracks of four-wheel enthusiasts who came out here in the desert to play.

With the help of a little monetary persuasion, his street sources had revealed that Leland recently moved his drug lab to a new location near the point where the riverbed became impassable to vehicles of any kind. It was the sort of intelligence cops never seemed to have, or maybe ignored, especially since these bikers were very good at not pissing in their own pool.

Cliff had been a cop long enough to know that a lot of police work operated on a live-and-let-live credo, with mutual back scratching as illegal tender. Leland was a master at playing the game. That didn't mean he'd hesitate for a second to protect his turf, or his rep, which helped protect his turf. Problems within his business would disappear, no muss, no fuss, no headlines, and never would violence be visited upon the innocent.

About a mile back, the dust cloud Cliff had been leaving behind all but disappeared. And sure enough, the farther he drove, the wetter the sand became.

He knew why because he'd read about disappearing rivers in a book. Not the fake streams people put in their yards, but nature's kind.

Beneath him, in a channel carved in the bedrock millions of years ago, a ribbon of water seeped along, pulled by gravity to some ultimate destination he could only dream of. The layer of sand and gravel between the tires of the LTD and the water was getting thinner. If the bedrock continued to get closer to the surface of the sand, he might soon be driving in water. That'd be cool, in more ways than one, but he hoped it wouldn't stop him from making contact with some of Leland's outriders.

Behind removable side panels in the doors, Cliff had stashed the four packages of crank Caitlin gave him in payment for services rendered. He turned over hard copies of the email and banking evidence, but when she asked where he got it, Cliff made it clear to her the experts were *his* contacts. Want some more? Caitlin knew his number and she could damn well put it on speed dial.

In the meantime, Cliff didn't believe for a moment that Caitlin was done. Or that Phillips wasn't hanging around sniffing at her crotch. But whatever either of them did, no way was Cliff going to turn down this opportunity, especially since he'd been tossed out like last week's trash.

And that didn't mean trying to sell the shit, which would bring way too much attention his way. He was capable of handling lots of situations, but he didn't have eyes in the back of his head.

It meant working an angle, first by handing the drugs over to the rightful owner, then asking only for a little of the action in return. Like filling in the gap left in the biker's drug business. Cliff only had a private pilot's license, but he'd logged enough flight time since then to build confidence in the basics: pull back on the controls to make the houses smaller, push forward to make them bigger. How hard can that be?

He smiled at that standard pilot joke. But if they gave

him a chance, he'd get some more flight training and take over distribution. And to that end, he'd left the sport coat, tie, and shirt at the motel. This wouldn't be a matter of head-faking anyone. Try that with these dudes and they'd send him home with some broken bones.

About a mile farther up the ravine, Cliff leaned out the open window. Sure enough, wet sand was being thrown up against the fender and rocker panel. Not long after that, the water quickly deepened into a nice stream, and he had to find a place to climb out of the channel onto the desert. The cactus and larger rocks were spaced far enough apart that he could maneuver around them, but if he misjudged the height of one and punctured his oil pan, he'd be on foot in the middle of nowhere.

He stayed as close to the water as he could, but that option appeared to be quickly running out. After a detour took him about a hundred yards to his right, he maneuvered back toward the stream, rounded the base of a small hill and hit a rock dead center that almost lifted the front of the LTD off the ground. He powered over it to keep up his momentum, the sound of his engine racing in low gear punctuated by the crunch of his undercarriage in contact with three more rocks in quick succession.

The engine died, hopefully not for good, as he stopped by the stream, now flowing over gravel, grass, and the military combat boots of a guy carrying an assault rifle.

Cliff's hands were on the steering wheel, where he willed them to stay as he leaned his head out the window. "Howdy."

"The hell you doin' up here, man?"

"Thinking about buying this car. Owner said I could take it for a test drive."

The dude almost smiled. "How's it workin' for ya?"

"About done, I'm afraid."

"Hate to tell you this, but there ain't no place to turn 'round up yonder. Reverse work okay?"

"Haven't tried it."

"Best do that now."

"How about taking me to see Leland?"

"Who?"

"I really enjoy the banter, my man, but could we cut the crap? I've got something he'll want."

"How do ya plan on provin' that?"

"Check in the trunk and behind the side panels in these doors."

The dude paused for a moment, then shifted his eyes behind the LTD and nodded slightly toward Cliff. His rearview and both side mirrors suddenly filled with biker types, all armed, all approaching the LTD. The guys on the right side and to Cliff's rear stopped a few feet from the car as the one on the left opened the driver's door and placed the muzzle of a sawed-off shotgun against Cliff's ear. It was very quiet, the only sound that of water, gurgling softly, in stark contrast to the pounding of Cliff's heart.

"Very slowly," said the guy by the door, "you're gonna ease out o' there and move away from the car with me. Got it?"

Cliff almost nodded, thought better of it with the shotgun pressing into his head. "Absolutely."

While the guy patted him down and removed the .45 Cliff told him he was packing, two guys removed the drugs and set them on the hood of the LTD along with the duffel bag from the trunk.

The dude in the stream walked up to him with his rifle slung over his shoulder. "So, you come all the way up here in that piece o' shit for what reason, exactly?"

"To talk to Leland. And I wouldn't want to be the one who stood in the way when he finds out I didn't." The dude seemed confused by that information, as if it had frozen his processor. Cliff nudged him with, "Maybe you ought to let him decide."

The dude's eyes shifted to Cliff, a bit of dim light behind them. After a moment he gave a quick nod. "The boys'll valet park your wheels for free."

NICK POPPED THE TOP on a bottle of local New Mexico beer and took a sip, remembering in part the description on the brewery's website that convinced him to try it: *Anything but a typical American Pale, Santa Fe Pale Ale is as full bodied as its most robust English counterparts, while asserting its American origin with a healthy nose resplendent with Cascade and Willamette hops.*

Whether Nick agreed with that or not, this was very good beer, and he always pondered better with a brewski. He sat in the motel-room desk chair with a notepad and pen to let his mind wrap around the task ahead.

He began scribbling notes, an obsession with him when planning almost anything, and he soon had an idea for trying to locate the missing ruddervator. He fully recognized and accepted the difficulties ahead, but technologies existed to increase the odds of success.

The problem could be likened to that of using knowns to make assumptions that could be used to solve for an unknown. The solution had to begin by defining the position of the Victory in three-dimensional space at the precise moment a catastrophic flutter event caused in-flight breakup. The NTSB had copies of the Air Traffic Control radar tapes with that information, and Nick's first task would be to finagle a way to get it.

The end point of the crash sequence lay in the wreckage debris field, mapped in detail by the investigators as they recovered each piece of the Victory.

Nick would use ballistic trajectory analysis to connect the start and end points of the three major pieces of wreckage the NTSB found: the fuselage with one wing attached, the other wing by itself, and the tail section. Then he would run a hypothetical trajectory analysis for a Victory ruddervator to predict the impact point of the missing ruddervator on the ground.

Prior to initiating a ground search, he would obtain an airborne survey of the known crash site and the predicted impact point of the ruddervator to map the position of any metal objects out there. In a perfect world, a metal detector mounted on a helicopter flying a precise GPS grid pattern would pinpoint the location of the ruddervator. Using a handheld GPS, Nick would drive/hike to the point and pick the damn thing up. In reality, he planned a far less expensive, and in some ways more reliable, multiple boots-on-the-ground search.

Nick suffered no illusions about the probability of success because ruddervators sometimes threw balance weights during a flutter event. So even if he found the flight control, he might not achieve the crucial goal of matching the cut-down balance weight from Parker's locker with its other half. But he'd never know unless he tried.

Nick's cell phone interrupted more note taking and he recognized the number. "Hotel, my friend, how are you and the Cedar Valley Gazette doing without me to keep you straight with my letters to the editor about your worthless column?"

"Much better, thanks. So is the flight school. Running smooth, making money without you there to muck it up. I've become a local celebrity now that everyone has heard about your comment in the Market that I'm going to play you in the movie. Most important, I just soloed in the Cub."

"Congratulations. How much is it going to cost to repair it?"

"Funny man. And shifting to another topic, I heard a rumor that Laurie moved out. I didn't believe it. Went by to check, and sure enough, it looks like a ghost house."

Of course. Privacy and small towns are mutually exclusive. "Sounds like the news has been slow and you're reduced to reporting rumor. Do me a favor and hold the presses until I get back."

"It's none of my business, but—"

"You got that right. Chill the beer, and while you're at it, do the same to yourself." He ended the call, plopped down in one of the two armchairs, leaned back and closed his eyes.

The origin of species had been a topic of interest to Nick for as long as he could remember, and one of the key differentiating characteristics among life on planet Earth was the ability to modify behavior based on experience. On what side of the line did he exist? Had he learned anything over the past two weeks? About life in general? Himself? Or marriage?

He knew people who believed love conquers all, but that was a self-fulfilling philosophy. If a couple stayed together through any adversity, they must love each other. If they split up, they don't love each other enough. He didn't believe life, love, or the pursuit of happiness could be reduced to such a simplistic view.

While looking in the mirror to shave every morning, he had long since acknowledged the face he saw belonged to a basically good man, but not without flaws. And the further measure of the man had to consider what he did or didn't do about his failings.

What does it say when he accepts them without resistance? Or if he honestly struggles to deal with them without success? At the end of the day, what's the scorecard going to read?

Nick had no easy answers to those questions because there were none. But the time had come to acknowledge that if he and Laurie had any chance whatsoever of salvaging their marriage, they both would have to step outside their individual comfort zones where careers defined who they were and allow the relationship to take center stage.

Absent that, reconciliation would remain elusive, and each of them would enter into a new phase of life no longer centered on the other.

THE STENCH SEEMED TO be everywhere. Cliff turned to his escort with the rifle. "How do you stand that?"

"By thinking about the money we make selling it. And always trying to stay upwind. Where we're going now." The dude led the way through some low scrub and stunted evergreens to the base of a cliff face where tents had been erected. Big ones, staked and tied down, with roll-up sides. One appeared to be a camp kitchen, another an office, with computers, cables snaking into the desert to a clear area with a satellite dish, and a four-wheel pickup with an enormous generator in the bed, idle at the moment.

The other two had cots and footlockers. It reminded Cliff of a military encampment, and it was obvious Leland ran a tight ship out here in the dry ocean of the high desert. This was no group of unruly biker gangbangers hanging around drinking beer, smoking dope and fighting whenever the mood struck.

"Wait here." The guy entered one of the tents where a man sat at a card table with the drugs and duffle bag resting on it.

After a short conversation, the man motioned for Cliff to come in as the other guy walked out of the rear of the tent.

Cliff approached the man, dressed in a blue denim shirt, black leather vest, jeans, hiking boots and a shoulder rig with what appeared to be a stainless steel Colt Model 1911 .45 caliber Officer's Model with a Pachmayr rubber grip. The pistol was cocked and locked. Serious hardware, but old school. Cliff liked him already.

The guy looked like a bookkeeper. "Who are you and what do you want?"

"My name's Yates. I'm a private investigator, but don't let that scare you. I have a business proposition."

"Let's hear it." He motioned to a folding chair leaning against the card table.

It took a couple of minutes for Cliff to present his case, that he figured the drugs might belong to Leland but got misplaced and needed to be returned to the rightful owner. If that wasn't Leland, please consider them a gift as a token of goodwill and the lead-in to a potentially beneficial business arrangement.

Leland listened, his eyes and face revealing nothing, like a real good poker player. When Cliff paused, he said, "Before I accept it and piss off someone who might take offense, where'd you get the product?"

Cliff smiled at Leland not admitting the drugs were his, but he was pretty sure the next part would come as a surprise and change things. "Out of a Victory. That crashed because it was sabotaged. It was sabotaged by the guy who maintained it. The same guy who had a deal with you to move the stuff around without drawing attention. And who did the opposite by shipping a load in the airplane after the sabotage. Stroke of luck the NTSB didn't find it and bring the FBI in here like stink on a crank lab. How am I doing so far?"

Leland lost his poker face and smiled. "How the hell you learn all that?"

"It's what I do. And I'd like to do something else. Diversify. How about I take over the shipping? Give me a chance to prove I can set it up and not leave you vulnerable in the process. Like Parker did, by the way."

"I was wondering about that. Why would he sabotage an airplane he worked on?"

"To murder the guy who flew it because his wife wanted him dead."

"Get outa here."

"Scout's honor. You know about that new cancer facility, right?"

"I work in the sticks but I don't live out here." He nodded in the direction of the satellite dish. "And in any case, we have an online presence." He laughed.

Cliff liked the dude even more. "This is soap-opera city, man. McAllister had a bimbo on the side, wasn't paying attention to business. His wife hired me to get the evidence to grab him by the balls so his heart and mind would follow."

That got another smile out of Leland. "Been there myself. Is there a punch line?"

"It's worth waiting for. The hubby gives up the broad, then recants, professes his love for her, tells his wife he wants a divorce, and you're going to love this. The wife decides she's had enough of his bullshit and decides to take care of it."

"'Take care of' as in . . .?"

"As in a box, man."

"Enter Parker."

Cliff smiled. "In more ways than one. He's been playing house with the wife."

Leland took a deep breath and exhaled with a chuckle.

"Christ! I am *not* believing this."

"Me, or the story?"

"Let's start with you. At first I didn't connect the name, but you're the cop who walked both sides of the street some years back, right? Got your balls in a vice? Barely missed a tour in the joint where the cons *love* to find a cop and pull his pants down?"

Cliff knew Leland hadn't been around back then, but his own reputation might still be fresh enough among the locals to give Leland pause about doing business with him. On the other hand, it helped remove suspicion Cliff might be working undercover. He was about to find out which side of the trust issue Leland would land on.

"That *used* to be me. Now I'm just an entrepreneur looking to provide a service. Consider the cash in that duffel bag as another token of my sincerity."

"How much?"

"Didn't count it."

"Where the hell you get it?"

"From you through Parker."

"What?"

"I'm guessing, but it's probably his Mule Air tax-free retirement fund."

"No shit."

"None whatsoever. So, how about my proposition?"

"I'll think on it and be in touch. As for the story, remind me never to get a chick pissed at me."

"Okay. In the meantime, you want that stuff moved?"

The look Leland sent Cliff's way said, *Back off,* better than he'd ever seen it done. He put his hands on the card table and scooted forward in the chair. "If your boys will help me get my chariot turned around, I'll be on my way."

CLIFF WOULD HAVE NEVER believed it, but two hours later the LTD was still in one piece, sort of, as he left the dry riverbed via a well-worn dirt ramp up to the highway. He was thirsty, hungry, and horny. On the way to his motel was El Barstool, a popular watering hole that served ice-cold beer, greasy cheeseburgers, mounds of French fries and onion rings, and bowls of fire-breathing chili. Two objectives down. Whether he could fill the third was anybody's guess.

He drank the last of the water Leland had given him and peered over his shoulder to check for oncoming traffic when his phone rang. He didn't recognize the number, but he had to answer every call to find out what kinds of opportunities might await

"Yates."

An unfamiliar voice said, "Got a job for you."

"Do we need to meet?"

"Nah. Simple game of hide and seek."

"As in, someone's hiding that you're seeking?"

"I only got a name. Need everything you can get, but quick."

"Then you're wasting our time."

"Say again?"

"The name, you idiot."

"Nick Phillips. Call this number when you have something."
Click.

Cliff stared out the dusty, bug-splattered windshield with the long crack down the middle that he hardly noticed any more. Might that have been Parker? The guy Cliff had just sandbagged with Leland? Was this call a complication? An opportunity? Or both?

This needed some thought, which he always did better with a few beers. He drove to the bar, ordered the heart-attack-on-a-plate combo and carried his first beer to the last booth. It was dark enough in the corner that he might not have to spring for a room if he got lucky later.

Later, belly full, his third beer in hand, and with no chick under the table to take his mind off business, he was pondering his next move when his phone rang. This time the one and only voice of the Balloon Bitch left no doubt that things might be getting even more complicated. Or opportune.

"What can I do for you, Mrs. McAllister?"

"If you can guarantee the same customer satisfaction you produced on our previous arrangement, I have another item I'd like you to handle."

"If I can't, you owe me nothing."

"You can count on that. It has come to my attention that someone has been snooping around the airport where my husband kept the plane. We've had the wreckage stored there temporarily until the salvage company can pick it up. I want to know who is interested and why. Can you handle that?"

Better than you would ever believe, bitch. "Yes, ma'am."

"Do you need a retainer?"

"I trust you."

She laughed, but Cliff got the distinct impression it had nothing to do with funny. "I thought you were much smarter than that, Mr. Yates. Goodbye."

Cliff tossed his phone on the table and signaled the bartender for another beer. The events of the past few weeks might well go down in his personal history as the chapter titled "Game Changer." Most intriguing at the moment was why two conspirators separately wanted information on one half of the dynamic duo, and how Cliff might be able to use that knowledge to his advantage.

He thought about that a bit and decided to offer pro bono the intel he already had on Phillips. It would be a small investment that might pay big dividends. If he could only—

"You're in my booth, mister."

And there stood about 5'6" of all woman, most of the good parts barely concealed, holding a tray with two frosty mugs of beer and two shots. Normally at no loss for banter, Cliff couldn't gain control of his tongue.

She smiled, nice teeth with one slightly crooked incisor. "That's okay. We don't need to do much talkin'. Scoot over."

CHAPTER TWENTY-THREE

Tommy Lee opened the rear door to his trailer for the first time in a couple of weeks and knew immediately one of those anomalies had paid a visit.

He stared at the floor below the slot in the front door. Where the mail should be.

And at a neat stack of envelopes on the dining table. Where it shouldn't be. Like a message, maybe?

We tossed your trailer and wanted you to know it.

He walked down the hallway to the second bedroom and peered past the doorjamb.

Cardboard boxes thrown on the bed, the closet door open, and his duster hanging from the middle of the rod rather than the end foretold loss of his laptop and the Mule Air cash long before he peered into the dark corner and saw the panel lying on the floor and the gaping, empty cutout in the wall.

Some sonofabitch had his ticket and was punching the shit out of it.

With the thought that he might as well have a cold one while being screwed front, back, and sideways, he returned to the kitchen, snatched a beer out of the fridge and plopped down at the dining table.

Beth would give him the money, but Tommy Lee had jeopardized the low-profile nature of Leland's gig. If the biker found out why the drugs were lost, and Tommy Lee wasn't flying the airplane because he'd sabotaged it, money wouldn't buy back Leland's trust. Nothing would.

Tommy Lee's temporary sterile cell phone began vibrating in his pocket. He pulled it out, recognized the caller ID as the private investigator Beth had used trying to nail McAllister's balls to his chair at the cancer center. The same PI Tommy Lee had called. Why she didn't want to reveal his name made no sense. The guy was a specialist and even had a few billboards around town. "Speak."

"I'm not complaining about easy jobs, but you owe me my standard minimum."

"I owe you nothing unless I get something in return."

"Then try this on for size."

Tommy Lee's heart tried to double-thump out of his chest as he listened to Yates' report.

Nick Phillips, the guy poking around Stillwater, was the same investigator who unraveled the Larchmont conspiracy a year ago. And he was working with Lawson's mistress? Coming after him? And they have the drugs?

Gotta be the same guy who found the balance weight. Sonofabitch.

Yates reminded him that his terms usually included a down payment, but under the circumstances Tommy Lee owed him nothing.

"Why not? What circumstances?"

"You probably won't be around long enough to pay me. And here's some free advice: Watch your back." *Click.*

With sweating hands, Tommy Lee dialed Beth's private number and tried to slow his breathing.

She answered on the second ring. "Why haven't you returned my calls?"

"What calls?"

"Three. To your cell phone."

"I asked you not to use that number, Beth. The guy who used to have it has left the building as far as everyone else is concerned, remember?"

"Okay, okay, you're right. I got a call from—"

"Yates?"

Silence for a moment, then, "How did you know?"

"Because he's got a reputation with lots of parts to it, not the least of which is the combination of being very good at what he does and not very discriminating about what that is."

They compared calls and agreed that Yates had gathered that information pretty damn quick to have started from scratch. They didn't know what that meant to them, but they had to do something, didn't know what that should be, and they needed to meet. Tommy Lee came up with a new join-up plan that didn't include renting airplanes and SUVs. Tonight, maybe. He hung up and sat very still in the dark trailer.

Why not just abandon everything? He had a pickup truck; a trailer not worth the gasoline to torch it; a debt to a drug dealer not known for violence but no stranger to it; and some guy on his tail that he'd heard about, who never gave up, and who probably had Leland's drugs and a chunk of lead that tied Tommy Lee and Beth to murder.

But after a few moments of trying to visualize a life on the run from multiple threats, he decided that his only option was to follow through with his original plan.

In his possession, the balance weight provided his only protection.

In the hands of anyone else, it left him totally vulnerable.

CAITLIN SIPPED THE CHARDONNAY and said to her waiter, "May I have a word, Raphael?"

His eyes registered the surprise she expected at hearing his name from a customer he'd served but once. "Certainly. What may I do for you?"

"Lean closer." When he did, losing none of his reserved bearing in the process, she told him of her expected dinner guest and that their meal was to be a very private affair, which was why she insisted on this table so far removed from the more crowded section of the restaurant. "We may be here for a while, and in consideration of your giving special attention not only to our meal but the solitude we require, you may expect a substantial gratuity."

"Thank you, but rest assured my service today will be of the highest caliber with or without that presumption."

"Of course. And just so you know, my guest will insist on paying, so please avoid any embarrassment or awkwardness and place the check well outside of my reach."

Raphael nodded, turned as if his feet were on a rotating disc, and seemed to glide out of sight behind a potted plant. The Oasis was a very nice restaurant, but Raphael's obvious training and experience would fit seamlessly in any of the upscale establishments Caitlin had enjoyed with Lawson and any of her clients.

Before inviting the Balloon Bitch to dinner, Caitlin had tried to talk herself out of such foolishness. The saying, *Nothing to gain, everything to lose* kept nagging at her as she made the reservation. But it was as if she couldn't resist the opportunity to look BB in the eyes and let her know what was going to happen.

And in the background, the possibility that being confronted by her dead husband's lover would trigger in BB the irresistible urge to take matters into her own hands, which might put them directly into Caitlin's.

Precisely at 7:30 according to Caitlin's last gift from Lawson, a custom Patek Philippe, Elizabeth McAllister entered the Oasis. She spoke a few words to the hostess, who signaled for Raphael. Caitlin watched as BB followed the waiter, her eyes scanning ahead, trying to figure out where he was taking her.

It was like reading BB's mind, noting her blatant curiosity about the trollop with the audacity to suggest that BB show up for a preview of how she will soon become the laughingstock of everyone she had worked so hard to impress. Caitlin appeared to have scored a bullseye, and the fact that BB even showed up spoke volumes.

She had stayed rail thin, probably had a chef and a personal trainer. But she ought to demand a refund on that facelift Lawson had told Caitlin about, and her hands told the tale of a woman barely south of 60 trying too hard to shave off a decade or more.

When eye contact was made, Caitlin had to give BB credit for holding it together well enough to smile, just a bit, with a look that said, Is this all you got, honey?

Raphael pulled out a chair and seated BB, whose eyes never left Caitlin, even when BB ordered a vodka martini with a twist.

"Thanks for accepting my invitation, Mrs. McAllister."

"I did no such thing. My presence here is nothing more than to deliver a response to your threat, which is to tell you go pleasure yourself some other way."

"This will suffice, actually, and I know that because you're here."

"Curiosity brought me. Reading anything more into it would be a mistake."

"Curiosity about what?"

"Lawson's last bimbo. I have to admit, you're a little above his usual forgiving standards, but—"

Caitlin laughed, the special one she layered with ridicule. "Nice try, but that dog won't hunt, as Lawson used to say. I focused my sights up. Yours targeted the gutter. An airplane-mechanic who lives in a trailer park?"

"I expected a foul mouth and you don't disappoint."

Caitlin held her response as Raphael brought BB's martini. While Caitlin ordered a curried-shrimp salad with grilled watermelon, BB downed the drink in a few swallows, then ordered another and a Cobb salad. Raphael refilled Caitlin's wine glass and floated off to the kitchen.

Caitlin sipped her wine, a Mer Soliel Chardonnay, and set the glass to the side. "We can sit here and scratch each other's eyes out until they close the place, but in the end you're going to deal with a problem because you have no other option."

"Is that so?"

Caitlin nodded and told BB that she had proof of a conspiracy to murder her husband. On the surface, it wasn't working. BB kept smiling, offering a little chuckle here, an Uh huh there, an Is that right? and an occasional Do tell? But her attempt to maintain a poker face wasn't up to the task of hiding a growing concern as the noose tightened around her neck.

Caitlin finally paused with, "So, how am I doing so far?"

BB scoffed. "It's a fairy tale you'll never publish."

"We'll see about that, and strange that you would mention publishing." Caitlin opened her handbag, removed a manila envelope with the sheaf of papers and set it on the table. "Have any idea what's in there?"

"Can't wait to find out."

"You'll have to for a little bit, at least until you open it, but here's a quick summary. The contents prove a clandestine relationship between you and the mechanic that began shortly before your husband was murdered. It includes communications and money."

"Total nonsense. I'm leaving you to your fantasies."

As BB reached for her purse, Caitlin stopped her with, "No you won't, or you'll miss the best part." She took out the balance weight in the plastic baggie and laid it in her lap. "I'm going to show you something. If you make any move whatsoever to reach for it, I'll pin your hand to the table with my salad fork. You ready?"

BB laughed. "If all I can do is sit still? Absolutely."

Caitlin placed the weight on the table, moved her hand to the side, and stared into BB's eyes. In rapid succession she noted confusion, recognition, and dread.

When the weight was safely back in Caitlin's handbag, she scooted her chair closer to the table and leaned forward, encroaching on BB's personal space to prepare her for what was to come. Especially since part of it was a lie that BB would never have the guts to challenge.

Against the background murmur of a large dinner crowd, the clink of dishes and silverware, and soft music, Caitlin said, "You think you're insulated by secrecy, but that's an illusion. That half of a balance weight is a perfect match to the other half we found in a piece of Victory wreckage the NTSB missed.

"And the guy who found it? You're going to love this. He's the same investigator who tracked another case of murder by sabotage all the way into the Oval Office."

In a voice that had lost most of its former confidence, BB said, "Pure fiction."

"Speaking of which, do you read much fiction?"

"None. What does that have to do with anything?"

"How about non-fiction?"

"Look, I don't know—"

"Like maybe a recent bestseller titled *Airborne Justice?*"

"Never heard of it."

"You have now." Caitlin had removed a thumb drive from her handbag while weaving the first part of her own web around the Black Widow, and placed in on the table. "There's a copy of the eBook on there. I recommend you read it and ask yourself if the main character has the persistence to follow through on an NTSB investigation that stopped a *little bit* short. Just like before."

BB's eyes shifted down to the thumb drive and back. "If you think—"

"Thinking has nothing to do with it. Especially since I know that your fingerprints are on this balance weight. It's tied to your boyfriend and fellow conspirator Parker through the Victory, which ties a nice little bow around the real cause of Lawson's death."

BB's face blanched at the word *fingerprints*. "You can't prove one ounce of that."

"I don't have to. What I've done, however, is let you know I can contact the author of that book, who would love to write a sequel to *Airborne Justice* with more of the real-life adventures of a famous crash detective. You mentioned publishing a moment ago? That author is a reporter for a juicy rag called *American Vigilante*. He's used to working on deadline, and he can have this story published before you can fully grasp and acknowledge what you know is true, that your boyfriend got you to handle this balance weight for a very good reason."

For the first time, BB appeared to be at a loss for words. She reached for her martini, tried to drink from an empty glass, banged it down on the table, started to raise her hand, then reached for her purse. "I'll put you and everyone associated with that garbage in the poor house."

Time for the knife in the heart. "Okay, but you need to plan on doing that from prison. The NTSB will use our evidence to reopen the investigation, bring in the FBI, and prosecute you for conspiracy to murder. Capital murder. With a death penalty option."

Caitlin finished her glass of Chardonnay, wiped her lips with a napkin, and lifted a hand.

Raphael appeared out of thin air. "What may I do for you?"

Caitlin stood. "Nothing, thank you. But my dinner companion appears to be a little dumbfounded. Another martini might help. Please bring her the check and remind her that I promised she would offer a handsome gratuity for services so elegantly rendered. Good evening."

THEY NEEDED AN ISOLATED location, but all of Tommy Lee's precautions of the past couple of weeks meant little now. No sense in trying to hide their movements from people who apparently knew everything they'd been trying to keep secret.

Beth's public exposure and reputation still deserved consideration, so they had agreed to use the McAllister hangar next to Stillwater Aviation's main building at the Adobe Wings Airport. Tommy Lee parked behind the hangar out of sight of Stillwater's office just in case Leo had decided to burn a little midnight paperwork oil, unlocked the back door, stepped into the empty hangar and glanced at his watch. Beth usually arrived fashionably late, even though fashion had nothing to do with wild and crazy sex with murder sprinkled on top.

Headlights flashed through a window on the Stillwater side of the hangar and became a halogen-white glow in the windows before disappearing near the back door. A car door slammed. Beth entered the hangar, saw Tommy Lee and strode up to him. He saw her arm moving back and knew what was coming, but figured he deserved it.

She slapped him with surprising power for a woman, damn near made his eyes water. He waited for the verbal assault he expected as a footnote to the slap. When her arm went back for the second time, he stepped close and pointed an index finger right between her eyes. "Only the first one is free."

Beth lowered her arm, tears streaming down her face, and screamed, "You sonofaBITCH!"

Tommy Lee nodded, "I know, but we need to put that aside and figure out a really good next move. Can we sit down?"

Beth looked around, marched toward the makeshift break area Tommy Lee had installed along one wall with a small table, three chairs, a refrigerator, microwave, cabinet and sink. She snatched a handful of paper towels off a dispenser and wiped her eyes. "Got any mind-numbing substances over here?"

"As a matter of fact, I do." He got bottles of tequila, Triple Sec and Gran Marnier from the cabinet along with two glasses, and from the refrigerator a bottle of margarita mix and the ice bin. Using a blender on the counter by the sink, he made a batch, poured two glasses and handed one to Beth.

"I like mine with salt."

"So do I, but we're roughing it. Cheers."

They clinked glasses, and after the first sip apiece, Beth said, "I'll never forgive you for that charade you pulled with the balance weight. In bed, playing me for the fool as you set up a way to implicate me in Lawson's death."

"Lawson's murder, you mean. That you arranged and paid for. I wasn't about to be the third on your list, and I needed leverage."

"There is no list, you idiot. All that speculation about Thomas' death being the work of a black-widow wife is nothing more than the mind masturbation of those who have nothing better to do than sit in front of a computer screen and network with others of the same ilk."

"Okay. One name doesn't make a list. But two would, which brings me back to my point of leverage."

"What leverage? Or have you forgotten you are no longer in possession of the single piece of evidence that ties us both to the murder?"

"Okay, my bad. But what about your insistence that I accept your checks as payment? You could burn me, use that legal team on your payroll to skate by on some technicality and leave me rotting away in a cell."

"Looks to me like we're even, goddamn it." Beth drained the rest of her drink and handed the glass to Tommy Lee.

He refreshed their margaritas, sipped his, so cold it made his head hurt. "We can spend our time bickering, or we can figure out how to do something more than sit around waiting. Do you have any suggestions?"

"As for as the drugs, the only thing we can do. Pour some of my money on the fire."

"And how do we prevent flare-ups?"

"Flare-up, singular. The drug deal isn't about blackmail. What're they going to do? Complain to the cops? Compensate them for the loss and it's done."

"Okay, but that still leaves Lawson's mistress and her bloodhound."

Beth took a long swallow of her margarita. "And together, they create two separate problems."

Tommy Lee had seen her do that before and wondered why the frozen slush didn't seem to affect her in the least. Probably because it didn't dare. "Why separate?"

"I read that vigilante article this evening and skimmed the eBook that caused all the stir. He's good enough to put us in prison or worse. We can't sit back and ignore the threat."

"What about the gold digger?"

Beth shook her head. "She's nothing more than an opportunist. It'll cost me some money, but she'll see the wisdom in taking a one-time payoff in exchange for that goddamn balance weight. Which, by the way, keeps it out of the investigator's hands."

"Then all we have to do is go after her, which will neuter him."

"Maybe." She stood and looked down at Tommy Lee, her face and eyes drained of any warmth. "You assured me that this could be done with zero exposure. Now we're having to deal with a problem you created by not trusting me. I'm going to fix it. You, on the other hand, are going to do nothing except find out how much it's going to cost to get that drug dealer off your ass. Understood?"

Tommy Lee nodded and watched Beth walk across the empty hangar and out the door. He poured the last of the margarita into his glass, picked it up, paused, set it down. From the cupboard he got a bottle of Jack Black, tossed a few ice cubes in a glass, poured a hefty shot and sat down.

In the glow of the bourbon's sweet burn, he tried to come up with a plan to get out of this mess and remain on the right side of the grass.

And after only a few minutes, he knew that Beth's *do nothing except* wasn't going to work.

CHAPTER TWENTY-FOUR

Cliff Yates woke up without a clue where he was, what he'd been doing, or what to do next. It was as if he had been transported off the planet into an alien universe without boundaries. The last thing he remembered—oh, maybe that's it.

The chick from the bar. Named Barbie, which seemed about right. At least the body. From what Cliff could tell, this Barbie's fashion sense included nothing more than tight tops, jeans, and cowboy boots. She came on to him stronger than a tornado, said she was the girl Willie Nelson had talked about in that movie. What movie? Oh, you know the one, where he tells someone about a gal who could suck the chrome off a trailer hitch. Cliff had laughed, told her to prove it, and goddamn!

That was how long ago? He opened an eye, just a little, and closed it.

Okay, the sun's up. Morning after? The morning after that? Who the hell knew?

Quickest way to find out was to check his phone. If he still had it. Where—?

A beep broke through the fog, which he recognized as due in part to a binge involving alcohol, the most obvious cause for the condition of his mouth. Nasty.

The beep again, the one his phone used to tell him about a

call. Or was it a text? Or a low battery? Way too many beeps in modern life, drove him crazy trying to keep them all straight.

He moved a little, decided it wouldn't hurt to try it again, managed to sit up and open his eyes.

Jesus. What the hell happened in here?

It was his motel room, probably, but with the worst redecorating job he'd ever seen.

He glanced to his left at the bed, pulled back the covers over a lump and yup, there she was. Miss Chrome Sucker.

Lord almighty. Boundless enthusiasm in a sexy little package.

Cliff got out of bed, went to the bathroom, then to the mini-bar. He drank a quart of water and searched for his phone, still emitting feeble beeps. At least one was the low-battery warning. He found his charger, connected the phone and discovered a voicemail.

A woman's voice said, "Mr. Yates, please return this call as soon as you can."

The voice was familiar. He didn't recognize the number, but that wasn't unusual. Most of his clients had ample reason to remain anonymous until they'd hired him. And sometimes even after. He didn't care in the least as long as the bills had Ben Franklin's portrait on them.

When Cliff finally climbed out of the shower, the lump in the bed still showed no signs of life. Except for the one eye he could see, which appeared to be not quite closed. It gave him the strange feeling that the eye might be tracking him.

Thirty minutes later in the motel restaurant, Cliff figured he might survive as well after a country breakfast platter and three cups of coffee. He asked the waitress for a refill, picked up his phone and glanced around to confirm that the booths closest to him were still unoccupied. The woman who left the message—had to be the Balloon Bitch—wasted no time.

"What took you so long?"

"I was being de-chromed. Who are you and what do you want?"

"A previous client with another job. When can we meet?"

"Name the time and place."

She did, and it sounded like she had some experience with arranging private meetings. GPS coordinates, yet. He waved to the server for his check, paid in cash, hurried out to the LTD and entered the destination in his portable navigator. It was still in New Mexico, but the lady liked seclusion. Cliff had to get moving if he wanted to be there before she arrived, a normal precaution he'd learned to take.

An hour and a half later, Cliff turned the LTD off the highway onto a dirt road. The woman had warned him that it would be a little rough, but no problem. He'd driven in a disappearing river with his trusty Ford.

After about three miles, he coasted to a stop and stared out the dust-covered windshield at a line of trees. The road should turn left to parallel the tree line and a dry riverbed for about a quarter mile and then make a hard right to cross it.

His portable GPS didn't show the road, but the distance to the coordinates of the meeting site confirmed he was—hello, what's this? Dust behind him in the rearview signaled a visitor. He flipped off the hammer tab on the shoulder rig and loosened the Colt in the holster.

The car was really moving, turned out to be a Range Rover that swerved off the road around him without slowing and signaled with two beeps of the horn.

Cliff followed a ways back and pulled under the trees about 20 yards from where the vehicle had stopped beside the river bed. The occupant climbed out, the Balloon Bitch in the flesh—figuratively speaking—wearing what appeared to be outdoor clothing that had never seen the outdoors. Cliff approached her and stopped a few feet away.

"Good morning, Mrs. McAllister."

"Mr. Yates. Would you join me, please?" She gestured to the passenger side of the Range Rover and slipped into the driver's seat.

He got in, shifted in the seat to face her, and noted what looked like a folded rental contract sticking out of the driver's side sun visor. Interesting. His heart almost came out of his chest when she suddenly reached under the seat. But before he could go for the Colt, she lifted up a plastic shopping bag and pulled out two black boxes about two inches wide by three inches tall and an inch thick. Cliff recognized them immediately and knew this wasn't just another surveillance job.

She held up both body wire detectors. "Pick one."

He did.

She turned hers on and motioned for him to do the same. "Either one of these finds anything to vibrate about, we're done. Agreed?

"You bet. Why are we being so sneaky?"

"Because we need to be. I hired you to obtain photographic evidence my husband was having an affair, one that he had successfully kept secret for too long. It took you a few weeks to finish the job, which told me you're a competent investigator. I'm not sure how private you are, but for the moment that will remain an open question.

"Then I asked for information about who was snooping into the crash of my husband's airplane, and you completed that in less than twenty-four hours. Which makes me suspicious, but maybe that's a good way to be."

"None of that answers my question."

"How are you at wet work?"

Uh-oh. Be very careful here. "Excuse me?"

"That's what you call it, right?"

"That's what I call what?"

APPREHENSIVE ABOUT MAKING THE call, Nick had been pacing around his motel room for about a half hour. He needed two crucial pieces of information and no way to get them without asking for help. Assuming that his recent Skype session with James Dickson meant their mutual professional animosity was truly a thing of the past, Nick finally sank into the armchair and dialed the number.

James answered with, "Should I tape this?"

"Hopefully not. It's going to be public record sooner or later, but I could really use a sneak preview. You know I'll never do anything that jeopardizes your position with the NTSB. And we're buddies."

James chuckled. "Hold on a minute."

Nick heard sounds of movement, a muffled voice saying something about taking a private call for a moment, and a door closing.

"What is it this time?"

"I'm running some ballistic trajectory studies for a client. To validate my findings, I need the location of that Victory breakup and a copy of the debris-field map. Can you help me with that?"

"Nick, if this comes back to me—"

"It won't. How about it?"

James finally agreed to use his personal email address to send Nick a PDF of the map and the geographical coordinates of the last Air Traffic Control radar sweep on the Victory. "I'll expect to see your name in the news before too long. The headline will be: 'American Vigilante Dispenses Airborne Justice Again.' I do not expect to see my name mentioned."

"Not to worry. This is very low profile and it'll stay that way."

James laughed. "That'll be the day," and hung up.

Memories of the Larchmont investigation were never too far below the surface of Nick's consciousness. One of them rose up now, when he was waiting for the package with the envelope the trooper found in the mechanic's jacket after his death in the automobile accident.

The thrill of putting pieces of a jigsaw puzzle together with a series of tiny discoveries had an addictive side to it. In this case, Nick didn't expect to receive from James anything like the key that solved the Larchmont case, but hopefully it would begin the process of unraveling a tale of conspiracy to murder.

He hadn't dialed the next number in so many years he'd lost count, but something told him it would still be a good one.

"Dr. Millbanks."

Nick had to swallow hard to get his voice to work. "Is this the same Rebecca Millbanks I once knew when I was an undergraduate student in USC's Aviation Safety Program?"

"We'll have to see. Is this the handsome devil who broke the heart of a teaching assistant on the fast track to a doctorate in aerodynamics?"

"It appears we may have verified the past connection."

"Just so. And to what do I owe the honor of a surprise call after all these years?"

"I need your help."

"That's where we left off the last time. I've never met a student who needed more."

"It's the same old me, I guess. What are my chances?"

"Let's hear it first."

Nick explained that by no later than the day after tomorrow he could have in Rebecca's hands the last known position of a Victory that broke up in flight, a map of the debris field, and the data readout from the flight data recorder. Could she write the code to generate a series of postulated ruddervator trajectories and their corresponding ground-impact predictions?

Rebecca laughed. "I thought this was going to be something difficult. I'll pass this along to one of my doctoral candidates. For no credit, of course."

Not a good idea. "Uh, it would be better if—"

"Relax, Nick. Just kidding. I read about your latest career change, by the way, and since this probably means you're on some kind of manhunt, I'll do it myself. Do I get a special badge?"

Nick really was going to find that journalist-turned-best-selling author and cut his nuts off. "You don't want one. They tend to draw unwanted attention."

"Good point. Where do I send the info?"

Nick gave Rebecca his email address, exchanged pleasantries for a bit, thanked her for the favor and leaned back in the armchair, the memories on an unbidden rewind.

His only objective from the first day in college had been to become an NTSB aviation accident investigator. The on-site kind, who sifts through wreckage and finds out what went wrong. All the formal training required to get there was nothing more than an obstacle in his path, to hurdle, bypass, or otherwise negotiate around as he pursued his goal.

With a degree in aviation safety, Nick was like a general practitioner. Rebecca, on the other hand, had as little interest in practical application of aerodynamic principles as he had in theory. She'd have to come out of the ether to produce what

Nick needed, but not for long. If what he remembered was still accurate, she could probably do this in less than a day.

The most reliable data in the aftermath of an inflight breakup came from two sources: aircraft performance parameters at the moment of the breakup as captured by the flight data recorder, or FDR, commonly called a black box, and the debris field where the physical location and orientation of the pieces had been carefully documented.

A major problem here was that airplanes the size of the Victory weren't typically equipped with a flight data recorder. Luckily, Nick had an alternate method for defining the starting point for this analysis. Although less precise than an FDR, Air Traffic Control tracking data could be used to determine with reasonable accuracy the airplane's flight parameters and position in three-dimensional space when it came apart.

Each piece of the airplane followed a ballistic trajectory from the point of breakup to the ground, during which time the only forces acting on them were the retarding effect of the air known as drag, wind speed and direction, and gravity. Trajectory analysis was far from rocket science, and the governing equations were well known. That said, the devil was in the variations, like the ones that caused the left ruddervator to go missing.

Rebecca's analysis would probably begin with finding the ballistic coefficient of the ruddervator, calculated by knowing the weight and defining characteristics of span, chord, thickness, and the drag coefficient. She'd use these to estimate ballistic coefficients for various orientations of the ruddervator to the airstream at the moment of separation. And that's where it would get tricky and require her expertise to avoid the garbage-in, garbage-out syndrome.

Like any flight control, ruddervators were shaped like

airfoils and generated lift, which wasn't accounted for in ballistic calculations. And after separation, the Victory's ruddervator almost certainly tumbled around as it fell, constantly changing its orientation to the relative wind and adding yet another variable to the problem by randomly varying the drag coefficient.

The only way Nick could wrap his mind around all of this techno-babble was to think of Rebecca's analysis as a series of runs with computer programs like BREAKUP or BALLISTIC if she had authorization to use them, or more likely with existing, readily available code and altering it to suit her purposes.

Each run would simulate the ballistic trajectory of a ruddervator at a given point in space, with a known altitude and velocity vector and an assumed constant average value for the ballistic coefficient. Varying the ballistic coefficients for successive runs then accounted for variables and created a series of ground-impact predictions to define the most likely area where the ruddervator might be found.

The rest would be relatively simple and exercise Nick's practical expertise: plot that area on a map and go look for the damn thing.

TOMMY LEE KEPT THE Maule at low altitude from the time he departed Adobe Wings until the GPS read two miles, when he climbed to 1000 feet above the desert and turned to put his destination about 30 degrees off to his left side. Leland had told him there was a runway there, hard to see, but that appeared to be an optimistic statement.

He circled the spot, and soon noted a dust trail approaching from the west. No way to tell who it was, so he waited until two off-road pickups charged up to where the runway was supposed to be. One stopped, the other continued about a half mile and skidded to a stop in a cloud of tan dust that immediately began drifting, a handy indicator of the wind direction.

A figure got out of the first pickup and stood in front of the bumper, but facing 90 degrees to it. With both arms, he gestured toward the other truck, a motion that Tommy Lee interpreted as a signal to *Line up this way.* He slowed, lowered partial flaps, and flew a low pass offset to the right of a line between the two trucks.

Well, I'll be damned.

The trucks pointed at the ends of a runway that looked like nothing except more desert, but it was hardly that. No rocks, cactus, rough terrain or anything else the Maule and the balloon tires couldn't handle. *If* he kept the airplane lined up in the middle of the cleared strip, which didn't appear any wider than about 30 feet. Get too far to either side and he'd have a problem. He also noted a stand of trees close to the end of the airstrip where the second pickup had stopped. Based on the wind direction, that would be the approach end of the runway.

He flew one more pass right down the runway to confirm he'd have almost no crosswind on final. A 180-degree climbing left turn put him on a downwind leg. Fuel on the fullest tank, mixture rich, prop full increase and the flaps full down, he turned final and pushed on the right rudder while he added left aileron to enter a slip, a handy maneuver that moved the nose out of the way so he could see better. It also helped control airspeed during a steeper approach to provide safe clearance from the trees close to the approach end.

Adjusting pitch and power to land just past an imaginary line extending from the centerline of the first pickup, he held the cross controls until a few seconds prior to touchdown, when he eased off the right rudder, leveled the wings, and closed the throttle. Without trying to finesse it, he touched down firmly in a three-point landing and pulled the yoke all the way back in his lap to plant the tailwheel on the ground. He barely needed any braking to stop after a short landing roll.

After repositioning close to the first pickup and pointed down the runway, he turned off the avionics master switch and shutdown the engine with the mixture control. When the prop came to rest, he turned off the ignition and the aircraft master switch, unfastened his restraint harness, lifted the backpack off the right seat and climbed out.

The driver of the first pickup approached. He had a very large pistol stuck in his waistband. "You packin'?" When Tommy Lee shook his head, the guy pointed at the backpack. "What's in there?"

"For Leland. His eyes only."

The guy seemed to be deciding whether that was a good-enough answer, then pointed at the passenger side of the pickup and got in the driver's seat. Tommy Lee hadn't even closed the door when the guy floored it. For the next 20 minutes they powered through the desert on a line visible only to the driver. Every time it appeared they would end up taking a boulder head-on, or a prickly pear cactus in the tires, or get hung up on the oil pad or transmission by a tall rock, the guy jerked the wheel to miss the obstacle and kept on going.

They stopped in the middle of nowhere and the driver led the way on foot into more rugged terrain with climbs, descents, and sudden turns along another invisible line. Leaving a rocky defile, they entered a flatter area with an encampment of tents under sparse trees.

The guy motioned for Tommy Lee to wait and walked over to what appeared to be the main tent, spoke to a man sitting at a table, turned, waved to Tommy Lee to come on. He entered the tent, put the backpack on the table, and sat in a folding metal chair.

After a moment of continued attention to a ledger of some kind, the man closed it and said, "You know who I am?"

Tommy Lee nodded.

"A few years ago when one of my guys brought me a proposition from a stranger about moving product a safer way, I had to think long and hard about that. Did some checking, tested the guy out with a few bogus deliveries. But hey, he did what he said he would. On time. No muss, no fuss. We moved on to real product, working great, and suddenly the fellow turns monumentally stupid. Am I to believe that's you?"

"Unfortunately."

"What're you doing here?"

"Bringing you this." Tommy Lee slid the backpack closer to Leland. "Thirty grand, small bills, used, unmarked. I'm guessing that's enough."

Leland unzipped the backpack, pulled out a stack of bills, thumbed through it. "We could call that square except for one thing."

"And that is?"

"I'm running a business. The delivery you *didn't* make put me in a bind. I don't provide a customer service line, but you can bet I heard about it soon enough. I also don't stock a bunch of inventory, so my production schedule has to respond. Manufacturing product is a tricky, and I can't do it on main street."

"I can get more money."

"You're dumber than you look. I just told you it isn't about money."

"Then what can I do to make it right?"

Leland leaned back in his chair and folded his arms. "I'm

telling you straight up I don't normally break bones and such nonsense because it's not good for business. But there's one exception. When I think it's not a matter of stupidity, but betrayal."

"I didn't—"

"Shut up. I know that. But what you did was, you got me spoiled."

Tommy Lee saw where this was going and knew that the move to simplify his life was going to do just the opposite. "With Mule Air."

Leland laughed. "So that's what you call it? That's great. And yeah, it's a valuable addition to my under-the-radar philosophy. You want to do something for me? Voluntarily, you understand, I'm not going to bring out the sledgehammers, get Mule Air back up and running."

Tommy Lee's brain entered into a rapid-fire *I-should-do-this-no-I-shouldn't* daisy-petal sequence that ended with, "I've got to settle a few things first."

Leland raised his eyebrows with a *no-shit?* expression. "From what I've heard, you got your work cut out for you."

A sudden feeling of doom settled over Tommy Lee, like he was about to enter the great unknown. "Like what?"

"Oh, nothing big. Just another dude who brought me the product you lost and wants to take over Mule Air's contribution to my business. A wealthy black widow way too close to you for comfort. A woman scorned out for revenge, and some guy looking to hang your stuffed head in his living room and nail your hide to his barn door."

Tommy Lee swallowed hard, his throat so dry it felt like he'd swallowed some of the dirt under his feet. "Got any water?"

Leland waved his hand and mouthed *Water* to the dude with the pistol.

Tommy Lee took the offered bottle, twisted off the cap, and sipped it slowly so his brain could catch up with the speed at which his life was deteriorating. Finally he said, "So now you've got the drugs *and* my money?"

The look on Leland's face sent a clear warning. "It isn't *your* money. Consider it a late fee. And about Mule Air?"

"What about it?"

"Let's just see which one of you subcontractors comes up with the better deal."

On the harrowing return trip to the Maule, Tommy Lee didn't hold on as firmly as he did on the way out because it didn't matter. Death in an overturned pickup would be a blessing.

The only way the drugs could have ended up in Leland's hands was if they passed through the investigator's. And Phillips had now decided to make a play for bringing Mule Air back to life? No way, which meant the missing link from the hidden compartments in the Victory to Leland wasn't missing at all.

Once airborne and headed back to Adobe Wings, Tommy Lee had no doubt that his only escape from this mess was to take control of his own destiny. He glared at his reflection in one of the gauges on the instrument panel.

You better do this right, asshole.

CLIFF SAT ALONE IN Barbie's usual booth, at least according to her, and polished off the last of his draft beer. One finger raised in the direction of CB, the bartender, got him a second boilermaker in less than a minute. The guy was really good, or maybe really bored, since it was not even 4 p.m. and the regular shit-kicker crowd was still digging ditches or laying concrete or taping and floating drywall in a new house somewhere. Cliff tossed down the bourbon and chased it with about a fourth of the draft, telling himself to slow down but not listening to his own advice.

What the hell was he going to do now? His PI gig had been paying the bills, if barely, since he was kicked off the force. Then the wealthiest client he'd ever get handed him a cut-and-dried nail-the-husband-as-he's-nailing-the-girlfriend job that turned out to be uncut and very wet. No local motels with this guy. He'd climb in his airplane and fly off somewhere, Cliff scrambling to get where he needed to be to snap those juicy photos.

But he did it and fell in lust with the girlfriend. He'd never seen a woman so close up and yet so far out of his reach. Drove him crazy. He even tried to make something happen with a sell-her-the-photos scam and ended up with a pistol in his face. Talk about surprised.

But that was nothing like the shock of her phone call and the meeting, Cliff trying to gain control of his tongue when she offered him a job helping with an elaborate scheme involving an aircraft accident investigator.

Then the drug connection and Mule Air and Leland and now this. Full circle.

Cliff had no clue how he felt because he didn't feel much of anything. Except maybe excitement, which scared him to think about hiring someone to put Caitlin Monroe and Nick Phillips on the midnight run to nowhere. He'd be able to leave all of his previous life behind with the money BB offered, easy street from here on out. And as often happened when decisions presented a crossroads, Cliff's internal dialogue began.

So, why are you hesitating, Cliff?

Because to hire someone puts me in the middle. If either end wants to sever connections, I'm the target.

So what? The world belongs to those who seize the moment.

And to the lucky ones. I've never—

Yeah, yeah. Blame it on chance and never admit you've been a loser since day one. Or you could change that right now. All you have to do is accept a new definition of luck.

Like when preparation and—?

That's the one. You're not so dumb after all.

Cliff drank more beer, set the mug on a soggy bar napkin and stared at it. Condensation coated the sides, looked like one of those beer commercials. Then he noticed where the foam layer was and the voice piped up again.

You're thinking it's half-empty, aren't you? No wonder you're nothing but a sleazy private dick with a few bucks in his pocket, no past to speak of, and no future worth even thinking about.

Cliff felt the anger rising up, the urge to lash out and shut that voice up once and for all, but he was too late.

Good. Now channel that and make it work for you.

He drained the last of the beer and leaned out of the booth to signal CB for another. And there she was, Miss Chrome Sucker, leaning against the bar and peering at him over the top of her sunglasses.

Cliff held up the empty mug and motioned with two fingers of his other hand. Might as well take advantage of this opportunity as the first priority of the new *Yates Enterprises.*

Watching her bring their drinks, unfamiliar warmth spread through him. He couldn't remember the last time he'd felt anything like it. Lust, yes, but this went way beyond a physical reaction because it affected his brain rather than his crotch.

She slid into the booth beside him, kissed him on the cheek, and smiled.

A little piece of Cliff zinged and seemed to foretell that his life was about to change in more ways than one.

CHAPTER TWENTY-FIVE

Nick taxied to the approach end of Runway 22 at the Double Eagle II Airport west of Albuquerque and completed his pre-takeoff checks just as the eastern sky behind the Sandia Mountains began to lighten with the approaching dawn. A forecast of clear skies and light winds along the route to the Dry Springs Municipal Airport near Phoenix allowed him to operate under visual flight rules and not talk to air traffic control if he didn't want to. Which he usually didn't. Just himself, his trusty steed, and except for the thrum of the engine through his noise-canceling headset, a relaxing silence he'd learned to cherish.

After visually checking the traffic pattern for other aircraft, he announced his departure on the common traffic advisory frequency, taxied onto the runway, eased the throttle forward and took off to the southwest into a gorgeous purple-black sky.

When level at his final altitude of 12,500 feet, he adjusted the engine manifold pressure, propeller RPM, and fuel mixture for a high-speed cruise. Normally he'd choose a more economical option, but today he didn't care about using the extra fuel because Caitlin was paying for it.

Stabilized in cruise and established on the centerline of the V190 airway course of 240 degrees, he made a final adjustment to the elevator trim and engaged the autopilot to hold his altitude and course. After a few more minutes tweaking the mixture and scanning the engine instruments for any indication of something not quite right, he removed a notebook from a chart pocket sewn into the sidewall upholstery and opened it to a page with the results of a Web search the previous evening.

The Grand Canyon Council of the Boy Scouts of America covered 22 districts serving communities of southwestern, central, eastern and northern Arizona. Nick had focused his search on the Thunderbird District, encompassing an area to the north of Phoenix near Peoria and Glendale, looking for names and contact information for Troop Scoutmasters.

With no idea what to expect, he had a list of names in no particular order and intended to start at the top and continue until a Scoutmaster agreed to meet with him. As far as Nick was concerned, that should mean he'd be sitting down with the first one for coffee in about three hours.

How could the guy resist Nick's proposal? There probably wasn't a merit badge for what he had in mind, but a day of hiking, the gift of a handheld GPS navigation device for each scout, a picnic lunch and a pizza party had to be an irresistible donation to the morale of the Troop.

And it just might help the morale of the Monroe-Phillips coalition as well.

Nick had considered landing at the airport in Wickenburg, Arizona, rather than Dry Springs for the same reason he'd parked his airplane at Double Eagle II rather than Adobe Wings. Best not to make access to his ride any easier than it already was by being in the same states frequented by a mechanic-turned-killer who was really good at sabotaging airplanes. Parker would have to show himself a lot more than he had so far, and that alone provided Nick some protection.

But in the end he decided this trip wouldn't draw any

attention, and hopefully he wouldn't be in Arizona long enough for Parker to find out where he'd gone or what he might be up to. Dry Springs was a lot closer to Phoenix and the Victory crash site, and he had a straight shot from the airport to Glendale and Peoria on US 60.

After an uneventful flight and landing at Dry Springs, he parked the airplane on the ramp close to the fixed-base operator who sold fuel, offered light maintenance, and provided other services to transient pilots.

Returning to the scene of his failed attempt to gain legal access to the Victory wreckage and logbooks added a little excitement he didn't expect, especially when the owner greeted him with eyes that seemed to say, *I know what you did here, so watch your step.*

Nick paid in advance for a spot in the hangar and asked for a fill-up, which usually got the courteous attention of FBO owners. Fuel sales were the bread and butter of making their operation successful. Based on the owner's reaction to the order, the tactic appeared to grant Nick a little slack.

In the pilot's lounge he bought a bottle of water and sat down with his cell phone and the list of local scouting contacts. The first two calls went directly to voicemail. Nick left a brief message with each, but the third number reached a real-person Scoutmaster named Darrell who seemed open to donations of any kind that would benefit his Scouts.

Nick rented a car and met Darrell at the Corner Bakery and Café in Peoria. After introductions, a cup of coffee, and a slice of cinnamon creme cake that Nick thought might be too addictive to risk a second piece, they got down to the business at hand.

"So," said Darrell, "you want to pay for a fun day outing for my scouts, give each one a gift of some kind, and stuff them on pizza and Cokes all in return for helping you with an activity you promise will not violate our law."

"That's correct. They'll be just as trustworthy, loyal, helpful, friendly, courteous, kind, obedient, cheerful, thrifty, brave, clean, and reverent at the end of the day as they were at the beginning."

Darrell smiled. "I'm impressed."

"Don't be." Nick showed him the little cheat-sheet card he had palmed with the scout law written on it, and they both laughed. Then he explained how each scout would be provided a handheld GPS with a unique pre-programmed course, all of which together formed a search grid of a moderately rugged area between Morristown and Wittmann on Highway 60 and the stretch of I-70 between New River and Rock Springs.

"Whoa," said Darrell. "How many square miles is that?"

"I'm not talking about the whole area, just a part of it that I will have narrowed down in advance."

"Where the gold from a train robbery by Butch Cassidy and the Sundance Kid might be buried, perhaps?"

"Don't I wish. You remember reading about a fatal airplane crash about a month ago?"

Darrell pondered that for a moment. "Uh . . . yeah. Some doctor with a cancer center in New Mexico."

"That's the guy."

"But the NTSB searched it all, right? What is there left to find?"

"I'm hoping the scouts of your troop are going to help me answer that question."

"When do you want to do this?"

"If I get the information I expect this afternoon, it could be as early as tomorrow."

"Well . . . the boys aren't back in school yet, but I might not be able to round up very many on such short notice."

"How many do you have in your Troop?"

"Typical size is between thirty and fifty. I've got thirty-seven on the email list, but not all of those are active at the moment."

"How about an email blast asking how many can commit to an exciting day of fun and adventure in the wilderness?"

Darrell chuckled. "I can do that."

They agreed that Darrell would canvas the troop and get back to Nick before the end of the day. He'd plan on about 20 boys. If fewer showed up, the troop would still get a donation of that many GPS units. More, and some of the boys would have to double up on a unit during the search, but he'd make sure that every Scout received one.

"How about transportation?" asked Nick. "It'd be really good to drive off-road and get as close as we can to the search area."

Darrell laughed. "This is Arizona. Four-wheel-drive vehicles rule."

"Most excellent."

They exchanged email addresses and agreed to confirm their plans as soon as possible and coordinate a rendezvous location. After Darrell left, Nick powered up his laptop, hoping that James Dickson and Rebecca Millbanks came through for him today. They hadn't yet, but he trusted them to do what they promised.

And when they did, he'd do his best to fill in the last piece of this murder puzzle, hand it to Caitlin, and wish her the best of success in yanking out a black widow's fangs.

UP SINCE 4 A.M., Caitlin finally reached her tolerance for pacing as the first light of dawn began adding shades of gray to the view out the window.

She had never known anyone who could slip as swiftly and completely into a mood of obsessive impatience as she often did. If she were inclined to explain it, which she wasn't, the blame would inevitably be assigned to others upon whom she relied and who were not capable of doing much of anything up to her standards.

In this case, her restlessness had nothing to do with lack of faith in Nick Phillips. Or with Yates, who as far as Caitlin was concerned, had fulfilled the terms of his employment and was back to snapping pictures of unfaithful husbands and wives.

The culprit was a pervasive sense of unfinished business. Not with BB, who would be dealt with soon enough, but with the mechanic who had planned and carried out a murder in the first degree and wouldn't pay for it except by extension from the fate of the woman who had hired him.

Which meant nothing. What the hell would he care if the Balloon Bitch lost some or all of her social standing? He'd never participated in any part of a black-tie existence before now and wouldn't in the future, no matter what happened.

No, this was entirely personal, no less than her decision to confront BB face-to-face. That had felt really good, and so would this.

She dressed in a black turtleneck, jeans, lightweight hiking boots, and a dark blue windbreaker. After checking for a full magazine, a round in the chamber and that the safety was off, she slipped the Walther into a soft nylon paddle holster that slid inside the top of her jeans slightly to the rear of her right hip. An extra mag with seven rounds of .380 ACP hollow points went on her left hip in another paddle-style holster made to hold the mag securely and allow quick access. A third mag in her right jacket pocket added a little weight and helped flip the jacket out of the way to draw the pistol.

Walking to the Mercedes, Caitlin pondered whether she had a particular reason for caution this morning other than her ingrained commitment to self-defense. By the time she turned the key and started the engine, she realized it did.

To paraphrase a saying, when you stare into the eyes of a killer, the killer stares back. And to assume so little response to their snooping thus far meant there would be no more to come seemed reckless in the extreme. Especially when she poked the killer in the eye with a stick.

A half hour later she peered through the windshield at the front entrance of Stillwater Aviation and almost couldn't believe that Lawson had kept his Victory at this out-in-the-boonies dump. All that money he had, with access to a lot more, and this was the best he could do?

She got out of the Mercedes, unzipped her windbreaker, and approached the hangar. The unlocked door opened into a front office smelling of furniture wax and a pine-scented cleaning product. Somebody was trying, but it seemed like dressing a pig in a silk dress. From down a hallway to the left of a reception counter came a gruff, "Hello?"

"Hello yourself."

A chair scraped on the floor, then footsteps approached and a big man in coveralls stepped out of the hallway. "Can I help you?"

"I'm looking for Tommy Lee Parker."

Leo, according to the nametag on his coveralls, seemed to process that for a moment. "He doesn't work here anymore."

"Where can I find him?"

"You'll have to figure that out for yourself."

"Do you know who I am?"

Leo leaned against the jamb at the entrance into the hallway and crossed his arms. "No, but I can make a pretty good guess."

Caitlin was sure she could feel the bad vibes flowing her way. A scornful disapproval, or maybe disappointment. Judgmental, like her many foster parents, hands on hips, ready to bring out the belt. Or worse. It made her right hand ache for the comforting heft of the Walther.

But she knew it wasn't about Leo, or the adults who fouled her childhood, or anyone or anything else outside of her own skin. His attitude reminded Caitlin of the way the ghost inside her stared back from the mirror.

It wasn't Leo's fault. But it wasn't hers, either.

Then, another part of her took control before she could stop it. "Just so you know, we loved each other." She turned on a heel and walked out of the office, nagged by regret that she'd made such a pitiful attempt to earn *Daddy's* acceptance for what she was, even with no apologies.

Sitting in the Mercedes, Caitlin renewed her commitment to confront a guy who could slink around in the shadows and tamper with an airplane to murder someone. Even with no specific reason to think he'd be there, it sent a shiver of anticipation through her whole body as she departed the airport for an unnamed trailer park on the north side of I-40 to the west of Albuquerque.

TOMMY LEE WAS LOOKING at a text on his phone while driving in his truck when he heard a horn, insistent, coming closer. He glanced up just in time to swerve back into his lane as a black Mercedes whizzed past on his left within inches. Heart pounding, he screamed at himself for getting distracted and nearly meeting an air bag up close and personal.

His heart rate had barely reached normal when he stepped

into the front office of Stillwater Aviation. From the back, Leo's voice said, "Be with you in a minute."

Tommy Lee barely heard it. He sniffed, then drew in a deep breath and immediately recognized the scent. Distinctive, sensuous, familiar, and indicative of how vulnerable he was if the dynamic Phillips-Monroe duo continued its snooping.

Leo appeared in the hallway. "I noticed you didn't get your tools before."

Tommy Lee nodded. "Had to leave suddenly."

"Come on back." Leo led the way to his office, opened the center drawer in his desk and pulled out an envelope. "Your last paycheck. It's from McAllister's account with us, covering the last two weeks of your employment."

Tommy Lee took it. "You sure—?"

"Yup. Not a problem." Leo extended his hand.

Tommy Lee shook it, started to ask if anyone else had been looking for him, immediately thought better of it. "I'd better get started. Thanks, Leo."

"You take care."

Tommy Lee drove his truck around to a side entrance into the main hangar workshop and backed up close to the door. He turned off the engine and stared out the windshield at the desert as his mind ran through a list of knowns, assumptions, and reasonable conclusions.

Unless Leo had taken to wearing perfume, that scent in the office was left a few minutes ago by the woman driving the car Tommy Lee almost ran off the road. It was the same fragrance from inside the Victory cabin. Countless women probably wore it. What was the chance one of them other than Caitlin Monroe happened to be in the front office of Stillwater Aviation today? Way too coincidental.

Why would she visit Stillwater?

She has to be looking for you.

Leo didn't mention it because he's a mind-your-own-business kind of guy. Tommy Lee could go back to the office and ask, but that would draw attention to the fact that he's aware of being hunted.

And why would Monroe do that? She had the balance weight and must recognize the strength of the hand she was playing against a very wealthy woman. And yet she wasn't content to wait for Beth to pay to get it back and cover up the unlawful death of her husband.

All of which meant, in spite of what Beth thought, this wasn't about the money. The sweet taste of revenge could make a person crazy. Unpredictable. And very dangerous.

Tommy Lee pulled out his phone. While waiting for Buster to pick up, his eyes roamed along the distant convergence of sky and desert.

Lots of desert.

CAITLIN FOUND THE TRAILER park and drove the length of the single dirt road to check out how many cars looked like they'd moved under their own power in the last decade. There weren't many.

At one trailer a relatively intact pickup sat in what she assumed was the front yard. She got out, adjusted the Walther forward on her hip, and walked up to the wooden steps leading to a small porch. The place looked like it could be either occupied or long-since abandoned, and there didn't seem to be any way to tell the difference between the two conditions with any trailer in the park.

As she put her foot on the first step, the inner door opened to reveal a hard-looking, ebony-faced woman in a tattered house dress with a cigarillo dangling from the corner of her mouth, a bottle of whiskey in one hand and a sawed-off shotgun with a pistol grip in the other, held muzzle down by her leg.

The woman stared at Caitlin suspicion. "Don't see many luxury cars around here. Thinking of selling it?"

Caitlin couldn't suppress a smile. "Before you make an offer, I had a fender bender once. It's all fixed now, but I wouldn't want you to think I was trying to hide anything."

"Never fear, girl. People tend to be real honest around Remmie here." She lifted the shotgun a little, looked like a Remington 12-gauge pump, and lowered it.

Caitlin glanced to her right, figured she could make it around the corner of the trailer before the woman got rid of the whiskey bottle, opened the screen door, and Remmie entered the conversation. "Now that we've got our intentions cleared up, I'm looking for Tommy Lee Parker."

"I been watching since you drove in. Didn't see you check his trailer. Think that might be a place to start?"

"Undoubtedly. If I knew which one it was."

"Ah. The girl seeks information."

Caitlin waited a moment, then slipped her hand into the pocket of her windbreaker and bought out a wallet she carried when the shoulder bag didn't go with her outfit. She slid a twenty into the space between two boards on the top step and put the wallet away.

The woman motioned to her right with the whiskey bottle. "Third one that way, but he ain't been around much lately."

Caitlin smiled again. "Just the way we sometimes like it, don't you agree?"

The woman laughed, a throaty sound laden with years of hard living. "You go on now."

"Thanks." Caitlin left the Mercedes where she'd parked it

and went to Parker's trailer, which was unoccupied and locked. She walked around to the back, tried a door, figured the lock wouldn't last more than a few sharp tugs. It appeared to have been recently damaged. Hand on the knob, she paused.

Entering this trailer doesn't make much sense. Yates had found evidence Parker might have visited the trailer recently, but nothing to indicate where he might be now. Did she expect him to leave a note with a forwarding address?

And if he was into drug dealing and had recently dabbled in murder-for-hire, his finger would probably be close to the pulse of local happenings. Feeling for things like who's snooping around, looking for him, stuff like that.

Maybe he'll come to me.

Caitlin walked back toward the front of the trailer, and as she rounded the corner saw a huge pickup with brush guards and searchlight bars parked by the Mercedes. She ducked behind the trailer, knelt and peeked around it. A big guy stood beside her car, shouting into a phone, his free arm waving around as if that would help him make a point. Caitlin couldn't hear what he was saying, but she didn't have to.

The guy walked up to the woman's trailer and climbed the steps onto the porch. He approached the front door and abruptly stopped, held both hands out to his sides and backed away. After a moment, he looked to his left toward Parker's trailer, pointed, then hurried down the steps, ran to the pickup, reached into the open driver's side door and came out with an assault rifle.

Caitlin jumped up, turned and ran into the desert in a direction she hoped would provide cover long enough to reach a patch of scrub vegetation about a hundred yards away. Halfway there, what sounded like hornets on steroids buzzed by her left ear, dust kicked up in the desert ahead, and the distinctive sound of a three-shot burst gave her an extra shot of adrenaline.

That rifle has been converted to full automatic.

She ran as hard as she ever had, abruptly changing directions, vaulting prickly pear, rocks, and short bushes as bullets struck the desert around her. After what seemed like an eternity, she reached the cover and scrambled behind it on her stomach into a shallow depression. One burst passed over her head. A few twigs and leaves landed on the ground in front of her face.

Except for the pounding of her heart resonating through her body, silence.

She peeked through the bushes. Didn't see the guy. *Gotta move while you can.*

Caitlin got up and began running as the distant sound of a big V-8 at high RPM reached out and seemed to say, *I'm coming for you.*

NICK DROVE FROM THE Corner Bakery and Café in Peoria to the Cabela's in Glendale and approached a cute, twenty-something female salesperson near a display case filled with all kinds of electronic gadgets designed for outdoor use. He explained his need for twenty handheld GPS units and asked for advice on which model to buy.

She looked at him as if he were from another planet. "Twenty? You must be planning an extra long trip. It's a lot cheaper to carry extra batteries."

"Uh . . . but I—"

"Just kidding. How much do you want to spend?"

"Cost isn't a factor, but I need to program a route between geographic coordinates."

"They all do that. When do you need them?"

"How soon can I get them?"

"Depends. I may not have twenty of the same units in stock. Do they all have to be the same model?"

"No."

"Okay. Let me—"

"And I need some help setting them up." He explained that when he took delivery, each unit needed a full charge and to be preset with a straight-line course between one of twenty pairs of geographic points. "I'll provide the coordinates, and I can probably have them sometime today."

Stacey, according to the embroidered nametag on her forest-green Cabela's knit shirt, paused a moment. "I'll have to talk to my boss about taking time away from the floor."

"Or, you could do it off duty. It'd be like overtime paid by me." When Stacey appeared skeptical about making an after-hours deal, Nick said, "Let's do this. You check inventory and get me twenty units. Mix and match, whatever. I'll pay for them right now and leave them with you. If you're willing to share a phone number, or better yet, an email address, I'll send you the coordinates. You charge and program the units this evening and bring them back here in the morning for me to pick up. Do you work tomorrow?"

Stacey nodded. "How much?"

"Two hundred bucks. Cash."

"What's this for?"

"If I tell you that—"

"Yeah, yeah. You'll have to kill me. I'll be right back."

Five minutes later, Stacey returned to the counter with the GPS units. "Follow me."

After making the purchase, Nick gave her the two Cabela's bags.

She handed him a slip of paper. "Memorize that email

address and then eat the paper. After you send me the coordinates, trash the email. The address will self-erase from your memory after twenty-four hours. We open tomorrow at nine."

Nick was smiling as he returned to the rent car. Besides being very easy on the eyes, Stacey had a playful streak. If he were only younger . . . then he twirled his wedding band and yanked his mind back from fantasyland.

Although Glendale had plenty of restaurants, Nick drove back to the Corner Bakery and Café for lunch. Well, maybe not for lunch so much as the Cinnamon Creme Cake. He found a table in a corner with an electrical outlet close by. After eating, he powered up his laptop and checked email.

How cool was this? Among the long list of annoying advertisements from online shopping websites, two gems appeared.

He opened the one from James Dickson. It read, *Remember to forget where you got this.* Nick saved the attached PDF to his desktop and opened it. Superimposed on the 1:24,000-scale USGS Baldy Mountain Quadrangle map was the official NTSB debris-field map of the area that contained the Victory wreckage. Using the zoom feature, Nick examined details of the terrain to familiarize himself with what he and his improvised team of Scout searchers would be dealing with.

McAllister had been trying to maneuver around a storm and land at a small airport northwest of Phoenix, Arizona. The aircraft passed over Lake Pleasant, then Baldy Mountain shortly before breakup. The center of an elongated debris field was located to the north of SR 74, an east-west highway between I-17 and US 60, in an area known as the Morgan City Wash.

Dickson had also noted on the map the last known position and altitude of the aircraft as shown on the radar tapes. Considering transmission delays, the breakup occurred at approximately 2700 feet above the ground. Based on the scale of the map, the debris field was no more than a mile long, consistent with the relatively short free-fall duration of the pieces from that altitude.

The email from Dr. Rebecca Millbanks said, *Next time, send me something worth my time.* She had inserted a little smiley face with the note, but Nick recognized the implicit message. Doing him this favor had bored her. He put a note in his day planner to send her an appropriate thank you. Unless her tastes had changed, a bottle of Longmorn Single Malt Scotch should do nicely.

To lay out the search grid, he needed a physical map to plot the impact points and the start and end points of the straight lines to cover the area containing them. A quick online trip to weogeo.com produced a digital copy of the Baldy Mountain Quadrangle downloaded to his computer. He copied the file to a thumb drive and motioned to his waiter.

The young man hurried over. "Yes, sir?"

"I need help with an errand. You got a break coming up?"

"No, but it's not like we're swamped with customers."

"Is there a copy place close by?"

"Heck, yeah. They're everywhere. Like daisies after a spring rain."

Nick laughed and handed him the thumb drive and three twenties. "Keep one of those for yourself plus any left over, get that file printed, in color, full size should be twenty-two by twenty-seven inches. What are you waiting for?"

The kid smiled, yanked off his apron as he ran back to the front counter, told the cashier he was taking a short break and dashed out the door.

By the time Nick had visited the restroom and refilled his

coffee from the self-serve urn, his waiter reappeared with the map.

"Was there enough left over for a bonus on top of the twenty?"

"Yes, sir. A nice one."

"Good." Nick put the flash drive back in his computer bag, spread the map out on the table and began plotting the predicted ruddervator impact points. With that done, he outlined the area in red marker, laid out the grid pattern of 20 lines and numbered them sequentially 1-20. Then he typed a list of the start and end coordinates of each line into an email addressed to Stacey and fired it off.

Next he compared the debris-field map from Dickson with the one he had made surrounding the most probable location of the ruddervator. The two impact areas were separated by nearly a mile, with the ruddervator area closer to the point at which the Victory came apart. Based on another incident of inflight breakup, that's what he expected.

On September 14, 1997, an F-117 Stealth Fighter participating in an air show was making a third high-speed pass over the airport at Essex, Maryland, when it suddenly pitched up, rolled inverted and plunged toward the ground. The pilot managed to roll the jet upright and eject safely a few seconds before the jet exploded on impact.

Most of the accident sequence was captured on video by a spectator. In real time, the cause could not be seen, but in slow motion, the left aileron clearly began to flutter. It separated from the aircraft after the first few oscillations and fell considerably short of the jet's final impact point. And as evidence so often proves, the first piece to hit the ground always reveals the most telling clue as to the cause.

Using Google Earth 3-D, Nick located and zoomed in on

the predicted impact area for a computerized aerial survey of the terrain. The search wouldn't be a walk in a city park, but these were Scouts, used to the outdoors and ready to tackle the challenge. Especially considering a picnic lunch, a free GPS, and a pizza party to end the day.

He zoomed out for a wider view and looked for a way to get the search party as close as possible to the target area before proceeding on foot. A Jeep trail off of SR 74 appeared to provide access to the Morgan City Wash, and from there to within relatively easy hiking distance of the wreckage area. Nick emailed Darrell with that information and confirmed that the search was a go for tomorrow as far as Nick was concerned.

Satisfied with the preparations, he closed his laptop and put it away along with the map and his pens. It was way too early for dinner, but not for an adult beverage. He motioned to his waiter and asked him to recommend a local beer.

"Four Peaks or SanTan."

"You pick it."

His waiter brought a SanTan. Nick sipped it and reconfirmed why he liked local beers, brewed in smaller quantities without preservatives or pasteurization. Like the River Rock Pale Ale of Cedar Valley that he was looking forward to when all this was over.

Then he remembered turning off the ringer on his phone and found four missed calls from Caitlin. He called her back and was informed that the cellular customer was not available.

Nick could never understand why people called multiple times, never left a message, and then turned off their phones. For all such folks, he'd try once, and then the ball was in their court. Besides, Caitlin was probably just being her typical over-controlling self and wanting an update on his progress. Hopefully, tomorrow he could file his final report and be done.

He could visualize it now.

He's out there with a group of Scouts, the boys having a ball with their GPSs, and he hears one of the adults calling his name. It's faint, and he's not sure of the direction until he sees in the distance someone waving his arms.

Careful not to twist an ankle or worse in the rugged terrain, he hurries toward the commotion, heart pounding in anticipation of walking up on the crumpled ruddervator of McAllister's Victory, the balance weight still installed in the horn. And the weight is about half size, with tool marks that perfectly match those on the other half he'd given to Caitlin.

He could feel the glow right here and now, sitting at a table in the Corner Bakery and Café sipping a local beer and thinking, *Gotcha!*

Chapter Twenty-Six

Cliff Yates eased open one eye, the most he could manage, and glanced at the clock. *Whoa.* 1:00 p.m. Barbie slept fitfully beside him, with what might be the beginnings, or maybe the remnants, of a smile. Good. He must have done something right. A pervasive attraction had begun to connect him to this stranger he knew very little about. Kind of scary, and he felt like running for his life about half the time, especially since she appeared to really like him.

After getting dressed he stopped by the bed, pulled the covers away from where she had tented them over her head, and found an eye open. Maybe she slept that way. Alert for something. He kissed her cheek, repositioned the tent, and walked to a café across the street for the Hungry Man Breakfast Special—served 24 hours a day—and the signature Bottomless Cup of Coffee. Thirty minutes after that, survival seemed a bit more certain and the time had come to make some decisions about the future of Yates Enterprises.

Two gigs beckoned, either of which beat the pants off being a PI gathering photographic evidence of infidelity. And although confronting a cheating husband with a handful of photos could turn dangerous in a hurry, running Mule Air and eliminating the Monroe-Phillips coalition introduced significant risks from the git-go.

Years of working narcotics cases and his personal behind-the-scenes shakedowns had taught Cliff that people dealing drugs could be loose cannons or as predictable as the sunrise. Like Leland. A savvy businessman, who had likely become so accustomed to the advantages of distributing his product through Mule Air that any reluctance to doing business with a stranger would be put on hold. And to help that along, Cliff needed to eliminate Parker as a competitor and offer Leland a ready-to-go operation.

Four flights in the Maule in the last couple of days had re-acquainted Cliff with the feel of an airplane. He hadn't been very precise on maneuvers, but the Maule was still in one piece, and an under-the-table incentive had encouraged the instructor to sign off Cliff's pilot logbook. The first venture of Yates Enterprises had already begun. The second possibility needed a bit more preparation.

Pumped up on alcohol last night, he'd envisioned popping a cap on Monroe and Phillips for the Balloon Bitch and walking away with a new life-start in a duffel bag. But in the light of a new day, sobering up on a full belly and a gallon of caffeine, all that macho Yates-the-badass bullshit became pure fantasy.

He was a scam artist with an exceptional nose for opportunity. That's how it all started. Take a little payoff here and there for doing a scumbag a favor, so what? Such a sweet deal until he got greedy. Tried to shakedown an undercover dude who knew how to hide in plain sight under a veneer of filthy rags, revolting body odor, and a mouthful of fake bad teeth.

And although the guy had helped usher Cliff out of the precinct and onto the street with no badge or legal gun, he also taught him a valuable lesson: how to get them looking at one hand while he picked their pockets with the other. Cliff's diversion wardrobe had served him well in life-after-cop.

Applying that principle to his current circumstances, he had to make the bitch believe in his willingness to commit murder for hire, which would help avoid having to. That meant manipulating Monroe and Phillips, and the key to their cooperation was to offer them something of value in return.

Cliff paid his check and left the restaurant. For a fleeting moment, he considered waking up his bed partner and checking her vacuum pressure, but the thought vanished as a message chimed into his phone. He fished it out of a pants pocket and read a text from Monroe: *Hiding in desert west of Parker trailer. Hunted by guy w/ rifle in pickup. Busy?*

It took only a few seconds for Cliff to absorb the message and conclude that this might be a great *opportunity*. He ran to the LTD, fired it up, and charged onto the highway toward the Adobe Wings Airport. Steering with one hand, he called his instructor. The guy was about to brief a student, but the promise of another generous cash incentive put Cliff on the schedule for the Maule and arranged to have the airplane out of the hangar, preflight done, and ready to start the engine.

He arrived at the airport in only ten minutes of hauling ass down the highway and praying for all the New Mexico State Police in the vicinity to be enjoying an early lunch. He skidded to a stop in the parking lot closest to the ramp, jumped out and yelled at the instructor, who was walking from the Maule back to the office. "Sign me out, okay?"

The instructor waved, and when he turned away, Cliff popped the trunk and hauled out a tactical bag with his very illegal full-auto M4A2 Bushmaster carbine in .223 Remington he'd confiscated for personal use while he still carried a badge. The previous owner saw the wisdom of not complaining to anyone.

He ran to the airplane, yanked the chocks away from the main tires, tossed the bag in the right seat, climbed in the left and followed the quick reference checklist: *Master switch on, ignition on, throttle open one-eighth inch, mixture full rich, fuel pump on five seconds, mixture lean, engage the start switch, mixture advance to rich after start, check oil pressure.*

The avionics master turned on the radios and nav equipment and he rushed through the after-start checks. During the short taxi to the end of the runway, he fastened his shoulder harness, checked that the pattern was clear, and then took off to the northwest toward I-40. Level at 1000 feet above the ground, he left the throttle full forward and let the airspeed increase.

The highway ran east-west, and on this heading he'd intersect it in less than twenty minutes. Finding the ramshackle collection of trailers surrounding Parker's would be easy. It sat on a plateau a couple of miles north of the highway between a cracked north-south asphalt access road and an escarpment immediately to the west. Monroe would probably have run in that direction for cover to avoid being caught in the open by the rifle-toting dude in a pickup.

Approaching the trailer park, he descended to 500 feet above the ground and flew over the top of it on a westerly heading to where the terrain dropped away. The slope wasn't too steep to negotiate on foot, and the vegetation down in a series of parallel east-west ravines grew in thicker clumps and closer together than up on the plateau. At the west end of the rugged slope, the ravines gave out onto a flatter area. Not like up on the plateau, but with enough vertical variation to offer concealment.

Cliff had no idea where Monroe might be hiding, but he didn't care at the moment. The ground here looked to be more rock and gravel than sand, and she wouldn't have left a trail visible to anyone but an experienced tracker. One of Parker's buddies charging around in a pickup? Forget about it.

The Maule's high-wing design and large windows in the doors allowed him to get a good view of the terrain, so he began a search pattern concentrated on the ravines.

FOR THE LAST HOUR or so, Caitlin had scrambled from one cover position to the next whenever the pickup was out of sight, and remained as still as a stump when it wasn't. She could picture the bottle of water in the Mercedes' beverage holder. The image tantalized her mouth into a dusty cavern.

Running from her first cover position on the flat behind Parker's trailer, she'd reached the escarpment at full speed and kept right on going over the edge, fell about five feet, landed on a slope of mixed sand and gravel, tucked her head and rolled, came up running again, her legs trying to keep up as she raced down the slope, frantically leaping over larger rocks, cactus and small bushes. At the first clump of stunted evergreens, she skidded to a halt and darted behind them just as the sound of the pickup's engine died out.

Silhouetted against the sky, the black snout of the beast appeared at the edge of the escarpment, then the man, scanning the terrain with binoculars. She lay very still, thinking he was either the world's worst shot, or he was herding her.

Which made a lot more sense. Parker needed the balance weight to eliminate the threat to him and the Balloon Bitch, and he had no way of knowing who had it. To paraphrase the woman in the trailer park, *"The man needs information."* It also meant Caitlin's plan to goad the Balloon Bitch and Parker into action had backfired big time.

The shooter disappeared, then the truck backed away from

the edge and began moving to Caitlin's left with the guy leaning out of the window looking for a place to drive down the slope.

The sound of the pickup's engine had just drifted away again when another took its place. Kind of the same, but different. If the shooter had called in reinforcements, this was not going to end well. Caitlin decided to move away from the last position of the pickup, located her next cover in the ravine, got up and jogged toward it.

The new engine sound varied from far away to closer, unlike anything she'd heard from the pickup, and then suddenly increased. Caitlin panicked, expecting to be run over when an airplane roared into view from behind the high terrain to her left, crossed the ravine, and disappeared. The damn thing couldn't have been more than a few feet above the ridges.

She sprinted to the next cover and crouched under the branches, heart pounding, convinced she'd never elude a ground-and-airborne tag team she had brought down on herself with way too much confidence in a Walther.

CLIFF THOUGHT HE SAW movement to his left as he passed over a ravine, but he lost sight of the area when the ridge on the other side blocked his view. He banked left and maneuvered up to the higher ground near the escarpment so he could fly down the ravine from the high end to the low.

He didn't see anything, so he tried it again. Still no sign of anyone, and he was about to continue his grid search when he saw a dust cloud in the flat area to the west of where the ravines emptied out.

After a moment, he saw a black pickup traveling at high speed and perpendicular to the ravines. He turned south to approach the pickup head-on and flew by it offset to his left so he could get a good look out the lower window in the pilot-side door.

Just another off-road beast as far as he could tell, jacked up, huge tires, brush guards and light bars. He turned back north to follow it and saw that the pickup had stopped. The driver was standing beside the open door, waving his arms. Cliff slowed, flew by again. The guy was motioning in what looked like an "over there" signal. Then it dawned on him he might have seen something to explain what was happening.

The flight log for the Maule had multiple entries signed by none other than T.L. Parker as the pilot. What if this dude thinks Parker is flying it? Which also would mean that the pickup wasn't just any off-roader out for a fun day in the desert.

Cliff flew over the pickup again and rocked his wings, an aviation signal that could mean many different things, and in this case was intended to communicate the message, *Follow me!* If he could lead the guy in a predictable direction, and Caitlin could see it happening, she might have an opportunity to run for it.

About a mile north, he found higher tabletop terrain that might serve for a runway. His instructor had been stressing short-field takeoffs and landings, although on a hard surface with more than enough length. Cliff did a flyby, looking for surprises like big rocks, logs, potholes and other hazards.

It appeared doable, so he slowed, extended the flaps, and set up to land toward the south. Down on the flat, the pickup raced toward Cliff's landing spot.

Doing his best to fight down the panic threatening to toss the remains of his breakfast special all over the instrument panel, Cliff put the Maule down with two spectacular bounces before skidding to a stop about ten yards short of a small evergreen.

No sweat. That's why they build them like they do.

He shut down the engine, unstrapped, snatched the bag off the right seat and climbed out. As with all of his weapons, he kept the Bushmaster ready to rock, but better cautious than sorry. He checked for a full magazine, round in the chamber, safety off, three-shot burst selected, and began running toward the edge of the tabletop.

Prior to reaching it, he crouched, duckwalked the final 10 feet to a little tree, and peered around it. The pickup had stopped at the base of the hill. A big guy was climbing up the rocky slope, head down watching where he put his feet. Cliff had never seen him before and was still guessing about who he might be until he noticed the strap that passed over the guy's right shoulder and under his left armpit. A rifle sling?

Cliff eased down to the ground and into a shooter's stance, put the Bushmaster's tactical scope on the figure. A big-bore pistol rested in a belt-slide holster on the guy's right hip.

Okay, but New Mexico is no different than many western states with an active gun culture. Here's a guy charging around in the desert minding his own business, sees an airplane roaming around a few hundred feet in the air, stops to wave hello. But Cliff adds meaning of his own, and is now about to shoot the guy for just being out here. Better hold off—*wait a minute*.

Over the guy's right shoulder peeked the distinctive shape of a flash suppressor of an assault rifle.

So what? Law-abiding gun lovers who'd never shoot anyone other than in self-defense can legally own assault rifles. This might be—

The sound of an engine diverted Cliff's attention to behind him. A four-wheeler, maybe? He turned around and stared at the other end of the hilltop. The engine was getting closer, revved up, the driver in a hurry.

Who the hell was this?

TOMMY LEE SLOWED HIS ATV and coasted to a stop at the base of the flat-top mountain where the Maule had landed. Putting it down up there was a gutsy move for a guy who, according to one of Leo's instructors, soloed in it day before yesterday.

Tommy Lee had called to schedule himself for later this afternoon and heard the story of an unusually rushed departure by none other than Cliff Yates, who had told Tommy Lee that Monroe and Phillips were investigating him.

Sitting on the ATV, the idle engine vibrating the seat and frame, Tommy Lee studied the slope. All-terrain didn't really mean go anywhere, but he figured he could make it to the top with a lot of full-throttle climbing, which would announce his approach. Not a good idea without knowing why the hell Yates was up there, especially considering the duffel bag his instructor had seen him toss in the Maule. Who needs a change of clothes to fly from Adobe Wings to a spot in the desert less than 50 miles away? Tommy Lee had only his 9mm Beretta, a peashooter compared to the weapon that might be in the bag described by the instructor: large, black, with *Bushmaster* printed on the side.

But Tommy Lee had to do something. He turned off the engine, shoved the keys into the pocket of his jeans, and started up the hill on foot.

CLIFF HAD CHOSEN THE hilltop because it didn't have many trees or big rocks. But now he had at least two guys to worry about and no cover worth the name. He glanced down at the big dude with the rifle and figured it would take him at least five minutes to make it up here.

Fire over the guy's head and get him scrambling for cover back down the hill? Maybe even try to disable the truck, except that a full metal jacket .223 round couldn't penetrate the engine block and would have to hit something softer and yet critical. Tires? The pickup could still move, but not far. Same for the radiator. He had an extra magazine, but was that worth the ammo to try?

Back away, run to the other end of the hilltop and find out for sure if he was being squeezed from two sides? The sound of the engine had died out, but the driver could be on foot. If so, what then? Get back in the Maule and haul ass? Could he get airborne before one or both of them made it up here? Risk a lucky shot from the rifle and whatever the other dude might be carrying?

Or to hell with being defensive?

Cliff turned to deal with the closest threat first and found that the guy had stopped and was shifting the rifle from behind his back to the front, eyes looking directly at Cliff. Or the tree he was hiding behind. Didn't matter. Especially when the guy yelled, "That you, Tommy Lee?"

He put the crosshairs dead center on the man's chest and fired a three-shot burst *BamBamBam*.

TOMMY LEE DIVED BEHIND a boulder and tried to get really small. But no rounds struck the ground anywhere near him. Maybe he wasn't the target. Or maybe the shooter was waiting, scope on the boulder, for Tommy Lee to uncover just enough.

He hated this crap, never intended to get involved in anything more than hauling product around behind the scenes, nice and quiet-like. But here he was, cowering, his heart pumping the blood so fast his ears felt it. He hated that even worse.

Pistol in hand, he jumped up and began running, the old moves from the gridiron coming back, fully expecting to be dodging angry pieces of lead spitting up gravel and rock chips around him. By the time he scrambled behind the ATV, he finally remembered to breath.

He quick-peeked the top of the hill. No sign of Yates, but he could be anywhere up there, hunkered down. Or maybe that was Buster's rifle, taking care of—*No, can't be*. Or could it? Tommy Lee couldn't remember if Buster's rifle had been converted to full-auto, but it didn't matter.

Peering over the top of the ATV's rear cargo bed, he picked a likely route up the hill with only one spot that looked dicey. With the pistol shoved deep into his waistband, he eased up, slipped the key into the ignition and started the engine. Eyes on the top of the hill, he climbed on, engaged the gear shift, cranked the throttle full open and almost flipped over on his back as the front wheels lurched off the ground. Once under control, he charged up the hill, fighting the ATV's efforts to buck him off.

THROUGH THE SCOPE, CLIFF watched the guy, twitching, his chest rapidly turning red, and wondered why he didn't feel much of anything. He knew cops who had used deadly force for the first time, and most of them talked about how the adrenaline rush from a sudden gunfight had messed them up for a while. Nausea, vomiting, and more than one had pissed himself.

But when he stood up, there it was, some dizziness and trembling in his legs. He gripped a branch of the tree and breathed deeply. If he could just wait here a few minutes—

The undulating growl of an ATV broke the silence. For a few seconds Cliff considered trying to get the Maule airborne, abandoned the idea as too risky and sprinted toward the other end of the hilltop. With each stride, the engine sound seemed to shift position, but the terrain and wind could do that. He also remembered that on his approach to landing, the far end appeared to have the most gentle and least obstructed slope.

Breathless, he finally reached the edge of the plateau and collapsed into a prone position. The ATV sounded like it was to his left, still climbing hard. Cliff had never driven one, but he was pretty sure that you couldn't do it with one hand and even fire a weapon with the other, much less with any effect.

He crawled to the edge and looked down. The driver had the ATV traversing from left to right, probably going for what looked like a natural switchback in the terrain. Cliff shifted position, put the scope on the switchback, lifted his cheek off the stock for a wider view, and waited.

When the ATV began the sharp turn to reverse direction, Cliff lowered his head, adjusted the sight picture and squeezed off two bursts low and in front of the ATV rather than at the driver.

TOMMY LEE HAD JUST eased off the throttle and yanked the handlebars into a hard right turn around a boulder when something kicked up three clouds of dust close in front of the ATV and a metallic *thwank-thwank* rose above the sound of the idle engine. Two holes had appeared, in the left front fender and the hood.

He scrambled off the ATV before it coasted to a stop. Pursued by three-shot bursts kicking up debris around his feet, he ran toward a group of trees. A sharp, stinging pain jabbed him in the calf as he reached cover and convinced him to keep on going. By the time he crouched behind a boulder big enough to hide a truck, he knew the shooter wasn't trying to hit him. Just like he told Buster to do with Monroe.

Where *was* Buster? That first, single three-shot burst would never have driven him off the hunt. The guy was relentless, feared nothing. The silence had to mean . . . *don't think about that.*

Tommy Lee checked his calf, found a slice in his cargo pants. The wound wasn't pulsing blood. Ignore it for now.

He crawled around the base of the boulder and found a slanted opening between it and the sloped ground. Through the gap he saw nothing at the edge of the hill above him, but that didn't mean anything. To his left, heavier vegetation covered the hillside. If he could find another way up through it and go on foot, Yates would have to be exactly in the right place at the right time to intercept him.

Ten minutes later, hanging on to an evergreen branch and trying not to slip on loose gravel, Tommy Lee heard the Maule's engine start up, then the roar of full takeoff power drifted down the slope from his left, passed his position, and faded to a distant hum in the still desert air.

So much for getting a bead on Yates. Now where was Buster?

Tommy Lee scrambled down the hill and trotted to the ATV. It started okay, and he gunned it around the hill to Buster's pickup. His crumpled body lay about 100 yards up the slope. Tommy Lee got out the binoculars from the under-seat storage box. The bloody sight in close up made his stomach churn, but he fought it down, along with the rage that threatened to overpower his ability to think this through.

What to do with Buster's body? He claimed no close family

and no friends to speak of other than Tommy Lee. Nature's cleanup crew would return him to the soil soon enough, but the guy deserved better.

Leland wanted Mule Air up and running yesterday. Tommy Lee had to deal with that soon or get the hell gone.

Beth might decide to work out a deal with Monroe. And maybe protect Tommy Lee in the bargain. But that was a really big *maybe,* especially since the protection of the balance weight went to the person who had the goddamn thing. In Beth's hands, it was like a dagger pointed at his heart.

And if Tommy Lee didn't find Monroe now, he wouldn't get another chance. She'd never again be foolish enough to put herself at a disadvantage and so vulnerable, and the balance weight would be more out of reach than it had been this morning.

What the hell was Yates doing here? Did Monroe call him? Did she know he was flying the Maule? If she saw it leave, what's her next move?

Tommy Lee shielded his eyes and scanned the ground between him and the highway to the south. He'd lived in the trailer for about ten years and considered the area below the rim of the plateau as his personal ATV playground. The terrain became more rugged closer to the highway. Monroe had run around in the desert for a few hours now, probably without water. The dry air, combined with the adrenaline pumping into her bloodstream, might make her dehydrated, confused and vulnerable.

He checked Buster's pickup and found the keys in the ignition. A quick inspection under the ATV's hood found no punctured hoses or engine damage. It wasn't quiet, but it beat the hell out of Buster's throaty V-8 and glass-pack mufflers.

Tommy Lee grabbed a gallon jug of water from the pickup,

tossed it in the ATV's storage box, slipped the strap on the binoculars around his neck, climbed on and raced toward the highest terrain between him and the highway.

CAITLIN CLIMBED THE LAST 50 feet of the hill on her stomach. A peek over the top revealed more of the same rocky ground with scrub vegetation and the occasional stunted evergreen. She'd been moving in a southerly direction toward the highway and away from the last known position of the pickup and the airplane, but she couldn't see the top of the highest terrain. She needed a bearing to be sure she hadn't drifted off course.

It was time to do that, but with her head resting on her crossed arms, she closed her eyes for a short rest. Then she would get up and make a push for safety.

WHEN TOMMY LEE REACHED an elevated point with a good view of the terrain, he stopped the ATV, rested his elbows on the handlebars, and scanned the hills, ravines, and everything in between with the binoculars. And while this could be like looking for a black grain of sand in the Sahara, rugged terrain on either side of the landscape up to the highway formed a natural funnel for hikers and motorized travelers alike.

After about five minutes, he noticed a dark lump that looked out of place near the top of a hill. It was in shadow cast by some trees, but he fine-tuned the focus to examine it more closely. After a few moments, he saw a head rise, drop, and a leg shift position.

Good afternoon, Ms. Monroe.

He picked out a route that kept to the dry washes and ravines and put higher terrain between him and the target. A handful of dirt tossed in the air drifted to his rear and confirmed he was downwind. Not that Monroe would sniff out his presence like a deer, but sound drifted with the wind as well.

It took about twenty minutes to reach a deep-cut dry wash that Tommy Lee figured put him within a half mile of Monroe. He checked the Beretta, slipped it into his waistband, got the jug of water from the ATV and began climbing. Nearing the top of a ridge, he knelt, crawled the last few feet and peeked over the edge across the ravine to the top of the next ridge.

It didn't look like Monroe had moved so much as a toe. For an instant, Tommy Lee wondered if she might have died. Maybe she'd been hit when Buster was nudging her deeper into the desert with his rifle. With the binoculars Tommy Lee looked for any sign of blood, didn't find it.

Okay. He'd rather not carry the water jug, but re-hydration might be the only way to get her on her feet. He had no restraints and didn't want to leave her while he went back for the ATV. Jug in one hand and the Beretta in the other, he crested the ridge. While shifting his eyes from Monroe's prone figure down to the ground and back, he carefully placed his feet to avoid sending any rocks tumbling down the slope.

At the bottom of the ravine he realized he'd need a free hand to steady himself while climbing. He removed his belt halfway, slipped it through the handle on the water jug and positioned it in the center of his back. With the Beretta inside the front of his waistband and both hands free, he ascended the slope.

Halfway up, he paused. Fifty feet above him lay the key to implementing the only solution offering any protection against running for the rest of his life. If not from legal retribution, then from a black widow who wouldn't hesitate for a second to sink her deadly fangs in Tommy Lee's back.

It had been so deliciously wicked, the seductive thrill of sneaking around with Beth McAllister, half-again his age and looking like half of it with a nip here and a tuck there, the best age reducers money could buy. But no more, even if the opportunity remained after the dust settled. He couldn't spend 24 hours a day looking over his shoulder and sleeping with one eye open.

Monroe raised her head and shocked Tommy Lee back into the moment. If he spooked her, she could be over the top of the ridge and down the other side before he could do anything. She was probably armed and would shoot to kill, while he had to make sure he didn't punch his ticket out of this mess before he had a chance to get that balance weight and disappear.

When she lowered her head, Tommy Lee climbed the rest of the way, one hand and one foot at a time until he was standing over her. Even covered with dust and wearing sweat-stained clothes, Monroe was a head-turner. Enemy or not, he'd hate to mar her beauty and hoped it wouldn't come to that.

But she had to think he would.

Chapter Twenty-Seven

Nick rolled over and slapped at the alarm until it quit nagging him. He seldom slept well knowing he had to be up on time or risk being late for something important. Especially in a motel room.

He peered at the clock, resisted the temptation to close his eyes for a few minutes, rolled out of bed, completed his morning ritual on autopilot, tossed his belongings in the duffel and dropped the key card off at the front desk.

First stop, a light breakfast, then the Cabela's in Glendale. He arrived at about 8:45, parked close to the front door and settled back to wait. About a minute later, the door opened. Stacey stepped out and motioned for him to come on in. An employee who arrives early and has initiative. Amazing.

She had 20 GPS units stacked in a box, with the packing material and accessories in another resting on a counter. "Each unit is numbered with a stick-on label, one to twenty. They're all fully charged and programmed with one of the coordinate pairs you sent me. The paper in this box shows the coordinate pair for each GPS. Number one is the northern-most pair, number twenty at the south end. I hope you find what you're looking for."

"I do, too. You've done a great job for me, Stacey." Nick pulled out his wallet.

Stacey shook her head. "You've already paid me."

"Yeah, but the way I look at it, customer service above and beyond deserves extra compensation."

"We had a deal. I did my part and so did you. That's the end of it."

Nick smiled, partly from the pure joy of meeting someone of a later generation who had apparently been raised with the same values he grew up with. He set two 50s on the top of the counter. "You can consider those as an anonymous gift to whoever finds them." He stacked the boxes and picked them up. "Or, you can accept them from someone old enough to be your father and who appreciates that you have given him a tiny bit of optimism that the world may not have gone to the dogs quite yet. Thanks again."

Nick was putting the boxes into the Jeep when he heard the front door to Cabela's open. He looked up.

Stacey tossed him a casual salute. "You're a good man, sir, no matter what anybody else says."

Nick waved and got in the Jeep. Fifteen minutes later, he arrived at the Corner Bakery Café in Peoria. The waiter who had helped get the quadrangle map printed yesterday seated him. Nick ordered coffee and a piece of that signature cake, asked him to check with the manager about his to-go lunch order, then called the Scoutmaster.

"Darrell here. That you, Nick?"

"It is, calling for an update on how many lunches to bring."

"Hold on." After some rustling and muffled voices in the background, Darrell said, "We've got twenty-five scouts confirmed, two probables, and five adult supervisors plus me."

"Okay. Will you be getting the boys together before you leave for the rendezvous site?"

"Yes."

"You might want to announce, and I'll mention it as well during my remarks and instructions, that we'll have only twenty GPS units for today's search, but each member of the team will receive their own."

"That'll work. Any ideas for what the boys without a GPS will be doing?"

"Glad you asked. We'll arrange the search line along a southeast-northwest axis so the boys advance on a southwesterly heading. That word picture may be a little confusing, but it puts the search line perpendicular to the last known heading of the airplane and spreads it out to cover a half-mile total width. I'd like to use the extra boys and adults as rovers in the gaps."

"Sounds good. You on schedule?"

"I'm picking up the lunches now, see you there about eleven."

When his waiter brought the coffee and cake, Nick asked him to tell the manager he needed 10 more lunches for a total of 35 and was that going to be a problem? He'd just finished the cake when the waiter said they'd have them ready in about 30 minutes.

He got out the map with the search area and grid lines plotted on it to familiarize himself with the terrain. The NTSB debris-field map and Nick's plot of predicted ruddervator impact points were both located to the south of the Morgan City Wash. Contour lines showed the average elevation to be about 2000 feet, and the distance between the lines indicated that much of the search area was relatively flat.

But they had to get there, which meant leaving SH 74 on an unimproved road to the northeast that curved left around higher terrain to the west and intersected another unimproved road in the wash near the Morgan City Well. From there, they could drive the wash to a point north of the search area and separated from it by a wall of steeper terrain that formed the southern edge of the wash.

Nick studied the contours and found a gap in this wall that should provide a shallower climb and put them onto the flatter terrain without requiring any special skills other than being careful. From there, he could organize the boys into a line and begin the advance.

And that highlighted a hole in his planning. He called Darrell back. "Do you have a bullhorn?"

"Are you kidding? Try controlling a bunch of Scouts with your unamplified voice and see how that works for you. It's not like herding cats, but close."

"It would be really helpful for keeping the line straight."

"Forget straight. Straighter is the best you can hope for."

Nick laughed and signed off. Darrell sounded like someone he'd like to have a beer with.

The lunches weren't ready yet, so he checked for messages and remembered the missed call from Caitlin. He hadn't been able to reach her yesterday, so he tried again and rather than reaching her voicemail, got the recorded notice that the cellular customer wasn't available.

He didn't know what triggered that difference. If her phone was turned off, he still ought to be able to leave a message, and she'd get it when she powered up the phone again. It might be worth a call to his service pro—

"Your lunches are ready, sir."

Nick glanced up and the waiter handed him the check. He paid cash and gave the kid another generous tip for carrying the bags to the Jeep. The on-board GPS route from the café to the coordinates for the rendezvous point indicated a trip of 35-40 minutes.

Staring at the screen, he realized that in about a half hour, he'd begin the final chore of this adventure into private accident investigation. And it would be his last contribution no matter what he did or didn't find. He'd made that absolutely clear to Caitlin. Which probably didn't mean much, come to think of it.

As he pulled away from the café, a troubling concern settled around him. He'd never before called Caitlin and not been able to reach her. Where was that girl?

PANIC WOKE HER UP, and the debilitating fear of the unknown. She was lying on her side, under covers, in almost total blackness. A pinpoint of pale yellow light seemed to be floating out there somewhere, shifting position as she stared at it, returning to the starting point only when she blinked. Muggy air surrounded her, tinged with the odor of moist earth. The only sound a steady humming. Electrical maybe, familiar and yet unidentifiable.

Caitlin pushed herself into a sitting position, felt around with her hands. Light blanket, sheets, pillow, probably on a cot. Behind her and to the left, metal. To her right toward the light, empty space. She leaned over, tentatively reached down and touched more metal.

She threw off the covers and moved her legs. No restraints. Her captor wasn't worried about escape. The thought sent a cold shiver through her body.

Mind videos began to play, scenes of running, bullets kicking up dirt and rocks around her, crouching behind bushes and under trees, and thirst. Her mouth so dry that she could barely swallow. Fatigue so immense she could only lower her head and drift away.

Then a voice, stern, commanding, a crushing knee into her

back, the pistol and magazines yanked from her waist, removed from her jacket pocket. Hands tied with a leather strap, a blindfold, then gentler hands rolled her onto her back, lifted her torso into a sitting position, and placed the most delicious water in the world to her lips.

After a while, a guided, stumbling hike down, then up, down again, and finally a hair-raising ride on a four-wheeler sitting in front of someone who seemed intent upon crashing the damn thing. Transfer to a vehicle, and the sound of an engine she knew all too well. She must have passed out of and back into this world a few times until all settled into nothingness.

Like now, except that she felt rested, wasn't thirsty, and really had to use the bathroom. Feet on the floor, she stood, shaky, and with her right hand on the edge of the cot and her left arm outstretched, she stepped toward the head of the cot until she felt the metal wall. To her left was the light, so she turned and with her right hand touching the wall and her left arm running interference, she slowly advanced.

By the time she came to a dead end at another metal wall, her hands had explored a series of obstacles built out from the wall: cabinets, a counter with stovetop, a sink and a faucet that worked, a shower curtain surrounding a wooden frame built around a toilet.

Right hand still on the intersecting wall, she moved along it, found a door frame, metal door, and on the other side of it the little light in a switch. Curiosity played tag with dread as she reached for it, wanting to see but terrified of what she'd find to confirm the image in her mind of a tin-can dungeon with all the conveniences.

Eyes closed tight, she flipped the switch. The inside of her eyelids lit up. A quick reverse blink caught a blinding preview of a metal tube turned into a room. Shielding her eyes, she opened them a tiny bit and waited for her pupils to adjust.

She was standing at one end of a room about 30 or 40 feet long and half that wide. The walls curved outward from the floor and back toward the center and joined over her head to form a ceiling about 15 feet high. A row of low-voltage light fixtures hung from the apex on chains. To her right along the wall she hadn't touch-explored, more cabinets, bench seating, a desk with a reading light and a chair, and at the far end by the foot of the cot, two more cots, folded and stacked against the wall.

Pushing down the thought of what she was doing here, Caitlin used the flush toilet, explored the room and found a well-designed and fully stocked survival environment for three. Canned goods, some cooking utensils, bottled water, ready-to-eat meals and spare batteries. The humming sound was probably a ventilation system, and it had to include some type of temperature control to keep the interior this comfortable. All of this was disturbing enough, but nothing like the plastic sack sitting on the counter by the sink.

Essential toiletries. Still in their packaging.

Stories of women kept for years as sex slaves filled Caitlin with a determination to be ready. She searched every nook and cranny of her prison and found nothing that could be used as a weapon except maybe the handles on one of the plastic spoons she found in a drawer by the stove. Or maybe the handle on the toothbrush if she could find a rough surface to use as a file.

She finally sat on the edge of the cot and cradled her head in her hands, summoning the strength to fight tooth, nail, hand, and foot to make the sonofabitch pay dearly for whatever it was he wanted from her.

A scraping sound, like shoes on concrete, drew her attention to the far wall and the door. Metal on metal, a key in a lock, clicking of a deadbolt, and the door swung open.

Caitlin looked up. The silhouette of a man stood in the doorway filled with daylight.

NICK HADN'T BEEN PARKED at the rendezvous for more than 15 minutes when a cavalcade of SUVs appeared out of the haze to the east and pulled up on the side of the highway behind him. A stocky guy with a head of unruly red hair and a mustache to match climbed out of the lead vehicle and approached Nick with his hand extended. "I'm Darrell."

Nick shook hands, liked the feel of a firm grip. "The boys ready for the big adventure?"

Darrell chuckled. "You might say that." He motioned behind him. "Right back there as we speak, the supervisors are reminding their Scouts not to open the doors and to remain seated with their seatbelts fastened. I'm surprised it's working, frankly."

"Eagerness is good. I'll lead the way to where this road," he pointed to the northeast, "joins the Morgan City Wash. We'll stop there for lunch and my briefing."

Darrell nodded, turned and walked back to his SUV, his arm rotating in a "round 'em up and head 'em out" motion.

Nick turned north off the shoulder of the highway onto a nameless paved road that turned to dirt after about a mile and a half, and shortly thereafter intersected the Morgan City Wash. The SUVs pulled up into a rough circle and the Scouts poured out. Darrell used the bullhorn to quiet them down with instructions on how to get fed while Nick introduced himself to the adults and distributed the lunches.

It didn't take long to eat, and no time at all to collect the trash into bags Darrell brought. Nick was impressed with the way the Scoutmaster controlled what could have become an unruly crowd of excited youngsters and assembled them, quiet and attentive, for the briefing. After the introduction, Nick explained in detail how the search line would work, the importance of staying on course, the job of the rovers, and then handed out the units. He formed the boys with GPSs in a numerical-order line and talked them through turning the units on and selecting their grid-line courses.

Then he passed out copies of a color photo of a Victory ruddervator with a yardstick lying beside it. "We're looking for a piece of an airplane that fell off in flight. It won't look like this undamaged one, but it gives you an idea of the shape and size, kind of like the wing on a small airplane. This one will be white, with stripes of red, blue, and gold, about five feet long unless it's very badly damaged. The point is that it should be relatively easy to see, but let's be sure to check any holes in the ground or caves in the side of a hill large enough to conceal something of this size. You boys carrying the GPS units can move left and right of your courses, but don't go so far as to cross another guy's course. And if you see something you think needs to be checked out, you can always stay on course and get one of the rovers to do it."

He asked if there were any questions, then after a final caution about safety he turned the briefing over to Darrell and the supervisors. They did a great job of emphasizing the team approach so important to Scouting.

Darrell turned to Nick. "I think these young men are ready to go."

"Agreed. Where's number ten?"

A freckle-faced Scout who Nick figured to be about twelve years old stepped forward, his expression serious and his back ramrod straight. "That's me, sir."

"What's your name?"

"Wilbur, but I don't like it."

Nick stifled a smile, wanted to say something like *I wouldn't either.* "Once we begin the search, you're going to be 'Number Ten.' But that's just for my convenience because I don't know everybody's name. Is that okay?"

"It's a lot better than Wilbur."

That cracked everybody up and got them off to a good start. Nick asked Wilbur to ride with him. Before they got underway as the lead vehicle, Nick explained that the GPS they had was programmed with the start and end points that defined the centerline of the search area. "Let's set it up to take us to the start point. Can you—?"

Wilbur lowered his head close to the screen, studied the buttons a moment, and commanded direct-to navigation in about three seconds.

Nick smiled and said, "Well, I guess maybe you'd better teach me how to use that thing after we're done, okay?" Wilbur nodded, and as they drove up the wash, Nick told him that his job was to monitor the distance-to-go readout. It would decrease until they reached a point in the wash closest to the center of the search line, then begin to increase. That's where they would proceed on foot by finding a way out of the wash up onto the higher terrain to the south.

Wilbur nodded, but his expression appeared to carry the message that the explanation wasn't necessary. Kids these days cut their teeth on electronic gadgets, and Wilbur probably entered the world texting a kid being born in the next room.

They had driven about a mile when Wilbur said, "Stop, sir."

Nick put the Jeep in PARK. "I'll be right back." He got out

and walked to Darrell's SUV, leaned against the driver's door and pointed at the high terrain forming the southern wall of the wash. "The search area begins about a half-mile southwest of us. There's a dry streambed just up there that looks on the quadrangle maps and satellite imagery like it might be a relatively gentle climb. I think we can find a way from there to head back east to the starting point without spraining any ankles. Or worse."

Darrell nodded. "Let's do it."

Nick found the streambed and parked on the northern edge of the wash. The team gathered around him and the supervisors checked each boy's clothing and water supply. When all was ready, Nick led the way and the supervisors organized the line by GPS number, positioning themselves and the young rovers in between boys with the GPS units.

After a few minutes of hiking, Nick remembered he intended to call Caitlin while he was still up on the highway. He checked his phone, found a good signal, and dialed.

The cellular customer he was trying to reach was not available.

Nothing he could do about it now, and that made him feel out of the loop and helpless.

TOMMY LEE STOOD IN the doorway of Buster's bunker, amazed anew that the apocalyptic folly of his friend's family had turned out to be so perfect for neutralizing Caitlin Monroe's threat to himself and Beth. The half-buried cylindrical survival shelter was built by Buster's grandfather and had been refined over the years by his dad to prepare for a continuing stream of end-of-the-world scenarios.

Time after time while growing up together, Tommy Lee

had to stand with Buster in the kitchen while his parents prophesied the next date it would all come crashing down based on Biblical references combined with mysterious cosmic alignments. Buster had never been the brightest penny in the pocket, but Tommy Lee couldn't for the life of him understand how anyone with a lick of sense could simply push the reset-date button when doomsday predictions failed to materialize.

The bunker sat in the backyard of Buster's family home, ignored by neighbors who had long since turned their collective backs on the crazies. Just the way Tommy Lee needed them to be as he stepped inside and closed the door.

Monroe stood in the right-rear corner of the room and reminded Tommy Lee of a raccoon in a trap. Ready to snarl and attack when a threat passed a do-not-cross line visible only to the raccoon. He wanted her wary and in fear of what was going to happen, but not to the point of desperation. She needed to see a way out. Not the best solution, maybe, but certainly not the worst.

He went to the bench along the wall and sat down. "Do you know who I am?"

"A murderer."

"Good. I'm glad you fully appreciate the nature of your predicament. But I also want you to acknowledge that if I wanted you dead, you wouldn't be here."

"Where am I, exactly?"

"Think of it as nowhere. And you'll stay disappeared if you don't come to your senses."

"Which means what?"

"You have something I want. Hand it over and you can walk away from this."

Monroe pulled out the chair from the desk near the end of the cot and sat down. "I don't know what you're talking about.

And even if I did, there's no way I'd trust you."

"You're gonna need to re-think that. Admit you have the balance weight and exchange it for your life."

"You're talking about that chunk of lead? The one in a plastic baggie? With the fingerprint that you planned to protect yourself with?"

"That's the one."

"I no longer have it."

"I wish that were true, and that your lackey Yates has it. Then I'd take it from the sonofabitch and get a little payback for killing a friend of mine."

"You mean the shooter who was trying to kill me?"

Tommy Lee shook his head. "His *name* was Buster. And if I'd told him to kill you, you'd be dead and buried."

"Thanks for nothing. And good luck with getting payback from Yates. As for the weight, I gave it to someone for safekeeping before I came looking for you."

Tommy Lee pulled Caitlin's Walther out of his waistband and held it up with the muzzle pointed at the ceiling. "Did you plan on shooting me with this?"

"Thought about it. Still am. But I just wanted to tell you face-to-face that I've figured out how you and that scheming Balloon Bitch did it."

Tommy Lee stood up. "I'm going to leave now. Into the sunlight with the freedom to go wherever I want and do whatever I want." He turned his back on Caitlin and walked to the door, then looked at her over his shoulder and smiled. "You, on the other hand, will remain here. For as long as I want you to. Until we talk again, you think about that."

With the door closed, barred, bolted, and padlocked, a process he intentionally made as noisy as possible, Tommy Lee climbed the steps to ground level, crawled out from under the camouflage netting, and walked toward the house.

With Buster's pickup in the detached garage, and the house looking vacant like it always had since Buster's parents died, Monroe's dungeon was invisible to the neighbors because of the family's reputation as kooks. No one would notice that Buster had disappeared, either. He'd effectively done that years ago, and in reality only yesterday evening when Tommy Lee had taken care of some hard business.

It was a nice spot for Buster to spend eternity. On his family's land, behind the bunker in a hole as deep as Tommy Lee could dig it before his back gave out. Stones from the property piled on top created a burial mound without announcing to the world that's what it was. He'd wanted to say some words before he walked away that night at dusk, but all he could come up with was, "I'll be seein' ya, Buster," before he turned his back on the past and returned to the present.

At the foot of the steps up to the back porch and the kitchen door, Tommy Lee paused to look at the rear of the property. The bunker really was invisible from this distance, and tough-girl Caitlin Monroe could stay in there until she withered into a fleshy sack of bones. But Tommy Lee knew it wouldn't come to that. A couple of weeks, maybe, and the isolation of solitary confinement would work its special brand of persuasion. She'd be begging him to take the balance weight.

In the meantime, without Monroe calling the shots, the scheme she'd cooked up would probably die of natural causes. And the accident investigator would go back where he came from. Unless she really had given him the balance weight. No telling what he'd do in that case.

But for sure, Yates was going to get what he deserved.

Then Tommy Lee could deal with Leland's demand to restart Mule Air.

And last, which based on the threat probably ought to be first, do *something* to protect himself from Beth's fangs.

CAITLIN SAT MOTIONLESS, STARED at the closed door and struggled to control the panic.

What a stupid thing to do. Get all pumped up with a false sense of invulnerability and hand herself over to this bastard. Who had probably never killed any one eyeball-to-eyeball, but didn't need to. He could just wait for stir-crazy to visit the bunker and convince Caitlin that she'd lost.

Less than a day locked up and already she was feeling the panic at not being able to open that door, walk outside and see the sky. She was trapped in here with only questions for company.

Did Yates get her text? And kill a friend of Parker's? The big guy with the rifle driving the pickup? Caitlin had assumed that Parker was flying the airplane, but he'd brought her here in the same pickup. How the hell did Yates figure into that? Even if he did, Caitlin couldn't *really* trust him not to sell her out.

That left Nick Phillips. If the Arizona desert held the final piece of the puzzle, Caitlin was convinced he'd find it. And when he couldn't find *her*, he'd try to solve the mystery of her disappearance with the same tenacity.

And walk right into a trap.

Chapter Twenty-Eight

Within a few minutes of setting up the search line, Nick discovered that the best place for him was close to Number-10 Wilbur. The Scout's GPS updated Nick on their progress, and with the bullhorn he managed to keep them in a reasonably straight line. They responded immediately to commands, and Nick was once again impressed with the way the supervisors had prepared the boys for the adventure.

He mentioned it to Darrell, who smiled and said that had been the easy part. "We promised them that if they did well, you would show them your badge and gun."

Nick didn't tell him the gun part would be no problem.

The line maintained a steady pace except for water breaks every hour and a mid-afternoon snack of granola bars. They had found a few small pieces Nick thought probably came from the Victory, but nothing even close to the size of a ruddervator.

At the 5:00 p.m. water break, Nick figured they had another hour to go, which would get them back to the Morgan City Wash about 7:00, a good half hour prior to sunset.

Shortly after the line began moving again, he'd resigned himself to failure when he heard a shout, glanced to his left and saw a total breakdown in the line. Two supervisors were waving and a group of Scouts looked like they'd found a trampoline.

He held up his right hand in a "stop" motion to hold the right side of the line in place. That entire half raced by him, cheering like a bunch of soccer fans at the World Cup.

A supervisor walked past and smiled. "So much for law and order, huh?"

Nick joined him, resisting the urge to run and doing his best to keep his hopes under control.

The Scouts had formed a circle so tight that Nick couldn't see what they were looking at. As he walked up, Darrell parted them with, "Make way for Agent Phillips, boys."

A Victory ruddervator, white with red, blue, and gold trim, lay on the ground at the base of an evergreen, wrapped around it by the impact. Nick had to wait a moment to let an unlikely mix of emotions subside.

Sadness at the thought of how this piece of mangled metal started a chain of events that killed two people.

Anger at the bastard who arranged it.

But most of all, the adrenaline rush of a successful hunt and validation of his reasoning that brought him to this very spot.

With his cell phone, he took multiple photos, then knelt beside the ruddervator and peered at the outer end. Where the horn and balance weight should have been. Mangled aluminum evidenced the violence of the event in which this ruddervator had fluttered itself to death in a split second.

And as sometime happens, the weight had ripped through the aluminum skin of the ruddervator horn. The drag caused by friction with the air in relation to the detached ruddervator's size and weight had caused it to fall well short of the major portion of the wreckage.

The balance weight, however, a dense chunk of lead a few inches long and about half as thick, would have dropped at a much sharper angle to the Victory's flight path at the instant of breakup.

Nick stood, turned, and looked back the way they had come. Somewhere between here and the starting point lay the companion to the half balance weight he'd given to Caitlin, with the matching tool marks and a fingerprint. From the Black Widow, maybe?

"Mr. Phillips?"

Nick looked down at Number-10 Wilbur. "Yes?"

"Did we do okay?"

The whole troop had crowded around, eyes locked onto him, faces filled with anticipation.

"You boys want to know if you did okay?"

In unison, "Yes, sir!"

"I could never have found it without you." When the cheering died down, Nick said, "How about if I have a special merit badge made up?"

Wilbur frowned. "Merit badges have to be approved."

Nick glanced at Darrell, who smiled, and whose expression clearly said, *It's your problem. Deal with it.* Nick put his hand on Wilbur's shoulder. "Tell you what. I'll have them made and you boys can work that out with your Scoutmaster, okay?"

Cheers erupted from the Scouts. Darrell leaned close and whispered in Nick's ear. "Thanks a lot, troublemaker."

After agreeing to let the adult supervisors help by taking turns carrying the ruddervator, Nick wrested it clear of the tree and handed it to a guy who looked like he could carry a Victory if he had to. "Pump a little iron, do we?"

The guy grinned. "Never. Got it from my pop, strong as a bull 'til the day he passed. Farm life will do that for ya."

"I bet. Thanks for the help."

The guy nodded and took off with the Scouts crowded

around, yammering and laughing about their successful hunt, interspersed with occasional debate about what kind of pizza to eat.

Nick followed with his phone in his ear, listening to another message that could have easily said, *We're sorry, but the cellular customer you are trying to reach has fallen off the planet.*

SITTING ON THE EDGE of the bed in his motel room, Cliff stared out the window at the sunset and tried to make sense of how he felt about the first few hours of the rest of his life after he had shot a man dead. No doubt the killing was justified under the principle of self-defense, which in police jargon he would have called it *righteous.* Even though he hadn't warned the guy first. So why did he feel like someone had wound him up like a play toy and turned him loose on a hardwood floor to skitter around banging into furniture and walls?

The answer to that question probably had to do with the adrenaline, which seemed to flow more every time he thought about the budding panic he'd felt watching a guy carrying an assault rifle coming up the hill toward him. And someone else behind him, both with intentions unknown.

Or maybe it was from watching through the scope as the guy went for his weapon as calmly as if he did it for real every day. Or maybe the feel of the rifle as it bucked and sent three bullets into the guy's chest. Or maybe the adrenaline had nothing to do with it.

He'd answered Monroe's call for help and then abandoned her to an unknown fate. Why did he even try if he didn't intend to see it through?

Because, said the other half of his internal dialogue, *you're no fool.*

Okay. Just a coward, maybe? Deep down where it counts?

No way. Monroe put herself in that mess and you didn't owe her a goddamn thing. Especially when you lost the tactical advantage. The only people who deserve that kind of risk are family.

Okay, but—

A knock on the door made him jump. He got up and looked through the peephole. Barbie had put her open mouth up close as if to suck the chrome off of it. The sight woke up his crotch, but not enough to prevent his inner voice asking, *Would you risk your life for her?*

And his confused answer, No . . . umm . . . well, you know what? For the first time in years, maybe . . . The recent unfamiliar sense of being connected to someone enveloped Cliff as he opened the door.

Barbie stepped inside, rose up on her toes and kissed him. "Get your business done?"

Cliff wrapped his arms around her and drew her close. When she rested her hands against his side, he said, "Hold me."

She did for a moment, then gently leaned back and looked at him. "What the hell is with you?"

With a forefinger, he tucked her hair behind her ear on one side, then the other. "You have really nice cheeks."

"I'm glad you like them, but you're freakin' me out." She tossed her handbag on the table and sat down. "Did you trade yourself in for a newer model while I was gone?"

"Same ol' me. You hungry?"

"Famished."

"Then let's take care of that."

They drove to El Barstool and entered an atmosphere Cliff found almost as comforting as home. He didn't smoke, but it didn't bother him. Sunlight streamed through windows that probably hadn't been cleaned in years, creating angled shafts of drifting white haze. It was cool, reasonably quiet, and the clack of billiard balls carried easily from the back room.

Cracker Bob, otherwise known as CB, owned the place. Quite a talker, he didn't mind telling anyone who would listen that he was proud of being as poor and white as his nickname implied. He spoke not a word of Spanish, but thought the name of the place should reflect its location. The fact that the word *barstool* didn't translate well didn't bother him a bit. He figured that the *el* took care of his obligation to setting.

While Barbie walked to the rear of the building to claim their booth, Cliff stopped at the bar. "Howdy, CB. A couple of usuals for me and the lady, please."

"Comin' right up, good buddy."

Sitting in the booth and drinking their boilermakers, Cliff and Barbie bantered about nothing much for a while until she scooted her back against the wall and drew her feet under her legs. "Have you thought about what's going on with us?"

"What?"

"It's a simple question."

The hell it is. Of all the questions a woman could ask a man, this one had too many layers to count. Cliff leaned back against the cushion and stared at the table, a scarred slab of wood with cigarette burns and the scribblings of countless drunks.

He really liked Barbie, and the thought of hooking up for awhile didn't frighten him like it had with other women in the past. Not that there'd been that many, but he always felt like he was being led by his dick down a narrow corridor with a prison cell called marriage at the end.

It did, however, challenge the wisdom of letting her into the world of Cliff Yates: disgraced cop; cut-rate private investigator; scam artist considering the potential of Yates Enterprises; and now, man killer. If he could separate one from the other, maybe.

And then there was that other thing, a kind of awakening that brought back memories of past feelings for another human being he didn't understand now any better than he had before.

He looked at her and smiled. "Order us another round while I visit the facilities and let's talk about that."

When Cliff returned to the booth and Barbie wasn't there, he looked over his shoulder toward the front of the bar and got a shot of mainline adrenaline. Three scruffy dudes wearing various leather fashion accessories had formed a half-circle around her. Back against the bar, she was obviously trying to free herself of their attentions and not having much success.

When one of the dudes reached out toward Barbie's breasts and she slapped his hand away, the guy shouted, "Don't ya love it when a bitch fights back?"

Cliff pulled the leather-covered lead sap out of his back pocket and palmed it as he reached into Barbie's purse for the stun gun. He'd discovered it the first night they were together. She was in the bathroom and he took the opportunity to check out this chick who came onto him a little too hard not to raise suspicion. None of his sources had anything on her, and a girl's gotta do what a girl's gotta do to defend herself, but it never hurt to be cautious.

Without looking at the trio, he weaved toward the front of the bar as if having had a few too many and he was leaving for home with no interest in anything else.

The dude closest to the door only glanced at Cliff and appeared unconcerned as he turned back to Barbie.

Approaching the group, Cliff flipped the slider to STUN, stumbled, and fell into the closest guy as he brought the stun gun up into his crotch and pushed the trigger button. The guy in the center backed away in surprise as his cohort began a spasm dance with a high voltage partner. That gave Cliff room to backswing the sap into the guy's kneecap with a satisfying *crunch*.

Cliff turned to face the only dude still standing and stepped in close. "Which one do you want?"

"Uh . . . hey, I didn't—"

"That's what all you pussies say. Assholes who play at being tough only when you're facing a helpless woman."

From behind him, Barbie said, "Helpless, my ass."

Cliff looked over his shoulder just in time to see her fire the Taser that CB kept behind the bar. After five seconds of zapping him to the ground, she kicked the dude in the crotch so hard it made Cliff's family jewels climb for cover.

CB hurried out of the back room. "The hell's goin' on?"

"Nothing," Barbie said. "We took care of it."

CB looked down at the trio, moaning and groaning with no attempt to harmonize. "Those fucks. I'll carry them out back to the dumpster and the next round's on me."

Seated in the booth with their free boilermakers, Cliff and Barbie toasted their successful varmint removal.

"You handled that really well," she said. "When you first staggered up, I thought you'd just broken the speed record from having a buzz on to being snockered."

Cliff laughed. "What really happened was a loss of all common sense. Three to one—"

"Three to two."

"And that was unfair of us to gang up on them."

Barbie smiled. "Fair's got nothing to do with it." After a sip of bourbon and a beer chaser, she scooted farther into the booth with her back against the wall. "What did you want to talk about?"

Cliff hadn't had time to think it out, so he didn't even try. "Want to hook up? For awhile?"

"Define 'hook up.'"

"Together. Mutually committed. No screwing around."

"Define 'for awhile.'"

"Open-ended. No advance notice required to end it. Any problem with that?"

"Absolutely not."

"Okay. But before we toast our arrangement, you need to know I've got a bunch of stuff going on that will take a while to sort out. I can't talk about it, and I don't want you to think I'm sneaking around behind your back."

"No problem. I've got a business to run. A merry-maid kinda thing, and you'd be surprised at the juicy secrets I have to keep."

"I'd rather not know. And one other thing?"

"Hmm?"

"I may be coming into some money soon, and . . . well . . . if that happens? I was wondering, just, you know, kind of like to test the waters?"

"Jesus, Cliff. What the hell are you trying to say?"

Cliff took a deep breath and held it, as if the sentence would need some forced air to help get it out. Then he exhaled with, "Think about whether you'd maybe like to go away. With me."

Barbie looked at him, astonished and speechless for a moment. "You just want me to *think* about it?"

"Uh . . . for now . . . yeah. But serious like."

She nodded, smiled, and Cliff was pretty damn sure no woman had ever been that open and genuine with him. He extended his hand and they shook on it. "Let's celebrate with double bacon cheeseburgers, CB's famous El Onion rings, a couple more boilermakers, and then get a good night's sleep."

Barbie smiled, a teasing, provocative one. "Except for the sleep, it's a deal!"

Later that evening, Cliff lay in bed, propped up on his elbow, watching Barbie as if for the first time without his being in a defensive posture. He couldn't tell if she was asleep or not until she whispered, "A watched woman never sleeps."

He lay back, closed his eyes, and fell asleep wondering if this might be a turning point to an open road in a life with too many dead ends so far.

NICK AND THE SEARCH team arrived back in the Morgan City Wash where the vehicles were parked just as the sun touched the higher terrain to the west. With the Scouts and their supervisors gathered around, he confirmed that Bruno's Pizza on W. Olive Avenue was expecting them, they could order anything they wanted and put it on Nick's tab.

"Even a Supreme?" one of the Scouts asked.

Nick laughed. "Knock yourselves out."

As the Scouts and supervisors walked to their vehicles, Number-10 Wilbur approached Nick. "Aren't you going to eat with us?"

He almost explained that he had too much to do and couldn't, but the look on the boy's face melted away any excuses. "Save me a seat by you, okay?"

"Cool!" Wilbur turned and sprinted away, shouting to his friends about how Mr. Phillips had asked to sit with him.

Nick had just put the ruddervator into the back of the Jeep when he noticed headlights approaching from the west. He stood by the open driver's door as a huge pickup with a jacked-up frame and massive off-road tires came to a stop beside him. The driver must have been at least in his 70s, with more hair on his face than his head, giving new meaning to the word *grizzled.*

The driver turned off the engine. In the ensuing quiet, he said, "What the hell ya doin' on my claim?"

"Good evening. Your what?"

"I own claim to this here land. All the gold's mine."

Nick wondered if that was intentional word play, decided not. He didn't know much about mine claims, but he was pretty sure that the old coot didn't have anything of the kind on public land. Best not challenge him, however. "That's wonderful. You're welcome to it."

The man's right hand moved beside him on the seat and came up with what looked like a Colt .45 single-action Peacemaker. He laid it in his lap and kept his hand on it. "I seen all them vehicles come in wi' ya. Whachalldoin'?"

The Glock on Nick's right hip felt about a thousand miles away from his hand. He glanced around to pick out an escape route, figured he might be able to duck to his left around the front of the pickup. He could probably have the Glock out before the guy put a sight on him.

Nick shifted position a little toward the front bumper, a black metal brush-guard monstrosity that could protect the radiator and headlights from a nuclear detonation. "You around these parts much?"

"I tol' ya it's my claim. I cain't work it sittin' on my ass at home watchin' the big screen like city fellers."

"Then you may know about that plane crash near here."

The old guy's head jerked as his eyes narrowed. "What bidness ya have wi' that?"

This was turning into an interrogation. Nick would soon run out of patience, but he wasn't ready to dodge .45 slugs just yet. "I'm an aviation accident investigator. I was running a search team out here this afternoon looking for a missing piece of an aircraft that might prove what caused the crash."

"I'll be goddamned."

You probably were long before now. "Now I need to—"

"Didja find it?"

"Yes."

"Can I see it?"

That took Nick completely by surprise, but in his peripheral vision he saw the guy lift the Colt and place it back on the seat. Handgun de-escalation was always a good thing. He smiled. "Sure. It's in the back of the Jeep."

As Nick turned his back on the old fart, the squealing sound of the pickup's door hinges split the quiet. He opened the lift gate to the Jeep's cargo area and stepped aside.

The man walked up and nodded at Nick. "Gotta put me some awl on them sumbitches." Then he peered into the cargo bed. "The hell is that?"

Figuring that an explanation of how ruddervators worked on a Victory would undoubtedly get him shot, Nick provided the short version.

The guy stepped back and crossed his arms. "So this plane come apart ina air?"

"Yes."

"That would'a been . . . 'bout a month ago, I reckon. I's out here prospectin' when a real gullywasher come a'callin'. Got my truck to higher ground and was sitting right up yonder waitin' her out when I seen some lights come over, a big flash 'o lightnin', and something slammed on top 'o my truck. Scared the fuckin' shit outa me, tell ya that."

Nick felt his whole body begin to tingle. "Something hit your truck."

"Damn near put a hole ina roof."

"Can I look?" When the guy nodded, Nick hurried to the guy's pickup and climbed up on the running board. Among all the other evidence of past collisions with hard objects, he found a depression that could have been caused by debris the size and density of a balance weight. Or a half-size one.

He got down and faced the man. "Can you show me where?"

"Git on in."

Nick got his GPS out of the Jeep and climbed in the truck. He couldn't find a seat belt, much less a shoulder harness, and he barely survived the old man's full-throttle charge up the slope to the north of the wash. After they stopped and got out, Nick asked how he knew this was the spot.

"Don't need one o' them there gadgets. Look 'round ya."

"What?"

"Ain't two places on earth the same. Just gotta pay 'tention."

"Right." This spot of desert looked *exactly* like all the rest of it that Nick had been tromping around in today, so he created a present-position waypoint in the GPS, then turned to face the direction the Victory had been flying to line up with where the Scouts found the ruddervator on the south side of the wash. Nick was searching for solid ground in a sea of conjecture, but not without scientific basis.

Falling from relatively low altitude, the balance weight would have had some residual forward velocity when it hit the guy's truck. That would put its final resting place lower on the slope between here and the wash. Or maybe in it. Or even on the other side, but not any farther. It was all a matter of the difference in drag coefficients between the ruddervator and the balance weight.

But he wouldn't be doing any searching this evening. Long shadows from the setting sun had enveloped the terrain. He considered trying to use the Scouts again. Even if the Scoutmaster agreed, that would take at least another day to set up, and he'd need to program a much tighter search grid into the GPSs.

In the meantime, he could come back to this spot and walk a spiral outward search pattern. Maybe with a metal detector? He'd never used one, and this ground was so hard that the weight would have bounced rather than bury itself. But would that make it easier for the detector to pick up metal that wasn't right under it?

Nick turned to the old man. "Thanks for your help. Just so you know, we might be back out here, but we're not looking to jump your claim, okay?

"Thought ya found whatcha been lookin' fer."

"Part of it. There's a piece still missing."

"I s'pose that'll be awright."

Nick accepted the danger of a ride back to his Jeep rather than risk running into a slithery devil-rattlesnake out for an evening snack. He opened the door to climb down, then turned to the driver. "You mind a question?"

"D'pends on what it is."

"What the hell are you really doing out here?"

"I tol' ya. Prospectin'."

"I'm sorry, but that makes no sense to me."

"That's 'cause you don' know nothin' 'bout it." The old guy turned off the engine. "Get out and lemme show ya somethin'."

He opened the tailgate. Two large galvanized water tanks for livestock were nestled in the front of the bed against the back of the cab. A stack of four aluminum half-cylinders about two feet in diameter and five feet long lay against the left side of the bed, three of which were fitted with wire mesh, graduated from course to fine. All had fold-down legs, sized from long to short, on one end. In the center sat an electric motor, a submersible water pump, a pick, a sledgehammer, three shovels and a length of PVC hose. A canvas tarp covered something lying against the right side of the bed.

The old prospector explained that using contour-line detail on quadrangle maps and the locations of every gold mine claim he could find in public records, he had plotted the most likely routes of water flowing downhill from local mining sites. In effect, he'd mapped an historical record of over 160 years of Mother Nature's placer mining in the area since the beginning of the gold rush days in the American West.

Gravel from the dry washes went into one livestock tank. He lived in a shack without electricity or running water, so he'd haul it to the house of a friend, the only one he had, apparently, and set up there. The water pump went on the bottom of the second tank with the hose routed to the highest aluminum half-cylinder. Each of the other three cylinders stepped down, ending over the tank with the water supply so it flowed in a continuous circuit.

The electric motor was clamped to the four-section trough assembly. He'd shaved some metal off the flywheel on the motor to make it shake a little. With the water running and the trough jiggling, he'd shovel gravel into the top section of the trough with no mesh on top. The water carried it down to the end of the trough and dumped it onto the mesh of the next lower trough section, then onto sections with successively finer mesh.

At the end of the trough assembly, only sand and any bits of gold would be waiting. All he had to do was add gravel at the top, keep the mesh screens clear of trapped larger rocks, and drink beer.

Nick had to admit that whether or not the guy had found anything worth more than a little pocket money didn't matter. He was spending his time doing exactly what he wanted, passionate about it, and offered no apologies. As long as he didn't shoot anyone to protect his bogus claim, it was a matter of no harm-no foul as far as Nick was concerned.

He complimented the prospector on his ingenuity and asked if he'd ever used a metal detector.

"Tough to find gold dust and flakes with 'em, but I'm always lookin' for scrap I can sell. Even found a few knives, spear points, arrowheads, buttons, belt buckles and such."

"Do you have to be right over the top of something to trigger the detector?"

The prospector thought about that a moment. "Dunno. Let's check 'er out." He reached into the truck bed, lifted the tarp, and picked up a metal detector lying on a pile of scrap metal. The device looked old enough to be an artifact, but it powered up fine. From the pile he brought out a piece of metal, dropped it on the ground and passed the detector directly over the top of it, then offset to each side to check the detector's response.

Nick's brain finally caught up with his eyes.

There lay a half-size balance weight from a Victory ruddervator.

TOMMY LEE DIDN'T HAVE time for this, but that didn't matter in the least to Beth McAllister. She called and wanted to know what he'd been doing for the past two days since she gave him $30,000 to pay off Leland. No cell-phone or email discussions. Get your ass to the house if you're not already there and wait for me.

"The house" meant Buster's, but Tommy Lee didn't need a story to explain Buster's whereabouts because Beth wouldn't even think about it. She steadfastly refused to acknowledge her young stud ran around with anyone like that, which was fine with Tommy Lee. Oil and water didn't begin to describe the incompatibility of his dual lives.

The fact that Monroe was imprisoned a hundred yards away didn't concern him either. She had truly disappeared and would remain so until it suited him otherwise.

Headlights flashed in the darkness through gaps in the front-window curtains. Beretta in hand, Tommy Lee went from the living room down the hallway to the kitchen and peeked out the window over the sink. Beth was getting out of what looked like another rental car. He slipped the pistol into his waistband at the small of his back under his shirt as he watched her approach the back door, then waited at the sink until she came into the kitchen.

To hug or not to hug? With or without kisses? He never knew, so he never assumed.

Beth tossed her purse on the kitchen table. "Anything to drink in this place?"

Aloof time with no physical contact, apparently. Tommy Lee got a pitcher of margaritas out of the freezer and poured two glasses. She accepted one and slouched into a chair, an unusual posture for a woman who always seemed to be conscious of presenting a straight spine, with shoulders back, hands and feet where they should be.

Her eyes, however, were as steel-hard as ever. "I don't appreciate your accepting thirty thousand in cash and leaving me in the dark about how it went with the drug dealer."

"It went fine."

"Not good enough. Define *fine*."

"I've still got all my original body parts in their normal places."

"It's hard for me to believe that's all there is to it. What about the Donkey Air thing?"

Tommy Lee tried hard not to laugh. If Beth thought anyone was having fun at her expense, *especially* him, she could make a Tasmanian devil seem docile. "It's called Mule Air, and we came to an understanding."

"Quit speaking in generalities and tell me *exactly* what you both *understand.*"

Tommy Lee wasn't about to admit that Leland was unwilling to let him off the hook so easily. "I agreed to assist in getting another airplane up and running. Then I'm out."

"Just like that?" When Tommy Lee nodded through a sip of margarita, Beth shook her head. "What about this 'in for life' gangster credo you hear so much about?"

"This guy's not a gangster, Beth. Yes, he's a drug dealer, and yes, he'll protect his turf, but whacking people isn't good for business. All you have to do is keep your word."

"Like when you put drugs on a sabotaged Victory and let Lawson fly it?"

"Leland doesn't know about that."

"Are you sure?"

"How could he?"

"I know of three people more than willing to tell him."

"Not including you, I trust?"

"That would make four, actually."

She smiled, and Tommy Lee wondered if female black widows did that as well just before consuming their mates. "Okay. Call it an error in judgment, or stupidity, whatever. It still isn't lying to or stealing from him. If I set up the transport again, he'll only be interested in results."

"And you'll be a key player in a drug operation."

"Not for long. He doesn't care who runs it, only that it's working."

Beth drained the last of her margarita, poured another, and topped off Tommy Lee's glass. "I'm getting very nervous about our other problem because it seems to have gone underground."

Just for a second, Tommy Lee's heart, stomach, and breathing all malfunctioned until he reminded himself Beth could not possibly know about what happened in the desert or who was in the bunker. He sipped the margarita and put down the glass. "I don't care whether they went underground, into the heavens, or somewhere in between so long as they're gone."

"You've become monumentally stupid in the last forty-eight hours if you think we're rid of them. We're hunkering down in a defensive posture and I don't like it." She stood, snatched her purse off the table, and poked a forefinger to within an inch of Tommy Lee's nose. "Mark my words, *partner*. You either handle this or I'll find someone who can."

For the next few minutes after Beth stormed out, he sipped the rest of his margarita and tried to come up with a play.

He agreed the best defense was a good offense, but the ideal way of dealing with his problems involved a head fake. If Beth thought he was being timid, she'd never suspect he had a solution in the works.

If she knew, Tommy Lee would lose control of the reins and the opportunity to regain the advantage of the balance weight. In his hands, no one could prove sabotage or even allege his connection to it, and Beth couldn't tie up loose ends by eliminating the only person who could do far more than attack her precious reputation.

The only lingering vulnerability he couldn't eliminate consisted of two carbon logbook pages that weren't burned along with the rest of the Victory records. But they represented a minor threat at best without evidence to corroborate the intention to sabotage an airplane.

Okay, then.

Beth knows about the bunker but has no clue what's in it.

Monroe insists she doesn't have the balance weight, but either she or Phillips does. She can't do any harm, and hopefully will be coming to her senses very soon in the dark isolation of her dungeon.

Phillips is probably up to mischief, but it won't matter if Tommy Lee gets his hands on the balance weight.

Leland will either accept Tommy Lee's apology and cash compensation or he won't, with or without resurrection of Mule Air. No sense in worrying about something he can't control.

And finally, Yates. Current whereabouts unknown, but destined for a lonely grave with a virtual headstone that reads *HERE LIES PAYBACK.*

Chapter Twenty-Nine

Nick was up early without relying on the alarm because he never really got to sleep. Of the two balance weights he knew as of yesterday afternoon had to be lying somewhere out there in the desert, to find the one Parker had cut in half made looking for the other one an exercise in futility. The thrill of holding the physical proof in his hand had not abated for about twelve hours now, and with his concern for Caitlin layered on top, Nick simply hadn't relaxed enough to doze off.

In addition, as if he needed another reason for not sleeping, his mind kept revisiting a disturbing thought: Tommy Lee Parker's sabotage had been a truly ingenious way to murder Lawson McAllister and get away with it.

To remove one balance weight would have maximized the imbalance and increased the likelihood of inflight breakup, but the difference in control pressures during preflight might have alerted Lawson. Removing only half of a balance weight lessened that risk, but still created dangerous inflight conditions based on Parker's private knowledge of how Lawson flew the airplane.

And the corollary question that popped up, like another mystery to be solved, was how did an aviation mechanic come up with the knowledge to target the balance-weight vulnerability inherent in V-Tail ruddervators?

Maybe Parker had an accomplice, as yet not visible to Nick's investigative radar. And who might that be? A PhD in aeronautical engineering who was vulnerable to blackmail? Sure. *Get a grip, Phillips.* Far more likely, Parker's source lived behind his computer screen. And why not? Nick had read that you could find out how to do almost anything online, and it wouldn't be long before the word *almost* would no longer apply.

Want to build a bomb? *Click here.* How about making a silencer? Or finding out which poisons are so hard to detect that only the most thorough postmortem can determine the cause of death? *Click here for details.* And what had to have been Parker's favorite: *MurderByAirplane.com.*

Philosophically, Nick supported the concept of free speech without reservation. But arrival of the modern equivalent in the age of the Internet had brought with it an online sewer inhabited by the scum of the earth, and the world would be a better place if those who lived in the light could nuke the darkness and be done with it.

On his mental To Do list, Nick added an item: *Find Parker's source.*

Following a hurried morning ritual, he grabbed a cup of coffee in the motel lobby and tapped a little bell on the counter. A kid who looked about 16 years old stepped out from the back office.

"Up early today, sir?"

Nick almost replied with something snide, like, *You mean it's morning?* But he caught himself in time and smiled. "Along with you, it appears."

"No, sir. My shift is about done."

"Good for you." Nick laid his key card on the counter. "Check me out of room two oh six, please."

The kid did that and handed Nick his receipt. "Have a nice trip."

"Thanks. Do you know of a shipping company between here and the Dry Springs Airport?"

"Don't think so. You need to head the other direction."

Nick thanked him and stowed his luggage in the Jeep. Sight of the crumpled ruddervator lying on the cargo bed with the rear seat folded down sent a revived tingle of excitement through him. It also turned his thoughts to the problem of getting the evidence to Albuquerque.

To ship it meant finding a FedEx or UPS store and waiting until they opened. Even with the obvious damage, they probably wouldn't accept it as is, which meant building a shipping container. Time wasn't necessarily a factor, except that the sooner he turned everything over to Caitlin, the sooner he could bid goodbye to an experiment in private aircraft accident investigation littered with mixed results.

The chance of losing it en route was too negligible to consider, but the best solution would be to take it with him in the airplane. He stared at the ruddervator and tried to imagine how he'd do it.

With tandem seating, the single passenger rode behind Nick and in front of the baggage compartment. He could remove the bolts that secured the rear control stick and the piano-hinge pins holding the rear seatback and baggage compartment door in position. This would provide a flat area for the ruddervator to lie on, one end behind his seatback and the other end extending into the open baggage compartment. The control stick, rear seatback, and baggage compartment door could lie on top of the ruddervator. One of the reasons he used a duffel bag was the ability to mold it into tight spaces, and he should be able to stuff it on top of everything else.

For this to work safely, he'd have to secure this unusual cargo to prevent it from shifting position if he encountered turbulence. But he had the rear seat lap belt and shoulder harness and some cargo straps in the baggage compartment. With a little creativity, he could probably tie everything down.

He stared at the eastern horizon, the glow of dawn just beginning to backlight the higher terrain of the Tonto National Forest and the Sierra Ancha.

Might as well try it. If the ruddervator didn't fit or wasn't secured well enough, go to plan B. He didn't have one yet, but he'd deal with that if and when he had to.

Nick drove to the Dry Springs Airport and hurried through all the departure preparations. Weather wasn't a factor, except for an area of forecast moderate to severe turbulence affecting his route over the mountains. He unloaded everything from the Jeep, turned it in, paid his bill for fuel, and began packing. One of the ramp guys walked up and asked if he needed help.

"Got it, thanks. This is not your normal cargo-packing algorithm."

"Huh?"

"Problem. I'm having to come up with a solution on the spot."

"I'll say." He pointed at the ruddervator. "What's this off of?"

"A Victory."

After a pause, *"That* Victory?"

"Yup."

"I'll be damned." He turned away with, "Have a nice flight" tossed over his shoulder.

With everything secured, Nick grabbed individual pieces of the cargo and pulled, trying to dislodge them, get them to shift around. Once satisfied, he climbed in and ten minutes later launched into the dawn.

Pockets of turbulence bounced him around during the climb. He'd planned to cruise at 8,500 feet, but it was so bumpy that he continued climbing and finally leveled off at 11,500 feet, the highest altitude he could use without supplemental oxygen when flying eastbound under visual flight rules. It wasn't smooth, but he'd have to live with it.

Once established in cruise with the autopilot tracking his desired course, the temptation to daydream crept into the cockpit and filled him with a sense of accomplishment. He'd made more progress than he would have ever imagined when he first contemplated trying to find anything worthy of being called evidence in the Arizona desert.

And at this very moment, strapped down within reach behind him, the ultimate proof of sabotage was on its way to serve a purpose known only to Caitlin Monroe.

The old prospector had been delighted with a handful of bills from Nick's wallet in return for a relatively worthless chunk of lead, and he admitted to Nick that his infatuation with gold was fueled far more by the anticipation of finding some than by any success at doing so. "I pays my bills sellin' scrap," he said. "The gold's goin' into my 401k."

Nick had made it to Bruno's for pizza with Number-10 Wilbur and the Scouts in time to spend over an hour listening to various adventures he'd somehow missed on the search line. It reminded him of how the fertile imagination of youth can transport a kid to far away places with very little effort.

Every call to Caitlin remained unanswered, and he'd been unable to leave any messages, voice or text. Pondering his best next move made him a little apprehensive.

First, he'd check her motel room. If she was still registered and he found no sign of her or her car, maybe he could get the manager to do a welfare check. But he might not do that for anyone but law enforcement. Unless some greenbacks could persuade him.

Who might have seen her most recently? Their last face-to-face, or any contact for that matter, had been in Caitlin's car in the desert about five days ago. When he turned over the balance weight and the drugs to her—*oh, shit*.

A traffic stop or accident? Cops found the stuff and she's in jail? But she would have called him. Or a lawyer. But she would have him call Nick, wouldn't she?

What if she tried to return the drugs to their rightful owner, who wouldn't want anyone outside his organization to know about it? Caitlin was confident enough in herself to try something like that.

Or did the Parker/McAllister coalition have anything to do with her disappearance?

What about Yates? Every time Nick had seen him around Caitlin, the guy had a predatory look, or maybe more like an aura, giving off a vibe that he was about to reach out and snatch her up.

Whatever the reality, Nick had to find it as the first order of business in Albuquerque.

Approaching 30 miles from the Double Eagle II Airport, he checked the weather and began a descent. The ride had smoothed out, so he let his speed build to the top of the green arc on the airspeed indicator, which provided a visual reference for the highest recommended speed in turbulent air. Any faster, and he'd be in the yellow caution arc, where a combination of turbulence and control inputs could overstress the airframe. It didn't take a V-Tail and flutter to bend metal.

Passing 10,000 feet, Nick felt a few bumps and then a sudden, intense jolt like driving a car across a speed bump at

50 miles an hour. It slammed his head into the canopy and he felt something behind him move.

He retarded the throttle and pulled back on the control stick to slow down, felt resistance, pulled harder, but the stick was jammed. He couldn't move it aft enough to control his pitch attitude and bring the nose up to the horizon.

When he tried to move the stick to the right to roll out of the left bank and level the wings, it wouldn't budge. He had more movement to the left, which meant that he could bank more steeply in that direction to increase his turn rate, but reversing direction into a right turn was impossible. He was trapped in a left descending turn.

The first rule for any emergency situation appeared in bold, red, holographic type between Nick and the instrument panel: *Maintain aircraft control.*

A glance at the altimeter and vertical velocity indicator combined with the average elevation of the terrain beneath him and quick mental math defined his immediate problem.

He had less than a minute to stop the descent.

And the only way to do that was counter-intuitive.

Nick rolled into a steeper left bank, pushed the right rudder all the way to the stop, and shoved the throttle full forward.

The rudder now acted as an elevator and yawed the nose up, up, up until it was above the horizon.

When the vertical velocity reversed from a descent into a climb and the altimeter began to increase, Nick neutralized the rudder, rolled out of the left bank, and held the stick hard against the obstruction to both pitch and bank. He was still restricted to a left turn, but with the nose above the horizon he had solved the immediate and most serious problem of insufficient clearance from the terrain.

Second rule: *Analyze the situation and take proper action.*

Did he have sufficient pitch control to position the nose up and down well enough to land?

Nick eased the stick forward and aft to test the range of movement and decided, *No*.

Could he eliminate the restriction and regain more pitch control?

Options raced around in Nick's head until he realized his only choice was to risk further restriction in an attempt to lessen the amount he had now.

Which meant trying to dislodge the obstruction.

The only way to do that was to move the stick away from what was jamming it, create turbulence of his own with aggressive flight control inputs, and hope that the cargo causing the problem would shift enough to allow more control.

But he needed more altitude for a chance to bail out if his makeshift solution made the situation worse. As he tightened his harness straps, the memory of bailing out of a stricken airplane over a Colorado forest came unbidden into the cockpit.

The feeling of complete helplessness as the ground rushed up, the split-second, irreversible decision to jettison the canopy, pound on the harness quick release, push and kick free of the potential coffin the cockpit had become, grab for the ripcord *where is the goddamn thing!* and yank it, hear the zipping sound of nylon on nylon and feel the most delicious pain in the world as the opening shock of the parachute threatened to rearrange his manhood with the crotch straps.

Shoving those thoughts aside, Nick continued the climb until the altimeter read 15,000 feet. That meant he was about 7000 feet above the highest terrain. He'd prefer to get twice that much if he could. But without oxygen he risked the effects of hypoxia, the first symptom of which was confusion, followed by euphoria, then deterioration of motor coordination and ultimately, loss of consciousness. To attempt a bail out under those conditions would be like, *Who needs a parachute? I can flyyyyyyy!*

With no reason to put this off, Nick eased the control stick away from both the fore-aft and left-right obstructions and stirred the stick with sharp movements while he shoved the rudder left right left right left right.

A clunking sound, barely audible through his headset, and a solid thump in the airframe.

The stick moved further aft than it had since the initial event, but it was harder to move than usual. In his mind, Nick pictured a shifting of the obstruction so that it now rested on top of the rear cockpit controls where the stick attaches to the torque tube rather than in back of it. That solved the most critical problem, but he still couldn't roll any farther right than a 20-degree left bank. Now what?

Third rule: *Land as soon as practical/possible.*

Double Eagle II Airport probably didn't have fire-and-rescue capability. Albuquerque International Sunport definitely did. Nick had no intention of needing it, but to attempt a compromised landing without fire-fighting equipment available was akin to playing Russian roulette.

He was about 25 miles from Albuquerque, and he had to get on top of the airport so he could fly a left, descending spiral to the runway. But trying to go direct while in a continuous turn was like riding a merry-go-round to travel from one end of a carnival to the other. The only solution was to use a slip, a common cross-control maneuver for crosswind landings, that he would adapt to this situation.

The airport had just passed his 12 o'clock position and was drifting farther right. He couldn't roll into a right bank and point the nose at it, so he continued the left turn until the airport was at his 11 o'clock and drifting toward 12. With the stick held as far right as it would go against the obstruction and the airplane in a 15-degree left bank, Nick pushed the right rudder to yaw the nose right and away from the direction the aircraft was moving. The slip effectively canceled out the left turn and allowed him to fly directly toward the Sunport.

He listened to the recorded airport information and confirmed typical mid-day weather at Albuquerque: scattered clouds, good visibility, winds beginning to increase and turn gusty. With the radio on Albuquerque Approach Control frequency, Nick monitored the radio traffic as the controller gave sequencing instructions to multiple aircraft in the landing queue. At the first pause, he made his initial call.

"Albuquerque Approach, Experimental Eight Five November Delta, twenty southwest passing thirteen thousand three hundred, VFR, with information Juliet, landing Sunport, over."

"Experimental Eight Five November Delta, Albuquerque, squawk two zero four five and ident."

Nick changed the code on his transponder from the standard 1200 for VFR operations to 2045 and pressed the ident switch.

The controller gave instructions to three other airplanes and came back to Nick with, "Experimental Five November Delta, radar contact nineteen miles southwest at thirteen thousand, maintain VFR, descend to and maintain ten thousand four hundred and report a three-mile final Runway Three Zero."

For efficiency, standard radio terminology allowed shortening radio call signs to the last three numbers or letters, and Nick began doing that now. "Albuquerque, Five November Delta, unable. I need clearance to high key for a forced-landing approach."

"You have an engine problem, Five November Delta?"

"Five November Delta, negative. Flight controls. I can't bank to the right."

"Are you declaring an emergency, Five November Delta?"

"Not at this time, Albuquerque."

Then in plain language, because there wasn't any standard terminology for a situation like this, Nick explained that he had an hour of fuel on board and could fly a left orbit above the airport while the controller adjusted takeoff and landing traffic to create a window of opportunity for his landing. This would effectively close the airport to all other aircraft while Nick flew a very non-standard approach. By rule, this granted him landing priority and necessitated declaring an emergency, which meant filing a report with the Federal Aviation Administration.

Nick didn't know a single pilot who disagreed with the aviator's version of the FAA motto: "We're not happy unless you're not happy." Once they had reason to put a pilot and an airplane under scrutiny, watch out. But with clearance to fly direct to the airport at or above 10,000 feet, he didn't need emergency priority because no other takeoff or landing traffic would be up there, and he was above the upper limit of the airspace assigned to the airport.

By the time Nick arrived at the Sunport and entered a left-hand orbit, his right leg was aching and beginning to quiver from the exertion of holding full rudder. While waiting for landing clearance, he used his secondary radio to check the winds, which were out of the northwest at 8-10 knots.

Of four runways at Sunport, he could land on Runway 30 with a direct headwind. Runway 03 would be the better choice because he'd have a 90-degree crosswind from the left. Pilots seldom had reason to choose a runway with crosswinds, but in this case it would help him land the airplane. During a lull in radio traffic, he informed the controller of his request to use it.

The problem facing Nick boiled down to how well he could fly a curvilinear approach all the way to touchdown. If the nose of the aircraft passed the runway heading at any time during the landing attempt, he wouldn't be able to roll out of the left turn to correct his heading back to the right. That would mandate a go-around and another try, while all the other traffic on the airport waited, like spectators at an air show, some undoubtedly expecting to witness a fireball.

The controller's voice filled Nick's headset with, "Five November Delta, Albuquerque."

"Five November Delta, go ahead."

"Descend at your discretion to set up your high key for Runway Zero Three. Contact Albuquerque Tower on one two zero point three."

"Five November Delta copies." Nick changed his radio frequency to 120.3 and checked in with the Tower. The controller told him to expect landing clearance in about five minutes.

The elevation at Sunport was 5355 feet. For his first attempt, he planned to hit high key, a point directly above the approach end of the runway, at 6300 feet, and begin a continuous, 360-degree left descending spiral to arrive over the end of the runway a few feet above airport elevation, with the nose either lined up on runway heading or slightly to the right of it. That would allow him to add right rudder to stop the turn, and any last-second adjustments would require only rudder and varying the amount of left bank at touchdown. Now all he had to do was execute the maneuver.

Nick had made two orbits level at 6300 feet and was setting up for the third when the controller cleared him to land and confirmed emergency vehicles were standing by.

That meant the controller had probably declared an emergency for him, and Nick shook hands with the reality that this could end up very badly if he didn't fly the maneuver exactly as planned.

Halfway around the turn back to high key, he glanced down to his left. Flashing red lights appeared to be covering the taxiways and run-up area at the approach end of the runway. All this activity just for him. A little frightening, and at the same time very comforting to know the personnel on those vehicles trained continuously to put out aircraft fires and pull survivors from aircraft wreckage.

He wouldn't be able to see the approach end of the runway when he arrived at high key because it would be underneath the nose, so he picked out a ground reference point off his left wing to begin the final 360-degree turn. Approaching high key, Nick lowered the landing gear, checked for three green locked lights, extended the flaps, confirmed the prop in high pitch and the mixture rich. Passing the reference point, he increased his left bank to 30 degrees, reduced the throttle, and lowered the nose to begin the descent.

After the initial 90 degrees of turn, the approach end of the runway and the numbers appeared over his left shoulder.

And from this point on, Nick's challenge was to establish in his mind's eye a curved, descending flight path that extended from his seat and ended on the white 03 on the end of the runway. All he had to do was put his butt on it and keep it there, "riding the ribbon."

The approach could end up in one of three ways: a perfect roll out on final and subsequent touchdown; an under turn with the nose still to the right of the runway centerline, which would require a last-second adjustment with a combination of rudder and left aileron; or an overturn, which forcing him to abort the landing and try again.

Nick's primary objective was to plan for a slight under turn, because he could correct for it during the last seconds before touchdown in spite of his flight control limitations.

As he approached 90 degrees to final approach, he adjusted pitch and power to slow without changing his descent rate, scanned the cockpit instruments, and checked the gear and flap position indicators one last time.

Passing 200 feet above the runway elevation, he was a little higher and faster than he wanted. If he kept turning at this rate, he'd overturn the runway.

He moved the stick to the right against the obstruction to reduce the bank to 15 degrees and slow the turn rate, and simultaneously added full rudder to hold the nose to the right of the runway heading. The maneuver lowered Nick onto the approach path he wanted and reduced his speed about five knots.

As the runway rushed up at him and the 03 marking on the runway disappeared under the nose, he pulled the throttle to idle, released most of the right rudder, and increased the left bank just as the left main wheel touched. In quick succession, the right wing lowered and the right main wheel touched. He eased the stick back to plant the tailwheel on the runway, added full left aileron into the wind, and used tailwheel steering to maintain directional control.

A normal landing rollout seemed a little anticlimactic, but he'd take it.

"Experimental Five November Delta, continue to taxiway Foxtrot One and contact Albuquerque Ground Control on one two one point niner. Do you wish to cancel your emergency?"

Nick glanced to his left at the parallel taxiway where a parade of emergency vehicles with flashing red lights provided his own personal escort. "Yes, sir, cancel the emergency, and thank you for your assistance."

As Nick turned off the runway, the vehicles turned off their lights in unison and scattered to various points on the airport they called home. Nick switched to Ground Control frequency and the controller asked where he wanted to park. The area serving general aviation was directly ahead. He picked one of the two fixed-base operators and taxied toward it. As is typical of larger airports with a lot of transient traffic, a FOLLOW ME vehicle darted out from the main entrance and led him to a parking spot on the ramp.

The line guy waited until Nick opened the canopy and asked what services he needed.

"Nothing at the moment, thanks. I'll coordinate with the front desk when I decide."

Nick unstrapped from the harness and parachute, climbed out onto the wing, and stepped onto the ramp. His legs began to tremble. He gripped the canopy rail, breathed deeply for a moment, and peered into the back cockpit.

The cargo had shifted position from the way he had packed it, but he couldn't see the fitting where the stick attached to the torque tube. He unfastened the restraints and lifted out the ruddervator. It had apparently shifted during the atmospheric turbulence so that it was jammed against the aft edge of the fitting. Nick's intentional turbulence had shifted the ruddervator just enough to rest on top of the fitting, which released the jammed condition and allowed full elevator movement, but with more friction than normal.

And there, beneath the floor plates, resting against the bottom fuselage skin below the fitting, sat half of a Victory balance weight. Nick stared at it, his mind replaying the packing of the cargo.

He had put the weight in an outside pocket of his smaller duffel and used it to elevate the ruddervator above the fitting. The duffel had been tossed to one side. The pocket was unzipped. And a chunk of lead that had caused a fatal crash very nearly claimed a second victim.

Weak knees threatened to put Nick on his butt, so he leaned against the fuselage, closed his eyes, and offered a bunch of *Thank yous* to Lady Luck.

It took about 30 minutes to unload the cargo, return the rear cockpit to its normal configuration, and secure the airplane for overnight. He flagged down a line guy and arranged for a rental Jeep to be brought on the ramp, then loaded the ruddervator and his luggage and parked at the FBO. After signing for the Jeep, he got a cup of coffee and sat in the pilot's lounge.

Now was not the time, but sooner or later he needed to have a heart-to-heart talk with a mirror and acknowledge a mistake that could very easily have ended in disaster. If the flight controls had jammed at lower altitude, an NTSB Aviation Go Team would be scrambling about now to find out why his airplane had suddenly slammed into the ground.

No one in the FBO seemed the least bit interested in him. From the activity visible out the front windows, Albuquerque Sunport appeared to be back to full operation as if nothing had happened. Nick knew that the response of the air traffic control system and the FAA to an emergency condition after the fact was unpredictable no matter who declared it.

He also knew that the Aviation Safety Reporting System, or ASRS, was a voluntary, confidential, and non-punitive method for pilots to "fess up" in advance of possibly being investigated for a rule infraction or doing something that violated the catch-all safety-of-flight standard.

Nick hadn't broken any specific regulation, but he could

be chastised for failure to secure the cargo properly. Having the ASRS report on file wouldn't prevent the FAA from taking official action, but it carried a valuable mitigating effect by indicating he wasn't trying to hide anything. He had 48 hours to do that, but in the meantime, he had other problems to deal with.

Another unsuccessful attempt to reach Caitlin elevated her safety to priority number one. Time to be proactive with something other than a phone.

He drove to the motel where she'd been staying, checked her room and the adjacent parking lot. No Mercedes, and he couldn't see anything through the closed curtain. He asked a housekeeper if the room was occupied. News that it was, but it hadn't been slept in for the past few nights, and yes, the guest had been staying here for at least a week, sent Nick to the manager's office.

The guy had the look of a squirrel faced with a new barrier added to his favorite bird feeder. "I'm sure your request is motivated by genuine concern, sir, but I can't give out the names of other registered guests. You wouldn't want me to—"

"Invade my privacy? Hell no. But if I'd been kidnapped, I might appreciate someone taking a less dogmatic view."

"Whoa, now. You didn't say anything about a kidnapping. Perhaps we should call the police?"

Easy, Nick, don't get this guy punching in 9-1-1 or 3-1-1 or whatever. He crossed his fingers behind his back. "Pardon me for exaggerating. But she has this . . . condition. A seizure kind of thing, and she could be incapacitated."

"Well, if so, it would have had to occur sometime after the housekeepers checked the room yesterday, and you said you haven't been able to reach her for days."

"Do they go all the way inside if the bed doesn't appear to

have been slept in, for example?"

"They're supposed to."

"That's not what I asked."

The manager sighed as if he'd just decided this was the mother of all anti-squirrel barriers. "Follow me, but I will be the only one who enters the room. Agreed?"

"Absolutely."

No Caitlin, only her luggage, some clothing and toiletries, none of which had been moved recently according to the housekeepers. Nick thanked the manager, apologized for being testy, and got a room of his own. With his luggage stowed in the closet and the ruddervator hidden under the bed, he tried to call Caitlin again. No luck. Time for another tactic.

Yates answered on the second ring. "Well what do you know? Did little Miss Walther Monroe point her gun at the pickle in your pocket and threaten to blow it off?"

Nick *really* wanted to respond in kind, but the last thing he needed now was a word fight with a jerk. "Do you know where Caitlin is?"

"Uh . . . she doesn't tell me squat. In the meantime, we need to meet. I've got a proposal and I'm not discussing it over the phone."

CHAPTER THIRTY

Nick walked into El Barstool and paused to let his eyes adjust. The place was deserted except for a big dude standing behind the bar. Light from an overhead spot reflected off the top of his bald head and threw a long shadow across his face. He put down a beer mug he'd been drying and nodded. "You're not welcome in here unless you're thirsty."

"I wouldn't be caught dead in a place like this unless I was dying of thirst."

They glared at each other for a few seconds.

The dude shrugged. "My name's CB and I own the joint. What'll it be?"

"Coffee would be good."

CB frowned, a scary sight through a mass of unruly facial hair. "This ain't no goddamn Starbuck's."

"But it's barely two o'clock."

"Who says?"

"My watch."

"It's lying to you." CB pointed behind Nick.

He turned and sure enough, a wall clock above the front door had a 5 at all 12 hourly positions.

"Well I'll be." Nick peered at his watch, shook it a few times, looked at CB and shrugged. "In that case, I'll take a draft. You have Santa Fe Pale Ale?"

"A what?"

Only then did it dawn on Nick how stupid that sounded. Kind of like asking a waitress at a roadside diner if they had any béchamel. *Of course. It's one of our customers' favorite choices to go with the fries.*

"Make it a Bud."

Yates had told Nick to sit in the very last booth. When CB brought the beer, he leaned over and said, "Just so you know, it's—"

"Barbie's booth. I have permission."

CB smiled. "Fair enough, my man. But if you're lyin'? Hold on to your balls."

About ten minutes later, a man walked in the front door and stopped to talk with CB. Nick checked him out, but couldn't see well with bright sunlight glaring through the window in the door behind him. A few sips of beer later, he glanced up and found Yates standing at the end of the booth with a mug of beer and a shot class of whiskey.

Yates motioned with the beer toward the empty side of the booth. "Join you?"

"I suppose so, since you're the one who told me I had permission to sit here."

Yates slid in, drank some beer, and stared at Nick. "What?"

"I have no idea. You wanted to meet."

"You're looking at me like you're confused or something."

"Well, yeah. I guess I am. Where's that hideous sport coat, shirt and tie combo?"

Yates leaned forward and smiled. "At the cleaners."

Nick didn't believe that for an instant, but neither did he know what to make of Yates' switch to normal clothes. "Bet you can't wait to get them back. What are we here for?"

Yates launched into a story about being offered a job by

none other than Elizabeth McAllister, to eliminate a problem she had by "disappearing" the people who were causing it. He hadn't accepted it, but said that he would think about how he might pull it off and get back to her.

"When was this?"

"Less than a week ago."

"Assuming this conversation means you won't be accepting the job, thanks for the heads up. Anything else?"

"How about we team up again? But this time, I'm calling the shots, because I've got the plan and the opportunity to carry it out."

"I'm listening."

Yates explained that if Nick and Caitlin agreed to drop out of sight and off the grid with no traceable cell phone use, emails, credit card transactions, and so forth, he would take the job, charge a life-changing fee, and in return present evidence to the Balloon Bitch to prove he'd taken care of the problem.

Then Nick and Caitlin could resurface and hang BB's trophy head on the wall. She'd have a very surprised look, kind of like a deer in the headlights. Yates had a good laugh over that and said he would also record a conversation to prove that BB had engaged his services in a murder-for-hire scheme. How about it?

"Let's say I agree. Providing proof of life is one thing, but faking proof of death seems a little harder."

"Not to worry. I'm into head-faking people. It might be as simple as handing her something I couldn't have gotten without prying it out of your cold, dead hands, as the saying goes. Let me worry about that."

"But that means we wait while you get paid running your scam. What's in it for us but delay?"

"You didn't listen well enough. I may not have been part of

Monroe's inner circle, but it's no secret that blackmail has been her only realistic objective from the git-go. Your circumstantial evidence of sabotage might be enough to threaten BB into paying up. But if I have a recorded conversation of her hiring me to kill you two, there's nothing circumstantial about that."

"Okay, but a recording like that has to pass specific legal—"

"I just told you to let me worry about the details."

"But why would you turn it over to us?"

"Jesus, Phillips. You're still thinking of me as the outsider doing my own thing. I'm proposing a scam that needs your cooperation to *disappear*. Temporarily, mind you. I do my thing, hand you something that helps Monroe do hers, and then we split the ultimate reward."

Nick laughed. "Ah, yes. You didn't mention that."

Yates grinned. "But it won't work for any of us if we don't collaborate."

Nick leaned back in the booth and played out the scenario as best he could to fit Yates' proposal into what Nick knew that Yates apparently didn't. Time to test that out.

"We've got a problem with your plan."

"Just one?"

"That's all it takes. Caitlin's missing." Nick watched Yates' eyes for any indication he already knew and saw nothing but surprise. Best not to rely on a guy, however, who Nick was convinced had mastered laying smokescreens.

Yates shook his head. "That doesn't mean anything. She isn't much for announcing her intentions."

"Granted, but no way she'd suddenly go hands off, drop out of sight, and stop communicating. We have to assume they've got her and your scam won't work."

"Why not assume they killed her?"

"Because that doesn't eliminate the vulnerability to

prosecution they believe is tied to the physical evidence." Nick explained how the balance-weight connected McAllister to Parker and both of them to the sabotage. "I gave Caitlin one-half of the puzzle last week, and I just found the other half. It's the smoking gun."

This revelation physically shoved Yates back in the booth, and Nick was pretty sure he wasn't faking it. "When were you planning to tell me that?"

"Not until I had at least some of your cards on the table. And because I don't trust you to ever reveal your ace in the hole."

"I'm glad we got that straight. But if she has half, and she's missing, what makes you think they didn't snatch her *and* the evidence? Bury both and be done with it?"

"Because Caitlin would never totally compromise her safety. She's hidden that crucial evidence somewhere, and it's her ticket out."

"Maybe not. Pain can be a great motivator."

"No argument there, but Parker and McAllister have done all their dirty work from a distance. I can't imagine that either of them has the stomach for torture."

"I bet Parker knows some good ol' boys who might *enjoy* it."

Nick shook his head. "Never happen. He and McAllister are trying to shut down the threat of exposure. Involving some loose-cannon psycho exposes them even more than they already are."

Yates picked up his empty beer mug and signaled to CB for another. "I'm still not hearing a plan."

"Then here it is, and the partnership you proposed, suitably modified, will be required to make it happen."

YOGI BERRA'S FAMOUS QUOTE about this being déjà vu all over again came to mind as Nick trotted through the desert, dodging rocks and cactus under the light of a partial moon and hoping he'd be able to see a rattlesnake in time to perform his own imitation of a Michael Jordan gravity-defying leap.

Arriving unbitten at the Stillwater Aviation hangar, he paused to catch his breath and slow his pounding heart. His objective was the locker near Parker's workbench that had a box with a couple of spare balance weights. He'd unlatched a window for access during his last illegal foray. Hopefully, no one had noticed it.

With a small flashlight he peered though the window. Someone had locked it. But the tire iron he'd used to pry the window open and had to leave behind when he escaped in such a hurry was still lying on the ground. He picked it up and tried to wedge it between the window and the frame, but the tip of the iron was too thick.

Then in the light beam he noticed the glazing in the pane had shrunk up so much that it didn't appear to be in contact with the frame or glass. He tapped it gently with the flashlight, felt it move, really loose.

With the tip of his knife blade, Nick teased away the glazing in a few minutes and the pane came out with gentle prying. He set it on the ground, reached in and turned the latch. Rusty hinges fought him, but he got the window open enough to slip through. Unlike the last time, he managed to contact the floor first with his hands rather than his face, and he transitioned quietly into a crouch.

A pause now, pretty sure Leo had no reason to have installed a security system in the last week, Nick listened until satisfied he was alone. Careful not to bump into any of the airplanes and sound an alarm of his own, he found his way to Parker's work area and—*uh oh.*

A clean workbench with a completely different tool arrangement surprised him. Once mechanics developed a system for a place for everything and everything in its place, they usually didn't mess with it. Fully expecting to find an obstacle for which he was unprepared, Nick stepped over to the equipment locker, which hadn't been locked before, and lifted up on the handle with two gloved fingers.

Clunk, the door opened. Not surprising, really. The total value of the nuts, bolts, washers, and other miscellaneous parts in the locker probably didn't warrant special security measures. He knelt and with the beam of his flashlight probed the right rear of the bottom shelf. There sat what looked like the same arrangement of cardboard boxes. He pulled out the first one, then the second and breathed a sigh of relief. Two spare balance weights remained.

If the half-weight he'd found in Parker's personal locker had any distinctive marks on the uncut surfaces not present on either of these, that might alert him that he was receiving a fake in return for releasing his hostage. Nick couldn't remember any marks, but at least he could make sure these weights didn't have any. He removed them from the box and examined them with the flashlight. They appeared to be the same, and identical enough to the half weight to pass a naked-eye inspection if Nick cut them carefully.

Now for a band saw, the most likely metalworking tool for the job. Nick went to the area in the workshop filled with the power tools used for cutting, shaping, grinding, and polishing metal. Like all the rest, the band saw had a gooseneck floodlight that could be positioned to eliminate shadows where the blade contacted the metal.

Using clamps and straight pieces of angle iron, Nick fashioned guides on either side of the blade, equidistant from it and spaced apart just enough to keep the balance weight from shifting during the cut. He found a piece of wood for a push-tool to keep his hands and fingers well clear and a pair of safety goggles someone had left on a nearby tool.

This would be noisy. Normally he'd wear ear protection, but it wasn't like he did this every day. His real worry was that he'd be totally engrossed in the cutting and wouldn't have a clue if someone showed up. He might wake up with his hand being presented to the band-saw blade and a question or two on Parker's lips.

With no choice but to do it, Nick flipped the power switch on the saw and spent about ten minutes dividing the two weights in half. He examined the cut edges and wondered if Parker had dressed the ones on the weight he bisected. If so, Nick would be able to use the half he found in the desert as a sample and do his best to duplicate any filing to smooth the edges.

Metal shavings lay all around the band saw. He found an industrial vacuum and cleaned the area, then returned to the locker to verify he'd left its external appearance exactly as he'd found it. Approaching his private unauthorized-access window, his heart went into high-pump mode as headlight beams appeared in the desert toward the front of the hangar and came closer to the window.

Panic tried to glue his feet to the floor as he ran to the rear of the hangar toward the mechanic's personal locker room where he found the half balance weight in the baggie. He barely made it as the sound of a rock being thrown through a window shattered the silence. With the door cracked open a tiny bit, he knelt, drew the Glock, and peeked out through the thin space between the edge of the door and the jamb.

Teenage voices, speaking Spanish, whooping and hollering, having fun. With all this commotion, he doubted they were professionals and spring-loaded to use weapons, even if they had any. But he couldn't afford to be wrong, discovered, and on foot. He needed a diversion to clear the way for an uneventful escape.

Behind Nick was a cot, probably for mechanic siestas, or rest periods during a rush-to-finish overhaul of some kind. He stripped off the blanket, found the center of the sheet beneath it, and cut out two eyeholes with his knife.

Back at the door, he confirmed the raiding party had left the hangar. Their voices drifted back from the front office. Nick slipped out of the locker room and found the welding station. The helmet hanging on a hook nearby was a design with a Darth Vader look. Nick tried it out, and smiled. It had an auto-darkening feature. Without it, he wouldn't be able to see much of anything not lit up by the bright glow of the welding arc.

He donned the sheet so he could see through the holes and slipped the helmet on his head. At the doorway from the hangar into the hallway, he paused to figure out where the raiding party was, and decided they must all be in the front office. He crept forward, Glock in hand just in case, and stopped short of the doorway. A quick peek confirmed they had piled computers, monitors, and a cash register near the front door, along with all the snacks and drinks from the machines in the canteen.

One of the raiders had found a Playboy magazine. He'd opened it to the foldout, and appeared to be telling his cohorts all the things he'd do to her if he got the chance, including some interesting pantomime with his lower torso.

Perfect.

Nick stepped back into the hallway a little bit, took three quick steps, and leapt into the office with a ferocious growl.

The front door wasn't open, nor was the doorway large enough to accommodate the surge when they broke though it in their frantic attempt to escape the demon from welder land.

Nick chased them far enough to ensure that they'd keep hauling ass into the desert for a while, then ran to their wheels, punctured all four tires with his knife, and returned to the office.

The scumbags had done some damage, but nothing that couldn't be fixed in a day or so. Nick figured he'd saved Leo more than a front door would cost, so he didn't need to leave a note explaining what had happened. Besides, the registered owner of the vehicle stranded by the back door could tell the cops all about it.

He put the helmet on the booty pile and laid the sheet on top. Leo would undoubtedly wonder what purpose the two holes had served the thwarted burglars. Their real function would be Nick's little secret.

It took about five minutes to find some duct tape, latch the window from the inside, leave through the busted front door, and tape the pane back in place.

Another tension-filled jog through the desert put him at the rented Jeep. He drank a bottle of water, started the Jeep and followed the headlights into the predawn darkness en route to more conspiring.

CHAPTER THIRTY-ONE

Following an unsuccessful attempt to catch a few hours' sleep, Nick poured his first cup of coffee from the self-serve breakfast offering in the lobby of a motel nowhere near the Adobe Wings Airport or the Los Orcones Inn. Yates wanted him off the grid, and both of those locations had become far too familiar to him and vice versa.

Back in his room, he set the half balance weight from the desert on the bathroom counter under a bright spotlight in the ceiling. Next to it he placed the four halves he had cut. Even without a magnifying glass, a combination of visual and tactile examination convinced him of two important details: the same band saw blade had made all the cuts, and there wasn't enough difference between the fake pieces to make Parker suspicious.

The weight from the ruddervator went into a small bathroom trash bag, which he stashed in the ice bucket with ice and soft-drink cans from the mini-bar. He put one of the spare weights in an outer pocket of his duffel bag, another under the mattress, and another behind some snacks in the mini-bar. If anyone came looking and found one of the three decoys, they'd probably stop searching and leave with a weight that would not match up exactly to the one Nick had stolen from Parker's personal locker. The last fake weight went in his briefcase.

Using a Google search, he found the location of the closest

toy store, and where he could buy a pre-paid cell phone. He didn't think the conspirators would have hired anyone to track his electronic signature, but if Yates thought it was necessary, so be it.

He drove to a Quik Stop and bought one. It looked like a kid's play phone compared to his super-smart 180-IQ gadget with all the bells and whistles, most of which he never used.

Next, a stop at a toy store, then back to the motel to create an essential prop, and finally a meeting with the last tool in this scheme, none other than Cliff Yates, chameleon extraordinaire.

CLIFF ANSWERED THE CALL from a private number and was shocked to find Nick Phillips on the line. The guy had taken his advice for a change and was actually trying to drop off the grid. Fancy that.

They agreed to meet at El Barstool. On the drive over, Cliff tried to predict what kind of plan Phillips had come up with and ran through various scenarios for how to protect himself and the interests of Yates Enterprises. No way could he reveal to Phillips the events in the desert and his private conclusion that Caitlin Monroe was either dead or being held captive by Parker. The time had come to do what he did best.

When Cliff walked in the door, CB greeted him with, "Do me a favor, will ya?"

"What?"

"Don't invite coffee drinkers to meet in here. I make about two cents per cup."

"Quit your bitching. Barbie and I have bought enough booze in here over the past week to fill your retirement fund two times over."

"Not hardly."

"Okay, that was an exaggeration. One time. Bring me my usual, will you?"

Cliff slid into Barbie's booth and nodded to Phillips. As CB walked away from delivering the boilermaker, Cliff said, "You have something for me?"

Phillips laid a plastic baggie on the table with a chunk of metal in it.

Cliff picked it up. "You had this fingerprinted?"

"I made it look like it *has* been. Used an Edu Science CSI Fingerprint Analysis Kit. Cost me about twenty bucks."

Cliff stared at Phillips with a new appreciation for the guy's ability to step outside his straight-arrow persona and into that of a hustler. But the scheme still seemed weak by relying too much on assumptions. Cliff knew the best cons were those with a hell of a lot more predictability. They worked because the mark couldn't resist going for it and you knew that when you set it up.

He voiced his concerns and Phillips responded with a tacky comment about him being a rank amateur in the presence of greatness, and they had to play the hand they were given. "Your scam was to offer something to the Balloon Bitch to prove you've eliminated me and Caitlin. Get a bundle of cash for yourself and a recording that incriminates BB in a murder-for-hire scheme. Hand that evidence over to Caitlin and stick around to see if there's another payday in your future. Right?"

"Sounds like a damn fine idea to me."

"Except it falls on its ass if they've got her, which is the most logical explanation for her disappearance."

"But that makes no sense. If they have her, why would BB have offered me the job in the first place?"

"I don't know, but what if *they* don't have her? Taking Caitlin hostage could be a unilateral move by Parker to protect himself. And the balance weights are the key to it all."

Phillips laid out a scenario in which Cliff would tell BB that Phillips and Monroe have dropped out of sight so effectively that he's been unable to track them. But while tossing an abandoned motel room still registered to Monroe, he found the key piece of evidence Phillips had been hunting for. It's the equivalent of a smoking gun, and BB can have it in return for a ridiculous sum of money. Even for her.

Cliff finished off the boilermaker and signaled CB for another as he considered how to handle this. He finally decided his best move was to mirror Phillips' concern for Monroe's safety. After CB had delivered the drink and retreated to the bar, Cliff said, "You're putting our employer's life on the line. Why should either BB or Parker release Monroe once they have control of the evidence?"

"Because you're not really going to give it to them."

"You mean I really won't give them the *real* evidence."

"That's not what I said. You're going to double-cross her, and we're not putting any of the real evidence at risk."

"What the hell good will that do?"

"Stir up trouble, hopefully. If I'm right about what this evidence means, once BB sees it, she'll stop at nothing to gain possession. And you're going to tell her that the price has just gone up. The cash *plus* Caitlin's freedom."

"That's a bullshit plan if I ever heard one. You can't box someone in a corner like that. They get desperate. Refuse to cooperate just for spite and no matter the consequences."

"But you'll offer a sweetener."

"What the hell you taking about?"

Phillips picked up the bagged weight. "It's important that you initially refer to this as the *single* piece of key evidence that will put BB and Parker in prison. But the big surprise is . . .

there's *another* chunk of lead, the perfect match to this one, that absolutely proves sabotage downed the Victory. You'll hand over both in exchange for the money and release of Caitlin Monroe. Then you get the hell out of there and leave her with nothing."

"Except she'll still have the money if she shows up with it like she's supposed to."

"Not if you manage to talk her out of it."

"If I do, it's mine, goddamn it."

"You're welcome to it. Want to know why?" When Cliff nodded, Phillips said, "Because the *real* half balance weight matches the one recovered from the Victory's ruddervator. It connects Parker directly to the sabotage. And the only logical explanation for the fingerprint evidence is to assume that it also ties BB to the sabotage through Parker."

Cliff smiled. "You're a hell of a lot sneakier than you look."

"You ain't seen nothin' yet."

BETH MCALLISTER DISCONNECTED THE call from Cliff Yates and sat motionless in Lawson's favorite armchair, an outrageously expensive masterpiece in leather as soft as her favorite jacket. The SOB had spent most of his time in this Albuquerque house while Beth ruled over the enormous emptiness of their Santa Fe residence.

House versus residence. Everyday, mundane existence versus extravagant, luxurious *living*.

She set the phone on the lamp table beside the chair and stared at the bookshelves lining the opposite wall in Lawson's study. Beth's decorator, hijacked by Lawson for almost a year, had filled them with books Lawson had never read. They were props, just like so much else in their communal lives. A facade of respectability designed to present a carefully scripted message to the rest of the world. What a pair.

A brilliant surgeon who had achieved all of his professional goals in the practice of medicine by the time he was 42, eager for a new challenge and hungry for more of everything, prestige, money, and a series of younger bedmates to satisfy his insatiable lust for any flesh but that of Beth McAllister.

And a three-times-transformed woman. Beth had grown up as a trust-fund-protected socialite until her booze-and-drug-addicted father squandered it all. She became a determined stalker of wealthy marriage prospects, and ultimately returned to a life of wealth and privilege through entrapment. Her target was the heir to an ancient-money fortune. A faked pregnancy triggered an honorable decision to marry her, and his untimely death made her a very rich widow.

Lawson McAllister and Elizabeth Blaine, the happy couple. What a joke. A con man working a con woman, both so blinded by their greed that neither realized they were playing both roles in a farce.

And now she was being threatened by Lawson's last sexual diversion, who had managed to become his one true love, or some such variation on a worthless theme. Beth initially thought Lawson was immune to such nonsense, another error in a series of miscalculations that led to her marrying the man.

To deal with Monroe and her pet investigator, Beth had approached Yates with a straightforward business proposition. Next thing she knew, he may have tipped them off and sent them into the bushes, but in the process he'd found something of far more value to Beth than taking revenge on a gold digger who had proven to be even more predatory than Beth.

Tommy Lee and Monroe. Hardly allies in fact, but certainly in function, and Beth's only option vis-à-vis both was to remain focused on a way to render each of them harmless with one move. The question was, how could she pull that off dealing with the likes of Yates, a man with a sense of loyalty not worthy of the name? His offer undoubtedly had multiple layers, and she'd have to peel them back one by one.

To prevent any more surprises, Beth needed to set up a meeting with a predictable outcome. Then with the balance weight in hand, she'd be protected from Tommy Lee's treachery and Monroe's threat to put the FBI on Beth's doorstep.

Left with nothing but empty accusations and threats, the bimbo might temporarily tarnish Beth's reputation. Or maybe not. The rumors and speculation about how her first husband had died hadn't affected her access to society. In fact, anyone could see that many of the onlookers were fascinated by the question.

Did she, or didn't she?

It gave Beth an edge, and she enjoyed using it.

The question now was whether she could avoid losing it.

Tommy Lee had been checking on his captive about three times a day, in part to prevent being surprised by a Great Escape, but also to give Caitlin Monroe the opportunity to compare his freedom to come and go with her inability to do the same. And although she maintained a hostile silence that on the surface appeared to be more resolute with each visit, Tommy Lee was convinced that captivity had to be wearing on her, especially since she knew this wasn't about saving her life, but regaining one outside of a prison cell.

He'd just secured the outer door to the bunker after his last visit of the day when his phone vibrated. Beth bypassed any preliminaries as she usually did. "We need to meet, and there's

394 ❖ Tosh McIntosh

no time for elaborate shake-a-tail tactics."

"Hold on a minute." Tommy Lee turned away from the bunker, climbed the steps to ground level, crawled out from under the camo netting and stared at Buster's house. Although he'd been staying there long enough to know the neighbors paid little attention to the property or its inhabitants, he didn't want that to change. It would be dark soon, which would help keep it that way.

"One-half hour, same place as last time."

He prepared the requisite blender of margaritas, poured himself one, took it into the living room and sat in a chair placed by a front window with a view of the driveway through the slightly open venetian blinds.

They had agreed from the beginning to minimize phone conversations, although Tommy Lee considered that precaution to be more than a little ridiculous. Not to be seen together was one thing, but who would be so interested in either of them separately or as a couple to intercept their calls? Hopefully no one. That kind of scrutiny could turn up secrets Tommy Lee didn't even know he had.

One thing he did know, however. This call wasn't one of Beth's casual advances that on the surface had nothing to do with sex and underneath had to do with little else. She was worried about something and that meant that he would soon be as well.

When headlights turned into the driveway, he went back to the kitchen and poured a margarita for Beth and another for himself. He hadn't yet placed them on the kitchen table when she came through the back door, tossed her purse on the counter, snatched the glass out of his hand and sank into a kitchen chair. Tommy Lee waited until she had begun to fortify herself with the drink before he sat down across from her.

She downed half of the glass and got right to it. "Remember your plan to use the balance weight as insurance against me turning on you?"

Tommy Lee sighed. "It wasn't—"

"Spare me. The weight has just become a steel spike pointed directly at our collective hearts."

"How so?"

"Yates has it, and he's offered to sell it to me."

Tommy Lee's insides shifted as if his core had just experienced a seismic upheaval. Maybe Monroe didn't have it after all. If that turned out to be true, he'd have a problem to deal with, but at least he could keep Beth out of it. In the meantime, getting his hands on that balance weight and taking care of Cliff Yates had just become his number-one priority. "How do you know he really has it?"

"I don't. The only way to find out is to arrange the trade."

"How do you know you can trust him?"

"I *don't.* That's where you come in."

Tommy Lee sat at the kitchen table sipping his margarita and tried to maintain a flat demeanor to hide his budding excitement as Beth told him Yates had offered to trade the balance weight for cash. How much cash? She was to bring whatever she was willing to pay. If it wasn't enough, Yates would walk away. If she wanted to try again, she would have to let him know and hope he hadn't made a better deal in the meantime.

Tommy Lee *really* needed this meeting to go down, but he knew better than to let Beth get a whiff of the eagerness he was certain had begun to seep out of his pores.

He emptied the last of the margaritas in their glasses and shook his head. "That guy is certifiable. What makes him think *anyone* would meet based on an open-ended price tag?"

"I don't give a damn what he thinks. All I have to do is

show up with some money and get his eyes on it. Greenbacks close enough to touch are very tempting. I bet he takes the deal on the spot."

"Would you?"

"If he brings the balance weight that Monroe stuck in front of my nose? You bet. The amount of money I'll bring is nothing to me, but it'll be more than that sleazeball has ever seen, much less touched."

"Don't be too sure about that. My guess is, with him it's never about what you see. He's all about what's under the surface, like the old hustler's game with a pea under the walnut shell."

"Who cares if he's running a scam?"

"I do. Question is, what do we do about it?"

Beth smiled, but it wasn't a nice one. "You're saying 'we.' Let me make it clear that your role is to do exactly what I tell you. Neither of us would be in this mess except for your monumental stupidity. *I'm* going to get us out of it, and then we'll see if there's any 'we' left. Have a problem with that?"

"It depends on what *you* plan to do if he refuses the deal. Or hasn't brought the balance weight. Or he pulls a gun and points it at your nose."

"No problem. I'll call in the cavalry."

Now it was Tommy Lee's opportunity to smile, and it *was* a nice one. "To do what, exactly?"

"Take the balance weight. If he doesn't bring it, find out where it is. Can you handle that?

Oh, yes.

CHAPTER THIRTY-TWO

Cliff didn't worry about waking Barbie with his early morning get-up, because he was convinced she really did sleep with one eye open. He could almost feel it watching him in the dark motel room as he dressed and walked out with his tactical bag.

At the LTD he opened the trunk, placed the bag inside, and unzipped it. He chose the .40 Smith and two extra magazines, but left the Bushmaster for now just in case anyone happened to be looking. With the pistol slipped inside his waistband and covered by a loose outer shirt, he shoved the spare magazines into the left front pocket of his jeans, closed the trunk, and climbed into the LTD.

Although he'd been to the same location the first time he met Beth McAllister, last night he used Google Earth to examine the terrain around the coordinates she gave him. The map view didn't help, but satellite imagery allowed him to get a feel for the vegetation and contours he'd need for concealment. He also found a likely spot to park the LTD well off the dirt access road and out of sight, but still within convenient hiking distance of the meeting point.

Using the portable GPS mounted on the top of the instrument panel, he found the turnoff from the main highway in about an hour and a half. The approaching dawn had just begun to soften the darkness, and his headlight beams provided enough contrast to avoid the rougher spots and occasional rocks that looked capable of taking out an oil pan.

Arrival at the meeting point a half-hour later surprised him. Somehow he'd missed the bend in the road and a stand of trees sitting in a depression off to the right he had picked out for leaving the LTD. Headed back in the other direction, he kept a lookout to his left and finally saw it. Getting the car in there took some doing, especially backing in, but he wanted it positioned for a quick departure. A precaution he *didn't* take with the Maule and damn well should have.

He climbed out, opened the trunk, and from the tactical bag pulled a small fanny pack with a basic survival kit and a baggie with a chunk of lead that might be worth enough to fund his retirement. He snapped the fanny pack around his waist below the pistol grip. With the Bushmaster slung over his shoulder, binoculars around his neck, and a gallon jug of water, Cliff hiked to the meeting point and reconnoitered an area to the southwest that had appeared on satellite imagery to offer concealment. He lay down facing the way he'd come and used the binoculars and the scope on the Bushmaster to check line-of-sight. He had to shift positions twice, but finally settled on a depression about twice the size of a man and deep enough to low-profile him against the desert when lying prone.

The morning sun had risen to about 30 degrees above the horizon at his right two o'clock position. Not the best for his purposes, but at least it wasn't in his eyes. He drank some water and used the binoculars to scan the road. A dust cloud would probably give him advance warning of McAllister's arrival, but even if it didn't, he'd be able to see her vehicle before she stopped in the trees where the meeting would take place.

He settled down to wait, and for the second time since his

aborted attempt to help Monroe, tried to convince himself he hadn't run away. He retreated. Which was different. Only a fool stayed around when the advantage shifted to an opponent. And if he thought about it enough times, maybe he would eventually believe that he didn't owe the woman a goddamn thing, any more than he was obligated to tell Phillips about trying to help her and that she was probably still out there in the desert. Or more probably, *under* it.

But whatever happened after he got the hell out of there, this morning was all about the future. *His* future. If it brought Monroe back from wherever she was, even more full than ever of bad attitude and obsessed with revenge, that was of little concern to Cliff.

It would have been *no* concern of his except for the possibility that he could stick around long enough to share in the reward when Elizabeth McAllister became separated from a boxcar full of cash.

TOMMY LEE HADN'T EVEN *tried* to get some shuteye. From the first moment Beth told him of Yates' call, his whole body felt like it was wired up to a 220-volt circuit. And since he figured that Yates would want to be in position early, Tommy Lee had made damn sure it wouldn't be early enough.

Through the scope on Buster's AR-15, he watched Yates settle into his hiding place. Reminded him of a dog he had as a kid, doing at least two full circles before curling up in his bed.

It would be so easy. At this range the .223 Remington had such a flat trajectory that the crosshairs and the impact point were effectively the same. His trigger finger found its way inside the guard and began to increase pressure before he snapped out of the fantasy, Yates lying in a pool of his life's blood, coughing, spitting up red foam, but with intact hearing when Tommy Lee said, *That's for Buster, you motherfucker.*

So he backed down, brought his eyes away from the scope, and surveyed the ground between his position, Yates' layup, and where Beth would park. From here, he wouldn't have clear line of sight to her SUV. If he moved to ensure that, he wouldn't have line of sight to Yates. Decision time.

Was Yates just being cautious? So he knew exactly what he was walking into when Beth arrived?

Tommy Lee smiled. *Good luck with that.*

Or did he intend to use that rifle from ambush? And if so, why?

Unable to come up with a single reason Yates would do anything to blow the opportunity for making some money, Tommy Lee very carefully retreated from his layup.

As THE **GPS** INDICATED three miles to go, a text-message alert tone sounded in Beth's earpiece. She pulled off the road, parked behind a stand of trees, and learned from Tommy Lee that Yates was armed and concealed about 100 yards from the meet point.

They had talked at length about what Yates would probably do, and this precaution seemed to be the most logical. They had no indication he would use an accomplice, and he knew full well two conspirators desperately wanted what he was offering and to see him eliminated as a future threat.

Beth stared out the windshield with unfocused eyes as her mind played out the challenge ahead, to convince Yates that although she wanted this over and done with, the money in *that* bag was her first and last offer. He could hand over the balance weight and leave with more cash than he'd ever seen, or refuse and Beth would take her chances.

This, of course, with the knowledge that once she had seen the balance weight, Yates wasn't leaving with it. He might think he had the upper hand, but in the end he would either walk away with the money or empty handed. His choice, offered to him by Tommy Lee at the other end of his assault rifle.

She texted Tommy Lee *5 min,* and drove back onto the road toward a meeting she hoped would de-claw Caitlin Monroe for good.

CLIFF HAD BEEN WATCHING a cloud of dust approaching in the distance and heard the car before it rounded a curve about 200 yards away. He lifted the binoculars. A Land Rover, looked to be the same one she had driven to the last meeting, with a female driver. No passengers. Visible ones, that is. The vehicle stopped at the meeting point. He focused on the driver as she got out. It was Mrs. McAllister, in the familiar posture of someone talking on a phone.

A sudden feeling of vulnerability and threat enveloped him. Who the hell was she talking to from way out here for a confidential meeting? Checking in with someone? Who might at the moment be—

Cliff's phone rang, startled him so much he almost dropped the binoculars. He'd forgotten to silence it, a stupid move that sent him scrambling to yank the thing off his belt. He put the phone on vibrate and found an unknown caller, maybe another client with a cheating spouse, but this was not a good time. He let it go to voicemail, waited for the notification and listened to McAllister telling him she'd wait only 10 minutes.

He decided to spend most of it watching and waiting, but with the binoculars focused on the terrain to the side and behind him. Not that he'd see anything—Parker was no fool—but it made Cliff feel a little better. Which made him the fool, actually.

With that thought, he got up, slipped the sling over his head and onto his left shoulder with his right arm through the loop to put the rifle at the ready position for his right hand. Head moving and eyes scanning around him, he began a zigzag route toward the Land Rover to keep what little cover there was as close as possible.

STANDING BY THE LAND Rover wondering where Yates was made Beth feel *watched*.

She'd been backpacking the one and only time with her first husband when they were both zonked out of their minds on acid. After sunset on the first night, he casually mentioned they needed to be careful about bears. Huddled by the campfire in a small sphere of light, anywhere she wasn't looking became filled in her imagination with monsters waiting for the perfect moment to rush the camp and eat them.

Five minutes of nervous pacing came to a halt as Yates appeared about 30 yards away from behind a clump of stunted trees.

Beth's eyes glommed onto the rifle, focusing on his right hand resting on the pistol grip, first finger extended beside the trigger guard. Tommy Lee had said Yates was armed, but *ARMED* was more like it. It took all her will to remain calm, and on top of that, add a bit of *attitude*. Like, *Who do you think you're kidding playing tough guy?*

Which was a lot easier to do knowing Tommy Lee was—at least she hoped—watching Yates right now and ready to intervene if something went wrong.

Yates motioned with the rifle. "Your partner in murder hiding out there somewhere?"

Don't let him see you shaking. "That's a stupid question, Yates."

He laughed. "How so?"

"You'd better have the answer to that question on you, or we're done here." When his face clouded over, Beth added, "The balance weight? In the baggie? Proof that Parker was hedging his bets with a dagger pointed my way? Are you with me, now?"

"Oh, I get it. You don't want him to get his hands on it."

"Well, duh."

He walked closer, head moving all the time, alert, edgy, nervous, and scaring her with that finger so near the trigger. About 20 feet away, he stopped and slowly turned all the way around in a circle. Facing her again, he said, "You bring the money?"

"You bring the weight?"

"I'll show you mine if you show me yours."

"A gentleman always goes first."

"Not through a door he doesn't."

Beth didn't come out here to banter with this jerk, but that appeared to be all she'd get unless something changed. Time to push a little. "You're the one holding a weapon, as if you need it to defend yourself against a woman. I'm the most vulnerable, and I accepted that because I don't think you're here to do any killing. So here's what I'm going to do."

She turned, and with shaking legs she hoped Yates didn't notice, walked to the Land Rover's rear passenger-side door and opened it. From the floor she retrieved the black duffel Tommy Lee had given her and placed it on top of the hood. She unzipped it, pulled out a stack of bills, and tossed it over the hood toward Yates. It landed on the ground about 10 feet in front of him.

"What's that?"

"Money, you dolt."

"Not nearly enough, in case you were wondering."

"There are one-hundred-ninety-nine more just like it in this bag."

That got his attention enough to step forward for a better look.

Interested now, Yates? "Two-hundred stacks of fifties, fifty per stack, total five hundred thousand. You get the bag, I get the weight. Then we part company. Forever."

"I need to count it first."

"You'll do no such thing until I see the weight." When he hesitated, Beth screamed at him. "You don't have it, do you? This is all a shell game by a two-bit hustler." She zipped up the bag and nodded at the package of bills on the ground. "Keep that for travel expenses." She lifted the bag off the hood.

"Hold it." Yates motioned to set the bag back on the hood.

Beth did that and watched as Yates stepped forward to the stack, bent down and picked it up with his left hand, his eyes fixed on her.

For the first time since he had shown up, his right hand came off the weapon to riffle through the bills. He pulled one out of the stack, held it up to the sky, and examined it. Then he reached behind his back and pulled a fanny pack around to the front of his body. Again with his eyes never wavering from her, he unzipped the bag and brought out a plastic baggie, heavy at the bottom with a chunk of metal. "Is this what you were expecting me to bring?"

"I need to examine it first."

"Fair enough. Here's how we're going to do that." He

explained that he would approach the Land Rover, lay the baggie on the hood and take the duffel. While she was examining the weight, he would count the stacks of bills. "Understood?"

Beth nodded.

Yates did as he said he would.

Beth picked up the baggie and peered at the weight, which looked like the one Tommy Lee had brought into the bedroom, crowing like a bantam rooster about how something that ordinary looking could trigger catastrophic damage to an airplane. Black powder coated the weight, along with a piece of fingerprint lifting tape that looked like it had a readable print on it, Tommy fucking Lee's backstabbing insurance policy.

Yates finished counting, zipped the duffel and stood up. Beth glared at him. "Is this where you shoot me and take it all?"

He smiled, lifted the muzzle of the rifle and pointed it at her chest. "Only the last part of that will happen, unless you *don't* put the weight on the hood and step away from the vehicle."

Beth's whole body began to tremble as the anger rose up from deep inside and fortified her resolve to stand firm against a thug, who thought he was going to take her money and the evidence and walk away.

She managed to return the smile, noted a slight furrowing in his eyebrows as if it confused him. It calmed her just enough to keep her voice from cracking. "Can you feel it?"

"Feel what?"

CLIFF WAITED FOR AN answer, wondering what the hell she was talking about.

"The crosshairs centered on your chest," she said. "You can't be stupid enough to think I'd trust you."

No way. He'd scanned the area continuously with the naked

eye, binoculars, and the riflescope from first light until just before he broke cover. BB *had* to be alone. Unless he'd been early-birded. That thought gave Cliff an itchy feeling. All over. Like his skin was crawling around, trying to rearrange itself. Parker *could* be out there.

What next, Cliff? said the voice.

And there was only one answer. He picked up the duffel and backed away, eyes on BB until he reached the nearest cover and broke line of sight. He crouched down, slipped his arms through the straps on the duffel to carry it on his back, and began jogging in a direction away from the LTD, and that allowed BB to watch him for about 100 yards.

Cliff would have never agreed to this location unless the terrain offered him a tactical advantage. He was confident, even if Parker had line of sight to him, he wouldn't be able to maintain it as Cliff retreated.

He had to assume they were communicating somehow. Cell phone? Spotty coverage at best out here. Walkie-talkie? Maybe, but with range restricted by obstacles just like Cliff planned to use on his way to the LTD.

Cliff knew how to judge the weight of money based on the denomination of the bills and the amount. Five hundred thousand in 50s should weigh about 22 pounds, and the duffle felt right as his retirement fund pounded against his back with every step.

Reaching the cover, he stopped to catch his breath and drink some water. To his right and about a half mile away was his next landmark, a dead tree easily visible against the skyline. All he had to do was reach it, then alter course again in a direct route to the LTD. All of his maneuvering from here on would be invisible to BB and Parker.

On the move again, he replayed a recent internal

conversation in his mind. The one about Monroe putting herself in the crosshairs. She wasn't family. Cliff had no obligation to risk his life to save hers, especially now that he had a new start thumping against his back and someone to share it with.

WHEN YATES APPEARED FROM behind a small clump of trees in the dry wash where the LTD was parked, Tommy Lee lowered his cheek to the stock of Buster's rifle and followed him with the scope. The bastard might have been smiling, which filled Tommy Lee with an additional dose of commitment to take revenge right here, right now, with no regrets and no turning back.

Finger on the trigger, he centered the crosshairs on Yates' head, a tricky shot for an amateur shooter, but at this range Tommy Lee was confident he'd hit something vital enough to put his target on the ground.

As Yates approached the kill zone, an open space with no cover closer than about 20 yards, Tommy Lee took a deep breath, let half of it out, and held it as he increased the pressure on the trigger, looking to be surprised when—

Yates stopped, turned his head, appeared to be looking right at Tommy Lee, raised his weapon with his right hand as he began to run, the duffel bag on his back bouncing around, slowing him up.

Tommy Lee tracked him with the scope, led him a little, squeezed the trigger three times, the rifle jerking in his hands.

Yates lay on the ground, twitched a little, went still.

After watching through the scope for a few minutes, Tommy Lee stood up from his sniper's position on the side of the hill and walked down slope to the body. Yates lay in a crumpled heap. On the other side of a small entry wound in his head, a large portion of his skull was missing. Another bullet had struck Yates' side. Blood leaked onto the ground, pooled around the body.

Tommy Lee knew he should be horrified by the sight, sick-to-his-stomach affected, but instead a calm settled over him. Buster may have been a lot of things, most of them not all that good, but he was Tommy Lee's best friend, goddamn it, and he didn't deserve to end up like he did.

Tommy Lee knelt, pulled the handles of the duffel free from Yates' arms, and with his knife cut the sling on the rifle and the strap on the fanny pack. He pulled a pistol out of Yates' waistband and searched every pocket, where he found normal, everyday personal items except for a small digital tape recorder connected to a lapel microphone that looked like an American flag.

It didn't surprise him at all that Yates would tape a conversation. The only question was, who, what, and why? When he opened the duffel to put everything inside, the amount of money surprised him. He had no idea Beth was going to offer that much.

Mindful of the blood, he hauled the body to the LTD and searched the interior, removing anything that would make identification of the owner an easier task, including the VIN tags in the edge of the door and on the glare shield and the license plates. After dumping the body in the trunk, he jogged to his truck and drove back to the LTD.

He always kept a length of rubber hose with the jack and jumper cables in case he ran out of gas and needed a siphon. With it, he transferred gas from the LTD's tank into an empty gallon water jug and poured it into the car's interior. Another gallon went on top of the body in the trunk. He put everything he took off of Yates into the tool box on his truck, locked it, and got a disposable lighter out of the console.

Shoving aside the thought that he should stop for a moment and ponder what he was about to do, Tommy Lee flicked the lighter, adjusted the flame to maximum and tossed it through the open driver's window. The interior lit up with a WHUMPH and the wall of heat backed him away, head turned to the side and lowered to his shoulder.

He climbed in his truck, but in spite of wanting to separate himself from the smoke plume and any attention it might receive, he stared through the windshield as the flames consumed the car, waiting for the finale when the layer of fumes resting on top of the gas in the tank would explode.

He hated to miss that.

BETH WAS PRETTY CERTAIN she'd worn a circular groove in the desert around the Land Rover with all her pacing. Tommy Lee should have shown up by now.

He was supposed to watch the exchange to make sure Yates didn't try anything, then intercept him on his way from the meeting site to his vehicle and impress upon him the wisdom of accepting a modification to the agreement. Like giving up the money. They didn't expect to need violence, because once the threat of the balance weight was neutralized, Yates had no motive to press the issue except revenge. That would be a really stupid move, and he was no fool.

For the umpteenth time, she scanned the high terrain to the west of the meeting site where Tommy Lee had planned to set up. About five minutes ago, she'd heard three faint popping noises, thought they might be gunshots, couldn't tell for sure.

But now, a plume of black smoke was rising from behind the hill. The urge to run from an unknown event too close for comfort fought with an intense curiosity. Indecision held her feet to the ground until she couldn't stand not knowing.

Movement in Tommy Lee's peripheral vision drew his attention away from the entertainment.

Beth's Land Rover was about a half-mile away, bouncing and lurching over the rough terrain toward him. Her course might put her in danger from shrapnel if the tank exploded as she passed the LTD. He started the truck, steered clear of the flaming vehicle and hurried to block her from coming any closer. Nose-to-nose with the Land Rover, he climbed out of the truck and met her between the two bumpers.

She stared over his shoulder. "What happened?"

"I torched his car. It's kind of pretty, don't you think?"

"I'm not nearly as interested in that as I am in knowing why you didn't follow our plan."

Thinking up believable lies on the spot had never been one of Tommy Lee's strengths, but he had no choice but to try.

"Spur-of-the-moment adjustment. You didn't park exactly where I told you. I couldn't see either of you very well from the vantage point and didn't know what went down. When he left, I climbed the hill and tried to pick him up on the other side. But he didn't appear where I expected. I got worried he might sneak past me to his car."

"Why didn't you set up here and wait?"

"Because I had no idea where he was. And I had to assume he wouldn't take a direct route or go anywhere near the car without checking it out. The last thing I wanted was for him to walk up behind *me* while I was waiting for him."

Beth looked all around them. "So you've left him out *there*, while we're standing in the open *here*, close to a bonfire."

"He has nothing to gain by attacking us. He's got the money, and that's all he's interested in."

"How do you know he has the money? You just said you didn't see what happened."

Careful. "The deal was, money for the balance weight. You're here and he's in the wind. It's a reasonable assumption."

She stepped closer and poked a finger into his chest. "But what if he's *interested,* as you put it, in transportation? What makes you think he might not want a Land Rover or a truck?"

"Trust me on this, Beth. No one in their right mind runs into a gunfight when they can run away."

"This is *not* what we planned! The balance weight *and* the money, you said. Convince Yates to forget about scamming us and be thankful for his life. Remember that?"

"Yes, but you don't know the whole story."

"Enlighten me."

"He's got to make it out of this desert on foot. But whether he does or not, there's a tracking device in the duffel I gave you for the money. I know where he's staying. Getting the money back isn't a sure thing, but you were willing to pay that much before I suggested a way to keep it."

Beth seemed to deflate, body language incompatible with her usual ramrod-straight back. "Yates took them both, goddamnit! You've let him scam us. Now he's gone, and your only answer is to rely on a tracking device and luck."

Tommy Lee's world began to spin. He put his hand on the hood of the Land Rover to keep from falling as his eyes darted back and forth between the flaming car and his truck.

He hadn't seen the balance weight. Wasn't even looking for it because Beth should have gotten it. Then it dawned on him that whether it was on the body and melted into a glob, or in the duffel or fanny pack and he'd missed it, he should be okay.

He reached out to Beth, but she slapped his hand away. He made a "calm down" gesture. "I'll take care of it, don't—"

A wave of heat and pressure punched him in the back as the gas tank on the LTD exploded.

Chapter Thirty-Three

Eager to separate herself from the events of the afternoon and excited about finally having the balance weight, Beth made it back to the Albuquerque house without remembering most of the trip. She went straight into Lawson's study where he'd kept a bar well stocked with flavored vodka and single-malt Scotch whisky and small-batch bourbon whiskey and she didn't give a *damn* that they were spelled differently. She just wanted *alcohol*.

The first choice she found was a squatty bottle in a sack embroidered with the word *Blanton's*. It had a statue of a jockey on a thoroughbred sticking up from the cork. With the thought of *how quaint,* she grabbed a highball glass and shoved it under the ice dispenser, which completely filled the glass before she could pull it away. She tossed out all but a few cubes into the sink and poured two fingers of the Blanton's, drank half of it and savored the burn. And smiled at the memory. Lawson thought that drinking *his* bourbons and scotches any way other than neat was to blaspheme, and it gave Beth great pleasure to take the master distillers' names in vain.

Settled into Lawson's chair, which gave off a hint of his scent, unfortunately dominated by his favorite cologne, she thought about her plan for the day and its surprising outcome.

Tommy Lee's trickery to get her fingerprints on the balance

weight proved once again what she'd known since childhood. It was a lesson she learned from her father, the idiot who squandered Beth's inheritance to support his various addictions. You have to protect yourself, because no one else will. And if there's any deception to be done, be the first to do it.

Although she might be second in line to dispense some treachery, in this case Beth had gained the upper hand by seizing the opportunity while Tommy Lee was playing loose with what had happened and why. It *could* have gone down the way he described it, but that was not nearly as important as the fact he never saw Yates hand over the balance weight.

Beth's sudden realization that she could claim he didn't had been a stroke of quick-thinking genius. The insurance policy was now in her hands with a change in beneficiary. And Yates slipping through the noose avoided the problem of having to convince Tommy Lee that the guy was lying through his toothpick when insisting he'd handed over the weight in exchange for the money.

Beth finished the Blanton's, decided she liked it, and poured another before giving her mind free rein to consider the all-important question of what to do next.

If Tommy Lee was right about Yates being smart enough to take the money and slink into his Gollum lair under a mountain, she could scratch the PI off her list of men who deserved neutering. To part with the half-million rankled her coin purse, but if it kept him quiet and out of sight, it was worth it.

Caitlin Monroe was another problem altogether. And maybe her pit-bull investigator-lackey, wherever he was. Speaking of whereabouts, Monroe's absence from the scene was a bit troubling because it might mean she had a surprise in store. Or thought she did, believing the balance weight was still hidden away for safekeeping.

Okay, so what's the wisdom to be found in this cute little bottle of Blanton's? In a purple bag, no less.

Sit tight and see what happens? Or do something to incite a move by the opposition?

Then the soft voice of reason, its words slurred from the effects of Mr. Blanton's whiskey, reminded her of sayings about not tempting fate with tiger's tails, hornet's nests, and fire ant mounds.

She stared at her reflection in the picture window overlooking the backyard with the pool no one had ever used, so far as she knew, and smiled.

So what if it didn't make sense? The time had come to stir the pot and see what floated to the surface.

Beth rummaged around in her purse for her phone and selected the list of recents.

TOMMY LEE NEEDED TO check in on Monroe, but that would have to wait. He carried the duffel into Buster's house and dumped everything out on the bed. Seeing all that tax-free money gave him goose bumps. He spread the bundles out in a single layer and couldn't believe how good it looked.

And unlike people he'd read about who went brain-dead stupid when they received a sudden windfall and drew attention like a fresh chicken carcass in an alligator pond, he could live quietly off of this for a long time.

The most important object of his search, however, was not in the bag. Yates would have had no reason to dispose of the balance weight on the walk back to his car, which meant he either didn't bring it to the meeting, or he had it on him when he died. Tommy Lee had searched the body and didn't think he'd missed it, unless . . . *shit.*

Yates was wearing cowboy boots. He could have stashed the weight inside the top of one. Uncomfortable, maybe, but an effective way to hide it from someone not well versed in search techniques. Or reluctant to put his hands all over a corpse. But still—

A buzzing sound. Like a phone on vibrate.

Tommy Lee traced the noise to Yates' fanny pack and pulled out a phone. It wasn't locked, and on the screen, a familiar number.

He fought down a sickening feeling in his gut. Why would Beth call Yates now?

Did Tommy Lee really believe Yates kept the balance weight?

Would he risk not getting the money and hold onto a chunk of lead worth nothing? Except maybe as a bargaining chip to exchange for someone he didn't give a shit about?

Someone he left in the desert while he ran for his life after killing a man?

If Beth had planned some kind of balance-weight shell game with that asshole . . . but that made no sense. She expected Tommy Lee to intercept Yates on the way back to his car and relieve him of the money, which he would have received in exchange for the balance weight.

She also knew if Yates really was running a scam and didn't have the weight, or never intended to hand it over even if he did, Tommy Lee would still get the money back.

After a few moments of staring into the kitchen without seeing anything but a confused, blurry image of Formica counter tops and an ancient gas stove, it was if a pair of 20-10 eyeglasses put the bottom line into sharp focus:

Whether Yates kept the weight, didn't have it to begin with, or gave it to Beth, what you see now is exactly the same.

Yates' phone chimed with a text message. Tommy Lee snatched it off the table to read what Beth had written, fully intending to play the part of Yates and text her back, mess with her mind big time.

But the text said, *How did it go?* followed by the initials *np*.

All of a sudden, each of the four corners of the kitchen seemed to harbor a problem.

Monroe was a liability he had to deal with one way or the other.

Beth had very likely become an adversary and was much too close for comfort.

Leland still expected Tommy Lee to set up a replacement for Mule Air.

And the big unknown at the moment, an investigator named Nick Phillips, in league with Monroe and texting Yates from out there in the shadows.

Then he remembered the tape recorder. He connected his earbuds and listened to the first of two recordings in the latest folder. Beth and Yates were talking about a contract on Monroe and Phillips to make them disappear. Tommy Lee had no idea she'd done that, but it didn't surprise him.

In the second recording, Yates was offering the balance weight and setting up the meeting, all old news until Beth ended the conversation with, *"If you're telling the truth and hand over the evidence, I may have another job for you."*

Tommy Lee had an intense dislike for any situation, airborne or not, in which he felt out of control. Unfortunately, such a time appeared to have arrived, and he could either sit here in Buster's kitchen and wait for disaster to show up, or *do something.* Even if it was wrong.

He got up, put all the money into the duffel and walked

into the guest bedroom he'd been using. The closet had a false panel in the back wall because Tommy Lee had encouraged Buster to install a hidden storage compartment for the same reasons he did in his trailer. It didn't fool Yates, but that asshole wouldn't be stealing anything from anyone ever again.

Behind the panel, Tommy Lee found no insulation because this was an interior wall. Spaces between the studs wouldn't accommodate the duffel, but there was plenty of room for all the individual money stacks, Yates' fanny pack, Beretta, and the assault rifle, placed vertically in the space between two studs, the sole plate and the fire block.

From the toe of a boot on the floor he removed Monroe's cell phone where he'd temporarily stashed it, turned it on and checked the battery level. About 50%, more than enough for what he had in mind. As he walked out of the bedroom, the phone chimed and chirped and dinged. Someone really wanted to talk to her, and Tommy Lee needed to know who it was.

Although it wasn't quite as dark as he liked when moving around outside Buster's house, Tommy Lee retrieved the morning's newspaper from the front yard and hurried to the bunker. Monroe had assumed her usual position curled into a sitting position on the cot, legs tucked under.

He marched directly toward her, and for the first time since putting her in the bunker, invaded her space. Got right into it to make the point he could do whatever he pleased and not to forget it. "What's the passcode on your phone?"

"Use your own. I don't have many minutes left this month."

He pulled the Beretta from behind his back and tapped her on top of the head with the barrel before she could dodge it. "The next one's going to hurt a hell of a lot more than that. What's the passcode?"

She glared at him for a moment, then spit the numbers

out with her jaw clamped down so tight he barely understood them.

He unlocked the phone and discovered Nick Phillips had been trying to reach Monroe for days now. He went into settings, turned the passcode off, and held out the newspaper. She didn't reach for it, so he shook it. "Take the paper."

"I don't read newspapers."

"Take the *FUCKING* paper!"

She flinched at the volume of his voice in the confined space, then took the paper in one hand.

"Open it, hold it up with the front page facing me."

Monroe took her time like a kid playing with the peas she didn't want to eat, and finally held it up.

Tommy Lee really wanted to club her senseless with the pistol, but he shoved down the urge. "It's upside down."

Monroe made a big deal of being surprised before she rotated the paper.

He snapped a couple of photos with her phone and left the bunker. Walking back to the house, he checked Monroe's phone for other missed calls and found one from a number that stopped him in his tracks. It was a single call from Beth. About an hour ago.

Jesus. She's trying to organize the efforts of all my enemies.

A nagging thought kept popping up about the balance weight. Without *knowing* it had been destroyed in the fire, he had to assume that it was still out there. And in the hands of anyone else, it remained a threat because Tommy Lee had no allies.

NICK DIDN'T MANAGE HIS life around the capabilities of a smart phone, and he even turned the damn thing off on a regular basis to free himself from its insidiously addictive tether to the world.

But ever since Caitlin had suddenly dropped out of sight, and now that Yates wasn't responding to messages or texts, Nick fondled his phone a lot. He'd pick it up, check for missed calls and texts, confirm that he hadn't silenced it, put it down, but never very far out of reach, and repeat the process like a nervous parent looking at the clock while waiting for a teenager to arrive safely home.

He would much prefer taking some action rather than sitting idle, but nothing could alter the basic reality. He was stuck in a holding pattern until someone else did something. Pacing around his motel room didn't help. Nothing he found on TV was worth the brain cells he'd lose by watching it. Every snack in the mini-bar had been considered and rejected more times than he could count.

In the bathroom brushing his teeth, he almost didn't hear the text message chime from the phone, left on the bed like the old Nick would do.

What he found stunned him in place, his mouth full of white foam and his toothbrush dripping on the bedspread.

The text was from Caitlin's phone. It included only a phone number, and she stared at him in a proof-of-life photo. He got rid of the toothbrush, rinsed out his mouth, sat down on the closed toilet lid and dialed.

"That was fast. The photo get your attention?"

"Who is this?"

"We'll get to that. You might want to write this down." The guy read off a series of numbers Nick recognized as geographic coordinates. "That's a dirt strip. From what I hear, you're a hotshot investigator-pilot dude, so it shouldn't be a problem. You can't make it today before sunset, so let's say one hour after sunrise tomorrow. The strip will be mostly in sunlight by that time with only a few shadows. Land to the west with the sun at your back and don't be late."

"Why am I—?"

"Bring the balance weight or don't bother showing up, and she's dead." *Click.*

Nick sat very still to let his budding panic subside.

That had to be Parker. He could be bluffing, but the consequences of being wrong about that weren't acceptable.

Nick jumped up, found the morning paper in the trash, laid the front page on the bed and zoomed in on the photo. It might be faked. He could transfer it to his laptop and blow it up more, looking for evidence of image manipulation and clues as to the location, but that was a long shot and he didn't have time for any false starts.

Although his airplane was perfectly capable of landing on unimproved strips, he preferred grass and avoided gravel because it played cosmetic havoc with the prop, undersurface of the fuselage and wheel pants. Then he remembered the scheduling board at Stillwater Aviation included a Maule for rent. With large tundra tires, named for their popularity with bush pilots in Alaska. He called Leo.

"It's available in the morning, Nick, but we need to check you out. For insurance purposes. When—?"

"We have another hour and a half of daylight. I can be there in thirty minutes. Will that work?"

"Hold on." Muffled voices filtered through a covered mouthpiece, probably of the old rotary phone that Nick had seen on Leo's desk. He came back on the line with, "I'll probably have an instructor available. If not, I'll handle it. Hurry up, though. I've got a date with a lady who gets real grumpy when I'm late."

"On my way." Nick grabbed his keys and hurried out the door to accomplish the first task in setting up a scam that would be all his own.

BUSTER'S HOUSE HAD A creaking and groaning personality Tommy Lee found disconcerting. He didn't know exactly when it had been built, only that Buster's great-grandfather had done all the work on the original structure and successive additions had more than doubled the size to its current modest dimensions.

Variations in the floor level between the front part of the house and the first addition on the rear, and between the rear and a second addition to the side, evidenced either a carpenter's level about a half-bubble off, or uneven settling of the separate pier-and-beam foundations. But whatever the cause, the building was seldom quiet. Especially at night.

Tommy Lee didn't have a superstitious bone in his body, but that didn't prevent him from being startled every time the building complained about something. To ease any concerns this night as he poured his third Jack Black over a fresh tumble of rocks, he'd placed the nicest chair in the house, *nicest* being a relative term, against an exterior wall so he faced the living room. Not because he was worried about aliens, zombies, or serial axe murderers, but simply cautious. Yeah, right.

As his thoughts drifted ahead to tomorrow, he felt confident the photo and conversation with Phillips had the guy's attention. Monroe denied having the balance weight, which, if true, meant nothing Tommy Lee could count on because all he cared about was where it *was*.

The only undeniable fact was that Phillips had stolen it from Tommy Lee's locker. Everything else was conjecture: Phillips might have turned it over to Monroe; Yates might have gotten his hands on it somehow, a possibility made more reasonable with Monroe locked in the bunker; Yates might have given the weight to Beth in exchange for the money and she was hiding that from Tommy Lee; Yates never had it, or kept it as Beth said, and Tommy Lee had missed his chance to get it by shooting first and never asking any questions. He needed a goddamn dartboard to help pick one possibility and act on it.

He sipped the Jack Black, rolled it around in his mouth, swallowed, and let the glow of a bourbon-buzz settle him a little more into the seat cushion. Tomorrow would be a turning point one way or the other, and he was so ready for it. If for no other reason than he was tired of feeling like a target.

Phillips would probably try something, but it wouldn't be anything complicated. Like calling in the cops to put the meeting point under surveillance. Even if he had the time to set it up, the fact the law hadn't been involved so far meant Monroe had good reason to leave them out of it.

Phillips couldn't use Yates for an extra set of eyes, and as far as Tommy Lee knew, no one else had been part of the snooping into McAllister's death. Phillips had run out of accomplices, which left the guy on his own to do what?

He could pretend to have the weight and try to bluff his way close enough to seize the physical advantage from Tommy Lee. Good luck with that.

Or maybe he'd bring a different weight and pretend it was the real one. Good luck with that as well, because Tommy Lee knew exactly how he'd cut the weight down. He even weighed the two halves and picked the lightest one to put back in the ruddervator horn.

The thought of that small detail brought a smile. In all the world's history of exchanges between adversaries, this would be the first one in which a digital scale would be used to determine the weight of anything so worthless as a chunk of lead.

Phillips might also show up without the weight, claiming no matter what Monroe told Tommy Lee, she had it because Phillips had given it to her. Then he'd offer to take her place as a hostage to exchange for the weight. That made Tommy Lee chuckle. Monroe was a taker. Pure, simple, no ambiguity. She'd consign Phillips to whatever fate awaited and laugh all the way to doing whatever she'd planned from the beginning.

Or as a last resort and in pure desperation, Phillips might do nothing more than make a plea for releasing Monroe. With an appeal to the goodness of Tommy Lee's heart, maybe. Where there used to be some, but not any more.

He reached for the Jack Black to pour another two fingers of brilliance and realized the bottle was empty. When he tried to remember how much was in it when he started drinking, his brain couldn't figure it out. But that told him he'd had enough, especially when facing an early get-up tomorrow. Time to get some shut-eye, but first he had to do something. What did he—?

Oh, yeah. Monroe's phone. Gotta hide it.

Tommy Lee stood, a little wobbly, picked up the phone from the coffee table in front of the couch, and started down the hallway toward the guest bedroom just as car headlights flashed on the front windows and down the side of the house next to the driveway. He stopped, confused.

Who the hell was this?

He hurried on rubbery legs to the bedroom, tossed Monroe's cell phone through the open door into the closet, and had just turned back into the hallway when through the fog of the bourbon it dawned on him. Beth never showed up without calling first. He sidestepped into the darkened interior of the bedroom, pulled his pistol from his waistband and brought it up into a two-handed grip, front sight on the back door.

A car door slammed. Footsteps on gravel, then on the four wood steps up to the back porch, three steps across it and the squeak of the screen door. The doorknob rattled.

"Who is it?"

"A serial killer who announces her arrival. Open up, you idiot."

WHEN TOMMY LEE OPENED the door, Beth immediately thought this might be easier than she'd imagined. He had that droopy-eyelid look of a man in his cups. But she also knew that he'd surprised her on more than one occasion by appearing to be ready for a booze-induced night-night, and he'd suddenly snap out of it, ready to rock under the sheets.

When he didn't move out of the way, she shouldered past, in part to see if he would maintain his balance. She dropped her purse on the kitchen table and turned to face him. He had closed the door and was leaning against the wall. Probably so he wouldn't fall down.

Tommy Lee's words sounded lubricated when he said, "You normally call be—"

"Tonight I didn't."

"Why not?"

"Why should I?"

"This is getting us nowhere."

"Which is where we're going unless we settle a few things, and I'm staying until we do. You thirsty?"

"Usually, but I've had enough."

"Of what?"

"Bourbon."

"Not like this, you haven't." From her purse, Beth brought out the Blanton's, put it on the table, and opened up the kitchen cabinets until she found the glasses. The refrigerator had been manufactured about a century ago, so she pulled out an ice tray from the freezer compartment, twisted it to release the cubes, and dropped a couple into each glass. Careful to position her body between the glasses and Tommy Lee, into one she sprinkled the powdered contents of a small capsule she'd hidden in her palm when she got the Blanton's.

Walking back to the kitchen table, she smiled at Tommy Lee. "You're never going to drink that swill again after tasting this." With her back once again to Tommy Lee, she listened to his skepticism about drinking anything from a bottle in a sack as she poured the Blanton's and stirred his glass with her forefinger.

Facing him, she offered it. "Here's to honesty in all things."

He began laughing so hard he almost fell, but recovered enough to step away from the wall, take the glass, and weave past her. "Come on."

Beth followed him into the living room, which had a strange arrangement of furniture with an armchair shoved against a wall and no consideration given to the utility of how it fit with the rest. Tommy Lee collapsed into it, motioned to the couch, and drank about half the Blanton's in one gulp. She felt like saying something about that being an insult to small-batch bourbon, along with the ice, of course, but the more he drank, the sooner he'd be taking a nap.

She sat on the couch, sipped her bourbon, and made eye contact with Tommy Lee, at least with what she could see of them at half-mast. "I don't think you were telling the truth about what happened between you and Yates."

"Ditto."

"Would you like for us to correct that?"

"Not particularly."

"Why not?"

Tommy Lee began rambling, his words fueled by the booze he'd consumed and already showing the effects of the sleeping pill. Neither of them had any illusions that their relationship would last a moment longer than it served a purpose: his, to get close to more money than he could ever imagine, stick out his hand, and get some; hers, to be the bad girl with a bad boy for a bit of lusty fun with no strings and no regrets.

By the time he blubbered the last syllable and his head sank onto his chest, Beth concluded that her stud-pet had summarized it pretty well. Too bad he'd miss this part.

An hour, maybe, more likely two, and she needed to be long gone.

In the spare bedroom she found the duffel that Tommy Lee had given her. The one she had filled with a half-million dollars in 50s. And had handed to Yates. And that was now empty.

She turned around, sank onto the bed, and opened her mouth to scream when she noticed the open closet door and a cell phone lying on the floor near a boot. An unusual place to put it. Clothes on hangars had been shoved aside to reveal a portion of the closet's rear wall. Which didn't look quite right.

Beth got up, pushed the clothes out of the way, and discovered Tommy Lee had been in the process of putting a removable access panel back in place. One corner was sticking out from the wall, however, and all she had to do was lift it out.

Bingo.

Her money, a pistol, an assault rifle, and another cell phone in a fanny pack that looked suspiciously like the one Yates had been wearing. The phone was scratched and battered, just like she would expect from the hard use it would receive being an essential part of a PI's life. Where the hell did Tommy Lee get it?

Kneeling on the floor of the closet, Beth's mind and emotions fought each other for control.

She'd never had any illusions about whether her relationship with Tommy Lee was dabbling in danger, especially when she conspired with him to rid herself of a disaster for a husband and his whore. But the elements of control and power were always in her favor because both were synonymous with money.

Then his dastardly trick with the balance weight, played at a time of vulnerability, when she was drunk on sex and wine and loving every second of it. The sonofabitch had turned on her when she'd given him no reason to think she would ever betray him.

Her job offer to Yates, to find Monroe and Phillips and deal with them, didn't include Tommy Lee, even though she'd thought about it. Nor did she hide Yates' subsequent offer to sell her the balance weight. It wasn't until she drove up on that burning car, listening to Tommy Lee's feeble attempt to come up with a story that made sense, that she had—*click, like flipping a switch*—come up with the idea of denying that Yates had given her the weight.

Now it was *her* turn to leverage evidence into protection, and Tommy Lee was about to learn who had the ultimate lever.

Beth transferred the money, Yates' fanny pack and phone into the duffel. Tempted though she was to take the assault rifle, chuckling at the thought of Beth McAllister as Mrs. Rambo, she tossed the pistol in the bag and hauled it out of the closet.

Then she remembered Tommy Lee had mentioned a tracking device in the duffel to follow the money in case Yates eluded him and made it back to his wheels. She emptied the bag, did everything but rip out the seams and found nothing.

Did Tommy Lee remove it already, or was this just another in a series of lies? It didn't matter, really, because the most important thing was that he'd never put his hands on this cash again.

The first phone she'd found was lying face down on the floor. She put it in the bag, and paused. It didn't look like Tommy Lee's phone. Back in the living room, she found his lying face down on a lamp table beside the armchair with Tommy Lee in it.

She got the newer of the two phones out of the duffel. It wasn't locked, and she stared at My Number in the Contacts list trying to remember where she'd seen it. After a moment, she grabbed her phone out of her purse, compared the number to her list of Recents, and felt an ice-cold knife penetrate her back when she noticed the match.

What the hell is Tommy Lee doing with Caitlin Monroe's phone?

And it didn't take long to answer that question.

Beth zoomed in on a photo of Caitlin Monroe holding a newspaper, recognized the headline from today's *Albuquerque Journal,* and struggled for a moment to make sense of what it meant until it all became clear.

She turned and stared at Tommy Lee, slumped in that ugly-as-sin armchair, sleeping like a little devil child with treachery for a heart.

CHAPTER THIRTY-FOUR

It had been no more than 12 hours since Nick received the photo of Caitlin and the offer from Parker to exchange her for the balance weight. During that time, the thought of sleep never entered his mind. Even if it had, he wouldn't have been able to shut down the "what if?" portion of his brain that had more to chew on than time to digest it.

Steering the Jeep with one hand, he popped the lid on another in a long series of caffeine keep-me-awakes and tried to stay on the road as he hurried to the Adobe Wings Airport and Stillwater Aviation. He was on schedule, but since taking his checkout flight in the Maule yesterday afternoon, he'd been able to think long and hard about what Parker was doing and why, and what Nick could do about it, if anything.

On the passenger seat lay one of the three remaining balance weight halves resulting from Nick's efforts during the foray into Stillwater's maintenance hangar two nights ago. It was in a baggie, coated with a layer of dusting powder, along with a print of Nick's middle finger on a piece of lifting tape. That seemed appropriate somehow.

This whole spur-of-the-moment plan had too many holes to consider them all, so he focused on what he wanted to happen rather than how easily it could turn into a disaster.

Handing over the balance weight didn't require a face-to-face meeting with Parker. It could be done in any number of ways that didn't involve one party arriving in an airplane. The only logical explanation was Parker wanted Nick to show up without having arranged for a tail and trying to tip the balance in his favor with an accomplice.

Nick had also considered the possibility that Parker planned to be the only one who walked, drove, or flew away from the meeting. Nick's decision to use the Maule rather than his own airplane helped avoid being left in the desert for the buzzards. It was the equivalent of saying, *Someone knows I'm here.*

Parker couldn't return the Maule to Stillwater when Nick had flown off in it. To leave the airplane in the desert would generate an airborne search-and-rescue effort as soon as Leo reported it overdue, and put a bunch of people on the ground within a few hours of spotting it.

It gave Nick a small bit of comfort to assume Parker intended to get the balance weight and then part ways. What he'd do then was entirely up to him, but Nick had a spiel ready, hopefully to convince Parker he could free Caitlin without jeopardizing himself, and almost as important, gain the upper hand over his fellow conspirator in the bargain.

The problem was, if Parker believed the balance weight was the real one, Nick would be relying on nothing more than wishful thinking and conjecture that Parker's next move wouldn't involve taking Caitlin's life.

Nick's only option, risky in the extreme, was to arrive for this meeting with only one objective in mind: Parker had to walk away from it believing that he *could* have the real balance weight in exchange for releasing Caitlin. That meant he'd have to see it, touch it, become convinced, and then Nick would have to get it back. Piece of cake.

A footnote to this guesswork read, *Where the hell was Yates?*

What if he'd met with McAllister, turned over the other fake balance weight, and Parker knew that? Nick would show up with what he claimed was the no-shit, I'm-not-lying-about-it weight and the whole scam would fall apart. He'd be right back where he started. Or worse.

He had just finished his latest mainline caffeine hit when he pulled into the lot at Stillwater. After a pit stop and signing the schedule book for the airplane, he hurried to the Maule for a flight into unknown territory.

TOMMY LEE WOKE UP with the sound of booze demons screaming in his ears, surrounded by darkness, wondering where the hell he was, what time was it, what did he do?

Oh, yeah. He was drinking Jack Black and Beth came by with some kind of special bourbon in a goddamn sack that knocked him on his ass.

Then, *Oh shit!* He could barely see his watch, much less focus on it. He jumped up, too fast, almost tossed his cookies on the living room floor, and barely made it to the bathroom in time.

Shaking, he ran water into the sink, splashed it over his head and neck and dry heaved a few more times before making his way into the kitchen. A digital clock on the counter with a display big enough to read from the street told him he had to hurry, but he could still make it.

He started a pot of coffee, thought about eating something and almost got sick again. Two bottles of cold water from the fridge tasted okay, and he was able to keep it down along with his first cup of coffee. The rest of the pot went into a Thermos. From the pantry he grabbed some food bars for later when his stomach could handle it and hurried to the truck.

Sitting in the cab with the engine running, he took a moment to drink some coffee and thought about his plan, which luckily didn't take much preparation.

He had his pistol, Buster's rifle locked in the tool box in the bed of the truck, a full tank of gas, the digital scale he'd used to confirm the exact weight of all shipments via Mule Air, a small backpack, binoculars, a magnifying glass, a pair of disposable gloves, and about three hours to make a drive that should take no more than two and a half driving the speed limit. The New Mexico State Police were like invisible aliens who could hide anywhere. A sober person could get drunk on the fumes he was blowing in the cab, and he'd peg the scale on a Breathalyzer.

Time to go, *and be careful for chrissakes.*

DURING HIS CHECKOUT YESTERDAY with Leo, Nick had taken to the Maule fairly quickly. Control pressures were heavier than in his agile rocket, but he soon got used to that. With no information about the runway where he'd be meeting Parker, Nick had asked for extra practice on three variations to normal takeoff and landing procedures: short-field, soft field, and obstacle clearance, which were the Maule's bread-and-butter capabilities.

The Maule had a panel-mounted GPS navigation system. But just in case someone with a reason to go digging could retrieve the data, Nick didn't want to leave a record of the trip to the destination waypoint coordinates provided by Parker. So he planned the extra time to stop by the Albuquerque Sunport for a portable, backup GPS he kept in his airplane, and plugged it into an electrical power receptacle in the Maule's instrument panel.

Parker had told Nick to be on time or forget about it.

Comparing the time-to-go readout on the GPS with real time on the aircraft clock confirmed he would be 20 minutes early. He decided to loiter for 15 minutes, then fly direct to his destination, take a few moments to check out the landing surface, plan his approach, and land.

Watching the digital readouts, Nick felt the anticipatory tingle of excitement that always accompanied doing something in an airplane with unpleasant consequences if he didn't do it well. The secret was to control the feeling and use it to enter a special zone in which he saw more, interpreted it faster, and combined it with the sound of the engine and slipstream over the airplane and the feel of it in his hands, feet, legs and butt.

When the time-to-go indicated he'd arrive about three minutes early, he updated the GPS with the direct-to navigation command and began searching the terrain ahead.

Aeronautical charts indicated the landing strip sat near the base of a hill on the eastern edge of more rugged country extending to the west. From his current altitude of 5000 feet above the ground, he wouldn't be able to see much in the way of elevation difference, but the GPS would put him directly over the airstrip.

When distance-to-go indicated two miles, Nick turned right 30 degrees, waited for a few seconds, and began a slow counter-turn to the left. He'd learned long ago to follow the rule of *big to small* when looking for specific points on the ground. This desert probably had countless fairly straight and flat areas where he could land the Maule, but only one with the exact relationship indicated on the map between the landing strip, the hill, a dirt road, and a dry wash.

Once he saw what looked like a runway, he descended to 1000 feet while maintaining the left-hand orbit. After one complete turn, he confirmed the GPS bearing and distance to the airstrip agreed with what he saw. He flew a slow pass offset to the right and parallel to the runway so he could look to his left and down through the Plexiglass lower portion of the pilot's door. Piles of dead brush and small trees off to the sides of the landing area indicated someone had manually cleared the strip of rocks and vegetation.

To set up for the landing, he repositioned to the west before reversing course onto a downwind leg, parallel to the runway, but on a heading 180 degrees opposite the runway heading. The maneuver took him to the other side of the hill to the west, and he caught sight of a black smudge under a stand of evergreens, stark against the tan desert. He'd seen enough aircraft fuel fires to wonder if that might be a crash site. He took a short detour to check it out and decided it was probably a burned vehicle.

Back to business, he checked the clock, congratulated himself on the skill and cunning of his flight planning, and set up for a landing that was going to be right on time.

TOMMY LEE HAD HIDDEN his truck under a stand of trees well removed from the primitive airstrip. It wasn't a matter of fooling Phillips into thinking he had hiked in, but if things turned nasty, he'd know where to find his wheels and Phillips wouldn't have a clue.

The bourbon in that sack must have had an unusually high alcohol content, like brandy, and he was paying the price now. Carrying the baggage of a hangover from hell, it took Tommy Lee about twice as long as he'd planned to climb the backside of the hill that stood between his truck and the meeting site.

At the top, he paused to catch his breath and heard the distant sound of an airplane. After a few moments he saw a speck on the horizon. He hustled down to a jumble of boulders surrounding a depression and crouched down. As the speck grew large enough to be recognizable as a Maule, his mind had to readjust from what he expected to process what he was seeing.

Maybe this wasn't Phillips? But it had to be. He had his own airplane but chose not to use it? Some sort of trickery?

Tommy Lee watched the Maule circle the landing strip, make a low pass, then alter course and fly to the west. Where Yates' LTD had burned, easily visible from the air at that altitude. Could this be someone looking for—?

The Maule banked left, turned back to the east and appeared to be setting up for a landing as the sound of the engine reduced and the airplane began to slow up. Had to be Phillips. If someone else climbed out of that airplane, they were both going to be in for a big surprise.

By the time Tommy Lee had scrambled down the hill to his vantage point above the meeting site, the Maule was on final approach. It appeared to be stabilized, with few bank and pitch changes, which spoke to the pilot's skill as he touched down close to the approach end, slowed immediately to taxi speed, turned around and, in a cloud of dust from the prop wash, repositioned at the end of the runway for takeoff.

Tommy Lee used his binoculars to watch the pilot get out, look around for a few moments, then sit down under the left wing. He waited another 10 minutes, looking for any signs of nervousness, as if that would tell him anything, and decided that the guy was acting like he flew into the desert to meet strangers every day of the week.

With the backpack on, the pistol in his waistband, and the rifle at the ready, he slowly descended the hill, careful not to slip on loose rocks and gravel. The pilot was facing away from him until Tommy Lee came within about 20 yards, when his head turned and he made eye contact. He got up, slow and careful, and faced Tommy Lee with his hands out to his sides. Good. He understood and appreciated the situation.

Tommy Lee halved the distance between them and stopped. "If you aren't Nick Phillips, I hope you have a real good reason for being here."

"We meet at last."

"Did you bring it?"

"No. I came out here for a picnic." After a moment, he said, "It's sitting on top of the left tire."

Tommy Lee glanced down at the tire and a plastic baggie with something in it. 'Tell me about how you found it. Don't leave anything out."

And by the time Phillips finished his account, Tommy Lee knew for certain this was the guy who had, by a combination of incredible luck and uncanny intuition, turned an almost perfect plan into a disaster. Impressive, actually, and a good reason to be very careful now. "Are you armed?"

"Always."

"Where?"

"Right-side kidney carry in a belt-slide holster."

Tommy Lee raised the rifle and pointed it at Phillip's chest. "I want you to very carefully take the weapon out and put it on the ground and—"

"Forget about it."

"You see this rifle?"

"I'm not blind. I also don't think either of us is stupid enough to end this in bloodshed. The only way I can free Caitlin Monroe is if you accept the balance weight in trade. Once that happens, we can't hurt each other and might as well call it even."

Tommy Lee laughed. "Bullshit. You and Monroe and Yates are like bubble gum on a shoe."

"Speaking of Yates, where is he?"

"I have no idea, and good riddance."

"Agreed." Phillips picked up the baggie. "I'm going to put this on that boulder and come back to the airplane and sit on the ground."

Tommy Lee kept the rifle trained on Phillips, then sidestepped to the boulder to place it between them. He set the rifle on the boulder with the muzzle pointed at Phillips and picked up the baggie. It looked like the balance weight from his locker, with the lifting tape and fingerprint powder.

Tommy Lee removed his backpack, placed it on the boulder beside the rifle, removed the digital scale and put on the vinyl gloves. He turned on the scale, took the balance weight out of the baggie and weighed it.

A SINKING SENSATION ENVELOPED Nick, as if the dirt under his feet were turning to quicksand. He never anticipated Parker had weighed the cut-down balance weight for any reason, much less carefully enough to identify the original one by putting it on a scale.

The rifle muzzle appeared to be growing larger. The closest cover seemed to be retreating all on its own, and he was positive his Glock would hang up on his holster if he tried to go for it. Struggling to remain calm, he chuckled. "Am I being paid by the gram?"

"You'll get paid with a bullet in the gut if you're running a scam on me." Then Parker took a magnifying glass out of his backpack and began an examination that would do "CSI" proud.

Nick began to sweat. What if Parker had marked the balance weight to make it unique? But if so, why? What purpose would it serve when he expected never to lose control of it?

Parker returned the weight to the baggie, put it and everything he'd brought into the backpack and slipped his arms through the straps. "I'm going to take this, even though I don't think it's the one you stole from my locker. It's a little light, and the cut edge isn't perfectly square to the short ends of the weight." He stepped out from behind the boulder, picked up the rifle and put one arm through the sling to carry it over his shoulder, an action that raised the muzzle and shifted it to the side.

Nick muttered a fervent, *Thank you* and rushed him.

Parker reversed movement of the rifle but the sling hung up on the strap of the backpack.

Nick hit him with a full-body blow, slammed him to the ground with all of his weight on top, pinning the rifle to the ground.

When Parker tried to roll toward the rifle, Nick pushed himself up with his knees straddling Parker's body as he reached for his Glock, yanked it out and jammed the barrel into Parker's ear.

Parker went as still as the boulder beside them.

With his free hand, Nick pulled a Beretta from Parker's waistband and slipped it into his own. Then he eased up, holding the Glock steady against the side of Parker's head. "Slowly now, keep your hands in view and roll onto your stomach." After Parker complied, Nick put his left knee in the small of Parker's back, gripped Parker's right ankle, pulled his lower leg up, bent it at the knee, then straddled the leg at the ankle to pin it there with his own body weight.

Parker gasped. "My knee!"

"That's the point. Lie still." Nick yanked the rifle away from Parker's body and patted him down, then ordered him not to move, stood and backed away about 15 feet.

"Roll over, sit up, remove the backpack and toss it over here. Then put your back against the boulder and your hands under your butt. Do it now."

Parker did that, glaring at Nick the entire time. "What happens now?"

"I'm going to take a wild guess and say that it's something you don't expect." Nick knelt on one knee and laid his Glock on the ground within easy reach. He ejected the magazines and chambered rounds from Parker's pistol and rifle and put the weapons beside the backpack, which he searched and found three full magazines, one for the rifle and two for the pistol. "Planning for a war?"

Parker shrugged. "You can never have too much ammo."

"Okay, but now you have none." Nick picked up the Glock and stood. "Have you ever heard of me?"

"Up until my world turned to shit, no. Should I?"

"Here are some key words for your brain search: Larchmont, conspiracy, murder, White House. Does that bring up any links?"

Parker's expression indicated confusion for a moment. Then, "Oh. You're *that* guy."

"A lot of people think I took the law into my own hands to rid the world of a stone-cold assassin. And here we are, all by ourselves out here in the desert, me with a reputation for being a vigilante, and you, a killer."

"People know I'm here."

"You can forget that bullshit. Want to know why?"

"You're not going to kill me because you're a pussy who can't stand the sight of blood?"

Nick walked over and knelt down close in front of Parker, knowing that while sitting on his hands and with his legs stretched out, any move would be telegraphed. "Listen carefully, tough guy. I think Caitlin Monroe is still alive. And while I very much like the idea of convincing you to tell me where she is, I don't have the stomach for torture, and I think you know that. So here's the deal."

He explained that with the exception of the ammo, he was going to leave Parker with everything he brought, including his fingers and toes, *and* the balance weight. Then he'd fly the Maule back to Adobe Wings and wait for Parker to release Monroe.

Parker laughed. "You expect me to believe that? Is this is some kind of big-shot investigator trick?"

"Quit being so stupid. You think I bought all that crap about checking the weight and scrutinizing the cut? That's the weight I took from your locker. It has Elizabeth McAllister's fingerprints on the lifting tape because you *tricked* her into handling it. So you could either blackmail her, or more likely, protect yourself. You knew that the minute you saw it. Your little charade was designed to get me nervous and fidgety. See if you could rattle me into revealing the deception you anticipated."

Parker's eyes reacted to the part about the fingerprints, a telltale as clear to Nick as if Parker had nodded in agreement. He waited to give the guy time to digest something he totally didn't expect.

It didn't take long. "If I'm the killer you say I am, why wouldn't I take the weight and put Monroe in a hole somewhere."

"Two reasons." Nick reached into Parker's backpack and removed the balance weight. "First, because I lied. I'm taking this with me. Second, you *can't* be naive enough to trust Beth

McAllister. Am I right?" When Parker scoffed, Nick held up the baggie a few inches from Parker's face. To give him a real good look. To make him *believe*. And want it so bad he could taste it.

After a moment, Nick backed away and stood up. "Aside from having this balance weight, Caitlin Monroe is your best weapon. I've been working with her for the better part of three weeks, and you can take this to the bank. She's so bent on revenge that all you have to do is turn her loose, sit back and watch."

"Like she won't come after me again."

Nick almost reacted to the word *again,* but managed to hide his surprise. He should have predicted Caitlin would try something like that. He pulled a piece of notepaper from his shirt pocket and shoved it into the backpack. "That's a sterile cell phone number. Do something smart for a change. You're *not* Monroe's primary target. Call me when you're ready to make the exchange. And if you've learned anything from our little chat, you'll destroy the balance weight or put it somewhere a hell of a lot safer than a locker with a padlock."

Nick backed farther away, about half the distance to the Maule, and holstered his Glock. "I'm going to leave now. You might as well gather your stuff, tuck your tail between your legs, and climb that hill. I can't say it's been nice meeting you."

He turned his back to Tommy Lee and had almost reached the Maule when two distinctive sounds stopped him in his tracks: A rifle magazine being rammed home and a charging handle chambering a round.

TOMMY LEE CENTERED THE laser sight in the middle of Phillips' back. "Let me see your hands and turn the fuck around."

Phillips did that, nice and slow, his face as white as his T-shirt. He looked down and stared at the red dot on his chest. When he raised his head, beads of sweat were trickling down his forehead. "What now?"

"How are you at tucking *your* tail?" Into the silence, Tommy Lee said, "Assume the face-down, prone position you subjected me to a little while ago." After Phillips did that, Tommy Lee planted his good knee in the middle of Phillips' back and jammed the rifle barrel into the base of his skull. None too gently, he searched Phillips and tossed everything he was carrying into a pile well out of reach.

He stood up. "Now let's try that other position against the boulder over there." Once Phillips was sitting on his hands with his legs spread wide in front of him, Tommy Lee held up the baggie and kissed it. "Welcome home." He put it in an outer pocket of the backpack and smiled. "Thanks for teaching me all that cool shit, by the way. How to control someone and keep them submissive. Where'd you learn that?"

"From your mother."

Tommy Lee waited a moment to let his temper back away from the edge and reduce the pressure of his finger on the trigger. "It appears the tables have turned. All because you didn't really listen when I told you there's no such thing as too much ammo. The magazine was in the top of my boot, asshole." He paused to let that sink in. "Move from there, even a little bit, and you're dead."

Holding the rifle's pistol grip with one hand and the laser sight trained on Nick's chest, with his free hand Tommy Lee put both of Nick's loaded pistols, the extra magazines, and the keys to the Maule in his backpack. He backed up to the airplane and locked it, then approached Nick and stopped at a safe distance.

"Take off your boots and toss them over here." Phillips did that, Tommy Lee picked them up and backed away to the base of the hill. "Do *you* have all your fingers and toes?"

"So far."

"If you want to keep them, don't move from that boulder until I'm out of sight over the top of the hill. I'll be checking on you often with this," as he brandished the rifle, "while I climb. Your boots and the keys to the Maule will be on the other side of the hill about a mile from here. Watch out for rocks, cactus, and critters that sting and bite. Understood?"

"Yes."

"Okay. Before I go, let's be clear. Right now I have no *good* reason to kill you. But if I even *see* you again, that's all the reason I'll need."

Chapter Thirty-Five

On the trip back to Buster's house, Tommy Lee's mind refused to concentrate on the driving and kept replaying the initial part of meeting with Phillips like a bad television commercial.

Using the scale and the magnifying glass had been nothing more than an act to see how Phillips would react. But all it did was convince Tommy Lee he had finally recovered the balance weight. Then he lost concentration, got careless, disarmed, and utterly humiliated. Sitting on his hands, helpless as a baby, waiting for what came next, and Phillips surprised the shit out of him by letting him keep his pistol and rifle.

And then, in a world-class brain fart move, Phillips turned his back as if he wasn't worried even a little bit that Tommy Lee could do anything to hurt him.

The rifle: *$1500 bucks as equipped by Buster*. The mid-quality magazine: *$25-35*. Thirty rounds of .223 ammo: *$17*. The look on Phillips' face: *Priceless*.

All Tommy Lee had to do now was deal with Monroe, and Phillips' suggestion was making more sense by the minute. Or maybe not. He was a sneaky bastard, far more dangerous than he looked.

A nightmare holographic image drifted up from the truck's glare shield: Tommy Lee at gunpoint, Phillips and Monroe with the balance weight back in *their* hands and laughing their asses off at how easy it had been to set the trap. Taunting him about how much he *wasn't* going to like prison. And them loving every minute of it while Tommy Lee dreaded every second of his future.

He should just load up his truck with the few personal possessions he gave a damn about, which were mostly his tools, and put this place and all his troubles behind him. Aviation mechanics were always in demand. He could find work easily enough no matter where he went. Or if he got really paranoid, get a job working on cars. Joining the ranks of auto mechanics would make it even easier to disappear.

In either case, he had the safety net of Beth's half-mil. He'd use it to live on until he could make ends meet with a salary, then sock away most of the cash for emergencies. Be smart for a change.

Bottom line was, Tommy Lee's role in the remote murder of Lawson McAllister had bothered him way more than he ever thought it would. The up-close killing of Yates had felt really good at the time, and the sonofabitch deserved what he got. But that was some heavy-duty baggage to carry around, and Tommy Lee wanted no more of it.

So why not just release Monroe? Maybe something simple, like one last visit to the bunker and make it sound like he was locking her in when he left. After a few days without a visit, she'd try the door. It would be like opening the gate on a chain-link fence to release a rabid pit bull into Beth's life. *How fast can you run, darling?*

By the time he rounded the curve in the road in front of Buster's house, he'd made a mental list of things to do and forgot everything on it when he saw a vehicle parked on the shoulder by the mailbox. Not just any vehicle, but a cruiser with the distinctive paint scheme of the Bernalillo County Sheriff's Department.

Turn around, keep going, stop at the house, call for a beam-up . . . and the next thing he knew, there he was, in the driveway. He climbed out, slower than normal, careful to keep his hands in sight of the deputy, who was standing on the front porch. "May I help you?"

The deputy stepped off the porch, approached Tommy Lee and glanced at a small notebook in his hand. "Are you Samuel Hayes?"

The question confused Tommy Lee until he remembered that Buster's given name was Samuel. "Uh . . . no, sir. My name's Tommy Lee Parker. I'm house-sitting for Bus—uh, Mr. Hayes."

"Do you know where he is? Or how to get in touch with him?"

Tommy Lee shook his head. "He doesn't tell anyone where he goes. I don't think he even has a phone."

"This is a welfare check. I need to look inside."

Tommy Lee's heart speeded up and felt like it was pounding hard enough to be visible through his shirt. He fast-forwarded through a mind inventory of each room and paused on the guest bedroom. Had he left the closet door open? Did he replace the panel on the hidden compartment? Leave weapons out? Was the money—?

"Did you hear me?"

"Uh, yes. Sir. I have a key right here. Follow me, please." Tommy Lee's legs didn't want to move, but he forced them to take him to the front door. He unlocked it and stood aside.

The deputy motioned with his arm. "Lead the way."

Tommy Lee began with the living room. The deputy stayed close and always positioned himself so he could keep Tommy

Lee in sight, even when checking the bathroom and a hall closet. Relief flooded over him as he entered the guest bedroom and didn't see a bedspread customized with bundles of Ulysses S. Grant greenbacks. The comfort vanished, however, when the deputy walked over to the closet and opened the door. Fully expecting to end up in handcuffs, Tommy Lee held his breath until the deputy closed it and nodded toward the hallway.

In the kitchen, the deputy peered out the window at the back yard. "Let's check the garage."

Tommy Lee's heart sank to the kitchen floor. He was pretty sure the deputy would never notice the bunker, but if he knew about it and wanted to check the interior, Tommy Lee was in some really deep shit.

He led the way and hurried to open the garage door. At the rear bumper of Buster's pickup, the deputy looked at the license plate and pulled out his notepad. "This vehicle is registered to Mr. Hayes. How's he traveling?"

"There's no telling, sir. Probably motorcycle."

"We don't show he's registered one."

Tommy Lee smiled, shrugged. "He's a little . . . uh . . . loose about stuff like that."

The deputy closed the notepad, slipped into a breast pocket, and handed Tommy Lee a card. "If he contacts you, tell him to call that number. Thanks for your cooperation."

Tommy Lee waited until the cruiser disappeared around the curve, then began breathing normally again as he put his truck in the garage with Buster's and hauled his stuff into the kitchen. He glared at the empty Jack Black bottle as if it were an enemy, tossed it in the trash and sank into a chair.

A welfare check? Someone had to initiate it. As far as Tommy Lee knew, Buster didn't have any family, at least not local. They'd all gotten as far away as they could when the apocalyptic survivalist bullshit took over and made the entire Hayes family out to be nutcases.

But what if it had nothing to do with Buster? What if someone wanted the cops snooping around Tommy Lee? Get his balls in a vice? Folks appeared to be standing in line to do that.

Whatever the cause, this place no longer had the anonymity he needed, especially with clear evidence of kidnapping so close by. The time had come to quit procrastinating and go with his gut.

SINCE REACHING THE AGE of 18 and being able to choose her own destiny, Caitlin had considered herself to be tougher than nails and ready for any obstacles that life might throw at her. But nothing could have prepared her for the helplessness she felt at having her freedom snatched away.

She wasn't chained to a wall, but she might as well have been for all the difference it would have made. And although she wasn't one of those people who insisted on being constantly bombarded with whatever they called music these days, her dungeon was so quiet she could appreciate fully the benefit of carrying on a conversation with herself just to vibrate the air.

One diversion turned out to be a slight echo in the room. She played around with various sounds she'd learned to make as a child, like cars and motorcycles. It provided some comfort, actually, to revive the few happy memories of her youth. She could do guns, too, and trains.

Props had provided her with interesting variations. A plastic picnic knife, which Parker had obviously missed, made a really cool sound if held on a table with the fingers of one hand and flipped with a finger on the other. Sliding the knife more onto the table or off of it varied the frequency. Not quite the entertainment value of Netflix, but it would have to do.

More important, she'd been sharpening the tip and edge of the blade on a piece of the metal cot frame and looked forward to using it on Parker if he ever dropped his guard.

Estimating the passage of time was another big deal. Outside didn't make it into the room with the door closed, and only slightly when it was open. She had no idea how long she'd been locked up. Parker's visits were no good for that, because he didn't seem to be on a schedule. Why should he? He wanted to break her will, and this room had enough food and water to sustain her body way longer than her mind would last. All he had to do was wait and let boredom convince her resistance was futile.

A scraping noise intruded. Caitlin jumped up from the cot and hurried toward the door. Then a metal-on-metal grating, like a large bolt being thrown. She ran to the kitchen counter, snatched up the knife, slipped it into the top of her right sock and sat on the cot.

Soft light framed the doorway when the door opened, but she couldn't tell what time of day it was. Parker stepped inside, closed the door, walked to the small desk, pulled out the chair and sat. He was less than 10 feet away, but she'd never get the knife out of her sock without alerting him.

After a moment, he said, "What if I said you can go free?"

"You'd be lying."

"Maybe this will help." He unzipped a fanny pack strapped around his waist, reached in and held up a plastic baggie.

Caitlin's normally tight control of facial expression and body language crumbled. She stared at the balance weight with its fingerprint evidence as her emotions rose up to betray her. All her leverage, gone. The opportunity for revenge, only a fleeting memory of what might have been. And the overriding question, *How did this sonofabitch get his hands on it?*

"Do I have your attention now?"

All she could do was stare at the baggie and force down the panic.

Parker slapped his hand on the table. It sounded like a gunshot. "Answer me."

"I don't believe you, goddamn it!"

"Okay. It's not important you do. But listen very carefully."

Caitlin barely managed to stay focused on Parker's words as he explained what was going to happen. The fact that Nick had found the balance weight was almost unbelievable. And although a tiny spark of hope began to warm her insides at the prospect that Parker might be telling the truth, the burden of monumental betrayal chilled her to the bone. Nick had given Parker the means to scuttle what was already a leaky plan.

As always, she was alone, unable to count on anyone other than herself.

And maybe, just maybe, on a white plastic knife.

HUMILITY, SHAME, A MONUMENTAL sense of failure, and very sore feet rode with Nick in the Maule on the flight back to Adobe Wings and in the Jeep on the way to his motel. He barely remembered stopping at a drive-through burger joint to pick up an infusion of grease and comfort, or buying the only six-pack of Santa Fe Pale Ale in the cooler at a convenience store. It had probably been in there for years.

He ate an early dinner in his room, opened his second beer, went into the bathroom and sat on the closed toilet seat to soak his bare feet in warm bath water as he contemplated all the unanswered questions.

Had Yates convinced Beth McAllister the balance weight was the real deal? And if he exchanged it for cash, where the hell was he? That was supposed to be nothing more than a down payment on the possibility of a much larger payoff when Caitlin threatened to expose the conspiracy to murder and destroy McAllister's precious reputation. Yates would never walk away from that.

Did Parker really buy Nick's argument that *this* was the real balance weight? It certainly appeared so, or Parker would probably not have left Nick standing upright on this earth, but prone underneath it.

Were Parker and McAllister still working together to keep the lid on? Somehow Nick doubted that. If Parker thought he had the real evidence and recognized the advantages of turning Caitlin loose on Beth McAllister, why would he need her?

And if each of them thought they were in sole possession of the key to protecting themselves from prosecution and their co-conspirator, would they keep the secret from each other to maintain the advantage in an alliance of killers? Or would they compare notes and figure out they were being scammed?

Only one combination of answers to these questions would bring about the outcome Nick wanted, and the uncertainty had wound him up. Pissed off at himself and the world, sleep was out of the question. Unless he could use boredom as a knockout pill.

TV seldom held Nick's interest any longer than it took to channel-flip through the choices and confirm most of the programming was junk. Not only that, but motel entertainment selections always seemed to be the result of using a rubbish magnet that repelled anything of quality. Tonight, however, he was so nervous and fidgety that he grabbed the remote and began surfing.

Two trips through the channel selection brought him to a local news offering. After listening to a reporter trying to use excessive voice modulation to add interest to a naptime story, Nick lowered the volume and cleaned up the remains of his dinner. Then he noticed a crawler that said: *Local man reported missing,* and barely heard the reporter say, "Authorities are looking for Samuel 'Buster' Hayes . . ."

Nick put down the wastebasket and sat on the bed. He'd heard the name "Buster" a little over a week ago while hiding in the hangar at Stillwater Aviation, linked to a big dude playing quick-draw with a pistol. He turned up the volume.

Buster's semi-invalid aunt had contacted the police five days ago when he didn't show up with the weekly delivery of groceries, cigarettes, and beer. According to the aunt, the police didn't care if she was about to run out of smokes, and they gave her some excuse about not considering someone missing who was only a few hours late with a delivery. Being told Buster had been as regular as clockwork for years didn't alter their procedures, and the aunt didn't care for their attitude. She barely avoided being hauled off to the drunk tank, apparently.

Then an on-scene reporter gave a short blurb on the Hayes family, including their reputation for believing in the apocalypse and advance preparation as the key to survival. The part about the family's failed business venture in selling shelters had begun to bore Nick to tears when the report included a photo of a shelter.

He jumped up and peered closely at the screen. He'd recently seen a corrugated surface just like it. But where? After a moment, he snatched his phone off the bedside table. The proof-of-life image of Caitlin that Parker had sent was too small to see the detail even when zoomed in. He transferred it to his laptop, examined the JPG and stared at the surface behind Caitlin. If it wasn't the same, it was close enough to be very, very intriguing.

Nick opened his browser, went to whitepages.com to look for an address, and crosschecked all the possibilities against Google Maps to correlate the rural scene behind the reporter with locations in Albuquerque. Only one Hayes seemed to fit, but it wasn't Samuel. Maybe his father? Did the reporter mention the elder Hayes' name when talking about the failed business?

A visit to the news station's website to watch the report again produced the name Harlon Hayes. Google Earth street views of the address and the house visible in background on the report were the same.

He zoomed out to look at the terrain around the rectangular lot. Based on the homes to either side, Nick guessed it encompassed well more than an acre, with the short side adjacent to the road. The rear of the lot included a cluster of trees dense enough to hide the ground.

If Nick were of a mind to survive the apocalypse, which he wasn't at all sure he'd want to do, those trees would be a very good place to put a shelter. Hide it from the prying eyes of aliens looking for earthling blood and flesh to fertilize their gardens, or some such horror.

He glanced at his watch and pulled up sunrisesunset.com., and timeanddate.com. Two hours to sunset and three days past a new moon, which wouldn't rise until after 4:00 a.m. If he stepped out of the Jeep about midnight, it would be plenty dark enough, and the neighbors would most likely be sleeping.

Parker had taken a move out of the Nick Phillips Playbook and left both of his unloaded pistols jammed muzzle-down in one of Nick's boots. The empty magazines had been shoved into the other boot, with one .40 caliber round balanced on the toe. Under the round, the slip of paper Nick had given him, with the phone number lined through and *For pain relief* written in felt-tip marker.

For that and a lot of other reasons, Nick had bought a box each of .380 ACP and .40 S&W at a sporting goods store before he stopped for dinner. He loaded both pistols and extra magazines, laid out his darkest clothing on the bed, and returned to the Google Earth image to plan his approach to the property.

That done, he set his alarm and tried to take a nap. It didn't work.

Images of rattlesnakes, pit bulls, and cautious landowners with shotguns tormented him.

Tommy Lee had never accumulated much in the way of material things. Not because he didn't want them, but as a Harley Davidson road warrior wannabe, he couldn't haul a lot of shit when moving on to the next place. The fact that he'd never owned a real Hog had nothing to do with it. The attitude was the only thing that mattered, and Tommy Lee figured he had that in spades.

Standing in the guest bedroom of Buster's house, he looked at the bed where he'd piled the clothing he was going to take. *Is that all?* And then, *That's enough for a lean, mean traveling machine.*

His tools were in the truck, along with a cooler filled with ice and drinks and lunch meat, a sack with bread, chips, mixed nuts and other munchies, and some camping gear. He could restock those supplies on the road and spend nights in rest areas, use the shower facilities at truck stops, and never spend a dime on a place to stay. What the hell, he could *live* out of that truck if he had to. Mechanically, it was perfect, and anyone who fixed airplanes could keep a truck that way without even trying.

And, of course, he'd take the weapons. The false bottom in the truck-bed toolbox was large enough for the rifle when broken down, and it would take a very careful examination to find it.

He pulled two duffel bags out from under the bed and began stuffing his clothes inside, along with a toiletry kit. He had some room left, so he went back in the closet and picked out a few more pairs of jeans, some T-shirts, and underwear.

Next the closet, but first, was there anything else? Oh, of course. Don't forget the booze. He went into the kitchen and got two bottles of Jack Black and a couple of shot glasses. He had no qualms about drinking out of the bottle, but whenever he did that, things turned really nasty inside his body the next morning. Feeling the need for a little hair of the dog that bit him, he sat at the table, filled a shot glass and sipped it as he reviewed tonight's planned activities.

His original idea about leaving the door unlocked so Monroe could eventually free herself wasn't going to work. She'd never seen the outside of the bunker and had no clue where it was located. Once she did, the connection from Buster to Tommy Lee would leave him vulnerable.

If Monroe fought against being restrained, he'd zap her with a stun gun. Then cuff her, do a little hogtie deal to control her legs, silence her with duck tape, blindfold her, haul her out to the truck and get her nice and comfy on the floor between the front and back seats. He had an air mattress, sleeping bag, and some blankets. It's where he slept when traveling, for chrissakes. Primo accommodations at the Parker Travel Inn ought to be good enough for Miss Monroe.

He planned to depart Albuquerque about midnight, head south on I-25 to Socorro, west on US-60 toward Magdelena, and south on SH-107 to a remote spot in the Cibola National Forest. He'd find a landmark visible from a distance and leave some food and water and a disposable cell phone. Then he'd drive a few miles away and drop Monroe off, blindfolded, hands loosely tied, and with instructions on how to find the stash when she managed to free herself.

Except for passing in opposite directions on the road to Stillwater Aviation, she'd never seen his truck and had no way to connect him to a particular vehicle. The registration did that, but going to the cops didn't fit into the plans of a blackmailer. If he could get out free and clear right now, he should be okay.

That said, Phillips had convinced him Monroe would never abandon her vendetta against Beth. And with that to deal with, Beth wouldn't have the time or inclination to come after Tommy Lee for taking the money. A partnership born in sex, deceit, and conspiracy would dissolve, and he'd consider himself lucky to have escaped with his head and other precious body parts still attached.

Time to get moving. He went back into the bedroom, removed the panel from the hidden compartment, and stared at an empty space that used to be filled with a half-million dollars and now contained nothing more than dust and spider webs.

BETH HAD SPENT SO little time in the Albuquerque house that she barely knew the floor plan. Her usual circle of friends and acquaintances probably didn't even know about the place, so when the doorbell rang, she ignored it and continued exploring the rooms, looking for *something* to show her who Lawson really was. She was damn certain she never found out while they were married.

When the ringing doorbell changed to incessant pounding, Beth decided she'd had enough. The pistol she'd taken from Tommy Lee's hidden stash was in her purse. She had little experience with guns, but enough to know that with a semiautomatic, a round had to be in the chamber and the safety off. It took a moment for her to confirm that under the light of a desk lamp. By the time she reached the front door, she was ready to pull the trigger on this asshole just for making such a racket.

Through the peephole appeared the distorted image of none other than Tommy Lee Parker. Beth stepped back from the door and considered whether her next move should occur at his instigation with this surprise visit, or at a time of her choosing. After a moment, *Might as well get it over with.*

With a lilting inflection, she called out, "Who *is* it?"

"Open the goddamn door, Beth!"

"Is that you, Tommy Lee?"

"I'm warning you. Open the fuck up."

Beth's hair-trigger temper snapped. She yanked the door open and leveled the pistol at Tommy Lee's face. "Consider this a warning in reply, you sonofabitch."

He stepped back and almost fell off the porch. "I didn't know you owned a gun."

"I don't. This is yours."

That appeared to confuse him, but only for a few seconds. He nodded. "Of course. Why not steal as much as you can when given the opportunity?"

"I wasn't *given* anything. I take what I want."

"Tell me something I *don't* know. We need to talk."

Beth lowered the pistol. "Wipe your feet." She turned her

back to him. To piss him off. To show she wasn't in the least bit worried. To be clear she held the upper hand in whatever happened next.

In Lawson's study, she got out the Blanton's, set it on a coffee table between two couches and sat down.

Tommy Lee had stopped in the doorway, his eyes wandering around the room. He seemed confused again, or maybe in awe of his surroundings. "I was in here once. When Lawson hired me."

"Spare me the tender reminiscence. Sit."

He bristled at that, just as she intended, but he stepped into the room and took a seat opposite her.

Beth nodded at the Blanton's. "Pour."

He did that and offered her a glass.

She nodded at the coffee table, picked up the glass after he set it down, raised it as if to make a toast, and sipped the bourbon. "So, are we celebrating the resumption of normal relations or is this the harbinger of a painful breakup?"

"The what?"

"A sign. An indication."

"We're way past that."

"How can you be so sure?"

"Cut the crap. You took advantage of my drunken state and—"

"Recovered *my* money? That you could have only gotten from Yates, and you told me you'd missed him in the desert. Try explaining that."

"I wasn't going to keep it."

"Stop lying to me! And if you hadn't been so goddamn intent upon protecting yourself against me, we wouldn't be in this mess."

Tommy Lee smiled, which convinced Beth she was dealing

with a deluded idiot. With a forefinger he motioned toward her. "*You* need to chill." Then he slowly pulled a fanny pack around to the front of his waist, unzipped it, removed a plastic baggie and held it up. "What mess are you talking about, exactly?"

Beth stared at the baggie and its contents as the rest of the room faded into a fuzzy, darkened background. There seemed to be an overhead spotlight pointed directly at it. All of her confidence was being pulled away and stuffed into the baggie with the balance weight.

She put down her bourbon, got up, went to Lawson's desk, picked up her purse and returned to the couch. Without trying to, she mimicked Tommy Lee's slow process of producing *his* little surprise. "Looks like we've both been deceived."

Tommy Lee's smile vanished as his eyes shifted from her baggie to his and back. He took a deep breath and sighed.

Beth tossed her balance weight on the couch. "While your overloaded brain tries to absorb what's going on, let me make it easier for you. We—"

"What the hell do you mean, 'we'? Real balance weight or fake, it doesn't matter. I can be out of here tonight and never look back. But you're trapped, aren't you? A prisoner of your carefully engineered reputation bought and paid for with all your money."

Beth sipped her bourbon. "It's a good thing you have certain mechanical skills with your hands and other body parts, Tommy Lee, because your brain has a major short circuit."

"What part of 'I'm out of here' do you not understand?"

"I understand the two most operative words in this conversation. Money, and *prisoner.*"

Tommy Lee's eyes flicked down to his lap, back up, around the room as he shifted position on the couch. "The hell you talking about?"

"*My* money, and *your* prisoner." That appeared to stop his breathing for a moment. "Wake up, you halfwit. I know you have Monroe. When were you planning to tell me?"

"Uh, I was—"

"Just stop it. You would have already left if you could. But you came here, whining about my taking back the money you stole to finance your disappearing act." Beth poured more Blanton's for herself. "You and I both know we're joined at the hip because each of us has what the other needs. It's a simple matter of exchange."

Tommy Lee picked up his glass and eyed it with suspicion before he took a sip. "This stuff will knock you on your ass. What kind of exchange?"

A familiar dichotomy settled over Beth, the opposite-pole contrast between who she was now and who she used to be, and yet still was when circumstances required. She didn't get to where she was by being timid, and she wasn't going to let anyone send her back.

"You kidnapped Monroe without telling me because you wanted to get the balance weight she dangled in front of *my* nose. That wasn't about protecting *us,* but providing you with leverage against me. Then you took my money from Yates and eliminated him, probably in that burning car."

"That was *personal,* goddamn it!"

"You think *this* isn't?" When Tommy Lee hesitated, Beth said, "You want the money? Help me get the real balance weight and disappear that bitch for good. Hopefully along with her pet investigator. No traces. Otherwise we part ways right now and you're on your own with dust in your pockets, living with the constant fear of when and where someone will tap you on the shoulder with a special message from me. Take it or leave it."

CHAPTER THIRTY-SIX

Nick left the motel at 11:00 p.m. for the drive to Buster Hayes' house. When his handheld GPS read one mile to go, he pulled off the road onto the shoulder and checked the map and satellite image he'd printed off the Internet. The closest homes were almost a half-mile away in front of and behind him.

Without encountering people or pets, he should be able to walk into the desert at a right angle to the road for about a mile, parallel it until reaching abeam Buster's lot, then walk back toward the road to the rear property line where he suspected a survival shelter was concealed under the trees.

He eased the Jeep off the shoulder into the desert using only the parking lights. Avoiding cactus and large rocks, he idled into the darkness until he couldn't see the road in the side and rearview mirrors, which meant the Jeep was all but invisible to anyone in a passing car. Then he turned around and shut off the engine. The dashboard clock read 11:37. He'd planned to start his reconnoiter at midnight, so he took the time to drink some water, eat a granola bar, and let his mind ramp up for what he was about to do.

For the majority of his NTSB career, Nick had always thought of the anticipation and excitement he felt when searching for clues as indicative of nothing more than a deep personal commitment to solving the mysteries contained in physical evidence. But his rogue investigation into the Larchmont crash, and now his probe of McAllister's, had changed that forever. The question of what happened and why as an avenue to enhancing flight safety had been supplanted by a compulsion to make the guilty pay for what they had done.

He stared out the window into the darkness. But not total darkness. Faint variations of black gave the desert an ethereal quality and just enough contrast to make out a fence post, a few shrubs, what might be a boulder.

Unbidden, the memory of a nighttime hunt in a Colorado forest joined him in the Jeep.

Night-vision goggles had helped, but only when Nick was stationary. They restricted his peripheral vision too much. There'd been a little more ambient light, and underneath an evergreen canopy it was as if nature had used a thousand shades of grey to provide a sense of depth and distance and detail that allowed him to quietly stalk a stone killer.

No snapping of twigs or tripping over rocks alerted the bastard that danger was headed his way, deadly menace in the form of a Sicilian shotgun in the hands of a vigilante who had never lost a minute of sleep. Because what he did was *justified*. Once. Nick never again wanted to encounter anyone who deserved Wilson's fate.

He glanced at his watch. This would be the eighth time in three weeks Nick had engaged in sneaky activity, and the fifth at night, when forays into the desert and the possibility of encountering a rattlesnake put his whole body on alert. He'd gone online and read they were active night predators in the warmer months. But tonight's current temperature of 63 and forecast low of 58 should keep the beady-eyed devils holed up for warmth. Or at least sluggish if they were out and about.

With the interior light turned off, he got out of the Jeep. He had the Glock in a belt-slide holster on his right hip, two extra magazines in a carrier on his left, and a bottle of water in a nylon pouch at the middle of his back. Using the rectangular course he'd plotted into the GPS, he began walking away from the road toward the first turn point of his route.

The desert at night had its own special brand of silence that wasn't silent at all. Insects and animals that shunned the light of day became active and filled the air with fluttering, scurrying, occasional evidence of predation, and all manner of sounds Nick had to ignore just to remain calm. He was an interloper in this world, and didn't like the feeling everything else out here knew exactly where he was. Hopefully he came across as a badass who deserved to be given a wide berth.

Approaching the turn point, off to his left a light flashed. He dropped to one knee and drew the Glock as he pocketed the GPS in his jacket to hide the glow of the screen. Occasional glimpses of light indicated movement from his left to his right, coming closer.

Retreat? No. Sit tight. Rely on darkness.

Voices drifted to him on the light breeze. Spanish. The scrape of a shoe on desert sand, a metallic clink of gear, then a thunk and a soft, "*¡Caramba!*" He didn't know what it meant, except that whatever had happened probably hurt.

Whether these guys were mules hauling drugs in backpacks or illegals en route to a better life didn't matter. He tried to shrink, slowed his breathing and held it as a line of five men passed within a few feet of him. His lungs were bursting before he finally sucked in a deep breath of sweet air.

The desert version of silence returned. Nick stood, holstered the Glock, confirmed his position and continued following the GPS course while checking over his right shoulder every few minutes, expecting to find someone sneaking up on him carrying a machete and wearing a malevolent grin.

At the turn point, he knelt and drank some water. From here on, he would advance toward what could be nothing more than the rear of a homesite with some trees, or as much as the location of a prison being used to hold a kidnap victim. In either case, the house on the lot might be where a killer waited, and a confrontation probably would involve more than angry words.

Nick glanced at the GPS and realized he hadn't reduced the screen brightness to account for his improved night vision. He adjusted the backlight until he could barely see the course line and the distance readout. After a few minutes, he checked it again. Satisfied, he got up and with careful foot placements began a slow advance.

He had picked the coordinates of his turn points from satellite images and maps and entered them into the GPS. Although a relatively imprecise method, it should be accurate enough to put him on Buster's property. Based on shadows in the satellite images, the vegetation where he thought the shelter might be appeared taller than that of the surrounding area, possibly indicating a depression that collected enough rainwater to support hardwood trees.

But when he arrived at what he estimated was the rear property line, details of the terrain he could make out looked like all the rest he'd passed through. He'd have to rely on the wooded area spanning the width of the lot, which reduced his chances of missing it completely as he advanced toward the front of the property where the house was situated.

After a few minutes of moving toward the road, he noticed the dry scraping of his hiking boots on sand, gravel, and rock had become softer. A familiar rustling. He knelt and placed his hand on the ground. Felt the brittle texture of dry leaves in a thick layer of seasons past. He looked up, surprised to find the black silhouette of branches and leaves against a star-filled sky.

The satellite image of the property indicated the house stood back from the road about 30 yards. An area of low, scrubby vegetation covered the front three-fourths of the lot. If he advanced until he reached the front edge of the trees, he might be able to see the house even if no lights were on inside. Sharp edges tended to stand out in vague silhouette against a dark background of nature's random shapes. At least he would know that if the shelter existed, it was behind him.

After checking the GPS again, Nick moved through the trees, looking skyward about every five yards to check for the canopy above, until he finally stepped into an open field. He couldn't be sure, but in the distance there might be a house.

For the next half hour, he walked a zigzag pattern from one edge of the trees to the other and from the front to the back without finding anything to even suggest the entrance of a bunker. Waiting until daylight wasn't an option, so he knelt just inside the front edge of the trees to take a break and drink some water before trying again.

In his peripheral vision, a flicker of light. He shifted position to face the house. Another flicker, then another moving from his right to left. Headlights on the road? About 30 seconds later, high beams appeared, turned toward the house and stopped. Had to be in a driveway, with the side of the house reflecting the glow from the headlights pointed at a detached garage.

The lights went out. Two faint door slams. A small light appeared, moving, a flashlight in the hands of someone walking. Coming this way.

Nick hopped up and retreated farther into the trees, found a spot to lie down and peered into the darkness. The light wasn't moving directly toward him. Looked like it might enter the trees at the mid-point. In a crouch he set a course to intercept the light.

When it appeared the person would enter the trees about 20 yards in front of him, Nick drew the Glock and lay down.

Soon the soft murmur of two voices. Man and woman. Nick's whole body came alive at the crackling sound of footfalls on dry leaves. He eased up, tracked the glow of the flashlight and moved parallel with it, counting on the sound of their movement to mask his own.

He hadn't gone more than 15 yards when the woman's voice said, "Did you hear that?"

Nick dropped into a crouch and froze as the flashlight began probing the trees, passed over him, jerked back and concentrated on the area around him. The urge to raise the Glock and put the light at gunpoint fought with the caution to stay very still. Movement was the enemy of stealth. He held his breath, certain that even that much could give him away.

Then a soft "C'mon" from the man. The light shifted away and began moving again.

Nick got up and stayed with it, timing his pauses to match whenever the light stopped moving. Suddenly couldn't see it. He froze, listened. Indistinct sounds, muffled by the trees, left him uncertain, confused. It was if the light had been swallowed up.

Very soft voices. Metal on metal clicks, a snap, then scraping and the squeal of rusty hinges.

THE SOUND OF THE locking bolt on the bunker door brought Caitlin out of a light sleep. She sat up, flipped the covers off her legs and crouched on the cot. No light entered the bunker as the door began to open. Parker had never entered the bunker at night.

Out of her sock she pulled the plastic knife, finally sharpened to a razor-sharp point, and slipped it into the long sleeve of her T-shirt at the left wrist.

A flashlight beam backlit the doorway, went out. The overhead florescent lights flickered, came on, and into the bunker stepped Parker and none other than the Balloon Bitch herself. She was smiling, and that made Caitlin's heart race at the thought of driving the tip of the knife into her carotid artery and watching her bleed out.

Parker carried a pistol and the Bitch had a black duffel bag. They approached the cot and stopped about 10 feet away. Caitlin's body tensed with the urge to go for one of them. Closer, and she might have tried it. Worth the effort, no matter what happened.

Parker nodded, a kind of polite hello, as false as the rest of him. "We have a proposition. The only one you'll get, so pay attention." Then he pulled out one of the desk chairs for the Bitch and sat in the other one, slightly behind and to the right of her. He held the pistol in his lap with both hands, way too ready for Caitlin to try anything.

"Nice try," said the Bitch, "but the scam with the fake balance weights is trashed. This is a one-time offer. Hand over the real one, I'll sweeten the deal with what's in this bag. You walk away, I do the same." She unzipped the bag, reached inside, pulled out a stack of bills and tossed it.

The money almost hit Caitlin in the face because the word *fake* had stunned her so much she could hardly move. She examined the bills to give herself a moment. Fifties, with a band around them. *Stall.* "How much?"

"Half-mil."

To feign being insulted required a full measure of Caitlin's acting skills. Nick Phillips hadn't found the real balance weight and given it up after all. She fanned the bills, frowned, threw them past the Bitch onto the duffel. "Not even close."

The Bitch laughed. "Perhaps you didn't hear me? The part about this being the only offer you're going to get?"

Caitlin nodded. "My hearing is fine. It's your math that sucks."

"Not so much, actually," said the Bitch as she put the bills back into the duffel. "I'm going to dial your lackey's number and hand you the phone. You will tell him it's the real balance weight for your life, and he's to call your number when he's ready to hand it over. Understood?"

"My comprehension is just as good as my hearing. Yours, on the other hand, is seriously flawed if you think I'm—"

The Bitch got up, reached into the duffel, brought out a wood chisel and a hammer and looked at Parker.

"Hold her down."

NICK STARED AT A faint glow. Coming from underground. Weird. He eased toward it on his belly and peered around a low shrub.

Camouflage netting? Covering a hole? If this was the entrance to the bunker, it had to be totally buried or—*wait a minute.*

While Nick walked back and forth through the trees, the ground in the center had risen gently to a peak and then descended on three, maybe four trips. At the time, it felt like a natural variation. But if you wanted a bunker to be virtually invisible from the ground as well as from the air, you'd put it deep. And plant trees on top. If Buster's grandfather had done that, they'd be full grown by now.

Inching forward, Nick began to see more detail. Squares in the netting. Fabric leaves of various colors and twigs, could even be real ones, slipped into the netting. Then it dawned on him that if he'd stepped *on* the netting, he'd have fallen into the empty space below it. Not exactly a stealthy arrival.

He reached the edge of the netting and peered through one of the squares. Steps. Steep ones. He'd have to pull the netting up and slip under it. At the bottom a small landing, lit by a sliver of light peeking past a partially open door. Faint voices drifted up, sounded like two women.

Nick's heart rate quickened as he backed away and thought about what the hell he should do next. If he could reach the bottom of the steps—

BARBIE SHOVED THE BARREL of her suppressed Sig Sauer Mosquito .22LR into the back of the guy's neck where a single shot would punch into his brain stem and put him down instantly and for good.

He froze, except for an adrenaline quiver.

She leaned over, whispered, "Don't even twitch without my say so. All moves very slow. Quietly now, stand up."

The guy did that.

She slipped her free hand beside a water-bottle carrier at the middle of his back and through his belt. Gentle tugs guided him in retreat about 20 yards from the edge of what appeared to be the entrance to an underground shelter. "Lie down on your stomach. You can use your hands, but once you're down, extend your arms out to the sides." After he did that, she relieved him of two pistols, stepped back well away from his legs, and put him at gunpoint with the Sig.

Who the hell is this guy?

Leland's instructions had been uncomplicated. No wet work, just watch Parker and Yates, report back on where they go, who they see, what they do. He was primarily interested in Yates, who hadn't ratted anyone out after he was caught shaking down street dealers and taking bribes. Problem was, the disgraced-cop-turned-private-investigator bit was also damn good cover for infiltrating Leland's operation.

Tracking devices in Yates' LTD and Parker's truck and a handy program called TrackEm allowed her to keep tabs on their movements. It also created a maze of connections that had nothing to do with her assignment. Additional devices linked Parker to a rich widow, another guy and another woman to Yates, back to Parker and the widow. The individual tracks had become a maze, and Barbie had given up on trying to make sense of the intersections.

Yates was especially cagey. Her ruse with the short skirts, cleavage, and barroom shtick had been designed to put him off guard. It was working, but then it backfired.

She would have never predicted it. With all the guy's rough edges and role-playing, he couldn't hide what Barbie felt had been something real. Even more of a surprise had been the unexpected response not only of her body, but her emotions. Usually kept stuffed into a mind vault with a combination long forgotten, they refused to remain there and had crept into the light.

Then he went into the desert and the tracking device stopped working. She had punched the coordinates of his last known position into a GPS and found the blackened hulk of an LTD and a charred corpse. A check of Parker's travels showed the intersect, and within Barbie arose a determination to unlimber the tools of her trade for a little personal retribution.

And now here she was, following Parker's truck, anticipating the satisfaction of looking into the sonofabitch's eyes as the blood flowed out, and she stumbled on this dude. Surprises being the nightmare of her profession, she took out her phone and checked the latest TrackEm data: Parker's device sat within a hundred yards, the one for a rented Jeep about a mile away.

Okay, then. Whoever this guy was, he'd just become a tool.

As she knelt down to let him know what was coming, a phone chimed, amplified in the quiet under the trees, and startled her so much she almost dropped the Sig. She leaned close, whispered, "Move and you die," hopped up and retreated into the woods.

After five minutes with no obvious reaction from the bunker, Barbie approached the prone figure, knelt beside him, whispered in his ear, "Where's that goddamn phone?"

"Right thigh pocket of my cargo pants."

Barbie found it, silenced the ringer and asked for the locking code.

"Hardly ever use it."

She shielded the screen and checked for messages. Someone had sent a photo. A right hand, looked like a woman's, with a ring on the third finger. Two hands gripped the wrist and appeared to be holding the hand down on a metal surface. Nearby, the business ends of a hammer and chisel.

The text message read: *She loses the first finger in 1 hour, another every hour until you deliver the balance weight. Call for instructions. Clock's ticking.*

Goddamn. Barbie killed for a living and had no qualms about it, but her methods ensured that the lights went out instantly. This threat indicted a level of brutality found only in sociopaths. Because they *enjoyed* it.

She told the guy to roll over and sit on his hands with

his legs crossed, and noted his reaction when he got the first glimpse of her full face mask. Protecting her identity was only one reason for wearing it. The other two were plainly visible in his eyes. Fear and submission did wonders for maintaining physical control of someone until she no longer needed it.

Barbie showed him the photo and message. "Recognize that number?"

His face turned white in the darkness as he nodded. "Who the hell are you?"

"You don't want to know. What *I* want to know is if you're here because of Tommy Lee Parker."

"More for the person who owns the phone that sent the message."

"Where are they?"

"Underground bunker."

"How many total?"

"Three. I think."

"Think?"

"Pretty sure."

"Describe the entrance." He did that and Barbie thought about how to do this, remembered the words of her first mentor: *Gift horses don't live in no barns, Barbie girl. Ya gotta be ready to climb on and ride with the wind, ya hear?*

"Okay. Listen up. You're gonna stand and lead me. I'll leave your hands free for getting under the net and down those stairs. Quietly. Silently would be even better." She held up the Sig. "If you do *anything* to hinder us, I'll use this. Got it?" When he nodded, she motioned him up with the tip of the suppressor.

CAITLIN SAT ON THE floor of the bunker with a dishtowel pressed against her nose to stem the flow of blood.

When Parker had come for her, she pulled out the plastic knife and jabbed it into one of his arms as the other punched her twice in the face. From that moment on, it had been a nightmare from her worst fears as he hauled her off the cot, pinned her hand to the floor, and the Bitch knelt beside her with the hammer and chisel.

Relief had flooded through Caitlin as the Bitch placed the tools beside her hand and snapped a photo with a phone. But the feeling didn't last long as reality returned with a vengeance when the Bitch had announced "One hour to *show time*."

And now she knelt in front of Caitlin and gripped her chin hard. Nose to bloody nose, she smiled. "If your manservant doesn't call back soon, we'll begin the cosmetic surgery. But don't worry. I hear some johns like their whores mutilated. The good news is, the longer he makes us wait, the more you can charge. Advertise yourself as the fingerless fuck."

Caitlin's hatred overflowed. She didn't care about anything except hurting the Bitch and hearing her scream. She tried to get up, slipped and fell.

The Bitch laughed. "What's the matter? Feeling a little woozy?"

"Damn it, Beth," said Parker. "Would you quit this shit?"

The Bitch turned on him. "You weakling. I should have known you're good for nothing more than the dildo you haul around between your legs."

She stood up, paced around the bunker for what seemed to Caitlin like an eternity, repeatedly glancing at her watch, becoming more and more agitated. Then she stopped, as if she'd turned into a statue. Except for her eyes. They flitted around the bunker like windows into the soul of a person losing it.

Caitlin glanced at Parker, who appeared to be worried for his safety. He coughed. "Maybe we should—"

"Shut the fuck up." The Bitch's words, soft, barely audible over the buzzing of an overhead light, frightened Caitlin even more. She was looking toward the front of the bunker, wondering if she could make it, when the Bitch said, "I'm through waiting. Get over here and hold her."

Caitlin tried to fight him, but quickly ended up face down on the floor with Parker straddling her body and holding her right wrist with both hands. She made a fist. Parker pried her first finger out flat on the floor, pinned it there, said to the Bitch, "Be careful with that goddamn chisel."

THE WOMAN STEPPED UP behind Nick, gripped his belt at the small of his back with her left hand, and leaned close. Past his right shoulder, she whispered, "Shove your hands into your front pockets and keep them there until I tell you to remove them for going down the stairs."

Before he could lift his hands, a terrible scream cut through the night silence.

Adrenaline and instinct took control as Nick pivoted to his right and drove his right elbow backwards, felt the impact with the woman's neck and shoulder as his left hand grabbed at the suppressor on the pistol in her right hand.

Pop!

A tug at his side, hit but not bad, his left hand gripped the suppressor—*hot!*—twisted the pistol to her right against her wrist. Her fingers lost the grip and he yanked hard, the pistol loose, jammed the grip into his right hand, brought it up and she was moving fast and gone into the night.

Nick turned and ran to the faint glow in the ground, tried to stop, slipped on the leaves, fell onto the netting.

Riiiiiip!

He landed on a concrete floor, the netting torn away from the bunker, but it softened the impact. He jumped up, quick-peeked past the edge of the door. Caitlin, Parker, McAllister all close together. Nick brought the pistol up, led with it as he shouldered past the door into the bunker.

Caitlin lying face down, blood from a scalp wound covering the left side of her face, Parker straddling her and pinning her right hand on the floor, McAllister kneeling and holding a chisel and a hammer. A large handgun on the cot behind them. Three heads turned toward Nick.

The pistol, probably a .22 or .25 caliber, felt awkward, muzzle-heavy. It wasn't as accurate with the suppressor, and he couldn't keep it from shaking. Hoping Parker and McAllister wouldn't notice at this distance, had to be 25 to 30 feet, Nick shifted the sight from one to the other.

CAITLIN COULDN'T SEE MUCH. One eye had swollen shut and Parker's knee was blocking most of her view, but the face of Nick Phillips behind a pistol with a very long barrel—*what the hell is that?*—and Parker and the Bitch looking at him, were all she needed.

She turned her head. On the floor under the cot lay the plastic knife. It didn't have any blood on it. *Need to correct that.* She reached for it, gripped the handle in her fist with the blade protruding toward her thumb, brought it close to her body.

"Welcome," said the Bitch. "You must be Nicky boy. Did you bring the real balance weight this time, or do I have to take one of the bimbo's fingers?"

"Try that and I'll shoot you dead."

The Bitch scoffed. "Not with that little thing, you won't." She turned to Parker. "Are you just going to sit on your miserable ass? Pick up your pistol and send this pest back where he came from."

"He knows better," said Nick. "Don't you, Tommy Lee?"

"Apparently he doesn't know anything of use," said the Bitch. "Even something simple. Like how to do what he's told." Then to Parker, "What are you waiting for?"

Time had stopped for Caitlin as the stalemate froze everyone in place except for Nick's shifting the pistol back and forth and one other crucial detail.

She felt a slight decrease in the pressure of Parker's weight on her back and his grip on her wrist. He was getting ready to move.

Wait . . . wait . . . NOW!

NICK CONCENTRATED ON PARKER and McAllister, ready for any moves that threatened Caitlin, and almost pulled the trigger when she suddenly rolled on her side and struck at Parker with her closed left fist.

He reared back, both hands reaching for something white sticking out of his throat, blood staining his shirt collar, and hit the floor on his back.

McAllister slashed at Caitlin with the chisel, striking her in the cheek, dropped the hammer and reached for the pistol on the cot.

Nick aimed, fired, *Pop!* Thought, *Is that all?* Fired again, and through the haze of gun smoke saw McAllister crouched down, hands covering her head. He'd missed with both shots, took a step forward to close the distance and froze when something hard jammed into his back. A hand reached around his body and took the Sig.

Caitlin rolled away from Parker, scrambled up and almost

478 ❖ TOSH MCINTOSH

fell, one hand pressed against her bloody cheek. She snatched the Beretta off the cot and placed the muzzle against the back of McAllister's head.

"NO!" shouted Nick. "It's not worth it, Caitlin."

Her whole body shook, the pistol wobbling in her hand as she hissed, "Look at me, Bitch."

McAllister turned to face Caitlin. "You don't have it in you."

Tears streamed down, mixing with the blood on Caitlin's torn cheek. The look in her eyes spoke of hatred and blood thirst.

From behind Nick, "Don't listen to her, honey."

ANOTHER WOMAN'S VOICE WEDGED its way into Caitlin's awareness and confused her. She looked up from McAllister to Nick and realized he no longer held the pistol with the long barrel. What was he doing?

Then she noticed a masked, black-clad figure behind him, barely visible in the dim light. Parker's Beretta felt like it had a mind of its own as she raised the muzzle from McAllister toward the new threat.

Two voices, Nick's and a woman's, spoke as one. "Don't."

Then the woman, her voice slightly muffled from inside the mask: "Put the pistol down or your *friend* dies. I won't tell you again."

Caitlin knew she was in shock and not thinking clearly, but who would want to hurt Nick when he was unarmed and she had the gun?

"Please put it down, Caitlin," said Nick.

She made eye contact with him, saw a slight head nod that seemed to say, *It's okay.*

Then in a surreal moment, knowing it was a risky move but not being able to stop, she held up the Beretta, grabbed the barrel to transfer it to her other hand, and slammed the butt down on the top of McAllister's head. It felt so good that she had to smile as she tossed the pistol on the cot. She peered at the figure behind Nick. "Can I pick up that towel for my cheek?"

The woman nodded. "But no more sudden moves."

Caitlin's legs trembled, her knees felt like they were knocking together. She moved away from the Bitch, who sat on the floor glaring at Caitlin through strands of hair blood-soaked from the scalp wound. Parker lay on the floor with his eyes closed, holding his throat. The blood wasn't pulsing through his fingers, and Caitlin regretted not having had better aim. With the towel held to her cheek, she lowered herself to the floor.

The woman pushed Nick forward. "Bring one of those chairs over by me. Sit in the other one and don't even twitch." In each hand she held a pistol, the small one with a suppressor, and the other looked like Nick's Glock.

When Nick was seated, she put the small pistol on the chair close to her and kept the Glock pointed at Nick as she circled everyone and got the Beretta off the cot. It looked to Caitlin like musical pistols as the woman removed the suppressor, put it in a jacket pocket, and slipped the small pistol in a shoulder rig. She shoved the Beretta into her waistband behind her back, picked up the Glock, walked over to Parker and stood over him. "Hey."

It was a soft sound, so gentle and caring that Caitlin wanted to scream at her to stop being nice.

When Parker didn't respond, the woman nudged his shoulder with the toe of her boot. "Look at me."

Parker opened his eyes, stared at the ceiling for a moment, then at the woman.

She nodded. "Good. You know that guy in the LTD? Out in the desert? The one you killed and set on fire?"

Parker grimaced, blinked a few times. Bloody bubbles foamed from his throat as he said, "Who are you?"

"His friend. We were on the way to being more, and you robbed us of that future. I wanted you to see this coming, you sonofabitch, and know who it was that sent you to hell." She lifted the Glock and fired twice into Parker's chest and once into his forehead.

Caitlin couldn't hear a thing even if there were anything to hear. But she didn't need to. Her eyes told her everything she needed to know.

Parker in a spreading pool of blood. Flowing toward Caitlin. She didn't mind.

The Bitch sitting on the floor, apparently unaware that Parker's blood threatened to reach her shoes. Nice shoes. Expensive. Probably ruined now. Served the Bitch right.

Nick in the chair, watching the woman as she retrieved the two shell casings from the small pistol, put them in her jacket pocket, then picked up the three from the Glock and sat in the other chair.

"Y'all listen up. I usually don't kill anyone unless I get paid, and I have no arrangement with anyone regarding any of you. This asshole right here was an exception, over and done with. I also never leave loose ends. Now I'm faced with three of them. Question is, what should I do about it?"

Nick pointed at Caitlin, then at himself. "As for us? It's already been done."

The woman stared at Nick for a long moment before she nodded. "Smart fella." Then she looked at Caitlin. "Do you understand what's going on?"

She really wanted to, but her brain wouldn't stay in the bunker.

The woman leaned forward, held up the Glock in one gloved hand and the Glock shell casings in the other, and looked deep into Caitlin's eyes. "To avoid a follow-up visit from me, all you two folks have to do is *not* make it personal between *us*."

Then she turned to Nick and nodded toward the Bitch. "Do I need to worry about *her*?"

"Leave her to me."

"Then I'll be saying goodbye."

When the woman stood up, Nick said, "Could you leave my backup?"

She stared at him for a moment, as if to read his intentions. "It'll be at the top of the steps. Don't pop your head up there too soon."

AFTER THE WOMAN LEFT the bunker, Nick waited as long as he could stand it, which wasn't more than a few minutes, and decided the woman had no cause to stick around and every reason to get the hell gone. He picked up the chisel and hammer and ordered McAllister to sit on the cot. "I'll use these on *you* and never regret it for a second, so stay put."

At the top of the steps, he found his pistol, checked for a round in the pipe and a full magazine, and shoved it into his waistband. The hammer and chisel disappeared into the trees as far as he could throw them.

Back in the bunker, he helped Caitlin into a chair. The scalp wound had bled all over the front of her shirt, but it had clotted. Her cheek wound was still bleeding and worried him. When he tried to ease the towel away from her face to take a look, she grabbed his hand and pulled it away. "Would you *really* cut off her fingers if I asked you to?"

"Just mouthing off. That wouldn't hurt enough, and I know you want her to suffer a long time."

Caitlin's face hardened. "Absolutely."

McAllister appeared to have regained her arrogance. "Pardon me for interrupting, but we're all in the same *bunker*. Looks to me like cooperation is required."

Caitlin scoffed. "In your dreams, Bitch."

"How about *your* dreams? The half-million dollars in that bag will buy some."

"Your math is still way off."

"I'll double it."

"You're not listening to me."

"Two million."

"You don't have enough."

"Try me."

"No. You want to know why?"

"I can't believe you're that stupid."

"Stupid is to think you can sabotage an airplane and kill your husband and get away with it."

"That's a load of crap. Balance weight or no, you can't *prove—*"

"The hell we can't." Caitlin pointed at Nick. "This guy has already told the NTSB about finding the evidence of sabotage, and he'll be helping the FBI fit you with a pair of shiny bracelets."

Nick was having a hard time keeping a straight face. Caitlin could win an Academy Award with this performance, and it looked like McAllister was barely holding it together.

Then Caitlin removed the towel from her face and leaned toward McAllister, who recoiled at the sight of torn flesh and blood. "But you want to know the best part? That center you've wanted for so long? It will never bear your name."

McAllister launched herself at Caitlin.

Nick reached out, punched McAllister in the chest with the heel of his hand and knocked her back onto the cot. "Don't try that again."

"Goddamn you to hell!" screamed McAllister.

"He probably will." Nick stood and helped Caitlin up. "Can you walk okay? And make it up the stairs?"

She nodded, but when Nick tried to guide her toward the door, she pushed his hand away. "In a minute." To McAllister, she said, "I'm going to take away everything you ever cared about."

To her credit, McAllister recovered her composure as if she'd flipped a switch. "Bullshit. It's all about money, honey. My attack-dog legal team will tear you and everyone around you into tiny pieces."

Nick grabbed the straps of the duffel and slipped them over his shoulder. When McAllister stared at him, with a *What the hell are you doing?* expression, he nodded toward Caitlin and said, "It's for her legal expenses."

They left her sitting on the cot looking like a deflated witch doll.

CHAPTER THIRTY-SEVEN

Nick locked the bunker and helped Caitlin up the steps to ground level. She wanted to walk to the house with him, but he tried to convince her to wait for him to get a vehicle.

She shook her head. "I've been cooped up down there too long. Need to walk away from that horror on my own. Look around at the landscape. See the stars." She marched toward the house, a little unsteady on her feet.

Nick followed close behind, alert for any sign that she might lose her balance, but she appeared to be getting stronger. When they got to the garage and he opened the right door, Caitlin said, "I know that truck. It almost ran me over when I left the airport on the way to Parker's trailer." Then she peered into the left stall. "And that one. The guy driving it damn near killed me. I never knew pickups were so dangerous."

Nick smiled at that small bit of levity in the midst of some serious shit and checked the registrations. "One is Parker's. The other belongs to Buster Hayes, the guy who lives here."

"You mean, *lived*."

"What?"

"Long story, but I'm pretty sure he won't be coming home. You see any keys?"

Nick found keys in the ignition of Parker's truck, backed

it out, helped Caitlin climb up into the cab. "Where's your shoulder bag?"

"Parker took it."

Nick searched the cab. On the floor in the back seat he found a large purse that contained McAllister's driver's license and credit cards. He tossed the duffel in with it. "I'm going to look in the house. Stay put."

When he turned to leave, Caitlin said, "Nick?"

"Yeah?"

"You're bleeding."

He looked down at his side, pulled his shirttail out and found a bloody crease just above his waistline. "I'll get something for it."

With no time to hunt for anything better, he grabbed some paper towels from the kitchen, removed his belt and used it to strap them tight against the wound. He discovered Caitlin's shoulder bag behind a removable panel in the wall of a bedroom closet. Clothes on hangers had been dumped on the floor and the panel hadn't been carefully replaced, or he would have never seen it. Caitlin's Walther and extra magazines went in Nick's jacket pocket, and he confirmed her driver's license and medical insurance card were in the bag.

A quick Google search with his phone identified the closest 24-hour emergency facility. On the way there he mentioned the need for a good spur-of-the-moment cleanup plan and learned that Caitlin had left the Mercedes at Parker's trailer park.

He thought about that for a moment. "He's probably moved it. Get it away from property that could be tied to him. Where are the keys?"

"Last I saw, in my bag."

Nick reached into the back seat and lifted the bag onto the console. "Which pocket?"

"The small exterior one."

Steering the truck with his knees, he unzipped her bag, brought out a key ring and held in the palm of his hand so Caitlin could see it. "Are these yours?"

After a moment, "Yes."

"What about the key to your motel room?"

"The keycard's in my wallet."

"Okay." And now for the biggie. "Where's the balance weight?"

She smiled. "Before I forget to mention this, the fake-weight scam was brilliant. Thanks for being so sneaky. The real one is in my room, behind the grate on the vent above the door in the bathroom."

"Where anyone who likes mysteries and thrillers would never think to look because it's so obvious. I'll get it from the motel room and look for the Mercedes. How are you doing over there?"

"I'd really like some happy juice. How much longer?"

"Almost there. In the meantime, please listen carefully. You walk into an ER with a bullet or knife wound? They'll report it to the police. But this? I don't know. Hopefully, they'll accept your explanation that it was an accident. But even if they don't and the cops get involved, you're not filing charges. We don't want any reports connecting you to events in the bunker."

Caitlin sat with her eyes closed, head against the headrest. "I can do that." She turned her head toward him and opened her eyes. "Speaking of which, what are we—?"

"There's no 'we'."

"But I can—"

"Forget it."

Approaching the ER, Nick suggested it would be better not to drive up to the entrance. "I should have switched to the

Jeep. But it's too late now, and we don't need security cameras connecting the truck of a dead man to us."

After deciding that all the parking areas were probably under surveillance, they parked around the block from the entrance to the ER. When Nick wanted to escort her, Caitlin objected. "I can make it okay. Let's keep your face away from cameras."

He got Caitlin's phone out of the duffel and put it in her bag, then took it back out and deleted the two incriminating photos and messages before returning the phone to the bag. He draped the straps over her right shoulder. "Your wallet's in the bag with your phone. I've got the keys to the Mercedes and the keycard to your motel room. Do you want me to check you out?" When Caitlin shook her head, Nick said, "Call me when you need a ride. Good luck." He watched from a distance until she disappeared into the ER, then headed back to the bunker, his mind racing through a hasty checklist with a full dose of emotion as a backdrop.

Body dumping. The purview of serial killers and at least one aviation accident investigator. How does a person get to the point of accepting that as okay? Well, maybe not okay, but necessary? Or justified?

For Nick, the only rationale he could use and still sleep at night without the demons hovering over the bed was to concentrate on the question of retribution. The application of justice in this case had come at the hands of a petite assassin who normally got paid, but considered her personal reasons sufficient compensation.

Not only that, but she had taken advantage of the opportunity for an insurance policy with a company named Glock. And three slugs, at least one of which was probably in good enough shape for ballistic analysis. Matching a slug to a pistol registered in Nick's name and with his fingerprints on it would connect Nick to a corpse. Of a killer. Nick didn't spend much time looking for Biblical explanations of anything, but the concept of *eye for an eye* seemed tailor-made in relation to Tommy Lee Parker.

Okay, so Nick had personal reasons as well. He wasn't perfect. Never had been, never would be. That said, he'd take whatever consequences judgment day brought knowing his actions a year ago and today were righteous, and hopefully would be in the future.

Nervous about driving around in Tommy Lee's truck, Nick finally arrived back at the Hayes house and parked in the garage. Then he took the minimal chance of attracting attention at 4:00 o'clock in the morning and trotted a mile down the road to where the Jeep was parked. He had to hunt around for a while, but the eastern sky had lightened enough with the impending moonrise to help him identify his tire tracks.

He drove back to the house and gathered up cleaning supplies and tore a sheet from the laundry room into rags. In the garage he found a tarp covering a motorcycle. A Harley. He didn't know much about them other than they sounded really cool, and this one looked like an older model cared for with loving attention.

It also directed his thoughts to Parker's biker connection and the drugs. And for some reason he couldn't explain, to a female hired gun with a personal grudge against Parker and a bad attitude to go along with it. That was a possible link Nick had no intention of exploring.

He wiped the interior of Parker's truck, put all the cleaning stuff in the Jeep along with McAllister's purse and the duffel, then remembered Caitlin's Walther, zipped it into the duffel with the money and drove to the bunker.

If looks could do physical damage, Nick would have lost his manhood and head at the same time as soon as he opened the door. He sat in one of the chairs and pointed to the other.

"*Gentlemen,*" McAllister hissed, "hold a chair for a *lady.*"

"Those are two good reasons I'm not doing that. Sit or stand, but listen very carefully. Are you listening?"

She just glared at him, but at least she didn't cover her ears and babble.

"This is a stalemate in terms of involving the cops because everybody loses if we do. I'm going to take you home, but you'll be blindfolded. You can accept that willingly, or I'll use whatever force necessary. Your choice."

"Some choice, you sonofabitch."

Nick vaulted out of the chair and put his face a few inches from hers. "And you're a murderer. So let's acknowledge mutual aversion and both of us will have to live with it. Deal?"

He didn't expect an answer and didn't wait for one. From the cabinet next to the cot he pulled out a pillowcase and tossed it to her. "Put that on and leave it there. You will lie down in the back seat, out of sight. If you sit up, or your hands get anywhere near the pillowcase, I'll cable-tie you into submission and the trip will become very uncomfortable."

McAllister's hostility seemed to vanish. She opened the pillowcase and placed it over her head. As he guided her up the steps to the Jeep, Nick reminded himself to be careful, like he'd be around a wild animal kept as a pet.

Using McAllister's slightly muffled verbal directions delivered through the pillowcase, he drove to the address she gave him and passed by to check it out, then parked on a street corner about three blocks away.

Now came a tricky part, walking with a woman wearing

a pillowcase over her head. This early he wasn't too concerned about someone glancing out a window, but he couldn't let McAllister see the Jeep and maybe the license plate number. She knew who he was, so the precaution offered only immediate protection. But at least she wouldn't be able to get the Albuquerque cops looking for his wheels.

He told McAllister what was going to happen and asked about the alarm system.

"I don't know a thing about it."

"Don't give me that shit. It's your house."

"Are you *blind?* I wouldn't ask my dog to live in this neighborhood."

"Oh. I see. So this is really the house of the Chief of Police, right? A little surprise for me when the door opens?"

"Lawson lived here, you idiot. I have a key in my purse."

"So is the alarm set, or not?"

"Not."

Nick pulled out his knife, flicked the blade out with his thumb. It locked with an oily *snick.* "You hear that?" When she nodded, he said, "That's a razor-sharp Spyderco. If you're lying, I'll use it to cripple you before I run."

He closed the knife, got a set of keys from her purse and put them both in his jacket pocket. Once out of the Jeep, he guided her around the corner and yanked off the pillowcase. She began turning her head to look behind them.

He gripped her arm harder. "Eyes *straight* ahead. Walk faster."

At the front door he handed her the keys. "Hurry up."

She opened it and they stepped into a quiet interior. Nick looked around him for the alarm panel, saw the green READY light and relaxed a little. "Where are the phones?"

She led him to each wireless handset. He shoved them in

his jacket pockets. In the kitchen, he pointed to a chair. This time she sat without protest. A resignation to reality? Or a head fake in preparation for punching the panic code into the alarm system once he cleared the front door?

After confiscating her cell phone, Nick stepped up close in front of her. She had to look up to meet his gaze. He lifted his knife, snapped open the blade, and with the other hand grabbed her hair to prevent her from leaning her head away.

With the point placed gently against her left cheek below the eye, he said, "It would give me great pleasure to disfigure you in return for what you did to Caitlin Monroe. And if you think my not doing that is a sign of weakness, consider this a promise.

"If you sound an alarm now, or in the future send the cops after me or her, I will see to it that you regret it for the rest of your life. You may think this is an idle threat, but know this. I have the resources to send someone who does this sort of thing for a living. Not like you, a rank amateur, armed with a hammer and a chisel. He will have much more creative ways to make it hurt."

Nick stepped back, closed the blade, and held eye contact with McAllister for a few moments, hoping she bought his lie. If he had to guess, he saw more fear than defiance. He turned, left the house, and just in case he was wrong, sprinted to the Jeep and got the hell out of there.

ON THE DRIVE BACK to the bunker, Nick had to pass through central Albuquerque. This early in the morning, he could attract the attention of a cop and be subjected to one of those thinly disguised "probable cause" stops that invariably include, *Do you have any objection to me taking a look in your vehicle, sir?*

Say yes and end up in cuffs.

He pulled over and transferred the contents of the back seat to the cargo area. New Mexico and Colorado had reciprocal concealed-carry privileges, but one of the weapons he had belonged to someone else. And although cops didn't usually check the registration of a weapon in the possession of a person legally carrying it, Nick had no intention of being on the wrong end of an exception.

Caitlin's Walther went in the spare-tire well along with individual bundles of cash from the duffel crammed into every available space. He replaced the lid and covered it with the cleaning supplies.

On the road again, Nick's mind began checking off items on the cleanup list. Disposing of Parker's body was next, and memories of details at a Colorado mineshaft resurfaced as fresh as the day Nick experienced them a little over a year ago.

Controlling the mule, skittish as a thoroughbred being led to the starting gate.

Cold, wet darkness in the horizontal tunnel approaching the vertical shaft.

The yawning black hole, barely visible in the gray floor.

Colder, musty air rising from the depths of the shaft.

And the terror of falling in, more debilitating than any fear he'd ever known.

A slow realization dawned on him. He couldn't do that again. He had to get rid of Parker's body, but not *that* way, and not in a grave dug by his own hands.

He had to protect himself and Caitlin at the same time, and he couldn't do that with a rag and liquid cleaner.

Nick was pondering another solution when he noticed what looked like a body lying under a streetlight. As he slowed, out of curiosity, or maybe civic duty, or compassion, the body moved and a homeless man appeared out from under a tattered blanket. Nick pulled to a stop with the headlights on him. The man shielded his eyes with one hand and held up a stained, creased and torn cardboard sign.

401k running low. Anything helps.

Without thinking about what the hell he was doing, Nick turned off the headlights, got out of the car and approached the guy. His face was covered with hair: a beard, mustache, and eyebrows that reached to the hairline of a coarse, matted lion's mane falling to his shoulders.

Nick nodded to him. "Got a cigarette?"

"Jesus, fella. That's my line." His voice sounded like it had been filtered through a Darth Vader mask.

"I'll pay for it."

"How much?"

"Twenty bucks."

The guy eased up straighter, fumbled under the blanket for the pocket of his filthy military-style parka, and pulled out a crumpled pack of smokes. Nick doubted any cigarettes could have survived that treatment, but then again, cancer sticks were like cockroaches.

"You wouldn't happen to have a fresh pack, would you?"

"I look like a fresh-pack kinda guy?"

"I suppose not." Nick got out a 20-dollar bill and handed it to him. When he looked inside the pack, almost cringing as he did, there were three smokes, each of which was bent into artistic curves but still unbroken.

He pulled one out and shaped it straight between two fingers. "Got any matches?"

"Shoulda let me know you wanted a package deal. Now I'll have to charge you full price for the extra transaction."

"What'll that cost me?"

"Twenty bucks."

Nick handed him another bill and examined the matchbook. It was from the Stardust in Las Vegas and had never been used. A collector's item. He thanked the guy, walked toward the Jeep, stopped, turned around. "Mind my asking a couple questions?"

"How much?"

"It's just conversation."

The guy blew his nose into the sleeve of his jacket, coughed up a wad of phlegm and spat. "What do you wanna know?"

"Where'd you get the matches?"

"People hand me all kinds of stuff. Sometimes it looks like they're just cleaning out the consoles in their cars. You got only one more free inquiry. Use it wisely."

"How'd you get here?"

"I walked."

"Before that. Back when you knew what a 401k was."

"Oh, yeah. Way back then. Stockbroker, financial advisor, which some people consider being a crook."

"Were you?"

The guy paused, stared into the distance for a moment, and nodded. "But that's not what got me." Nick gave him a look that asked what did, and the guy replied, "Nose candy. Ever hear 'Cocaine' by Eric Clapton?"

"Yeah."

"Well, he's right. She tells lies."

BUSTER'S OVERSIZED GARAGE LOOKED to Nick like a contradiction in both appearance and function.

The outside had a run-down look of neglect that spoke of abandonment. But the double doors had been reinforced and adjusted so they swung open with only a light touch and closed with about a quarter-inch space between them.

One half of the interior appeared to be a catchall for every bit of discarded junk collected within all of Bernalillo County. Lining one wall of the other half was a workshop full of machines and tools that probably had been designed around customizing motorcycles.

Nick recognized an English wheel, a tool for shaping metal that he'd seen used on a TV program where a guy constructed a gas tank for a chopper. No way any work could be done with two vehicles inside, but emptied out, it would be a custom builder's wet dream.

It didn't take long to discover that Buster kept gas in a 50-gallon drum with an old-fashioned hand pump. Nick found a couple of 5-gallon plastic containers, filled them and put them in the back of the Jeep. At the bunker, he hauled them down the steps to the landing, then went back to the Jeep and tore the rags he'd made for cleaning and wouldn't need any more into thinner strips, then tied them together into a single piece about 10-feet long.

At the door of the bunker, he paused to collect his emotions and shove them into a lockbox. Then he opened the door and forced himself to walk up to Parker's body and look at it. He didn't know why, exactly. Maybe due to a vague feeling that he should. To give himself a chance to back out if somewhere deep in the core of his conscience a voice spoke up in protest. After a moment, he wanted to hawk up a throat full of phlegm like that homeless guy did and spit on Parker's corpse. Apparently, that's how he really felt about the asshole. So be it.

It took about 15 minutes to build a pyre with bedding, paper, boxes of wooden matches, and anything made of wood that was portable and he could easily move. One end of the sheet strip went on the pile, weighted down with some paperback books. He checked the authors and mentally apologized, even though he didn't know any of them.

The other end of the sheet went at the base of the open matchbook, propped vertically between two more books. He tore the filters off three cigarettes and pushed them down into the matches to hold them vertically and stepped back to assess the sequence of events.

Do this wrong, and end up a human torch. Or maybe in the next county if the fumes ignited before the gas.

Do it right, and be far enough away to never know it happened until it reached the news.

Option two seemed best.

One last inventory. He had the money, two pistols, every phone he could find in the bunker and the house, and had been very careful not to leave fingerprints. Hair and fiber evidence in the bunker would never survive the heat. Parker's DNA might, or his dental work, but identification of the body wouldn't be a catastrophe. And Nick had been in the house so short a time that he doubted anything could be used to place him there even if they tried really hard to find something.

Okay. Time to do this thing.

Then he thought of one other precaution and ran up the stairs to the Jeep to turn it around facing the road and leave it running.

Back in the bunker, he got a box of wooden matches and carefully lit each of the three cigarettes, blowing on them gently to get the tips fully afire.

He brought the gas cans into the bunker. Quickly now, with his heart beating in his chest so hard he thought it would burst, he soaked the pyre and saved the last bit to pour on the sheet fuse up to the base of the matchbook propped between the two books. He was counting on the gas wicking up to the end of the sheet. But hopefully not quite yet.

Nauseous from the fumes, Nick paused at the door to the bunker and bade a silent farewell to what happened here and what was about to happen. He propped the door open for a source of air to feed the fire, knowing that the heat would escape through the smokestack vents in the bunker ceiling, creating a vacuum effect and drawing in more fresh air.

Then he climbed the steps and got in the Jeep. Just in case a neighbor might notice and to avoid looking like he was running from something, he idled out to the road, fully expecting a shock wave and searing heat to roll over him. At the speed limit, he drove to his motel, making full stops at signs, not running any red lights or even coming close, using his turn signals, and without tailgating any of the few other cars he saw. It was the most law-abiding trip he'd made in years.

He got a beer out of the fridge in the mini-bar, sat down, couldn't stand not moving, hopped up, drank it and one more while pacing a groove in the carpet. Then it dawned on him that the fire might have been reported by now. He turned on the TV, discovered that *KOB Eyewitness News 4 is your best source for Albuquerque news, Santa Fe news and New Mexico news, weather and sports.*

That sounded good, so he left the channel there, lay down on the bed just to close his eyes while waiting for some *good* news.

A MONSTER WEARING A hideous mask and howling with blood lust had strapped both of Nick's hands to a table and was sharpening a huge knife with savage strokes on a whetstone. Nick was jerking against the restraints, trying to drag the table with him far away to safety when the creature raised the knife high above his head and slashed down with all his strength on Nick's right wrist.

He woke up screaming, sweating, and safe in his motel bed. He got up, took a shower, made a cup of coffee, and glanced at the TV where an on-scene reporter stood beside a mailbox with the house visible to her left side. Behind her a red glow flickered in the trees, gray-black smoke climbing skyward with white accents as the water from the fire trucks turned to steam and water vapor.

Nick watched for a few minutes with a strange sense of accomplishment, wondering if that's how an arsonist felt. He ignored the other thing, figuring that he'd deal with it soon enough. Probably with more nightmares like the one he'd just endured.

He called Caitlin's phone and left a message, then decided to take care of some lingering details by first removing the soft drinks from the ice bucket and pouring out the water. There in the bottom sat the half-balance weight that had been thrown from the Victory ruddervator. With his backup weapon temporarily serving as his primary inside his waistband, he slipped the weight into his ankle holster for safekeeping. The three diversionary half-weights went in an outer pocket of his suitcase. They might make good paperweights for his desk at the flight school. And remind him on a daily basis to use better judgment the next time someone offered him a job looking into aviation sabotage.

Then he moved the Jeep to a corner of the parking lot as far from the motel as he could get it. With the rear shielded from curious eyes by a stone wall and row of bushes, he transferred the cash and Caitlin's Walther from the spare tire well into the duffel bag and hid it as best he could under the ruddervator.

At Parker's trailer park he found the Mercedes, worse for

the wear with the tires and wheels gone, a window busted out, the interior a mess. He called Mercedes Benz of Albuquerque and arranged to have them pick it up and get it running, fix the window, and deal with cosmetic issues.

He visited Caitlin's motel room and carried a desk chair into the bathroom to stand on.

Four screws out, he lifted off the grill vent and peered in.

His heart tried to stop beating.

The balance weight wasn't there.

Steely-eyed investigator/pilots don't panic, but Nick felt as if he'd just lost his membership in that elite club. He looked around the bathroom. There were no other vents. This had to be the one.

Peering into the vent, Nick positioned his head to let in as much light as possible from the bathroom. His spirits sank again until he noticed a slight glint, a little sliver of what might be light reflecting off a baggie. He reached in as far as he could. His fingers brushed what could only be a baggie, most of which was hidden behind a 90-degree corner of the ducting. With two fingers pressing hard together, he tugged on the baggie and felt the weight move. The sound of it sliding on the ducting warmed his insides as he pulled it all the way out.

Sitting on the bed, Nick held in his hand the baggie with the *real* half balance weight, lifting tape and powder residue from Parker's locker. He reached down to the holster strapped to the inside of his left ankle and pulled out its mate from the ruddervator and held them side-by-side.

Staring at them, he wanted to remember what this felt like.

As a counterpoint to the dilemma.

Knowing this evidence could prove sabotage and point directly to a murderer.

But as a private crash detective, unlike a PI ferreting out

the truth behind a homicide and putting usable evidence in the hands of a cop, Nick could never call upon legal redress.

Closing the door satisfactorily on any investigation would have to be a rogue action.

Maybe the *American Vigilante* journalist was right, that commitment to justice demanded a willingness to stray outside the boundaries. A lot farther than a little B&E.

And if Nick had a problem with looking at himself in the mirror after crossing way over the line, he had no business being right here, right now, or anywhere near it ever again.

NICK HAD JUST FINISHED lunch, an unhealthy but scrumptious cheeseburger special with curly fries, when he received a text from Caitlin: *Took a cab to the motel. New room number 145. Where are you?* He texted back *on my way*, arrived there in about 20 minutes and parked as close to her room as he could. Both balance weights went in the duffel. He carried the ruddervator to her room and left it on the sidewalk while he went back for the duffle.

When she opened the door to an EXECUTIVE SUITE, according to black lettering on a gold plate, he felt himself pull back involuntarily at the appearance of her face.

"That bad, huh?"

"Uh . . . no. You make butterfly bandages look pretty good."

"Liar." Then her eyes shifted past him and down to the ruddervator lying on the sidewalk and immediately teared up. She turned around, ran through the living area into the bedroom and slammed the door.

Nick stepped inside, heard Caitlin crying, and felt like a complete jerk for not anticipating the emotional impact of being confronted with the crumpled physical evidence of the crash that had killed the man she loved. He put the duffel on the floor of the closet and leaned the ruddervator against the ironing board, then stood in the middle of the room, wanting to comfort her but not having a clue what to do. So he waited, staring at the closed door.

The room became very quiet. After s few minutes, Caitlin came out of the bedroom. Her eyes were a little red, but she had recovered her composure. "Where did you put it?"

"In the closet. I'm so sorry I didn't think—"

"It's okay, Nick, really. There's a lot of stuff running around in my head right now and the sight of that . . . it . . . it just took me by surprise. Have a seat."

They sat on a couch and sipped bottled water because Caitlin was still taking pain medication, and Nick had tentatively planned on flying back to Cedar Valley later that afternoon.

He wasn't at all sure what to talk about or where to start, so he decided to deal with aftermath logistics like the Mercedes, her pistol, the cash, and the balance weights. With those topics covered, he moved into unknown territory with, "Will there be a scar?"

"Too soon to know. The chisel made a pretty ragged cut, and it depends on how much cosmetic surgery I elect to have."

"Why wouldn't you choose to make it disappear completely if you can?"

"It's complicated."

"The surgery?"

"The *issue.*"

Nick picked up on Caitlin's tone, which shutdown *that* topic, and asked about her plans for Beth McAllister.

Caitlin's expression lost any emotional vulnerability it may have had before. "I'll make it a point never to call her by any names other than the ones she deserves. I'll keep the threat of legal action in her face until I find that she's aware it's an empty threat. And last, but first in importance, I'll visit the offices of *American Vigilante.*"

She explained that the journalist/author of *Airborne Justice* was going to receive the surprise of his life. And under Caitlin's direction, he would drive a word-stake through the heart of the Balloon Bitch, pinning her Black-Widow core to a shattered reputation. If she refused to retreat into the loneliness of counting her money and made good on her threat to sue the world for slander, Caitlin would spend every minute of her life and every dime she had or could get her hands on to make revenge an unwavering life goal.

Nick had told Caitlin more than once, but it seemed a good idea to do so again. "Sounds like you have it all worked out, but let me remind you that I've got nothing to do with any payoffs and I won't cooperate with this book thing."

Caitlin nodded. "Noted for the record. But you need to wake up to reality. You're a hero. The public loves you. People are fascinated with a guy who risked his life to go after a man trying to hide behind the unbridled power of a big white house, and *especially* with the continuing mystery surrounding the disappearance of the assassin when you were the last person who can place him on this earth."

Nick squirmed, hoping he'd been able to hide it. "That's great fiction hiding behind the illusion of truth, but it's in the past. What you're talking about happens in the immediate future, and it shines bright lights on events best left in the dark."

"Speaking of which," said Caitlin, "I heard some of the nurses talking about a fire and I watched a TV news report. Want to tell me about that?"

"Absolutely not."

"But I—"

"Forget about it."

"It'll help to get it out."

"You misunderstand. It's not about my feelings, but about three people who have dropped out of sight over the past two weeks."

"Now *you* misunderstand. This book will be about *her.* The rest is collateral damage in the realm of rumor and speculation."

"But it will get them *looking.*"

"So what? The Balloon Bitch will hide in her mansion to mourn the loss of her precious reputation and won't say a word about bodies. Yates killed Parker's friend Buster. Parker killed Yates. And all of that died with him at the hands of the little lady with your big pistol. All we have to do is keep her out of our lives. Based on the news reports, I'd say you came up with a way to do that. But you can't let it fester, Nick. It will eat you up."

Nick sighed. "Thanks for the advice, but this one's all mine."

He stood. She followed him to the door. After an awkward moment, he said, "Goodbye, Caitlin," and reached out to shake her hand.

She ignored it, moved in close and hugged him. "Thank you for everything."

Nick didn't trust his voice, so he didn't say a word.

When she stepped back, he looked into her eyes. The urge to dive in almost overwhelmed him. But he smiled, nodded once, opened the door and walked away.

Part of him stayed behind.

By the time he was packed and ready to depart Albuquerque for home, Nick chose to wait until the morning. Approaching darkness and the prospect of a night flight over mountainous terrain, combined with an almost debilitating fatigue as he descended the backside of an experience that left him questioning himself and what he stood for, made the decision a no-brainer.

He ate dinner at a small café that served a to-die-for tortilla soup and sandwiches with homemade bread. The waiter had turned his back on the legality of sending Nick out the door with two unopened bottles of *Santa Fe Pale Ale*, which he covered in ice before he took a long shower and put on a pair of sweatpants and a favorite t-shirt with the head of a bald eagle on it. The same eagle that graced the engine cowl of his airplane.

Then he opened one of the bottles and plopped down in an armchair, rested his bare feet on the seat of the desk chair, and took a long swallow of the beer. At reflective moments like this, his eyes usually lost focus on the nearby reality of the physical present as his mind sought out images from the past in an attempt to connect them with a thru-line to the future.

But this evening, the process had a short in it. Kind of like hooking up a wire to the wrong terminal and singeing his eyebrows. Then he'd try what *had* to be the right connection and get zapped again. Current wouldn't flow no matter what theory said because the present wouldn't let it.

Over the past year, Nick had accepted the reality that no matter how strong he thought his connections to family had been in the past, unintentional neglect was no less cumulative and destructive than its deliberate cousin. He could never go back again. All he could do was try to forge new bonds with the three people in the world for whom he cared the most. But first, he had to answer a few prerequisite questions.

Could he cram the spirit of a hunter into an emotional lockbox and throw away the key? Did he want to? Would it make any difference if he did? And what price would he ultimately pay to ignore his passion for uncovering the truth about what caused an airplane to end up in pieces?

If Nick could rewind his life a couple of years, the answers might come more easily. But the Larchmont and McAllister investigations had altered forever the core motivation that defined his professional goals during his career with the NTSB.

And at the end of *this* day, he knew that searching for evidence to prove pilot error couldn't even begin to compare with shining the bright light of truth on airborne murder.

CHAPTER THIRTY-EIGHT

Cooler weather and autumn leaves heralded Nick's favorite seasonal transition. But for the first few weeks after his return from what he now thought of as the misguided adventure that changed everything, only his immediate thoughts and emotions mattered. It was as if whatever happened *out there* escaped notice.

About the second week in October, Nick felt like he'd just awakened from an inadvertent nap. At the flight school, Ashton continued handling the day-to-day operations and proved that Nick could have faded into the woodwork without being missed. In and around town, friends and acquaintances, including Hotel, kept a polite and respectful distance with nods, casual greetings, and less than normal eye contact.

Heaven forbid a volatile question like, *How you doing?* With the possible exception of his neighbor's cocker spaniel, every resident knew full well something was seriously amiss in the life of the valley's most famous, or infamous, inhabitant. All of which was fine with Nick. He didn't want to be in anyone's limelight.

Then the book came out, and he experienced first-hand the true origin of the word *buzz*. They might have to change the name of the town. Which would allow Hotel's regular column to appear in the *Murmur Valley Gazette,* especially since he'd begun a series on one particular impact of eBooks on the publishing industry.

Using the astonishing success of *Airborne Justice* and the brand-new *Black Widow Unveiled* as examples, Hotel had illustrated how rapidly the public's interest can be exploited before the limited attention span of modern society embraced the next titillating story. Hotel had expressed it as the ability *to lure, capture and hold the attention of a vast readership for as long as possible.*

Elizabeth McAllister's multiple lawsuits, which appeared to have been filed against the entire world, injected sales of the second book with steroids and rejuvenated the first with a fresh run of its own. Rumors of a movie in the works would not abate.

Although Nick was tempted to read both books, he refused to yield control of his recollections and allow them to be tainted by the speculations of others no matter how well researched they may be. He knew the truth, after all, and he didn't need to read the fiction.

Early one evening in late October, Nick built the first fire since his return. Not because it hadn't been cold enough, but he couldn't wrap his emotions around memories of evenings in the living room with Laurie as the soothing aura of the fireplace filled them with peace and contentment. Like if he didn't *look* at the empty spaces left from her departure, he didn't have to deal with it. Sitting in his favorite chair, he watched the flames from the kindling crawl up the sides of the pine starters and begin to lick at the Douglas fir logs.

Deep in the core of who he was, Nick knew the time had come to face the reality of loss. To deal with the grief. To put it behind him and move on. He'd read that grieving was a process, with steps that ultimately led to closure, but that didn't feel right. He had no intention of terminating anything to do with his family.

The challenge was to accommodate himself to new relationships with Laurie, Stephanie, and Brad, and Nick refused to accept that the love they shared over the years couldn't survive the transition. He would reconnect with his family and build new links to a shared future.

He'd just decided to begin life-after-Laurie with a redecoration scheme to fill the physical vacancies left by her absence when headlights flashed through the blinds on the front windows. No one had been in the house except Nick since Laurie had moved out, so he wasn't expecting anyone. When it dawned on him he hadn't closed the garage door, he stood and walked toward the kitchen.

The front doorbell rang and diverted him to the peephole, filled with the face and upper torso of Caitlin Monroe, wearing a fuzzy hat, a brilliant red scarf tied in loop fashion around her neck, and what appeared to be a full-length leather coat that gleamed in the pale glow of the porch light.

He couldn't move, even if he wanted to. Backward into the living room. Forward to open the door. Run and hide in the attic. It didn't matter.

The doorbell rang again, then a knock, and after a moment, "I know the peephole in the door is fake, Nick, and you're peering at me through that sneaky one in the jamb. Nice touch, by the way, but you can relax. The Walther is still in my bag."

Nick took a very deep breath, held it for a long time, and exhaled in a rush as he slipped the deadbolt and opened the door.

No amount of breathing and exhaling could have prepared him for the smile he received. Caitlin's face had lost the persistent anger that, even when she was playing nice with others during the investigation, had always shown through in the set of her jaw and the fire in her eyes. He noticed the scar, tried not to look at it as he stepped aside and invited her in.

The fragrance of Ambush trailed her into the foyer. Nick wondered if she had a license to wear it in Colorado. "I was about to open a bottle of Sauvignon Blanc. Join me?"

"No thanks. But if that glow from the living room means what I think it does, I could use a little sit-by-the-fire time."

"Follow me." Nick hadn't replaced Laurie's chair, but he'd positioned a couch-and-armchair arrangement with a coffee table on the other side of the circular fireplace. He motioned to the couch, stoked the fire with a poker and added a new log as she took off her coat and sat down.

As he sat in the armchair, Caitlin was looking around the room. "Is there furniture missing?"

"Laurie took some with her."

A shadow passed over her face. "What happened?"

"Mutual but incompatible love, unfortunately."

Their eyes met for a moment. Caitlin nodded slightly. "I'm so sorry, Nick."

"Me too. So, what's up with you?"

She caught him up on events in Albuquerque after he left and told him the short version of her dealings with the journalist. "I know you won't have anything to do with him, but he's the writer's version of you."

"What the hell does that mean?"

"Total commitment to a goal with no hesitation, doubt, indecision, or other evidence of a namby-pamby attitude."

He grinned. "Oh, well. He and I might have something in common after all. Are you going to win this lawsuit?"

"Who cares? Did you see the latest about the cancer center?"

"I've been trying not to."

"Okay, but you might like this. That was to be her crowning legacy, right? With your help, I prevented her coronation and delivered the ultimate blow. Last week, the board of directors voted to change the name to the Lawson McAllister Memorial Cancer Treatment Center."

Nick chuckled. "Now *that's* a case of award-winning poetic justice. But I hope it lasts. She's got more money than she can spend in a lifetime of lawsuits."

"Agreed, although her real vulnerability lies in how important *perception* is to her. And you want to know the absolute, most perfect, it-can't-get-any-better-than-this outcome of our collaboration?"

"If you put it that way, sure."

"She's disappeared."

"What?"

"From the social scene. From management of the center. And from *anything* to do with life outside of a psychiatric hospital."

"Voluntary, or was she committed?"

"Not sure. Her lawyers are doing everything they can to keep it under wraps. And while it might seem overstated to call her obsessed, I can't conceive of a situation in which she would give up. The woman was crazy before, and I'd bet she's a raving lunatic now."

As if by silent acknowledgment, they sat quietly, both staring at the flames licking skyward into the chimney.

Caitlin broke the spell with, "I'd better be going."

The goodbye felt awkward to Nick, as if so much had been left unsaid, but he pushed it into that lockbox where he kept the other things he dared not think about too much.

As he reached for the door, she put her hand on his forearm and gently tugged it around her waist. "Hold me."

Standing as one in the foyer, with her head resting on his shoulder, Nick breathed deep of Ambush, leather, and a hint of vanilla.

Time didn't mean anything. Or the house. Or Cedar Valley, or Colorado. For all Nick knew or cared, nothing mattered except the molded physical connection between two people standing in space with no attachment to anything else.

When Caitlin lifted her head, he almost said, *Don't go!*

She reached up to his face with both hands and guided his lips to hers.

Nick's whole body tried to melt, and it would have except for knowing the difference between true attraction with the real possibility of a future together and being on the rebound.

But even if that didn't stand in the way, the other reason would, symbolized by the burning sensation on the ring finger of his left hand.

He eased away and started to say something without a clue what it was going to be when she placed a forefinger against his lips. "Shhh."

Then with the hint of a smile, she nodded, a tiny movement that seemed to say, *I know.*

As the taillights of the Mercedes disappeared into the night, Nick sighed, trudged back to the house and walked into the living room.

Her fragrance remained, a hint of the surprise attack that could easily have rendered Nick forever lost and seeking even more that he couldn't have.

Before he knew it, he was sitting at his computer with his browser page on Amazon's Kindle store, typing *Airborne Justice* into the search field.

He one-clicked the purchase, then did the same for *Black Widow Unveiled.*

At the corner of the desk sat his new Kindle Fire. He didn't even know why he bought the damn thing, but now it began to make more sense.

When Nick brought it out of sleep and found both books waiting on the carousel, he realized he could have ordered them directly from the device. Glad his kids hadn't seen him act like a low-tech dinosaur doofus, and yet wishing with all his heart they were here, he clicked on the cover of *Airborne Justice* and glanced at the table of contents.

The first sentence of the Author's Foreword got his attention.

This is the true story of retribution delivered by the talons of an eagle.

# # #

About the author:

Following graduation from the University of Washington in Seattle with Bachelor of Science degree in Psychology, Tosh entered the Air Force with the intention of serving a four-year commitment as a pilot before deciding what he really wanted to do with the remainder of his professional life. One ride in a jet trainer consigned that plan to the scrap heap.

Twenty years of flying jet fighters (including two combat tours) remain the highlight of his aviation career. Another twenty years as a commercial airline and corporate pilot and current enjoyment of sport aviation in light aircraft have embedded within him a passion for sharing with others his unique perspective of what it means to be an aviator.

Pilot Error is his first novel in a series that interweaves a life-long fascination with writing and thousands of flight hours in pursuit of one goal: to create stories that entertain and put readers up close and personal within his world of the cockpit.

Red Line continues the adventures of Nick Phillips as he hunts for the elusive clues to solve another case of airborne murder shrouded in a smokescreen of pilot error.

Connect with Tosh online:

http://toshmcintosh.com/

www.ingramcontent.com/pod-product-compliance
Lightning Source LLC
Chambersburg PA
CBHW031050260626
47172CB00001B/7